Changes

4: Greening the Valley

Francis Oeser, born 1936 in St. Andrews, grew up in Australia, went to UK in 1967 retracing Alexander the Great's tracks from Taxila to Athens. Now he lives on Aigina island, Greece.

He has collaborated with artists and musicians as poet and librettist, published a score of books since 1983, poetry, art and prose.

Work in progress:
The Seasons, Shakespeare's Songs, Portraits, Time & Memory, Greece, The Language of Social Dreaming.

Changes

4 : Greening the valley

by FRANCIS OESER

Sicnarf Press

London, Melbourne, Ithaca : 2010

Also by F.Oeser & The Sicnarf Press:

O for Love 2 (with Ann Dowker) 2010
Giants, Divas and other stories 2009
Reflections 2008
Orchestra 2008
Outrageous Fortune 2007
Loukoumia 2006
Africa Sung to 2005
After you've Brushed your Teeth (Bunyip Stories) 2005
48 Evening Ragas 2003
Your Whispered Name (with Ann Dowker) 2003
Eyeland (with Akiko Fujikawa) 1997
Scenes from Childhood 1997
But (with Akiko Fujikawa) 1996
Persephone 1996
O for Love (with G. Wickham) 1994
You, Me, We 1993
Social Dreaming & Shakespeare 1992
Bay Break 1991
Africa Sung (1). 1987
Seasons End 1984
Black Notes 1983

British Library cataloguing-in-publication data.
A catalogue record for this book is available from the British Library.

ISBN: 978-0-9552974-8-9

Printed & bound by TJ International, Padstow, Cornwall, UK.

Mixed Sources
Product group from well-managed
forests and other controlled sources
www.fsc.org Cert no. SGS-COC-2482
© 1996 Forest Stewardship Council

Foreword

THIS NOVEL is part 4 of a five book sequence collectively titled "Chages", and set in Australia, Greece, Venice and a Pacific island. As fiction, it should be enjoyed as such. Notes at the end may be useful to readers wanting background information not in the text.

Acknowledgements

THANKS to Priscilla Hall for vital early editing advice (CH1); thanks to Judge Graham Frike for help with the trial scene (CH1), to Warren Simmons for clarifying the law relating to children (CH3). Thanks to June van Ingen for help with German and Italian in the early stages (CH1&3). I am glad to pay tribute to Angela Matheson for her fine translation into Italian of Ossian's Venice song (CH4), and to the late Tom Matheson for his support, plus advice on Feminism, as well as Shakespeare. Pauline Cohen and Dr Frances Gilley were insightful on the interpretation of dreams (CH1&4).

To my forebearing wife who thought, as I did, the tram-stop meeting was to be a short story, thank you.   It's all my fault.

1-

JO STOOD AT THE WINDOW of her rented room in a colonial terraced house near the university. She was naked. Two puppies had burrowed under the fence and were romping below in the small rear garden. Rolling, biting with milky teeth, growling and chasing happy tails. She imagined Symph's "mates" as he called them causing the same delightful havoc on his verandah in her family's distant country property. She sighed.

An elegant back held by her shapely bottom, her long hair shimmered water-falling down seductively screening her body. Her legs, glowing with sun, spoke of the treasure they held. She had the slimness of a boy, the succulence of a woman and a carefree delight in sex tantalising her many lovers.

There was a groan from her bed. 'Are you coming, Jo?' A young man lay there undressed except for underpants.

Jo turned and smiled. 'You're not quite ready, Ian.' she said. 'Take them off! I like to see what I'm in for.' She appraised the bulging underpants with pleasure, then enjoyed the unveiled phallus. She stood over him.

He lay looking up through her legs, her neat pubic triangle to her upright breasts and smiling face, and stretched.

Jo knelt and lingeringly licked the rearing sex. She sucked the naked head clean of its oozing juice and whispered. 'Are you a Jew, Ian?'

'Not at ALL.' He came. 'I had a problem as a baby and they circumcised me, that's all. My dad's the same.'

'No problems now. Feel better?' Jo asked.

He weakly nodded.

'It'll be more fun now.' she said and lay down.

He kissed her tentatively. 'All right?'

She yearned towards him. 'Oh, yes.'

He caressed her, kissing her from neck to navel.

She raised her hips, pushed his head into her groin until he found the pleasure she longed for. 'Oh, Ian. Yes.' she moaned.

He felt down her legs and up to her breasts, wallowing in the power and her growing sense of bursting, as he was. With a flurry of desire he pulled himself up and drove into her with ferocious hunger. The floor drummed.

Bursting, she cried out. Her ecstacy drowning his panting as he died on her. She caressed his sticky flesh. 'Wasn't that great?'

He recovered, amazed at their freedom. His fingers eased down the wet crease between her buttocks and fondled her anus. 'Do you do it there?'

'I haven't. Tell me, you've been fucked?'

Ian blushed at the directness.'A bit. At school.'

'Poor boys. Nowhere to go. You and all the others.' She watched his confusion settle. 'Do you still want it that way?'

He trembled. 'Um, yes. Would you let me?'

Jo nodded. 'Perhaps, If there were more time.'

'More time?'

'What we just did was so good. I need those feelings. If there was time to explore, more might happen.'

Ian breathed excitedly. 'So, you need sex?'

Jo kissed his stubbly cheek. 'Yes.' She rose and went to the bathroom. Sitting on the WC she fingered her puffy labia savouring the pulsing inside. I need it all the time, she thought.

Ossian, her young brother, found them sitting in the kitchen. He looked a school boy, too young to be at university, too brilliant not to have been accepted by the music faculty.

'This is Ian.' Jo said.

'Ian?' Ossian said. Thinking, Another of her blokes. He grinned, shook hands and stamped along the hall, dumped his books and music on the desk and fell on his bed. They, and the sun had gone when he woke.

Jo had left some money and a note for him: "Nothing in the flat, go and eat somewhere!" Ossian sauntered to the main road lined with shops and sidled along a side street to a small Italian restaurant. It was homely. The wife cooked, the husband and their teenage daughter served. The girl ushered the fresh young man to a small table in a corner, removed a setting and cheerfully smiled.

'Would you like a drink?'

'Aqua minerale con gas per favore.'

'Nienta problema.' the girl chuckled surprised by his confident Italian, hurrying to the back where the sound of cooking, washing-up and Italian gossip issued. Ossian sipped the water and ordered calamari, rice and zukinis in a tomato sauce. Then he settled down to study a score of a new oboe sonata his friend Tasmin Baker had written for him.

The girl brought bread-sticks, and craned over his hunched shoulder. Soft grey eyes regarded her. She blushed. 'Oh, it's for oboe. I'm learning at school.'

Ossian grinned gently.

'Do you play? she pleaded.

Ossian nodded.

'Do you know about reeds? My reed is terrible.'

'Bring it here. I'll have a look.'

She brought a neat black box lined with blue velvet.

He assembled the instrument, pursed his lips, masticated the reed,and played. Cats screamed, or some awful nocturnal murder cry resounded. The girl's father hurried out in alarm as a grey-eyed student was shaking his head at his daughter. 'You're right. It should be scraped.' He turned to the man. 'Have you a bottle I could break?' The man looked doubtful, only his beaming daughter convinced him this was not another student prank.

'And a stout plastic bag.' Ossian called as the man disappeared, soon returning with both. Ossian put the bottle in the bag and smashed it against the wall. He removed a sharp shard and carefully scraped both faces of the reed, feeling it with knowing fingers until he nodded, stuck it back in the oboe and blew again. A thin piercing note filled the restaurant. The man smiled; the girl, almost speechless, 'Wow, it sounds good. Could you play something, anything?'

Ossian looked at her. She was young and fresh, another Miranda, but darker. He played a short gigue by Handel. Two women stood wiping their hands on voluminous aprons in the doorway to the kitchen. When he finished there was a chorus of 'Bellissima!' Then they chided the girl. 'When your music is as beautiful as the boy's, then you'll be a star.'

Ossian understood the Italian and replied in Italian, 'She is as beautiful as music. The rest depends on practice.'

The girl was enraptured.

The door to the street opened, people, curious about the music entered. The man nodded them to tables and begged. 'My young friend, please play once more, prago, prago!'

Ossian looked at the girl winked at her and played a longish solo by Benjamin Brittain based on *Syrinx*, a flute piece by Claude Debussy. It was haunting, virtuosic, longingly amorous.

The girl's eyes shone with tears as her secret dreams swam whispering around her. 'Mille, mille grazia.' she blurted as Ossian handed her back the now magic instrument. He was touched this small sweet stranger felt music so deeply, for yes, it was about dreams uniting souls, the sighs of nature.

The girl loved him: the eloquence of music from so young and beautiful a player. The family felt him special because he spoke Italian. Their dreams encompassed him. There was no bill. The restaurant was full due to his siren songs.

Ossian decided to go when the girl was threatened with bed. He stood up and grinned. 'Would you like to go to a concert of wind music next Saturday? It's not long.'

'They won't agree. It's our busy day. Ah, Mama?'

Mama too was touched by the grey-eyed angel, and trusted him, she knew not why. She gave her permission.

The daughter flung her arms around her food-scented neck and kissed her heartily. 'Buona note, mia amore mama.' Before going to bed the girl ushered her grey-eyed god out into the night.

'I'll pick you up at seven. A little practice now.' Ossian called unnecessarily, for after this glimpse of Heaven, she would play her heart out.

The concert was fun. The music, both tuneless and melodic was sumptuously carried by the rich variety of wind instruments. The sounds filled Angelica. She had her very own programme. Her new friend introduced her afterwards to Jiri, the brilliant oboist as 'This is my friend, Angelica Salvatori.' "My friend!" he had said, *and* the concert *and* sitting with the players afterwards talking and drinking bewitched the girl, *and,* best of all, Ossian held her hand all the way home so her feet never touched the ground.

The Salvatoris saw the joy. They were grateful. It was tough running a family business. They longed for their girl to be carefree as she became that evening.

'He's a nice, almost-Italian boy.' Mama confided to her sister as they dished-up scrumptious left-overs for the youngsters whose mood infected the patrons who smilingly ordered extra coffees and liqueurs and some whispered to Senior Salvatori 'Will he play tonight?'

An old man approached Ossian. 'Are you by any chance related to Timothy Macknight? You are his spitting image.' He had a kindly face and his wife a faded beauty.

Ossian smiled. 'He's my father.'

The old man grinned to his wife. 'I told you so. Please remember us to Tim and Sophie. 'I am Dr Alan Martin, I saw them through the Department many years ago. How nice to have his handsome son here now. You are enjoying the Conservatorium?'

'Yes, it's great. I graduate this year; then I'm going to do conducting and composition for post-grad and finish my anatomy and music engineering extras.'

The old man laughed. 'You're another wild Macknight, I see. Wonderful. I don't suppose you'd like to come and play for us some-time, probably too busy, eh? Your dad charmed us, even if his bassoon was a bit growly, whereas your oboe could chirp cheekily. It would be like old times?' Shakily he handed Ossian a card. 'Ring if you want. I can pick you up. Ossian, is it? It would delight us, yes, perhaps after your exams. I do understand,' He shuffled back to his beaming wife.

Angelica gasped. 'We thought you were at school.'

'I know, I am young. But I'm studying music.'

'No wonder, you're so good.'.

Ossian had tired of the sex-tinged admiration of the faculty. He longed for a simpler friendship Angelica represented, sharing passions and dreams without adult complications. He put his hand over hers. 'Please let's be friends. Music-friends. Angelica?'

Her head swam. It was all she'd ever wanted. Music and this wonderful boy. Now, "the curse" had bloodied her she missed the sureness of childhood. Ossian was the bridge she needed to step over the yawning canyon separating childhood from womanhood. She blushed with longing and relief. 'Friends, Ossian. Friends, yes.'

He leaned forward and lightly kissed her cheek. It burned for hours afterwards.

The father intervened. 'My friend, play for us again? Per favore.'

'Only if Angelica will play too. I'll write out a simple tune and we'll play it next Saturday?'

Father and daughter and mother and aunty were delighted.

He wrote *Twinkle, Twinkle Little Star* on the paper table cloth. They sang it together until she was sure. 'Play it until you know it by heart; because otherwise I'll confuse you.' he said.

The girl nodded. It was their love-song; she twinkled in his sky of soft grey eyes and hand-clasps "How I wonder what you are" her heart sang all week. To wonder with him was everything.

The problems were delicious. There were so many clamouring to dine on Saturday, the usual patrons plus a hoard of cheerful students, for the word was out Ossian was up to something, so they turned up to hear this charmed young man. The Salvatoris kept one room in its sedate arrangement of separate tables. In another, hurriedly rearranged, all the tables were pushed together like a refectory. Everyone was accommodated. There was suddenly a special 'student offer' fixed menu at a bargain price.

Ossian had asked the advice of his old dance teacher, Lettuce Marr, about minimal fancy dress. Lettuce rummaged, handed him two jester's hats and long colourful scarves.

'Nothing like an old trick. Go round the tables jesting and playing. Make it theatrical, my dear.'

Angelica was nervous waiting through Ossian's medley of solos. He was so good, his music danced and lilted until she had to smile as the drink-loosened students banged time on the table with fingers and cutlery.

Afterwards, Ossian waved his oboe for silence. 'Now Angelica and I will play, but only for the children here. The rest must be quiet and just twinkle.'

There was a roar of merriment.

Ossian whispered, 'Take your time, mia Angelica. Keep going until I nod, then finish at the end of your tune, just as we practised it. He smiled winningly and nodded-in the quaking girl.

A sheepish star breathlessly twinkled, but gathered courage and tone in the expectant hush until some of the diners joined in, humming softly.

Angelica's best friend from school was there with her

bemused parents, very impressed indeed. 'I'd never stand up and do that.' she whispered to her mother.

Then a quaint wispy oboe-echo embellished the tune. It grew in force and frenzy until a shrieking syncopated hiccuping drowned the tune remaining faint and steadfast, like love surviving the storms of life. Then the second oboe mellowed. It wove sumptuous decorations around the simple tune until everyone mellowed, and the wine decanters were replenished. Then it became a bass line as simple as the tune itself, and the harmony of two became one. Then Ossian nodded. Angelica played the tune alone and for the last time. Its sweet and plaintive air left everyone aware of the rich journey they'd shared. There was a moment of warm silence, then applause.

Signora Salvatori wiped a tear with her greasy apron and whispered to her sister. 'In one week she is a star. What a blessing.'

Food and wine were heaped on tables. After *Dolce*, before coffee, Ossian played again. There were clamours for more twinkling. So Angelica donned her silly hat and scarf and stood with her god and played just for him the glories of sharing, of music, of love of a happy twinkling ending.

Ossian was by now tipsy, his embellishments were wilder and more extreme delighting the music students, some of whom added other harmonies and rhythms until the polyphonic complexity confused other diners. When a classical bass line heralded unity the others fell silent. It was a touching duette, and a sweet lonely ending as one plaintive voice finished where it had all begun.

Eventually Jo led her very tipsy brother homeward. 'That little girl's besotted.'

Ossian smiled happily at the stars. 'She's in love with music; just like me.' He lay in a bed swimming rather alarmingly through chuckling skies, or was he chuckling? shivering to Jo's vibrating bed. Then he slept, dreaming of shooting into warm dark space with his arms filled with laughing, wondering stars. He travelled far, returning in the morning with a headache which only his landlady, Sophia's double espresso and an Italianate cuddle in her kitchen, lightened.

2-

IN THE AFTERNOON Tasmin Baker dropped in waving some sheets of manuscript. 'I recorded you last night. It was wild. I tried to write some of the variations down. It's almost impossible. It's interesting how, like jazz, played as distinct from read music, is very hard to notate. But you owe Dohnányi a small debt.' *

Ossian grinned. 'I thanked him before I got drunk. I bet the second run-through was harder to annotate than the first.'

Tasmin smiled. 'Well, not all of it. You relaxed with the booze and made clearer themes - less clever hopping about.'

Ossian hopped about the room laughing.

Tasmin sighed patiently enjoying his usual feverishness. 'How's my sonata?'

Ossian hopped to a standstill and nodded. 'It works quite well. There are a few places I'd query. Shall we look at it now?'

They clambered up the stairs. She sat on the bed as he played the questionable bits. She nodded, scribbling notation in place of the original. She sat back and sighed. 'I'll change the piano part too. Can we have a run-through next weekend?'

The phone rang. One of the students downstairs called up 'It's for you, Ossian.'

'Hello. It's Wendy. I'm ringing from the County Hospital during my break. Peter thought you should come home for the weekend. Things are difficult. Symph died and it's created problems. He thinks Will and Miranda need some support. Can you come, Ossian?'

'Why me?'

'Peter thought because you're so close to Will you could help him. It seems he's made Miranda pregnant. They want to stay in the

---
* See notes at end.

valley. Your Mum and Dad are upset because they're so young and were talking of going to Uni. It's a bit of a mess Peter says. He feels they should be allowed to make up their own minds. But perhaps you can pour oil on very troubled waters? I think Trish Maxwell is coming. Will needs you.'

'OK, Wendy, I'll get the afternoon train on Friday.'

'Good! I'll meet it. I'm driving home then. Thanks Ossian. Peter will be relieved.'

'How are things?'

'Darling Peter. Married life, I never see him. We're both so busy. But when we do meet it's bliss. We're OK. I love the valley, the family is thriving. See you Friday.'

Tamsin was waiting. 'What's wrong?'

Ossian shrugged trying to lift the weight off his slim shoulders. 'Our Old Man of the Sea has died. A terrible silence. And it's Will again. More trouble. That boy is doomed. Peter wants me to go out. It must be serious. No sonata rehearsal next weekend. Oh, shit, I'm sorry Tamsin.'

Tamsin kissed him.

Both were surprised. Both comforted. To love music makes one love musicians, Ossian thought later still warmed by Tamsin's understanding kiss and the radiance of Angelica. But he worried, this time music would be no use to Symph, or Will.

Ossian clambered off the train. Wendy was waiting in her sporty yellow car. She kissed Ossian warmly. They drove through the town and out into the country where Wendy speeded up making Ossian nervous. There was a big flashing light and a policeman at the top of a long rise. 'Shit!' breathed Wendy. 'It's a speed trap.'

'Could I see your licence, Ma'am.' the officer said, shaking his head in disbelief at the speed recorded and the flashy car. 'Oh, hello, Ossian, how's things?' he softened.

'Hello Charlie.' Ossian smiled. 'Do you know Peter's wife, Wendy? She's a nurse at the hospital, just finished work. There's a problem at home. You know how it is.'

The officer grinned at Wendy. 'Yes of course! I've seen you there. Once in Emergency when I brought a crazy drunk kid in who smashed up his dad's ute. Your job's not easy, even worse that mine.' He inspected the car and whistled. 'Nice set of wheels.

Trouble at home eh? Sorry to hear that. Well, you'd best be on your way. There'll be no report this time. But take it easy. Hey, Greetings to your old man.' He returned Wendy's papers, winked at Ossian and waved them on marvelling at the music of the super-charged exhaust and how sexy Peter's shiela was.

Wendy drove to her house. 'Have a cuppa before you go?' She sat Ossian down in the living room, remembering Will's greed, and her own. She enjoyed his gossip about Jo and all her men, about the wild Italian music night. It all sounded fun. City fun, a long way from here, she thought.

Ossian rose and put his empty mug on the tray. Wendy went out onto the verandah and put needy arms around him. She kissed him. 'Thanks for quashing the speed-report. No licence, means no work. You were amazing. No arguments, just a little chat. I see how you charm your orchestra.' Reluctantly letting him go, she leaned against the door frame watching the trim figure slope away towards Symph's empty house on the track to Ararat.

Ossian saw movement in Symph's house. There, on the verandah were Miranda and Will lying on a couch surrounded by dogs, too comfortable and familiar with the visitor to do anything but wag welcoming tails. Ossian walked over. The lovers leapt up and fell happily on Ossian's neck, dragging him onto the verandah into a chair while his sister brought them tea.

In spite of her grime from working the land, Miranda looked ravishing. Ossian was taken aback. Will too was firmer, warm in his pleasure at having him there. Ossian was embraced by their happiness, entranced by their talk about their new life in the valley.

Will beamed. 'Miranda and the valley are the most precious things in the world.'

Ossian nodded. 'This is the music of love.' he told himself.

Shyly they told him about their child. 'We made it in a magic place Symph sent us to deep in the Bush.' Miranda whispered so as not to over-excite the baby.

'It's what we both want.' said Will firmly. 'It's "the new start" we talked about when we did the *Erlking*.'

Ossian sighed. He looked at their radiant faces. 'Are you really happy? What about your other plans?'

'Really happy. At last.' they both said laughing.

Miranda leaned forward and kissed him. 'Even happier you

have come home.' It was a full, fleshly embrace. It reminded Ossian of his own brimming joy singing in one of Bach's ravishing motets. Then he knew these very dearest siblings had to be defended.

'I'm happy to be here with you.' Ossian said.

The tea finished, they rinsed the mugs, shut the door and walked down the track to the main house. While the two love-birds showered, Ossian sat with Tim and Sophie. He demurred at more tea. Soon wine loosened tongues.

Ossian understood his parents' distress: the lovers' immaturity; the shattering of plans for the future; the dead-end they would embrace if they settled. Sophie was the spokesperson, his father seemed torn between support and doubt. Their sadness was evident. It was the other side of the coin he'd shared with Will and Miranda.

Ossian glanced woefully at the trees. 'I'm here for the weekend. Let's try and have a jolly supper and enjoy what we can tonight. Perhaps in the morning a solution will be found.'

Tim nodded and sighed.

Nina and Ant came in, followed by Miranda glowing after showering. 'Let me help with supper.'

'I can manage.' her mother said.

But Miranda, too happy to notice the slight, set the table with Ant and Nina, finished the salad and put a pile of plates in the oven to warm, shouting to Will to open more wine and for Ant to get glasses. Tim and Ossian looked-on savouring the lovers.

It was impossible not to enjoy the meal, or to ignore Sophie's distress. But having Ossian home was balm.

'Trish will sort them out when she arrives tomorrow.' Sophie told herself, mellowing with wine.

In the middle of the meal, Adam arrived. Delightedly a place was made for him. His talk of electronics and student goings-on leavened the tension. Ant felt cheered at last.

'Hey, it's great having Ossian home.' Adam cried gazing at the ruddy wine-tinged faces of his family and swallowing another glass. 'You and Will must dance for us tomorrow, dance our valley.' Adam ordered, beginning to join a floating world, whispering to Ant about the buxom girls and all the fun waiting for him.

Ossian felt tired so he too went when Ant and Nina left for bed, walking along the verandah looking at the serene sky mirrored in the lake, the drooping trees and the warm patches of light falling from the house.

Nina looked shyly at her big brother. 'Ossian please tell Ant and me a Bunyip story.'

Ant sighed. He remembered many happy occasions snuggled into someone's bed sharing Bunyip's adventures. He nodded. 'If you and Bunyip aren't too tired.'

Miranda who had routinely followed to see them tucked in, caught them up. 'Can I come?'

Everyone snuggled into Nina's bed. Ossian began:

The scratch at the window was urgent. The smallest girl jumped up and let Bunyip in. He looked sad. They clustered around him as he whispered. 'Somehow we must make the Myrror folk well again. They are so very, very unhappy. You must help me.' So all the children grasped paws and Bunyip leapt into the night sky, flying way past the clouds and the stars, far far away to the land of Myrror.

There, they were confronted by disgruntled folk without their usual smiles. And no jokes. No laughter. A dark silence trapped them.

'We don't want to stay here.' many of them cried. 'We want to go over there, where the grass is greener and the sun warmer and life is easier.'

'Then make a bridge, and go!' said the boy who knew something about structures. (Yes, that's Ant, Nina). It was he who helped them gather lots of grass to be woven into long plaited ropes. When they had made enough, one of the strongest wound the ropes around his tummy so he looked like a grass ball, then others tied the free end of the rope to a high tree, took him back and then ran with him, throwing him into the air where he swung over and bounced on the other side where the grass was greener and the sun warmer and where life would be easier. Although making it was hard work, eventually the bridge was ready. All the disgruntled Myrrors rushed over, swaying the bridge.

It swayed so much it broke. But luckily the last few had tied themselves on so their friends could pull them up to where the grass was greener, the sun shone more warmly and life was easier.

The remaining Myrrors sighed. They felt even sadder now their friends had gone. 'It's not much fun here now.' they wailed.

Bunyip nodded concernedly.

While on the other side, the rest tried hard to be happy. But there was no disguising the fact, as one of the smallest Myrrors whispered, 'It's no better here. If anything, it's worse.'
Now, they disregarded the sun and the grass, for they missed their friends sorely. The Myrror children began to cry.

Then the parents cried. because someone pointed out although the grass was greener it was too short to make ropes. So they could not return. Soon everyone was crying and life seemed harder, not easier!

Bunyip and the children on the other side had an idea. They gathered the remaining Myrrors together and suggested they form working-bees to make another set of ropes to rescue their friends.

The little Myrrors danced and sang. It became fun, thinking they would all be together again; it was infectious. Now all the grown-ups were happily harvesting and plaiting the long grass into strong ropes. They began to sing:

> Cut, cut, cut the grass.
> Trim, trim, trim the grass.
> Plait, plait, plait the grass.
> Knot, knot, knot the grass.
> Bridge, bridge, bridge the pass.
> All, all, come home to us!
> All, all come home to us!

Until quite soon the happy workers had made a new bridge, wound it round the biggest of the children and thrown him like a grass ball to the other side where supposedly the grass was greener, the sun warmer and life easier.

Then they secured the bridge at both ends and, more care - fully now so as not to set it swinging again, all the adventurers returned home, just as the song had wished.

There was great rejoicing. Then a great party with lots of music and dancing, eating and drinking until everyone was full to bursting and one of the more garrulous Myrrors made a speech ,

praising the skills of the children and thanking them for showing
them something so simple they were ashamed to admit it, the very
important lesson to be repeated every day from now on, that:

> **Where you are, the grass is greenest, the sun**
> **warmest, and life and love are worth more than**
> **anywhere else in the whole wide world.**

Then Bunyip smiled for the first time for ages. He took the
work-worn hands of his dearest children and lovingly took them
back to their beds.

And, do you know, each one of them snuggled down
happily thinking, 'This is the greenest, warmest most wonderful
bed in the whole wide world.'

Miranda kissed her little sister. 'It's true.'

Nina's arms encircled her neck. 'I know.'

Ossian accompanied Ant to his room. Watched him strip and slip his long legs and slim hips under the covers. He opened the covers to pull Ant's tee-shirt down, seeing the rising excitement crowned in a nascent shadow of fur. He ruffled his brother's hair acknowledging his new power. 'Sleep tight, dear Ant.'

'I *am* interested in structures.' Ant whispered.

'I know.'

'I want to be an architect like Ray Rubbo and one day build a house like this one.'

Ossian looked fondly at his brother, once so carefree and now troubled by growing pains. 'Ant, I'm so glad. You will be terribly good.'

Later, Ant masturbated and slept soundly in the warmest, greenest grass-bridge bed in the whole wide world.

Ossian found hugs and talk in Miranda's room. 'I'm just telling Will your story.' she said.

Ossian sat with them. They were soft in a way he couldn't quite articulate. It's as if they've melted together, he thought. He enjoyed their unguarded warmth. 'They relate in exactly the way they'd play chamber music. It's the duet they hanker after' he mused. Rising he brushed a hand over rumpled hair. 'You are so lucky, wanting to share the greenest, warmest loveliest place in the world. I envy you. Know you'll always have my support and love.'

Will whispered. 'Oh, Ossian. We love you the same way.'

A few of Miranda's joyful tears escaped. 'Yes, darling Ossian, for ever.'

But instead of going to bed, Ossian returned to the living room where his parents were listening to Adam regaling them with news of his college and his plans to start an electronic~computer consultancy with a friend with a national mail order 'fix-it' section.

Adam winked at his brother. 'By the way, I hear there are plans to build a communications tower that will extend services to the valley. Don Bayne and Jeff Dean have signed-up. Has anyone been in touch with us?'

'A form came.' Tim murmured. 'I haven't done anything about it. After all this time without, it seems an extravagance.'

Adam looked surprised. 'Surely to be able to telephone, now we are all so far away would be better?'

Tim shook his head. 'I know Will is keen, after being persuaded by Don and Jeff. But we're all right. Anyway, I don't want to be at the beck and call of everybody.'

Adam looked sharply at his silent brother.

Ossian shook his head in disagreement. 'Although Symph had his birds, I think he would have welcomed a telephone here. Will's right. For all our sakes, get hooked-up.'

A wall of resistance strangled discussion. Ossian took a deep breath. 'There's something I'd like to say about the valley. It's really about the future of the valley, now things are changing. I'd like to have my say and leave it until tomorrow so you can sleep on it. For I'm afraid I agree with Miranda and Will. Their plan to move into Symph's place and extend it into a family house is sensible.'

Sophie sniffed angrily.

Tim gently shook his head.

Ossian's brow creased. 'They told me how Symph sent them away to find themselves. What they found is amazing. I think Symph knew - his understanding of us and the valley was extraordinary - that's why he's gone, leaving them his house. They love each other they're wedded to this place. Staying becomes inevitable.'

Sophie burst. 'Rubbish! They're kids playing with dreams of adult life. Their futures will be ruined. Both have great promise. For once, Ossian you're wrong. So mind your own business. Symph was a silly old dreamer taking advice from parrots, who imagined a leaky shack and a pack of scurvy dogs was enough. He meddled in their lives disastrously.'

Ossian shook his head. 'I suspect Symph saved Will's life; he and his dogs and his deep understanding of us and this place.'

Tim nodded. 'Darling, I think Ossian's right. Symph always watched over us as a sort of defender of the valley. There was something peculiarly powerful about his abstracted presence, difficult to see until he'd gone.'

Sophie scowled. 'Well, it doesn't make Ossian right.'

Ossian's brow darkened. 'Will and Miranda are no longer children. They are lovers and parents just as you once were. They're the new defenders of our valley. You are blind and thoughtless. Who else is there now Symph has gone? Peter and Wendy have half a life in the town. Don and Jeff have other concerns. Adam, Jo and I have other lives. Anyone who escaped here in a trunk, survived the brutalities of Ruddles, who loves us and the valley and wants to make a life with Miranda is quite amazing. His bravery and bruises and his wonderful, shining love must convince you. Also, Miranda's life-long involvement with him surely show you they're the most precious people here? What they stand for is everything you and Dad have struggled for. Here, in front of your noses and you deny it. I am disgusted.' Ossian jumped to his feet and stormed out.

Never had he been angry like this. Never fought so vehemently. And for what? Adam felt his brother had assumed the wise power of Bunyip. He rose. 'I think we should all sleep on it, eh?' He kissed his parents and sadly went to bed knowing the usual comforting Bunyip-aftermath was unlikely in the morning.

Trish Maxwell arrived quite early. She was perplexed by the conflict. Will and Miranda's plans sounded rational, if unconventional (they showed no interest in marriage ceremonies). He had the financial resources to extend the house and, as Peter had pointed out, they could extend their education when they wanted, as he had. There was work and income for him, Peter promised. Their love was the fulcrum for any decision. Adam sided with Ossian. Tim, Trish realised, was torn between his love for Sophie and his intuitive respect for the children. Trish acknowledged Ossian's wisdom, the pair had a right to make their own lives.

Trish suggested Peter and Wendy, Tim and Sophie have tea

while the rest were visiting Symph's grave beyond his vegetable garden. She asked each of them to tell her something about their present life, hoping for a glimpse of underlying issues.

Peter and Wendy expressed frustrations of having too little time together. They nodded ruefully when Trish murmured 'Try to find more time for each other. It can make or marr a marriage.' But their involvement in challenging lives was heartening.

What struck Trish about the Macknights' life was its gradual unwinding. She had seen it: parents whose children had left, lost vitality. Trish said gently. 'Sophie you look tired.'

Sophie said flatly. 'First it was Tim, then the children, then moving and worries, and now this. It's too much.'

Tim put his arm round her. 'Easy, darling.'

Angrily she shrugged him off. 'Oh it's all right for you, poncing about. I was left to clean up the mess, day in day out. "Defender of the valley" indeed. I've done nothing else for years.'

Trish looked thoughtful. 'You and Symph?'

'Yes, if you like, Symph and me picking up the damaged kids and dogs, making them beds and food, always being here while others fucked about with trees and each other and talked about reclaiming themselves. What about me? When is it my turn?' Sophie burst into tears of rage and of disquiet knowing it was only half true.

Trish nodded Tim to comfort her. 'It sounds as if it's your time now. Maybe a break? Maybe reflecting on others lending a hand, and the sort of life you want to lead now some of that vital and fantastic living has been accomplished? For you and Tim have done a marvellous thing, don't you agree, Peter?' (He nodded.) 'Now it's your turn. What about a holiday? Any ideas?'

Sophie wept because she felt loved and cared for, because it was true, and she wouldn't have changed much. She was worn out. She sobbed. 'It's a good idea. Get away and see it more clearly. Find myself.'

Wendy saw the stress. 'I found myself and Peter in a hut on the beach. It's wild and lonely, beach-combing, being together in such a beautiful spot. I'm sure my friend would lend it to you. If that's the sort of place you want?'

'Like when we were with Simon, Peter's brother and the school librarian with whom he was having a secret affair.' Sophie muttered. 'I'd love that. Oh, Wendy, do ask. I don't want crowds.

I never have. To be with Tim like years ago.' She cried as her love overflowed with her regrets about times past, and from somewhere deeply hidden, niggling fears about a bleak future without anyone.

Trish smiled at Wendy. 'Maybe you two should go back there soon?'

Peter hugged Wendy. 'Ask for that too, darling. I'd love to burn my fingers again, freeze in the surf and be together.'

Wendy laughed. 'It was the best honeymoon ever.'

Peter smiled at Tim. 'Leave us some wood, won't you. The nights are cold. But that's not the problem. It's the cooking. One must stoke up for the nights.'

Laughter broke the spell.

When the children returned, they found the problems diminished. Happily they offered to take care of everything in all of the houses, including the black snake, when the others went away on honeymoons.

'Then, what about us?' cried Miranda cheerfully.

'You have to get married first.' Trish admonished savouring their joy.

'Our honeymoon's here.' Miranda murmured.

Nina snuggled up to Mummy; she was upset by the tensions and needed reassurance. She sighed. 'I'll help Manda, so don't worry Mummy.'

'We'll cope.' breathed Will.

Tim looked fondly at him. 'I'm quite sure you will. I depend on you. We all do.'

But Ossian worried, nothing really had been settled. But the new mood heartened him, so he sat-out his fears. For in this beloved valley, things had a way of resolving, helped by moon-light and stories, he had found during a life time living there.

3-

THE COAST WAS WILD and uninhabited. The broad beach stretched away in both directions lost in haze. The wooden hut lay, 'leaned on tip-toe' is a better description, on the landward side of scrub-covered sand hills. A corrugated iron tank held water from the roof. Wood was stacked under the hut and in an untidy pile outside. One end was buttressed by a stone fireplace and gable wall. A flight of rickety steps led up from the sand onto a verandah and then to a small lobby and three rooms: a living/dining/kitchen, a bathroom and a large bedroom with bunks for six.

The hut was surrounded by gaunt trees, twisted by the wind. The surf boomed, sea birds' mournful calls entwined with sighing trees. Sophie listened intently. There was nothing but Tim's axe cutting wood and her breathing. First of all he had lit the fire. Soon she took a hot cuppa out to him, stopping his work with a hug. 'I do love you.' she whispered. It sounded loud. Her hands strayed down to his fly, cupping his sex with rediscovered intimacy. 'It feels so good already.' she murmured. 'Tim, let's sleep in the living room? I'll put two mattresses in front of the fire?'

Tim kissed her. 'I'll sleep anywhere, if you're naked.'

When they'd unpacked and stowed everything, they draped towels around their necks and followed a faint track over the dunes to the beach. The sand was warm. They ran towards the water. The waves, gifting froth and shells, were streaming up the shore and bubbling into a myriad of minute holes. It looked like a maturing cheese.

Sophie pulled off her clothes. 'Come on, Tim, let's swim.'

Tim stood watching. Her neat bottom and strong back still delighted him. When she returned goose pimpled, he dried her down and hugged her.

She teasingly wiggled her bottom into his erection. 'Do you think the fish care about little things like that?'

Tim cupped his hands over her surf-cool breasts.

'I thought they might be jealous and nibble bits off. I want it all for tonight.'

Sophie turned looking seriously into his face, still beautiful if rather lined. 'Can I have all of it too?'

'Well, it depends how good the food is, and the drink.'

He helped her dress and they wandered far along the beach scuffing the virgin sand, sometimes chasing one another, sometimes walking hand in hand against a stiff wind which blasted bare legs if they ventured into the loose dry sand at the foot of the sand-hills. Sometimes they gambolled in the shallows or looked for treasures in rock-pools. They stopped at an invisible line agreeing they would turn back but sat for a time enjoying the sea-fresh emptiness.

Sophie leaned against him. 'I was thinking about Symph. I feel lonely without him. As if I've lost my father. I think the children feel the same.'

'I do too. He was the guardian of the valley. He allowed us in, showed us its secrets and blessed all we did in some strange way. Without him, we have become more vulnerable.'

Sophie pushed against his stolid torso. 'I guess, I panicked over his death and Miranda's pregnancy. It was extreme, trying to deal with both.'

'Two events over which we have no control.' Tim said. 'Death and life.'

'I'm a bit envious she is starting, as I'm finishing.'

'But Symph is showing us there are no "ends" in the valley, only extensions. Life changes. Will and Miranda will carry on where we leave off; we must now find other tasks,' Tim gazed at the surf. 'In a funny way, I feel Symph's like Bunyip, he'll be there when we remember or need him.'

'I wonder if you'll always be there. Stories are not the same as life.' Sophie shivered. 'So, do we accept these silly careless children, let them stay and propagate in the valley?'

Tim sighed in a distant dream. 'Remember darling last time you lost your cool, that xmas at the Baynes. We were careless. What riches that brought us.'

'That's not fair, Tim. That was different.'

'Was it? I doubt it. Yes, life has changed, but the feelings driving it are the same. Then, we fell in love again. Miranda and Will fell in love so deeply a baby grew out of it, just as we made Jo.'

They sat leaning against each other until he kissed her cheek. 'Let them green our valley. It's so very important. We must join with all the children in celebrating that. Funny, our kids showing us what to do. Darling, we'll enjoy having the house filled again with mud and shouting, music and feasting, the whole valley danced in, swum through, picnicked, those warm flat rocks bedding lovers, the birds carrying messages of joy to all their relatives wherever they may be, and Bunyip scratching on the windows, won't we?'

She cried. Because he was right. Because he was there and because, in the pristine beauty of their foot-marked beach, she was reminded of the love she had chased all her life and finally, she acknowledged, found with her family in their greening valley. 'Yes.' she sobbed.

They went back gladly, their fears teased out by the fresh breeze. The fire still glowed. Tim revived it with twigs and blowing. Soon the smoke was burned up by flames hungrily dancing under the billy.

'Darling, play for me while I prepare supper.'

Tim sat on the dilapidated couch hugging his bassoon until the music ceased. 'Enough, I'm tired.'

She wiped her hands on her apron and came to him. Kissing his thinning wind-ruffed hair. 'Darling, no wonder. You packed the car, drove all the way and cut all that wood and told me not to be a silly duffer. That's enough for today.'

He packed his bassoon away, exchanging it for the griller bulging with steak. He set it over the hot coals and played chef, nursing the potatoes in their silver jackets, watching his wife bustle about with plates and salad and wine. He wanted to tell her something about feeling contented. But was silent. He wanted to lie with her and feel his age wash out.

They ate with little talk. When finished, she pushed the chairs back and dragged two mattresses in front of the fire. He sat enjoying the aftermath of feasting and wine.

She emerged from the bathroom and slipped naked into bed, lying on her tummy watching the fire-pictures until he kissed her little cleavage. Turning she saw her lovely aroused man kneeling at her feet. She opened her arms. They shared lips as he eased into her.

He came quickly. 'Sorry, Soph.'

'Darling it was lovely, so gentle, so needy. Perfect.'

'You didn't come?'

'No. It doesn't matter. It was good feeling you whoosh and then relax, loosing seed and worries.' She kissed his eyes until they closed. This is all I want, she thought. Then she slept.

In the early morning he peed off the verandah and woke her with ravenous lips and caresses. She was consumed by glittering clitoral climaxes and pulled him in. They cried with pleasure, panted with the struggle towards climax. Each erupted. Shouts and whimpers shook the hut. They slept until the sunlight slipped through the window and tweaked open their enchanted eyes.

Tim put small twigs and a tent of bigger kindling on the few red coals and retreated back to Sophie's body where they waited for the billy to boil to start another day.

She began thinking ahead. 'We are starting a new group in the Hospital, a weekly discussion between women. There are many who are damaged. Either men brutalise them during sex, or brutalise them by denying them. They're hurt and confused. Just like the kids we talked to at Francis Wynn's inner city practice; it's the same in the country.'

'Where kids find more to do.' Tim turned and kissed her soft nipple. 'Ours are no exception.'

'Why do innocent women and children bear the brunt of sexual ignorance? Truncating our love? Our life denuded by guilt and masculine brutality?'

Tim felt her nipple harden as he ringed it with his tongue. '"Innocent"? I don't agree. Women are as caught in our sexual mores as men. Each expresses confusion in different ways. Darling, last night you let me fuck you without much return, enjoying my enjoyment; not lying there stiff and critical at the selfish, sinful pleasure a male brute was stealing from you.'

She started. 'I love you using me. I love your excitement, your seed coming. You know that. I still regret knowing so little of your desire when we kissed on the beach as raw school kids. I gladly would've helped you. I felt your need but didn't understand. It's taken years of embarrassed experiment to find how to love you.'

Tim ran his finger through her slimy labia. 'Darling, no one told us much, it was the hidden school of lovers that taught us. I struggled to free myself from the monsters haunting me; it was wild, immoral/illegal but essential to join all the bits of love together. In the process I learned something about our different pleasures. You are a fantastic lover; you allow such play! Remember, carrots, boy-sex, quickies under trees, in water, lovely long gradually intensifying fucks leaving us more in love, more hungry and starry-eyed than before? You took wonderful risks which bound me to you and saved me and gave me this life.'

Involuntarily her thighs opened as pleasure nudged her. 'Darling, that's so good! Please. Not too much, I want to talk. Oh, It's good. You bastard, you know the way to . . .' She placed her restraining hand over his. 'From the outset, I knew I wanted you. With no rules, except your need and its satisfaction, and mine which you discovered admirably.'

He moved his slippery fingers onto her anus. '"No rules" is the key. We agreed love was the prime rule: what's done with love is usually safe. The other confusion you implied is making love, which is more than having sex. But we managed the messy feelings of jealousy and complaints. Well, you did. I don't know how you accepted my playing away.'

She raised her bottom, allowing his finger to slip in. 'Darling; I like that. You were at it before we met and all those years of growing-up. The only time I wept was seeing you and Fran, so happy and hungry. And that was well before we coupled. I remember her picking you up outside school and wanting whatever she had so as to be able to share it with you. I found it during our hike: sharing everything in the world it seemed like. Then you had Don; it was a fragile and tumultuous affair tinging both of you with golden cheer I wanted to share, not let jealousy exclude me.'

She trailed her fingers down his chest, over his soft tummy to caress the saddle above his hip bone.

He shivered. 'And Agnes?'

Sophie felt his growing excitement. 'I guessed she was the mother you missed. Such balanced power. I wanted you to go back so as to be able to come to me. I'll always remember your pleading afterwards we share digs at Uni. Because of Agnes you were enabled to accept me. I couldn't be all the people you needed; I had to be myself. I was fascinated by the changes in you after you came back from each of your loves. I never doubted one day you would be mine. That's why I helped you disengage from Will: neither of you needed that sort of love. You see, my darling, I knew you had arrived. Not that there would be no others - I don't mind that - but let them be what they have always been, mutual lovers. He was so little, so damaged, so in love with you, with us all. We agreed at the time the dance was essential, but enough of a connection. Will seems to have weathered storms as bad as you and to have found a mate who understands him. I suppose, as Ossian and Trish argued, that is a great achievement.'

Tim saw the fork in the road. It was too long. He wanted her again, and both the family and her ideas about social work needed airing. But not now. Only small delay was bearable.

'But the women in your new group don't see it as you do? They are imprisoned by rules. Anti-feminine and anti-pleasure rules cripple them. Whereas by taking what you want you manage feelings they are too crippled to cope with. They allow their husbands only the bit women need; they deny anything extra. They judge, misjudge ordinary needs and punish themselves and their mates for them. In their despair the unfulfilled men punish them. So, the guilt circulates. So, personal and sexual freedoms are castrated. You must preach the old anarchy we once aired to those inner-city kids and their beleaguered parents. But Soph, no more now. I need you. You've really stoked me up!'

He turned her and plunged in. She was hungrily waiting and trembled with pleasure as he erupted and fell on her. Afterwards she whispered. 'Can I be your boy again?'

'If afterwards, you're my earth mother.' he whispered kissing her so gently some of her melted.

Afterwards, she longed to make him breakfast and cavort into the day's brightness filled by a wind inducing laughter in the trees, lascivious wavelets licking the beach, and the haze making distance like a dream, and them, at the magic centre of it all.

While she prepared breakfast Tim cut wood, collecting all the chips in a basket he deposited in the bathroom. 'They're enough chips for the bath heater. We can have a hot shower later.' He took his rod and fishing basket from the car. Then they trundled up over the dunes to the pristine beach; the high tide had erased yesterday's footprints.

She helped him find bait then, from the lea of a huge boulder, watched him scramble out over the slippery rocks to where the tide was gnashing before it turned, gathered itself and rolled in to consume everything. There, he fished until driven landward by rushing waves. 'Bloody fish.' he called. 'They love the bait, just suck it off the hook. Tomorrow I"ll try something firmer. Maybe mollusks rather than cunjevoi.'

Before the tide advanced fully they stripped and swam in a large rock-hemmed pool until waves broke over its edge. They sat higher up watching them engulf where they'd walked, until boisterous waves rushed at their feet and licked their shins, driving them to a still higher rocky platform. They surveyed the wild waters rushing in whacking the stolid rocks and turning into spouts of foam, watched sea gulls swoop down to skim the surface of the sea hunting in its beneficence, saw the kelp writhe like boiling brown snakes and touched each other with delight washed by tides of feeling.

Sophie took his salty hand. 'Tim, thank you for this morning. You helped a lot.'

Tim grinned. 'Although you allowed me my extra playfellows, you are less easy-going with Miranda. She has found love and you want to deny her with your plans for her future when she seems to have already made them.'

Sophie grimaced. 'That's what Trish said. She also asked me whether I was holding on to an old role in order to save my own life as mother, wife and so on. Maybe she's right. It's very hard to let go, allow their ways and to find another life for myself. Tim, I get frightened sometimes thinking you are all leaving me. If you did, I'd die. I do try to deal with this fear but sometimes it overwhelms me.'

Tim nodded, hugged her. 'Darling, I'm not going anywhere when such delicious feasts are offered. You must stay and stop me starving to death.'

'How long do we have?'

'All our lives.'

A gull landed nearby, its orange webbed feet planted firmly on the uneven rock. It wolfed Tim's abandoned bait, looking sideways at them, not with alarm but as if saying 'It's foolish feeding fish cunjevoi, it's meant for the gods of the air.' It crooked its neck and screamed warnings to other hovering gulls, letting out a cry so obscene no one challenged its feasting. Then it was lifted by invisible hands to float out over the heaving sea without even a backwards glance.

'And our storm-bird, Will?'

Tim smiled. 'Miranda is the spitting image of her mother. When she chooses, not even Hell can change her mind.'

She looked to the horizon. 'And Will?'

Tim sighed. 'I love him. How could I deny him? He is wonderful. Clever, loving, committed. To us, to the valley. We should trust the children's judgement, particularly Miranda and Ossian.'

Sophie frowned. 'I've never seen Ossian so incensed. He raged at me so fiercely, Tim, I was frightened.'

'He loves Will. I mean, really, deeply, beyond understanding. After all, he partnered Will in every single struggle with his Horribillies. Remember *Kookaburra Films'* scene with them walking naked through the long grass? It summed up the intensity and intimacy, the beauty of their love. Dan and Kim picked up what we missed although it flowered right under our noses. Ossian is still caught in that dawning love. Jo says he is oblivious to everyone around him who chase him like dogs after a bitch on heat. He only sees music. It's a strange irony: the boy who was a man so very early is now a man imprisoned by boys' dreams. Dearest Ossian. He was defending all he loves: Will, the valley, eternal youth (ours and his), everything from which his music stems. It was the fierceness of a lioness defending her litter.'

Sophie gasped. 'It felt like that. My poor little darling. Perhaps he'll never find love again. It comes only once. Maybe he's gay; some musicians are. Oh, Tim. I love our naked little god. Perhaps he should have stayed at home. He was too young to go away to university.'

'Too brilliant not to dear heart. That he has loved so intensely gives me hope. He'll find a mate one day. I'm sure.' He took her chilly hand and squeezed it. 'Darling one, Ossian, more than all of them, returns feelingly. He brings all of himself. We must take it as it comes and love him deeply and without judgement; let him grow in his own wonderful way and feed off all the love and peace we and the valley can offer. It saved Will. Ossian has always demanded the best from all of us. Never forget: he is our naked little god, nor the power of love to bless his life. We must never diminish our resolve however changed his or our lives become.'

She sat looking into the endless haze of the beach until the breeze flicked water from her eyes. 'What now?' she whispered facing the immensity of absent family, the eternity of her future.

'Now we hurry home for a cuppa and a snack. Then we try the bed round the other way and see if my bum gets as hot as my head did this morning.'

Sophie sniffed. 'Sex, sex sex. You sex maniac.' She pulled down his shorts and buried her face in his crotch until his penis stiffened. She jumped up gleefully. 'Keep it for later, sex maniac.' She ran away from him over the rocks and along the beach, making for the track up the dunes marked by their foot-prints. There, he caught her. She fell in the soft warm sand squealing as he kissed her face and neck so passionately she drew back in wonder. It was Ossian's love. Yet hers.

So, the days passed, growing carefree with lessening reviews of the past and increasing discussions about the future. By the end of the week, Sophie was helping Tim gut and clean his catch: small rectangular slim silver fish, colourful leathery ones with spiked foreheads and small mean mouths, fat luscious parrot fish with coarse scales. In far pools at the extent of low tide they harvested abalone which, cut from their mother-of-pearl shells, bashed flat and fried in batter, were delicious.

The hut became a treasure trove of shells, driftwood in evocative forms, smooth stones gifted by the beach, and the golden fronds of grass with feathery tops gleaned from behind the dunes.

Sophie responded to Tim's sudden and various sexual needs as she used to. They sloughed off the dross of years. He enjoyed her demanding temptations. They grew unkempt, careless in dress and time-keeping as inner strengths sharpened. Towards the end of the second week the weather deteriorated. They spent more time indoors, he playing bassoon and reading, she finishing a large patchwork quilt she had decided to give to Miranda and Will for their bed. They sallied forth rugged up in hooded jackets to stroll far along the beach, returning with wind blushed faces, hungry for tea with its extra tang after such excursions.

The last days were glorious. Warm with only a slight breeze. They fished, swam and played naked over the rocks and along the beach content with sexual contact rather than sexual fulfilment, long free days reminiscent of their shared youth.

On the way out, Tim let the car roll to a halt at the rusted gate in the boundary fence. They looked back revelling in memories. The hut looked derelict without smoke issuing from the chimney, its window-eyes shut, no human detritus spilling off the verandah. It seemed to reflect the bent and wind-bent trees under which it sheltered: a small gnarled gnome devoid of life.

'We sucked it bare of joy.' Sophie whispered.

Tim smiled and squeezed her leg. 'It helped us find the Eden in ourselves like a parent would. We all get tired and lose touch with our inner Edens. We'll remember its nurture. It will surely remain because it is cared for.'

4-

OSSIAN ARRIVED BACK IN THE CITY LATE. He was washed out. He went to eat at Salvatori's Restaurant. It seemed bleak and empty. Sitting at at his usual table, He lay his drooping head on the table.

A hand softly touched his arm. 'Ossian, are you all right?'

He looked up into the concerned eyes of Angelica.

He shook his head and stammered. 'Problems at home. Terrible row with Mum. Terrible, terrible.'

She winced. 'Eat something?'

'Yes.' he murmured.

The girl hurried away and told her mother who emerged from the kitchen and bustled to the wan young man and hugged him. 'Don't worry my dear. It's family life. Why, my Leonardo is always shouting at Angelica. Tears and shouts. But it's soon over. We mothers get angry because we love you, Now I will prepare a little veal and a mixed salad to cheer you up.'

Ossian nodded gratefully. They were gentle, fond words.

Angelica returned with a glass brimming with Chianti and a fistful of bread sticks and whispered. 'Write saying sorry. That'll help.' She looked so worried he felt easier.

'Yes.' he muttered, aware how much he needed to share.

He lightly kissed her hand. 'Thank you.'

She stood transfixed, wanting his wonderful liveliness to dawn and the soft grey of his eyes to flood her with warmth.

'I'm writing us another duet.' he said. 'I hope to finish it tomorrow. Come over and we'll go through it?'

She blushed. 'I finish school early. Can I come at three?'

Her warmth roused him. Ossian finally smiled. 'Don't worry

about your instrument you can use mine. There're many things to do before we play. Try to be punctual; I've a rehearsal later.'

Angelica sat watching him. He quaffed the wine too fast. She refilled his glass. He ate the meat using his knife with a surgeon's precision, leavening it with the salad, elegantly scooping it from plate to mouth. She was bewitched by his delicate sadness.

Her mother sallied forth with a special *dolce* for the dear, distrait child and a command that Angelica stop hanging about like a bad smell and go up to bed, immediately. Happily she obeyed, seething with expectations about tomorrow's tryst.

Ossian called for the bill

'The wine is on the house.' Leonardo said gruffly.

Ossian paid and reeled home. He was unwilling to get involved in answering Jo's enquires. He slouched to bed. It was a troubled night, dreaming about flying with a gentle hand guiding his arm and spilling red wine into a blushing sky.

He finished the duet, a folk song for two oboes. Then he wrote to his mother saying he was sorry they had fallen out. It was important and he loved her. He felt wretched. Nothing helped. It's as if something had died in me, he thought.

Ossian was glad Angelica was early. They sat on his bed. He encouraged her to sing her part. 'Angelica, G-sharp, it's A major, three sharps, What are they?'

She looked hurriedly at her music. 'A major: F,C and G sharp.'

Ossian played an A, asking her to sing the scale. 'See, you are singing those three sharps.' he said.

She smiled.

'Now, your tune again.'

They sang it together. He explained some of the awkward fingering and rhythms. Her confidence grew.

'Well done. Let's leave it.' he murmured. 'You should be able to play it now. Let's meet again and try it through.'

'Yes.' She sat waiting. 'Oh, yes.' waiting.

Gently Ossian pushed her until she lay on the bed. He lay beside her.

Her eyes shone, he noticed. 'Is this all right?'

With beating heart she breathed, 'Yes.'

He traced the outline of her nose until his finger pushed over it and into her unresisting lips. She yearned towards him. They kissed. 'Your heart is beating like crazy.'

'So is yours.'

His hand burrowed into her tee-shirt and rested below her breast absorbing the beats.

'Do you mind?'

She frantically shook her head.

'Can I see?'

She nodded, and watched his dancing eyes as he gently drew off her top.

He bent and kissed her naked breasts.

Each trembled.

He stripped off his tee-shirt and lay against her. She felt his penis pressing against her thigh. She was breathless. Emboldened by his nervousness, she touched his firm chest and moved her hand down onto his tummy. Ossian winced with lust.

'Shall I stop?'

He shook his head. His lips opened. He panted.

Nervously she touched his fly, feeling response thrill through his body.

Angelica unknowingly knew his landscape, although she had never lain with anyone before. He knew of her, because he had often seen his sisters naked. But feelings swept them beyond this, and into ancient experience lying fragmented in their sinews, which sang now, blinding yet guiding them.

She let him peel off her jeans, watching as he pulled his own down. They lay together, arms finding caress and new silky feelings from exploring skin. Only their brief underpants kept them apart. He pushed his down with a toe. Willing her to cradle his balls she was washed by their softness as he gasped.

'Am I hurting?'

'No. Oh, no. I love you what you're doing.'

She gingerly felt for his erection. It swelled under her touch and stretched towards her. As her fingers peeled back its fleshy tip, it spouted sticky fluid.

Ossian groaned. 'I couldn't stop it. Don't be disgusted. Oh, Angelica, I'm sorry.'

She felt tension ooze out of him, saw relief and a bashful tenderness steal over him, was astounded by his flowering beauty.

She remembered all their exchanges, suddenly aware what had just happened she had unwittingly sought. And she was glad.

'Ossian. I don't mind. Are you better now?'

He nodded and kissed her, worshipful thanks.

She lay with him for a long time. He was her baby just for a magic moment. She was his woman; his first, he whispered into her disbelieving ear.

Before she dressed he pulled her pants down and kissed her furry triangle.

She shivered with longing and guilt. 'Is that where you want to go?'

He nodded. 'We must wait. I know that Angelica. But let's be friends, please?'

'Oh, yes, Ossian, yes.'

'For always?'

'Yes. For always.' She had never granted so much.

They met often. Sometimes they repeated his messy release; sometimes they clung contentedly; sometimes there was only a chance for a swift kiss. She doted on him. He longed for her because she stood in both his boyhood and his future: a caring unpretentious partner. Each was delirious and melancholy.

Eventually the Salvatoris realised. Mama was aghast, Papa, resentful. 'She's far to young for that.' they agreed and bought aeroplane tickets for Angelica and her aunt to go to Italy for all of the next long school holiday while they moved to a house in an outer suburb, beyond his leery reach.

In losing her, Ossian lost his only sexual connection to a social world. So he immersed himself in music, ignoring the advances of women and of men; the boy within was adamant.

'He's probably asexual.' some said.

Jo saw his stained sheets which trumpeted his need. But he was locked away. She shrugged. 'I guess it's what he wants. He's brilliant, famous, lauded. So why worry.'

Ossian's professional life was hectic. He was playing, conducting, recording and composing. His passionate, involvement was profoundly admired. This new force was gossiped over, reported on and photographed. Ossian Macknight, a new star.

'So young, so beautiful, so mysterious' the crowd decided.

5-

WHEN OSSIAN STOPPED being busy, he felt an unfamiliar gnawing. Hopefully, longing for the intimacy of his family, he returned to
the valley ostensibly to complete his first symphony. Miranda,
grown very rotund, clamoured he stay with her and Will in the new
wing Ray Rubbo had made adding to Symph's old house. 'You will
be our first guest, before Nick is born.' She cried happily, kissing his
wan face into a soft smile of agreememnt.

Ossian melted into Will's strong embrace, nervous about
longing for companionship; nervous, because the tender relationship he had had was tinged now with a hunger for more. He studied
Will's well-filled fly, wanting to see him naked, to feel his sex, to lie
as they once had, naked and comfortable. 'I long to feel comfortable
again.' Ossian mused, watching the light dance in Will's brown eyes
turning their deeps golden-warm. 'I love you.' he murmured.

Will grinned. 'I know, Ossian. It saved my life; I feel the
same.'

But Ossian felt it was not the same; now, hunger made his
love gross (the outside world would say he compromised the expectant parents).

But when they sat at the grand piano in the music space,
Ossian persuaded Will to don his scanty leotard. He hungrily
watched him strip, gloried in his thick fertile sex; savoured Will's
fine maturing body revealed by the thin fabric; he marvelled after
brushing a shy hand over Will's crotch at his erection lifting and filling it. Its straining power thrilled Ossian who haltingly confided in
Will his sadness about losing Angelica. 'Perhaps she doesn't care.
The thrill of Italy and growing up pulling her to forget.'

Will kissed him. Some of his vast unexpressed joy trickled
into Ossian who said, 'Let's dance our valley and our love Will. I
have a Tchaikovsky piece, for you.'

The lush warmth in the music, its elongated melodic lines, its longing fused with plenteous dreams, grew in the dance: the light shining the river into a sinuous snake, the reflection of trees on the still surface of the lake; dust whirling as a car bounced over the rutted tracks, the silence of sky, the dappled shadows seething under trees; the peace and the comfort, the happiness, the longings they shared with a love newly touched by raunchy energy.

Nina watched the dance. She sensed some of its mood.

Later, helping Mummy she sighed. 'Will loves Ossian and Miranda. Can you love like that?'

Sophie kissed her maturing daughter. 'Love is a gift we give to someone precious, darling, perhaps the best gift of all. Love is blind. Why we love is as complex as whom we love. But its power transforms us. You have just witnessed that between your bothers. Wasn't it a fine thing?'

Nina nodded. 'It was wild.'

Ossian was restless. 'Something stops me working, Will.'

Will grinned. 'Remember how you made me dance what I felt? Well, you must write those feelings into your music.'

Ossian grimaced. 'I'll think of you and the valley since the first movement is carefree; then I'll suffer for the second! Then the third might emerge.'

Will nodded encouragingly. 'Do you remember playing me Monteverdi's L'*Orpheo*[*] with its happy sunny string breeze contrasting the dark murky fog of his all-leather Underworld wind-band; could that inspire you?'

Ossian's eyes twinkled. 'Wow. Will. What a brilliant idea. Zeus' sunny realm contrasted with Persephone's and Hades' shadowy under-world. That's exactly how I feel, except there is no 'bridge' joining them for me.'

'Then don't compose one.'

Ossian hugged him and rested his head on Will's shoulder. 'We are good together?'

'We always will be.'

'Life out there is not easy, brother.'

'Then come home to us whenever you can. You will soon

---

[*]   See notes at end.

41

have a nephew for music lessons. We want a sextet.'

'I'd like to buy land next to you. Do you think it's possible? Although I have to find money for the work to my proposed city pad, I'm making enough now to think about a simple shack in the bush. Can you and Peter sniff out the forestry commission, see if they'd release a block or two?'

Miranda and Peter were overjoyed by the idea.

'We must get Ossian here.' everyone agreed over supper.

Tim waved for silence. 'Ray thinks there's room for shacks to the north of the main house. Ossian can start there if he wants.'

Sophie smiled happily. 'Darlings, you are all coming home. Oh what a wonderful bother.'

'I wish Ossian would find a partner!' she said softly.

Then Ant heard about Ossian's plans. 'Me too. Get land for me, Please. Help me, Dad, I'm broke?'

Tim so loved his gregarious boy .'Son, tramp around a bit; why not also ear-mark a piece of land to the north of Ararat, discuss it with Ray. Make one of your famous models. Your Mum will be over the moon.'

6-

ANT HAD MATRICULATED very young, but wanted to work for a year before starting architecture at the university. Ray Rubbo had agreed to take him in, both as an apprentice and as a surrogate son, company for his own, who, although of the same age, was at school, and destined for architecture having been named Philip after Philippo Brunelleschi whose dome graces Florence.

Ray had set Ant to model-making saying it was the best way to envisage a building, and good training for the craftsmanship of construction. Ant also worked part-time on site under a foreman on one of Ray's jobs; it was invaluable training and replaced the physical labour he missed from his life at Ararat.

Ray generously included Ant in all design work in the valley. Ant shared most of it with school boy Phil, whom he treated with the warmth he once showed Will. But it was that relationship in reverse, for Ant instigated most of their adventures, as ignorant apprentices and as tear-away teenagers. Thus, they shared school and architectural matters while indulging at home in the secret games of late childhood.

Ant engaged with Ray's discussions with Miranda and Will about extending Symph's house for their family.

'We must make a flexible plan; the future has to be guessed by architects.' Ray advised.

'I like your idea of new bedrooms making the foot of an "L-shaped" plan. It's like open arms.' said Ant.

'The plan and roof protect, welcome and nurture.'

'So do the natural materials used in Ararat.' said Ant.

'Yes, they link us to the natural environment; working with elements such as verandas, bridges between in- and out-side.' Ray grinned, impressed by the boy's thoughtfulness concerning his own firm belief that design must respond to human *and* to environmental needs. 'For example,' Ray said. 'What Mother looks at from the kitchen, distant views, also overseeing children's play; where visitors come from, contained by entry protocol; whatever delights my clients; also, where the sun rises and sets, planting, prevailing winds, topography. All contribute to life and wellbeing.'

Ant was dazzled. 'I thought is was simple to design.'

Ray looked fondly at the grey-eyed stripling. 'The simple solution is beautiful only if it is arrived at through the complexity and mystery of all such considerations. Think how easy it is to kiss and how complex the feelings which lead one to express them.'

Ant was startled. 'Has Ray talked to the foreman? Was that kiss on site, seemingly simple, more complicated than I thought?'

When he and Phil had last worked on site, Micha the foreman had asked if they kissed. The boys denied it. But Micha had urged them to kiss. So they had. Then he said. 'There was this filum on last night about two boys who kissed and did other things too, as far as I could see, like girl- and boy-friend, but two guys. I didn't believe it. But you two look the same. I never did those things. There was a bloke in my village who paid me and my friends to take our trousers down. But that was all. No funny business. Not like the priest, the filthy bugger.' He scratched his neck.'You two hunky lads, get up to larks like that?'

'No. Of course not.'

But it wormed into them. Phil asked Ant to kiss him that night as they bedded down in his room. They had started the arrangement to surf the internet late, thinking no one knew. Anyway it was fun before sleep - although getting up was hard.

Ant kissed Phil squarely on the lips. Phil put a tentative palm behind Ant's head and held him until their tongues slid together and their erections sprang up. They fondled each other, finding relief, excitement and a nervous joy.

Ant pulled Phil onto his bed. Soon they were naked. Soon, Phil fell back and whispered. 'Finish me, then I'll do you.' Ant obligingly brought him to climax then lay back for similar treatment. They slept, waking as the house stirred, Phil leaping into his own bed to avoid discovery. 'Like Micha's film.' he whispered later.

This mutual pleasure fed their needs most nights.

'Ant, this is what gays do.'

Ant, who had enjoyed Will for years was more sanguine, 'Sex is a way of talking. Not only gays. Everyone. Well, not every-one, but friends and that.'

'Have you done this before?'

'When I was little.'.

'I do it at school. One boy fucks me sometimes. It hurts a bit, but it's wild! Would you do that?'

'I don't want that.'

'If I'm careful. I promise to pull out if you say?'

But Ant, after his hurt by Will, wouldn't. So hand-play was resumed. Yet they savoured sleeping together.

'It's nice to see them happy; they are becoming quite close friends.' Ray's wife observed, watching the boys larking with a hose on the back lawn. 'Look, a couple of puppies romping and wetting everything.' she crooned in relief; teenage moodiness had become instilled in the household until Ant arrived.

Ant started university just after Miranda's child was born. It was a girl, to everyone's surprise. But Nici's welcome was joyful. 'Let's call her the girl's version of Nick, Nicola.' Miranda had suggested to a baffled Will who thought a mother's prediction was reliable. He proudly loved his tiny daughter.

They giggled helplessly when Sophie confessed she and Tim had expected Jo to be a boy and had similarly re-jigged the name.

'You men always surprise us.' Miranda said, rubbing Will's erection almost nightly until her body had readjusted to being empty again, enjoying the hot splash of his juice which calmed demands and heralded sleep.

So Uncle Ant continued his studies of architecture at the uni-versity, occasionally meeting Jo who was completing medicine as an internee at a hospital. He lived with the Rubbo's all that year and the following when Phil started the same course. They remained involved in Ray Rubbo's practice and shared much else besides, including a busy social life with a gradual involvement with girls.

They were serious and energetic students, yet remained playful puppies to the delight of the Rubbos who secretly hoped the two boys would eventually join Ray's practice.

'It's not just their skills or youth; but because they're already seriously engaged in combating the thoughtless, greedy destruction of the world we have struggled against all our life, as have Tim and Sophie.' Ray said one evening when Phil had borrowed the car to go to a bar-b-q with a couple of girls, Ant promising only one of them would drink.

'I love them both.' his wife had whispered as the boys' cheerful barracking was silenced by the slam of a door and the rattling retreat of Ray's beloved old banger.

'So do I, my dear.' said Ray. They both want to work here during the next vacation: part on site, and the office. Their technical drawing needs attention. But Ant's free-hand drawing is spectacular; I guess it's all the studies he made for Peter. Not only does he have a good eye, his spatial imagination is breathtaking: he thinks in three dimensions, not two like most of us, including Phil. His love of materials has a practical basis, probably living with rocks, trees and water all these years. Ant's other asset, apart from good looks and charm, is his verbal dexterity: he can articulate what he feels, and describe complicated concepts. This spurs Phil. The happiness they find is formidable. I hope the barbarians never blunt their spirits.'

His wife worried. 'My dear, let's send them away for a tramp in the bush as well. They often talk about it. I think such a break would refresh and reward their hard work. I talked to Sophie last week. They're willing to lend the boys one of the 4-wheel-drives so they can go further afield. What do you think?'

Ray grinned. 'Kiffy, you mothers are right. A break is a good idea. Perhaps you should mention it to them now. Give them a chance to plan or invite friends if they want. I suggest the last few weeks, so they return to uni. fresh for the new term. Maybe we could get away as well, with Rose?'

Kiffy shook her head. 'Our daughter grows less interested in dirty camping, preferring the smart life. She's invited a girl friend to stay. I think we can risk leaving the house to them. But my dear, let's have matches; your silly old tinder box is not fun and games.'

'You drive a hard bargain, madam. Replace the tinder box with fun and games. I suppose so.' Ray chuckled and pecked her cheek.

7-

RAY RUBBO WAS OVERWORKED. He relinquished tackling the alterations to Ossian's town house to Ant, promising full support. Ant was thrilled. He and Ossian talked until hoarse. Eventually, he took some preliminary sketches to Ray.

'I like your ideas. The open studio space upstairs where walls are easily removed, the living areas underneath where walls can support the loads from above - grand pianos, on three points are frantically heavy.' Ray observed.

He gently chided the boy about costing and working drawings until Ant realised it was beyond him. Ray again gently offered the facilities of his practice. 'Although Ossian is unconcerned about cost, we must be. Lean on me whenever you need, I believe you can deal with the project, trust me. It's a great challenge. Remember model-making. This job cries out for one. I suggest you make a model in two colours: red for structural elements and blue for non-structural. Then we can sort out what is available for support. I think you should look carefully at the gable dormer-window structure at the front. Its triangles are naturally shaped to carry and distribute loads; it might generate a fine system for supporting the roof, making Ossian's studio rather special. I agree with you, a roomy private space is just what he needs.'

Ant liked sharing. Ray was kind, imaginative and easy-going. They talked a lot about what Ray called The Analysis of both need and structure. He prodded the boy to think about how to get a grand piano to the upper floor, about sound proofing, about the play of sunlight, about the dead-weight storage musicians need for music, the even environment keeping pianos and oboes in tune, and surfaces to embellish sound.

Ossian, familiar with the multitudinous detail in

music-making, was patient and responsive.

Ant began to read avidly about acoustics and inner and outer environments. He visited other architects and talked to many of Ossian's musical friends. Some laughed at his intensity. But Ray was always encouraging. 'The questions may seem silly, but the end result should be our focus. Keep at it!'

Ant made many drawings sending them off to the local authority for approval. Les Stevens, the engineer Ray used, took charge of the structure. Ant responded to Ray's comment about the triangular dormer and devised sets of triangles supporting the main roof beams as well as others holding a beam with pullies so Ossian's piano could be hauled up and into his studio directly from the street.

Les loved balks of timber. He warmed to the boy's idea of a forest of struts and devised practical solutions.

'The men'll enjoy constructing this lot.' Les grinned.

Ray nodded. 'I have a team in mind. Ant, another way to achieve quality is to allow enthusiastic craftsmen to shape our buildings. I thought Micha and his lads would do a lovely job, what do you think?'

Ant looked from one to the other. He was excited. He glimpsed the rich milieu in which buildings were made. He was part of a team. Team Leader they called him. His elation was infectious. He liked Micha, the kissing foreman. He and Phil giggled about 'Micha giving the kiss of life to Ossian's house.' Ant felt relieved.

Ray took Micha aside soon afterwards. 'He's a bright lad. But he needs help. He's not the type to get uppity either. So if you or the lads have any suggestions, mention it to Ant, as you would to me. And Micha, ring the office any time. We and Ant are available, as always.'

Work started the week Miranda and Will's second child was born. They called it Kim, after the *Kookaburra Films* cameraman. Sophie had laughed when they announced it. They cheerfully retorted. 'Of course, dear Mum, we know it can also be a girl's name. But our boy will grow strong with a huge willy, so there.'

When Ossian moved in to camp in his own house, Ant took over his rented room. Sophia and Toni were delighted to have another Macknight tenant. Ant was hauled in to feast on pasta and wine, fresh salads and *Tiramasu,* a sweet made with Marsala, amid talk about children, Italy, hard work and lots of laughter.

They found Ant more approachable than Ossian. 'More like Tim.' they remarked over the washing up at midnight when 'all the children' had been sent to bed - including Ant. They were particularly delighted he intended staying a second year for his final which entailed a lot of work.

Ray had suggested his graduation thesis be "A house for a musician" so Ant could capitalise on the research done for Ossian's house. 'You'll have to rejig the drawings. The architecture school requires a certain style for graduation theses.' Ray said. 'Just get it done. You deserve the piece of paper, another year there will not do you much harm, or good.'

Ant set up his drawing board and re-arranged Ossian's old room, an airy one upstairs at the front of the house. He filled it with books and models, large prints on the wall and a three-quarter bed: he enjoyed sharing it. He kept a mattress underneath for any friends who stayed over after parties or work. Ant still liked to share his room. Not in order to frighten off the Horribillies, but he had grown used to people around him.

One afternoon he bumped into Phil's sister, Rose who asked if he'd take her to a party. It was in an outer suburb. He picked her up on his motorbike around eight.

It was an evening of drinking and dancing. Ant didn't know the crowd. They were rich and well connected. He charmed them with his good looks and cheerful banter. Rose seemed a bit put out by the attentions lavished on him. Ant and she had a familiar relationship growing out of family life, so he didn't fret.

It was late. Rose buttoned her coat. The bike would be chilly. 'On the way, can I see your new room?'

So Ant drove them back there. She was drunk and agreed to a coffee to settle her spinning head. Ant returned with two mugs to find a pile of clothes strewn on the rug and Rose nestling in his bed.

Rose, what are you doing?'

'Waiting for you; come on.'

He sat on the bed. She reached out and began to strip off his clothes. Naked, he slipped in beside her. They hugged. She slid on top of him, took his head in her hands and kissed him deeply, sliding down so his erection was nudging her vagina. She opened her thighs and jiggled over it until it slipped in.

He reached up and kissed her nipples. She shivered and

started bouncing on him until she climaxed.

Rose let herself be turned over. Ant entered her again with long delicious thrusts. She climaxed again, letting out such a shout even distant Horribillies must have heard. Fountaining into her, Ant was almost oblivious. Whimpering with ecstatic effort he died. They drifted away, together.

In the morning they woke and dressed without a word. He stood at the door fiddling with his ignition keys. 'I'm sorry, Rosie, I'll take you home.'

She looked out the window and blurted. 'I wanted to see if you were gay.' She shuddered, embarrassed by feelings.

Ant took her shoulders and turned her into his arms.

Rose cried weakly. 'No I didn't. But I know Phil and you sleep together I saw you.' She whispered more to herself than him, 'Boys fuck with anyone. They don't care.'

'I don't fuck with anyone, Rose, I make love.'

She was shivering. She looked at him distraught with confusion. 'You love Phil that way, don't you?'

'No Rose. We were boys. Friends, yes. Anyway we didn't fuck. Ever. It was ages ago.'

She sobbed. 'I didn't mind then.'

Ant was startled. 'Rose, do you think last night was like me and Phil when we were school boys?'

She nodded.

'I saw only you.'

'And you made love?'

'Yes, Rose.'

'But I love you.' she whispered.

Ant held her. A wild pleasure raced through him. Carefully he took her clothes off, then his own and led her to bed. He kissed her until she shimmered. She fondled him until it became unbearable. He plunged in for more and more until her shouts burst and he burst and they lay in a victorious embrace.

He whispered. 'Oh Rosie, is that better?'

She smiled. 'Much better.'

'Are you hungry?'

Rose smiled. 'Famished.' They found some left-overs in the fridge and tip-toed back to bed where they fed each other like children at a naughty mid-night feast. Then she saw his excitement. Rose clasped his erection feeling it swell and harden in her palm.

'It's talking to me.' she whispered.

'Don't listen otherwise you'll be on your back again.'

'Oh, Ant don't be mean. He's the only friend I've got. Let him come.'

He straddled her, taking weight on his knees and elbows so he frisked around her labia until she pulled him hungrily in. He held it there pulsing and prodding with minute movements until she melted groaning with climax after climax, with visions of this most beautiful of men floating before her with ravishing promises. He stirred and thrust. Then all his riches were hers. Her love flowered.

She held him. 'I didn't know it could be so good.'

He raised his sweaty head. 'Oh, Rose, Rose.'

'What happened to the power of the giant? For now I can hold it in the palm of my hand?' she said. 'Is that love? Can such a small word blow us away?'

In discussing their holiday tramp, Phil and Ant delighted at the idea of each taking a friend.

'Hopefully a girl.' Phil said.

'Would you mind if Rose came?' Ant asked embarassedly.

'Won't she cramp our style, unless she brings a friend too?'

Ant blushed. 'What I mean is, she comes with me.'

Phil gasped and pushed Ant off his chair and onto the floor. 'You sneaky bastard.' He guffawed. 'I thought sis looked happy, with a new stud. But you. That's amazing.'

He fell onto Ant and rolled with hilarity until the carpet was rucked and they, dusty.

'Oh, Ant, I'm really glad. Glad for both of you. My favourite people snogging in the tent next door. What larks we'll have.'

Ray and Kiffy were bemused by the boys' plan.

Ray shook his head. 'Well, what a holiday. All our dear ones. An extension of home, really. I wonder what Tim and Soph will say.'

Kiffy took her daughter aside. 'Darling, are you sure? There'll be pressure to pair, particularly with Phil bringing his girl friend?'

Rose smiled archly. 'Oh Mummy. Ant and I are hardly strangers; anyway we both want to go.' She darkened. 'Ant's a special friend. A very special person.'

Her mother sighed. 'Darling, he is. I hope it'll be a wonderful holiday. You three together makes me much less worried than those two gadding about somewhere on their own. You know what clumsy puppies they can be.'

'No, Mummy, they're all right; it's being alive. I love their joyous energy.'

Kiffy nodded, impressed by her daughter's understanding. 'You're quite right, my darling. Their spirits make them precious. It is a rare energy all of you children seem to radiate. And you're right: maybe my worry was your being left out as so often in the past. It should not be a man's world. We women have equal rights to life and adventures. But I do believe a sexual balance keeps life manageable.'

'A "balance." Do you mean love?'

Her mother gasped. She was silent. 'Yes, darling. That power transforms the ordinary person, the ordinary life. My dear, you *are* teaching your old Mum to think clearly.'

Rose laughed.

They hugged. It was an intimate moment, mother and daughter connecting again after the estrangement during adolescent years. Both dimly acknowledged in their managing this balancing power lay acceptance of a beloved phallus.

8-

RAY'S OFFICE occupied the first floor of an old terrace house, owned by a consortium of three architectural practices, two on the ground floor. Below, at the rear, was the common staff/lunch room, also used for client meetings. It had access to the back garden where people congregated in good weather. Ray's double front room was a drawing office where everyone had a work station. The rear room was a shared library and secretary.

Because of lack of space, Phil worked in the library. But there was a lot of traffic as the boys conferred often. Ant was both a better draughtsmen and a better designer, helped by his earlier start at uni. There was little rivalry, rather a good humoured collaboration, the spirit Ray encouraged throughout the building.

The boys longed to be out working on site. Ray pressed them to work in the office. 'Our pencil skills must come first.' he said. Yet he seldom left the office on site visits without them.

He also persuaded them to help the secretary. They began to deal with the administration of building work. Their enthusiasm and cheerfulness helped bridge any irritation over mistakes so inexperienced a pair inevitably made.

Ray sent them regularly as workers to Ossian's house nearing completion. 'Help-out. Look at everything. So you get an inkling of another layer of our work: constructing from drawings.'

Micha fell about when, on the first day Phil cried 'And no kissing this time, please.'

'No, lads. That was a one-off.' Micha said. But he wanted to kiss them. They were so willing, so mature now, and so handsome. Spirits were buoyant on site, particularly as everyone knew Ant was not only the architect for the job but was interested in their site problems. They called them the 'Tootees', from 2T's , or two twins or two tee squares.

'The architect and the son of the boss. That's OK.' Even the young labourer agreed.

The boys couldn't keep up with the workmen when everyone adjourned to the pub on Fridays after work. They usually reeled back to Ant's room and slept it off, arriving still somewhat groggy the next morning to follow-up any site matters in the office where Ray usually popped in inviting them for lunch out or a client meeting. He laughed and roughed Phil's hair one bleary Saturday. 'Listen son, don't compete. They're old hands with the grog. Settle for what you can take. No honour lost, and no hangovers.'

But the boys enjoyed the riot of Friday afternoons. It washed some of the stress away. 'We're not as good as them on site or in the pub. Luckily it's not far to Ant's place. But it's fun.' Phil told his father.

'Well, and why not?' said Ray who then told them their pay packets would be bigger. 'You're earning it.' he said. 'And that calls for a drink.' his eyes twinkling almost as much as theirs.

9-

KIFFY RUBBO DROVE the four youngsters to the train. Ant, Phil, Rose and Phil's friend, Nadia. They had bulky packs even without the fresh food they intended to buy after Peter Sloan met them. He took them to the town super market and then to Ararat for the night, before they set off in the Macknight's 4WD.

Ant's plan was to follow the track outside the gate to the needles rocks, traverse the flank of the mountain and then drive along the ridge, through the cleft in the rocky summit and on towards the tallest peak called Mount Skene, leave the car and explore.

'It's fire-spotters' territory, so look out for smoke from their huts and a welcome.' Tim said.

It was Symph's route. But nothing was said about the sacred pool. A carefree student holiday should not be darkened by inner spirits, the Macknight family decided.

Everyone swam. The guests were at first bashful with nothing on. But the peace and gentle landscape washed away some of the city-stuffiness; the reverential unconcern of the house-hold seeped in until physical pleasure and freedom loosened reserve.

Ant shared his room with Rose with hearty interest from Tim and Sophie; Phil and Nadia took Miranda's old room next door. Both couples were subdued in so intimate and open a household.

'What if they hear?' Rose whispered.

Ant started thrusting deeply and whispered. 'They've heard it all before.'

She gasped as pleasure tinged with risk swept her.

They set off the next morning. By lunch time they had reached the split rock summit and decided to snack there. Ant found the remains of a fire. He wondered why anyone had camped there.

After lunch they drove on, bouncing over the rock scree and snow-line plants, reaching the base of the summit of Mount Skene where they set up camp.

It was windy on the saddle. Phil dug a pit for the fire. The others, after collecting wood, found stones to hold down the tents discretely separated by a large rocky outcrop.

They ate in the dying light. Then sat drinking wine as one by one stars peeped through their darkening velvet veil. Faces, ruddy with wind and firelight, seemed fragile in the immensity of space. Nadia had never camped this way was glad of Rose's camaraderie.

Phil's sexual licence unnerved her. The vast untamed space chimed with the untamed willfulness in which soon she would indulge so the stars were accusing eyes and the wind howled threats. Rose's feminine presence calmed her.

But once she was in Phil's arms little else mattered. Stars swung around her, the wind sang in delight. Her body opened. Soon they were fixed together bucking and groaning. Then the warm world exploded to fall around them with delicious sleepy sighs.

During the following days they explored the groins each side of the ridge to which Mount Skene was sentinel. It was peaceful tramping through the silent forest, a relief to be out of the wind. On the southern side they eventually found water, but although they pushed through boundless tangled scrub it remained pools rather than running water, although Ant thought it was the headwaters of one of the big rivers. 'It's the moist warm-up to sex, rather than a climax.' Phil ventured as they struggled up-hill back to camp.

When they tackled the mountain it was a warm quiet day. Snow still huddled in crevices away from direct sunlight. The rocks were worn by ice and winds, tiny plants nestled under them. The four delighted in the shy display, minute colourful eyes aware only of eagles in this airy place and the need for shelter. From the summit they spied a small hut perching on posts off the ground and looking nakedly awkward. It consisted of two stories, the second, a small glassed look-out from where fires were spied and reported to a radio base in a distant town. The smoking chimney proclaimed its resident fire-watcher. As the four were running short of water, they decided to drive there and beg some from a big round tank beside the door.

'The name's Mervin.' said a bearded man in surprise at the

delegation. 'Water? Sure, no problem. Help yourselves while I make a cuppa. Wash if you want.' While he stoked the sleepy fire into life the youngsters stripped and bathed with speedy hilarity. They filled their water cans and trooped inside.

It was a bare space with four timber posts supporting the upper look-out glimpsed up a steep staircase. A long table stretched between two of the posts. One end was stacked with a clutter of VHF radio equipment. The other served as kitchen bench and table. Merv pushed a pile of car magazines aside and invited everyone to take a seat, handing around mugs of steaming tea.

'No, there's no water hereabouts.' he told them. 'Yes, it sure is windy. A constipated place, all wind and no water.' he grinned. He readily agreed to their tents being erected nearby and to the girls offering to make them all a feast.

It was a jolly evening. After much talk about Merv's bush larks and student rags and after clearing up, Merv played his guitar and sang some of his favourite songs, indisbursed with songs every-one joined in. The wind rattled the thin walls, howling under the floor like a demented ghost.

The hut was shrouded in thick cloud when they opened the door to depart, Light from the door beamed through the swirling mist. Beyond the short flight of steps a beady pair of eyes gleamed. Nadia screamed.

Merv chuckled. 'Probably one of the nighties out fossicking. No worries, darling. It's more frightened than you.'

The four trod carefully, avoiding monsters lurking in the shadows and thankfully scrambled into tents and into each other's arms.

During breakfast Ant said, 'I'm sick of the wind. Let's go back to that chasm in the rock-summit. I understand why there was an old camp-fire there. It's good shelter.'

Rose nodded. 'We could explore from there, couldn't we?'

Everyone agreed.

'We'll have to tramp much further down if we want to find water' Phil said. 'We only have about four day's supplies. It would be great to camp by a creek.'

They drove along the rough ridge to the cleft, set up camp and divided into two search-parties exploring each side.

Ant and Rose turned left down the steep slope, kicking loose stones with their boots until reaching the scrub below winter's snow-line. It was difficult pushing onward, but eventually Ant saw lighter patches in the solidity of trees. 'Maybe the trees are thinning because there's a water course.' he panted. They hurried forward to find a trickle. Bounding over the rocks spewed in the groin they found larger pools and more flow.

Ant hugged Rose. Happily they pulled off their scant clothes then slipped together into a pool of water gilded from seeping through the earth. He wanted to enter her but it was too cold. So they scrambled out and fell on their clothes. She loved his ardour and his rushed coming. Loved the brightness of his body dancing with tree shadows, rippling with sex. Loved the freedom of their embrace in this unguarded peace, the freshness of meeting. Afterwards they lay on their backs and watched the clouds parade through the dancing leaves, bathed by blueness, burning after so cold a dip. Very happy.

'Can we spend time together like this?'

Ant rolled over and kissed her until his erection recovered. 'Let's explore down stream later. I'd like that.' He looked shyly at her. 'Did you mind?'

She grinned. 'Ant, it was the best.' and rubbed his erection, jumped up and dressed. 'Keep it for later.'

Phil and Nadia were slightly put out. They had struggled through the dense undergrowth, struggled through the forest, finding no water. The solitude was wearing.

It was an excited supper, a luscious night's rest and an early morning start, lugging very heavy packs down to a larger pool, more distant than the one which stopped Ant and Rose. With care-free haste they erected the tents, collected fire wood and made mattresses of ferns, lit the fire and, while the billy boiled, fell laughing into the clear golden pool, washing self-consciousness away, and with it, mores about nudity and sexual arousal.

Phil found it unsettling seeing his sister, who had had an invisible life since puberty, become visible and unabashed with his dearest friend. It invited similar behaviour he and Nadia gradually adopted.

So, happiness became tangible. With it, a wish for some private time. So when Ant mentioned exploring down stream, Phil and Nadia grinned broadly. 'Yes, you should go. We might stay here for the day. Don't rush back.'

When they had walked some distance and the camp was indistinct, Rose took Ant's hand. They walked down the verge of the stream carpeted in grass, green from proximity to water.

'It's like a Japanese garden, the grass patterned by rocks.' said Ant happily. 'Do you know *Ryoanji*?'

Rose nodded. 'It's one of Dad's favourites, the raked marble chips and the mossy rocks bounded by a low wall; he was in Japan last winter. He said the courtyard was awesome, the swirling snow reflecting the swirling patterns raked in the white marble.'

Ant enjoyed watching her. She's such a lovely girl, he thought. His shorts fly bulging. 'We need green rain today.'

Rose had spied his glances and his arousal. She loved his buoyant moods. '"Love is green" Lorca says. Will that do?'

He stopped. Studied her warmth, pulled her into his arms. He kissed her, pushing his erection into her groin.

She whispered. 'I do love you, don't you believe me?'

Ant held her, rocking them both in a gentle swaying motion and humming quietly *'Someone's in the kitchen with Dinah, some - one's in the kitchen, I know-ow-ow-ow, Someone's in the kitchen with Dinah, playing on the old banjo.'*

'That's why you want to be my boy?' he asked.

'I want everything with you, to be me and Phil. I feel free with you, Ant. Free to be crazy and weird, all the bits of me alive.'

He looked searchingly into her blue eyes and melted, stammering. 'I feel free with you, Rose. I'm so happy this holiday. I want to sing and to jump and shout.' He paused. 'And be everything with you. I've never felt like this. Have you?'

She shook her head, hair shadows dancing over her face.

He muttered. 'Let's get on to the water. I must take your clothes off and be with you that way.'

She grinned. 'I know what you want you over-sexed fiend. To be in the kitchen with a naked Diner.'

He openly wanted her. They both knew. She wanted him, it was also obvious. Her heart was beating with excitement, wanting to be in the kitchen with Ant, up to her chin in love-food and the aroma of love-cooking so they stuffed themselves falling faint with joy under the kitchen table where no one saw what delicious fare they quaffed.

They hurried on. Where the stream split, they took the upper branch, soon coming across an expanse of flat rock over which water trickled to fall into a large pool below. They tried to cross the rock. Ant slipped on the moss, pulling Rose after him to splash into the pool. They struggled out wet through, his small shoulder pack oozing water. Laughing they stripped off their soaking clothes, opened the pack, put everything out to dry.

Ant up-ended the pack over Rose's head emptying water. She screamed and pushed him into the pool. There was much frothing and shrieking and laughter as they swam and chased each other until she wrenched the sodden pack from him, filled it with water and upended it in retaliation. Then she clung to him, her knees gripping his waist. He was transfixed by her passionate kiss. She felt his erection pushing hungrily at her vagina. They scrambled out and continued their explorations bringing ceaseless pleasure until he touched her anus and whispered, so the nosy birds wouldn't hear and tell the world, 'What about this way, now?'

Rose nodded nervously. 'Be careful.'

Ant eased greasy fingers in until she relaxed and he entered her, Bit by bit until her buttocks pressed against his hips. He felt her relax, admitting him. He was over excited; a couple of deep thrusts and he ejaculated.

Afterwards they agreed it was weird stirring up shit, but intimate and exciting.

She looked curiously at his fallen face. 'Is it the same with a boy?'

Ant lay beside her silent. 'A similar tight richness, with no sense of domination, or of mingling of identical bodies. But the same wild pleasure in the forbidden.'

'Does it make me a slut?'

Ant started. He shook his head vehemently. 'Shit Rose, it was my desire. It's wonderful to play. I wonder whether I'm gay, still liking it.'

Rose sighed in contentment. 'Maybe I like gay boys. You are the most beautiful man-man I've ever met, if that's any comfort.'

He lay, nursing his indeterminate regret: possibly of having crossed into adult territory, of losing the lustless play of childhood or being suddenly more alone. For this act differed from the ending in an easy sleep after boy bed-play with Will; for now a shadow lay across them which a thorough wash afterwards did not loosen. What disturbed Ant it was the same dark shadow garnered from his rape, from which he knew he could never escape.

They lingered, he finding solace in the reflections dancing on the face of the pool, and indulging in her questing fingers as she caressed him. She watched his penis swell and wilt as his inner moods swung; watched the secret life in his balls as they stirred on his thigh; watched his tummy swell with his tightening lungs; watched him watching her with a pensive fondness until his familiar infectious smile warmed her.

'I could easily stay here all day. Except I'm ravenous.'

She bent and kissed his shrunken foreskin and jumped up for the packets of sandwiches they had prepared.

They were sodden. Petulantly they threw them away.

'Oh well, let's go back.' he said.

'One last splash. I want to fall from the mossy rock.'

He watched her clamber up and launch herself into the pool. It looked fun. He scrambled up the rock and slid into the water with a mighty splash scattering the floating remains of their lunch. Shivering and laughing they dried each other and walked demurely back to camp. There was no sign of the others. They livened up the fire for tea, and sat chewing on the last bread and greening cheese.

'Love is green, cheese is green, grass is green, moss is green, mould is green.' sang Rose.

Ant looked at her. She's gorgeous, he thought. A sunny smile lit his face.

Phil and Nadia, restless in camp, had struggled up the slope through the undergrowth to another ridge from where they admired the view but were buffeted by the wind. They had felt dwarfed by the mountains and hugeness of sky.

'I don't think we'll go there again.'

'Come down stream. We'll show you the moss slide.'

'Sounds fantastic. Yeh. Trust you to fall in gear and all. That's what city boys do. Nadia, we've a couple of city slickers here. Better pack them up and send them home.'

Ant grinned. 'We didn't know it was so slippery.'

'Exactly.' cried Phil. 'Tender-foot, tender-foot.'

'Well, we were boy scouts today' his sister said archly. 'I don't mind, as long as I don't have to fall in next time.'

Ant grunted, acknowledging her double-talk.

It's over Phil's head. Thank goodness, Rose thought leaning delightedly on Ant and nursing her tender bottom.

The expedition to the slippery pool next morning was cheerful. Phil was captivated by all the challenges he invented for sliding the full height of the rock face and making the biggest possible splash. Nadia, reluctant about nudity, found his boyishness infectious; she surreptitiously watched the others, and thrilled at the occasional erection, savouring the cuddle, sometimes penetration, but all at a gallop during the water play. Imperceptibly she sloughed off her self-consciousness and began to lark about as well.

Eventually, when Phil hugged her from behind and poked his erection through her thighs she wriggled and opened herself so he pushed in, thrust a little and backed away to scamper up the green rocks and career down into the pool, his swollen pole wagging triumphantly all the way down.

Ant tired of the games; he was restless, like his adolescent years: looking distractedly for an invisible something. He suggested he and Rose take their lunch and explore further, leaving the others fooling around the pool. She agreed.

Phil and Nadia sprawled sunning themselves and panting. Ant bent and kissed each surprised face. 'See you later, crocodiles.' He took Rose by the hand: they left following the course of the creek and soon disappeared.

'Ant's sort-of happy.' breathed Phil. 'Isn't it fun here Nadia?'

She nodded shyly. 'It gets better every day.'

Phil grinned mistaking her emphasis. She eagerly accepted him when he rolled over and into her, crying as her excitement burst and she forgot the growing-up dogma dogging her. Finally, she floated as fee and untouchable as the tiny puffs of cloud slowly unravelling above them. The grass bordering the stream bent under her, the birds relished her sighs. The sun smiled on her contentment in the silence of trees, rocks and pools.

Ant took Rose down the valley. Birds carolled, a slight breeze sighed endearments in the grass and through the crowns of the trees. The sun burned their backs; everything danced. Then the creek vanished. Carefully edging towards a precipice, they gazed down into a gigantic well in the rock into which water fell.

'It must be an old volcano.' Ant said in awe. 'Look there's water at the bottom.'

Rose gasped. 'Its green, love-green.'

'Better than *Ryoanji*. Let's find a way down.' Ant whispered, looking carefully round the precipitous rocks. 'Let's try over there to the left. See, there's a tiny ledge or is it a path?'

Rose was aghast but followed. He moved with nervous care along and down the cliff face until he reached a small twisted tree growing from a fault in the rock. Here he paused and helped Rose to clamber down and join him. He held her arm, stiff with strained descent into Hell behind her man. Ant panted. 'Nearly there, eh? You're a brave girl.'

Rose smiled wanly. 'I'm no good with heights. Come, let's go on.' She followed his lithe form inching down, down away from brightness and chirping cheer of the forest, away from her brother, their familiar camp. Small black birds fluttered around them making barely audible warning cheeps. A silver thread of water from a lip in the sky was falling to its death. The silence confounded them.

'It's as if we are in the middle of the earth.' Ant breathed, as at last they stepped onto a secure, horizontal shelf of rock overhanging the water and bathed in sunlight.

'The water really is green.' she murmured. 'Look, you can see the sky reflected. It's like a green lens and we are looking right through the earth to the sky on the other side.'

He stood stock still. Glanced at her face trembling with sunlight and feelings. 'Come on let's swim.' He peeled off his clothes and stood like a god, looking carefully into the depthless water. Then he dived, emerging with a shout, 'Wow, it's cold.'

Rose watched him swim across the limpid water and dally under the silver threads falling from above.

'He's being baptised.' she said softly. In the silence she found herself talking to? To herself? No, the voice was unbidden. It told her Ant's baptism was a vital event in his life, that she too must take it. It told her to look deep into her heart and see whose image was there - it was Ant's. It asked her if she was happy. She replied without hesitation, 'Oh, yes, certainly yes.'

'Then you must reach out and embrace him: his light *and* his shadow, the whole you've been discovering.' The voice was butterflies pulling her. 'Then you'll embrace your own light and shadow, because that's the way it must be for both of you, because he'll feel the same, if you dare to ask him.'

Rose undressed; suddenly aware of her body, particularly seeing its sinuous reflection in the disturbed surface of the green pool. She saw her swaying breasts, fulsome and bountiful, the broad boned hips, the neat triangle of pubic hair proclaiming the entrance to her womb 'Where he will plant seeds for your offspring.' the voice murmured.

She was hot inside with a knowing emptiness. She was happy. Her body, her love, her fountain of life, all her dreams joined, self-contained yet linked to the mysteries of the earth. She half-remembered the old Greek story of the sky lying on the earth to make everything. He was her sky; he would press onto her, bringing light and warmth to her darkest recesses; she, bringing him to life, nurturing the newness propagated; how it had always been. They, heirs to a fabulous heritage of love and making.[*]

Her head swam. She dived blindly. Cold shocked her back to reality. She swam breathlessly towards the filagree waterfall and Ant's head bobbing in its pitter-patter.

Rose reached up and marked his brow. 'You're being baptised.' .

'I know. Draw the letter A. Then I'll draw an R on yours.'

They heard the voice. 'The most sacred names in the universe. Now return to the rock and join A with R.'

Shivering, they paddled back to dry one another and warm-up in the sun.

Rose saw the most beautiful man: lean and tall, sun-bronzed with a shining halo of fair hair, with dove-grey eyes and a mouth as merry and ample as his velvety sex.

Ant saw a woman of soft muscular proportions with perfect breasts crowned with generous nipples, big-hipped for childbearing, strong thighs framing the loveliest mound of pubic hair, able hands, sturdy legs, feet and a face so tender, so strongly formed, he gasped.

He kneeled over her thighs and gently lowered himself down until he hovered like the sky over the undulating land, soon

---

[*] See notes at end.

admitting him to shower it with fertile rain.

Joy was intense. They laboured. His whimpering ecstacy mirrored in the goosepimpled water, until her shout unsettled the tiny birds which rose in clouds and wheeled in the amphitheatre overhead their shadows dancing over the lover's supine bodies.

Later she found herself and him. He was perched on a crooked elbow looking intently at her.

'Will you marry me?' he whispered.

'Now?' she stammered.

'Yes.'

'I must think. Give me time.'

But all her doubts and questions, the reason, logic, sense of everything in her life became mired in the voices inside and around her crying, 'Yes. Yes. Yes.'

Never had she lost herself like this. Never had she been so elated. Rose struggled to her feet, pulling Ant up with her. They stood at the edge of the rock moulded by the love of those before them and looked into the love-green water finding two lovers gazing at them in bemused wonder. She took his hand. With a sob of joy she whispered. 'Yes.'

The four lovers embraced, each pair becoming two souls melded into one. They sighed, or was it someone else? The voice of the earth? Their voices? Even years later after reflection they admitted they remained confused. But married, they had become, and witnessed. Of that they were certain.

They briefly swam again, chilled to the bone, but their unquenchable cores blazed. Ant stuffed their clothes in his pack and helped Rose on with her stout boots. They climbed up towards the light greedily feeding delighted eyes on each other as if counting every treasure they had just acquired.

Tired and scratched they reached the top. Nothing had changed, except the waning day. Hurriedly they dressed and tramped up the gurgling water course, past the deserted slippery pool and on up to their camp. The others had begun supper preparations. They smiled welcome.

'So you had a good time?' Phil said jocularly.

His sister kissed him. 'Very good!'

'Should we go?'

'Sometime. Later.' she blinked. 'We married.'

Phil whistled. 'Married? You mean you decided . . .'

Ant hugged him. 'We married.'

Nadia screwed up her nose. 'Why?'

'Because we love one another.' Ant answered.

'There was no other course.' Rose said.

'You could get an abortion.'

Rose smiled. 'Nadia, it's not like that.'

Ant squeezed Phil's waist. 'We want to be together.'

'Like the sky and the earth, free yet joined.' Rose murmured.

'Feeding each other.' Ant compounded the perplexity.

Phil let out a whoop and tugged Ant round in circles.

'They could be prancing round the garden again, wetting everything.' Rose smiled.

'We must celebrate.' shouted Phil happily. 'They're a few bottles left. Let's make wooppee.'

The firelight made the night dance until the four youngsters danced and hurrahed themselves into their tents as the moon serenely sailed over a distant ridge. Ant and Rose lay in a tender embrace listening to the tipsy efforts of the others in uninhibited love-making.

'We've done that.' she whispered.

'Not that we won't try again.' He snuggled into her warmth until sleep wafted them up to the rocking moon which crooned all night long.

Everyone woke early. The fire smoked from the shadowed floor of the forest to distant blue as sunlight slipped fingers deeper round the rocks and plants and the campers.

'We're staying put today.' announced Rose. 'Ant wants to sketch our house behind Ararat ("Our House", eh? thought Phil gleefully.) 'and I'm going to study natural colours for my next fashion collection.'

'It's fun moping about camp. But we've done that. Let's go back down the creek for another slippery time.' Phil cried.

Nadia shook her head in mock disapproval. 'You like everything slippery, you tender cock-foot.'

'Oh, I wish mine was as big.' groaned Ant.

Phil chuckled. 'You can't have everything.'

The girls looked-on at this masculine bravado, grinning as their men flashed winks and grins. Nadia packed snacks, towels and a plastic ground sheet, for sliding down the moss.

'Tea, Jeeves, at three o'clock.' Phil called as they left.

Over lunch Rose showed Ant her collection of leaves, rocks and flowers and sketches for a range of jackets and skirts using the colour scheme.

'I want a pair of slacks and a shirt. You know Rose, I really like the idea of letting nature influence colour. Will you make gear for our babies?'

She blushed; babies had invaded her thoughts since her ravishment, keened by their naked trek to the top when she had savoured his body, including what was usually hidden, such as the shy hair under his arms, the shadowed crease of his bottom, the way his sex swung and collided with his inner thighs; she imagined drying all his crevices and kissing him there as she would her baby now her womb was clamouring, as she was, for lodgement.

'I'll make clothes for all of us.' She flushed with pleasure. 'But only if I can live in our house. Show it to me.'

Ant turned serious eyes on her. 'It looks like this: **A⋀**. Each A-frame is structurally stable. The outer ones are roofed, the right A, our living areas, the left A are bedrooms: ours on an upper level above the kids; the space between is bare, a deck, a sort of courtyard where we eat and play. I want to leave the ground unscarred, so only the feet of the A's are in contact with it. If we need more room, we can roof the centre. I thought I'd position a verandah along the front to link it all, provide an entry as well as shielding us from the fierce western sun. What do you think?'

'It's a tree-house. Sky-living. Fabulous. Leaving the rocks and letting the ground flow underneath is perfect. Oh, Ant, can we really have our own little house in the valley? Fill it with books and music and friends and our children? Can we have a studio above the living area, like our bedroom? Then we can make babies, clothes and buildings? Oh Ant, I love you.'

Ant nodded. Then smiled. 'Your Dad suggested I thought of a village: making a cluster of houses around the upper entry level of Ararat; ours, Ossian's and one or two more. The space becomes like a village green where we meet and play, hugged by the buildings on its perimeter. Your dad is so brilliant: no flashy architectonic ivory towers, just the nerve to build in response to and support family life off the earth. I hope he approves.'

'Does it matter?'

'Yes it does. He's the best architect in the country. I don't care what institutes and the chatterers say.

'But it's ours, surely if we like it . .?'

'Ray sees into the future, like any good architect. It's beyond present opinion. The future must be accommodated. He will help me walk round the house and the green in a hundred years. He's like Symph, he talks to the birds.'

'I know he thinks you're very good.'

'One day I want to be as good as he. If you'll help me.'

Rose looked into the soft depths of grey, seeing her happiness reflected there. She snuggled up to him and whispered 'Always. Ant, I always will.'

After lunch they lay in their tent, soon naked and floating on a sea of desire; eventually they made the longest and gentlest love.

'All the softness in your balls washed me.'

'All the sweetness deep inside welcomed me'.

They slept in a green aura of ecstacy hazed by bird-song .

Ant half woke because insects were invading his crotch. Phil had found them. He ruefully acknowledged their peace, so shook a long frond of grass to wake Ant and entice him down-stream for a swim. 'Nadia's resting with a headache.' he whispered as they bounded over the rocks.

After a teasing active swim the two boys sat quietly in the soft shadowed afternoon sunlight.

Ant put an arm round his shoulders. 'Glad you came?'

Phil nodded unresolutely.

'I'm so happy sharing with you. Everything. The chores which you do without complaint, and all the fun and games.' He felt the stress. 'What's wrong, Phil?'

Phil sighed. 'I'm glad you're happy. Hey, I love sharing with you; I wasn't sure you wanted me around.'

Ant rocked them both. 'Because of Rose?'

Phil nodded embarassedly.

'I love Rose. I love you. I always will - my best friend, my brother. I don't know quite what happened here, but I found I needed Rose, and she agreed to have me. I've known I needed you: we've been mates for ages. Nothing changes that. But you know, Phil, it's as if I've been imprisoned by a shadow only Rose can free me from. It probably sounds daft, but I can't put it any better.'

Phil nodded blindly finding his own inner shadow newly grown. He savoured Ant's warmth. 'I do know what you mean.' he stammered. 'I feel a sort of silence. Once I just laughed and ran about. Now it doesn't work. Neither does sex. Something's missing. Is that what you felt?'

His reserve broke. He fell into Ant's lap, aware of sexual proximity, yet distrait enough to outface its challenge. 'Rosie and you are happy. I can't find that with Nadia, she fucks but we don't really love. Shit Ant, I'm lonely.'

He looked away down a shapely pair of sun-tanned legs to hide his distress, not only about loneliness, but seething feelings of wanting Ant to inseminate him with the power, beauty and solidity he'd always yearned for.

Ant caressed his damp hair. 'Naturally. If it's any comfort, one day you will find somebody to share with. You are a fabulous guy. She's out there. We must try to find her. It's odd how it happens. One day Rose was just my best friend's sister and the next we fall. Both of us. I don't think she was surprised, certainly not as much as I.'

Phil turned and looked into his gentle face. 'Did you mind what we did when we were boys?'

Ant stirred. 'Mind? We loosed frustration; but sleeping with you through the night was the best. It showed me how much I needed to share with you. With Rose, with everyone. I'm glad we stayed together. Really glad.'

Phil almost smiled. 'Me too. But I still need it.'

'So do I. I suppose we always will. When you're a kid you gambol through childhood; then you realise how few connections there are. Then you get scared and lunge for anything reducing loneliness, particularly because out there, contempt howls, and carelessness.'

Phil pushed himself up on an elbow and sucked Ant's penis into his mouth feeling it harden. 'I haven't done this for years.'

'It's just as good now.'

'I still want to fuck you.'

'I know. I don't mind now.'

Phil shivered with shamed desire. 'But we're men.'

'Men need each other. Well, some men. Maybe the woman in us needs reassurance or maybe we need to know another so as to know ourself. As a boy I loved you for sex and friendship. I don't need the sex as much as you do. I had a lot growing up. But I still love you a bit that way.' Ant hesitated. 'I never told you I was raped. I couldn't cope with those ghosts. Rose shooed them off; now I'd trust you too.'

'How could she fuck you there?'

'No, I fucked her. It was terrific; for us both. She wanted to be a boy. I think she envied our friendship; she asked if we'd fucked. She said she saw us in bed looking angelic. I think she treasured that. I said no and left it at that.'

'My sister doing those grubby, wonderful things?' Phil ruminated. 'But why me? I'm a plodder; you're brilliant and beautiful. You don't need me.'

Ant looked down over his sturdy body; his generously endowed sex; his big, open face; his inextinguishableness. 'Why do you have to measure and weigh? We are friends. That's enough. I love working with you. I love our larks and our talks. I love you, silly. That's why.'

Phil loved too, this clever, sensitive brother. The only person who saw shadows and anxiety; the only one he could share them with. He wanted to say, 'I love you.' But it stuck in his throat. His erection throbbed. He dragged himself clear. 'We will be brothers when you marry.'

Ant looked happily at him. 'We are married. We told you, brother. This place makes us say and do things deeply. My marriage, our love. Here we face truths. Don't you see?'

Phil stood wanting to swim, wanting the flush of water to caress him, clear his head and soften his desire. He stood over his friend. For an instant his feelings overwhelmed reserve. 'I love you.' he shouted. The Bush rang with his cry and the two huge splashes crowning it.

Ant stood him in the shallows, bent down, plunged his hand

into the water and wrote a P on his forehead. 'There, now you are baptised.' he said 'Put an A on mine so we'll be friends for ever.'

The two girls were talking by the camp-fire when Phil and Ant returned arm in arm. Rose looked up seeing such contentment and smiled for them all. Another marriage, she thought happily. More magic.

Then she knew her brother would build the shack next to theirs in the valley. She wondered how long it would be until he knew. 'Boys come so quickly; why does it take them so long with everything else?' she mused cheerfully. 'But Phil couldn't love him as much as I do!' she decided, shivering with tumult.

Next morning, after the dip, prelude to a morning cuppa, Nadia took some photos. They stood naked and dripping with water and cheer dwarfed by tall, slim trees marking the course of the creek like sentinels allowing the sun to reach the floor of the forest and bathe the camp in dancing light.

They were loathe to venture far on this last day, feeling time would spin more quickly. So they pottered around the camp, the girls washing scant clothes, airing the bedding while the boys lugged more wood out of the forest and chopped it up for the fire, or buried the burned rubbish in a pit. "Leave nothing behind but your thanks" Ant cajoled.

Unconscious of a shift in habits, they left their clothes either drying or in their tents, preferring nakedness, and the lusty interest this engendered. The girls started the masculine game of appraising penises, having played the feminine one of sizing up busts. The Rubbo's won both contests; nobody was aggrieved. The beauty in variety stunned everyone: rocks-breasts, trees-penises, gilded pools - their sparkling eyes, trees shivering with wind - their shivering lust; the arching sky giving freedom to birds, freedom to them all. It was so simple, this naked pleasure of nature.

But in the afternoon Ant took Rose away. They followed the gambolling water to where it tumbled into the chasm which held the love-green lake.

They gingerly clambered down. At last, they stood mirrored in the lake. She saw his arousal; he, her sigh of love. Taking her hand he jumped into the water. They swam to the waterfall. As needles hammered their heads they kissed. Chilled, they splashed to shore and made their way back to the flat rock.

After drying, he placed the towels and dreamily laid her on them. Kneeling, as before he paused worshipping; she trembled, opened and yearned him into entering. She cried as he penetrated deeper. He tensed over her, thrusting further.

Each gasped and laboured, searching for the hidden core in the other, longing to be united into one wondrous green lake interwoven by silver threads of lust, held by the embrace of warm rock and pubic wisps of grass and moss. Her mounting orgasms burst. She shouted release to the sky as wee black shadows fluttered overhead. He boiled and shot waterfalls of seed far into her clamouring womb and fell whimpering and wrung. The settling surface of the lake reflected clouds and love.

Everything sighed. Swooning in ecstacy, they were deaf even to thumping hearts. In the depths of their minds each knew the marriage had been consummated in this primal place. They had been joined promising to found a life together. Tomorrow they would journey home carrying within their own green lake.

Excepting appearances, everything was changed.

10-

THE CAMP WAS DISMANTLED. Leaving nothing but "thanks", the four youngsters battled up the rise to the car soon packing it. Ant found the battery was flat. 'It may've been the front door not fully shut so the light stayed on.' he groaned. So the other three got out and manfully pushed it over the rocky ground until to their hurrahs, the engine burst into life. Phil gladly drove all the way back too preoccupied to notice the quiet at the back where Ant and Rose nestled. Nadia decided they 'are terribly in love.'

Ant and Rose were dropped off at Symph's place, as it was still called. Miranda, Nici and Kim greeted them. Over a cuppa punctuated by children's play, Miranda said, 'Something happened?' Ant nodded. As they were telling Miranda about the love-green lake she leant forward and stopped their lips with her fingers.

'I know. Symph sent us there. Will and I found each other there.' Miranda smiled warmly. 'What about you?'

'We married.' Ant said

'So did we.' Miranda said. 'That's where Nic was made. Rose are you?'

Rose grinned. 'I'm not pregnant. But we're married. Ant wants to finish Architecture and I've, my fashion degree. Then we'll decide.'

Miranda frowned. 'You saw the truth. Was it scary?'

Ant and Rose looked at each other with soft smiles. They shook their heads.

Miranda gauged their happiness and nodded understand-ingly. She jumped up and hugged them both, dancing around them joyfully. 'I'm so glad.'

Nici looked up from her play. 'Mummy, is Aunty Rose

having Ant's baby?'

Miranda kissed her. 'Darling, they are very happy. So one day Rose and Ant will make a baby. Then you will have a new cousin. Won't that be wonderful.'

'Then why is Rosie crying?'

Miranda smiled. 'Darling heart, sometimes we are so happy we cry. Just as sometimes if we are very sad we can only laugh.'

Her daughter nodded. 'Sometimes when you make babies with Daddy, you cry. Is it like that?'

Miranda nodded, put her arms around them all and hugged until Nici complained it hurt. She unclasped and turned to her brother. 'Do the others know?'

Ant shook his head. 'They know we're married, but don't understand. Maybe it should remain private for the moment.'

'More secrets?' Will called, having kicked off his dirty boots on the verandah and slipped into the house.

'Will, they married in Symph's secret well.'

'Wowee. Then we best go and tell the old fellah.' Will picked up his children, one under each arm and shepherded everyone to a mound strewn with flowers under a gnarled tree at the edge of the vegetable garden. They sat around it as Will was told about the adventure. Then Ant stopped. 'Will, the past has gone; please now let's be friends like before?' He licked his finger and drew a W on Will's brow. 'There. Now it's forever.'

'Badness can take a life-time to eradicate.' Miranda whispered. 'Symph's power still protects us.'

Will struggled silently with joy and pain and relief. All he managed was, 'Another dream another sister.'

Nici squirmed. 'Daddy, cry. Because you are very very happy.'

Will's face trembled.

Miranda beamed. 'A sense of trueness stays, we found. It reminds me every day how blessed I am.' She bent down, kissed Symph's flowers, took Kim in her arms and hurried back to make everyone a snack, realising her blessings were becoming too numerous to count, including another twinge in her womb which, it seemed, only Nici anticipated.

After a simple snack enhanced by bird-song, Ant took Rose

back to the main house. Although she wanted to accompany him and her brother during their tramp over the future village green Sophie prevailed upon her to share some of Nina's school-work entailing an investigation of natural colour schemes.

Nina intuitively wanted the intimacy of the love her dearest brother and Rose radiated. She enjoyed having this special time together. They adventured through the valley with fresh eyes, finding rocks and plants, shadows and shapes, returning so Nina could assemble sheets of colours and sketches.

'Put them on brown paper.' advised Rose. 'The colours keep their intensity that way.'

When Nina had finished, Rose showed her the collection she had made in the magic valley. Nina was dazzled by the clothes. 'Rose you're brilliant. Like Ant.'

Later she said as much to her mother when showing-off her own work. Sophie was surprised by Nina's vehemence; she looked more carefully at her youngest son and his partner, deciding something had happened in the Bush - as it had to her and Tim, Miranda and Will in years gone by. Sophie managed a private moment with Rose: 'Did you find Symph's canyon?'

Rose blushed. Her feelings overflowed into the mother she dreamed of becoming. She whispered. 'Yes. We are married. Please don't be cross. We didn't sneak away for that. It just happened.'

Sophie hugged her. 'Darling, Ant and you have chosen well. It's your life. I'm delighted. You know Tim and I have been fond of you for years. How wonderful to have so delightful a daughter.'

Rose had admired Sophie and Tim who seemed, especially during her stormy adolescence, ideal parents. 'I have loved Ant for a long time.' she whispered. 'It grew. The love-green lake forced us to look into ourselves; we found each other, if that makes sense?'

'Perfect sense, my dear. The same sense I found with Tim, and Miranda found with Will. But did your man take a little longer to face the inner facts?'

Rose looked at Sophie, so assured, so motherly. 'No Ant knew. For he asked me. It took time for me to say 'yes' to a life with such a fabulous man.'

'I'm glad you see Ant that way. He's such a happy person and enjoys sharing. He may be a little free/wild by some standards, but I know deep down he'll always come home to you, probably bringing all sorts of treasures, as he always has, from his many escapades, the dear, dear boy.' Sophie started. 'You should tell your father; did you know he's arriving today to discuss a new staff building behind Ararat with us? You and Ant might want to take him for a walk. The poor man will be overburdened by all the projects we're hatching.'

Rose kissed her. 'Thanks Soph. He likes Ant a lot already.'

Sophie smiled. 'Kiffy and he may feel it's premature. Tim and I were inculcated by Will and Miranda and the others, so now we try to leave matters to you children and to Symph's magic canyon; I like your description of "a love-green lake". For that's what it really is.'

Rose blushed. 'Lorca says love is green. And I'm not pregnant, if that's what you're wondering. We want to be together for the coming year; maybe having the other wedding after Ant graduates, or even waiting until I finish.'

Sophie laughed and kissed her. 'Well, at least you contemplate "the other wedding". We can't get Miranda or Will to consider such a step. They say, our valley, having blessed them doesn't care; Although society beyond, might.'

Ray Rubbo duly arrived. The boys grabbed him at once, dragging him off to argue over the village green. They stood at its centre and glanced about and talked and settled on an outline plan.

'I like your house, Ant.' Ray said. 'But remember, those hefty rocks just beyond the back of Ararat call out for a pavilion - I have plans with me to discuss with your parents - So the siting of yours should be adjusted. Because it sits free of the ground (as this new one does) you can freely move it about. Why not tuck it into the gap in the rock teeth, some distance away? Its delicacy fits well there, a kite snared between boulders. At more distance, you and your girlfriends could make love unencumbered.'

Ray noticed a grin between Phil and Ant, dismissed it as smutty male humour and murmured. 'Have you noticed, Phil, that Ant's house has an A frame, A for Ant, structure? R's and P's are more difficult.'

'He's such a clever bugger.' Phil cried.

Ant demurred. 'Honest, I didn't think of that. It was a simple timber frame I wanted. Honest.' But he was delighted with the signature of his forehead being on this first building.

When he inspected Ray's proposal for the pavilion he saw the sense of its simpler form, a strong colonial hip roof with verandas which demurred to and counteracted the scale of the main house as well as the massive rocks flanking it. His seemed diminutive and frilly; he suddenly doubted his design.

Ray shook his head. 'Your house brings some human delicacy to the village. I know all the children in the future will love it as an architectural ant, as fine as their uncle, their father or whosoever he will be by then.'

Ray noticed again the fleeting smirk which leapt between his two boys, as he often called them. Yet was unprepared for the revelations which Ant and Rose announced during their walk. Then Ant said. 'Ray, I love her so much.' and Rose threw her arms around him, kissing him fervently. 'And I love him so much too.'

Ray secretly admitted holding a similar dream of such a family. But he prevaricated. 'And Phil, won't he be put-out: his sister running off with his best friend?'

Rose giggled. 'Does he look put out?'

'No.' said Ray.

'He's not.' Ant beamed. 'We are bestest friends now. Brothers, really.'

'Good.' Ray smiled.

'Well, there you are.' cried Rose happily. 'Oh Daddy. Won't it be great? All of us? Ant and I want to live together until he graduates. After that we may wait until I finish. Then we can marry and make our little house here and do work in the city and see you and Mummy and Phil. Oh, I'm so happy.'

Ray wagged his head. 'So what more do you want? It seems unnecessary to give you permission; you've taken the decisions?'

Ant swallowed. 'We want your blessing.'

In quiet Rose whispered with inner green-voices. 'Yes. Yes.'

Ray put a hand on each shoulder. 'My dearest children. Blessing. You know you have a thousand. May this dream of yours make you happy for ever. Kiffi and I will be there for you whatever and whenever you need. One family. Phil too, I'm quite sure.'

Ant stammered. 'Will you still help me with architecture? You make things so clear so much better. A-And we need some rent so Rose can take Jo's old room when she moves out next month?'

'Ant, your ideas are strong, clear and delicate. I've noticed, between you and Phil, there's little left for me except some tidying and some help with the production side. Please do come to the office whenever you wish, use it as Phil does. I enjoy working with you both; your talents delight me. Let me pay all your rent, keep your side to help with the day-to-day, further, why don't we renovate Rose's room at home for the both of you, it should reduce the travelling; you know Kiffy is frightened about your motorbike. Tim's accident makes us wary. That is, if this little lady agrees to the architectural rape of her room? I thought a high bed-platform releasing all the space underneath for study/ relaxation.'

Rose giggled. 'Well now, the best two architects in the world. I'll have to watch costs. I know you don't care what it costs, or how long it takes. Only a woman's eye can deal with such perplexities. Oh, Daddy. It is a good idea, isn't it Ant?'

Ant grinned. 'Complexities, surely? It just might be possible. But only if the soft furnishings are designed by the famous RR, and she consults me and the Bush about colours.'

They were bursting with happiness. Everyone gathered at Ararat for supper, including Peter and Wendy, Miranda, Will, and the two tiny-tots who fell asleep on the sofa. Phil was inveigled by Ant to ask his father to renovate his room as well.

Ant insisted. 'Your turn is coming. Remember, we promised it would be the number one anti loneliness project this year?'

'Double fees.' Ray said.

'Double cost.' Phil said.

'Treble pleasure.' Ray said.

Peter looked fondly at Ant. 'Will and I have been talking. Students like Ant have no money. We are both rolling in cash, so let M-S landscapes do the minimal groundwork and get the timber structure erected and roofed. I can get materials cheap, so will supply whatever finishes Ant wants, and lay on a man to help him finish. Will pays for materials, we for labour. Wedding present if you agree. If that would help?'

Ray nodded. 'Ant can use my office for all the admin., approvals, specifications, all the accounting and so on. BUT after he's finished his thesis.'

Ant looked suddenly troubled. Rose took his clenched hand and squeezed it as he stammered. 'My house, my very own? Will you, are you serious?'

Rose waited until she burst. 'He wants to thank you. But it's difficult. You're so wonderful, aren't they Ant?'

He nodded.

Phil grinned. 'I'll help you Ant.'

'And me.' said Rose.

'You're all amazing.' Ant muttered. 'I'll never be able to thank you. It's every xmas that ever was.'

Ray whistled. 'Hey talking of Christmas, you've forgotten the fireplace. How can Santa scramble down a non-existent chimney?'

Ant relaxed. 'We don't need any other presents.'

Phil sniggered. 'But your kids will.'

Everyone laughed.

'But Ant has the right windows for Bunyip.' Will said. 'That counts far more in our valley.'

Nina slipped away to bed vowing. 'When I grow up I'll have a house and children and a chimney and love a man and be as happy as that.'

11-

OSSIAN'S CITY HOUSE was finished enough for him to move in. He was delighted by the comfort of the ground floor living areas, thrilled with his first floor studio: the flanking walls of old red bricks picked free of plaster and re-pointed in a cream mortar. The floor and ceilings were of rich, warm hardwood and the end walls white painted plaster reflecting light in soft auras from sky-lights in the roof. The ceiling boards were separated by gaps behind which lay soft absorptive insulation balancing out the reflective surfaces. Ant's crane structure worked. The grand piano came up from the street like a huge black beast much to the neighbours' excitement.

Long hangings, also serving as curtains helped absorption; these had been designed by Rose, using her research from the secret valley, and then hand painted in long, flowing tree-lines on fine thick cotton which complemented the brick and timber.

'I feel I'm in the Bush.' Ossian cried happily. 'You two are amazing. This is better than a dream. Not only does it look beautiful, music sounds ravishing. Maybe I'll let it out for recording. Ossian gazed at the warm brick walls, the mellow floors and ceiling. My second symphony will start here in this lovely space: simple, natural, warm and vast enough for sound to start to fly. Me, flying with music.'

'The ground floor cries out for someone else.' Ant murmured.

Ossian was crestfallen. 'I know.' his face dropped.

'We'll add you to the list with Phil, what the boys call their "anti-loneliness project", see if we can find a nice girl for you too, or a boy if you prefer.' said Rose gently.

Ossian sighed. 'I met such a nice girl a few years ago; she was whisked off to Italy when her parents discovered us. I still think about how happy we were.'

Rose squeezed his able hand. 'Is that why you look sad sometimes?'

'I suppose so'.

'Someone will turn-up.' said Ant cheerfully. 'Rose and I promise.' He hugged his brother. 'One day soon we'll all be happy.'

'Dearest Ant, my dear Rose, you have brought enough happiness. How can I ever thank you? I've been away so much, but now with this place, I want to come home. It holds me softly, lets me breath, it wants me to sing. I guess that sounds daft. You'll never know what a precious anchor you have given me.'

Ant looked bashfully at Rose. 'Ossian, you couldn't have said anything better. I want you to come home and sing, so does your house, so does Rosie. Maybe I really can make buildings like Ray. Maybe one day I'll make you a music school so everyone comes there and sings.'

Ray was proud of them all. 'A good client, a good architect, a good builder and, darling daughter, you have a real talent for dressing buildings, so if the rag trade fails, turn to it.'

Ray sent his practice photographer in to make sets of both black and white and colour pictures, then unbeknownst to Ant, submitted it for the bi-annual architecture medal in the category of rehabilitation of old buildings as well as sending it off to America for the annual Review of Buildings published by a glossy magazine.

But the the music establishment spread the word. Ossian's friends visited, played and raved about it.

'It's an instrument.' proclaimed Robert, Ossian's old piano teacher. 'Good on Ant. Imagine, that scruffy cheerful little imp making this gem.' He kissed Ossian warmly. 'I'm jealous my dear, Always have been, bless you.'

Ossian's first symphony was due to be performed in a couple of months, so the media began agitating about new talent emerging from national policies about music. Ossian thought it all rubbish, but agreed to a joint photo interview for music magazines and the TV with his brother, "another talent nurtured by National Policy", they proclaimed. 'Also rubbish.' growled Ossian. 'It was our valley. National Policy turns children into zombies.'

But he and Ant leaned on the shiny grand and discussed architecture as frozen music and the need for unpretentious naturalness in both, included in the arts news in a piece headed "Our clever kids." Even Rose was mentioned as "Ant's partner" of which she approved.

Ray was distressed by being labelled architect, Ant being relegated to "designer".

But Ant didn't care. 'It would never have been built without you. If you want call it a collaboration. You were fantastic.'

Ray looked admiringly at the lad. '*You* were fantastic; I was the drudge. But you, me, Rose and Micha are a great team.'

The staff at the architecture school were convinced Ray Rubbo was the author: 'It has his hallmarks, brick and timber and his usual obsession with sunlight.' they agreed.

The students knew Ant had done most of the work, using Ray, who helped so many of them, lending his office after hours for those unable to work elsewhere or who were talented enough to want support. In the three faculties of Music, Engineering and Architecture Ossian's house became a cult building, and Ant, a hero.

Phil was the gossip pipeline, bringing snippets home and relaying, particularly to his student friends, much of the complexity Ant had tackled in arriving at his design. He shyly admitted his minor part in the proceedings, secretly hoping he and Ant would be partners one day, and enjoying being his brother now Rose had nabbed him.

The three were inseparable. They worked and played together. Ant and Rose spent hilarious times at parties discussing suitable anti-loneliness-project persons with Phil, who shuddered over all of them. Until one night he disappeared.

It was a party by the river. Lots to eat and drink, a live band with some brave ones dancing on or through the rank grass, lit by a giant bonfire. It was there they found Phil watching the sparks spin in the darkness' 'Red stars mating with white ones.' he murmured shyly, adding when he saw he was discovered. 'Ant, Rose, this is Katia. She plays the oboe and knows Ossian, isn't that nice. And she grew-up in Eliza Beach near grandma and grandad Dean. I've offered to take her to see the masterpiece next week. Ant's the architect. Rose did the fabrics.'

Katia was well-built and pretty. She sat easily with Phil. 'They make a couple.' whispered Rose scheming.

Katia had finished an engineering course and was working

in a big practice in the city. She played in an amateur chamber orchestra and taught oboe to a few pupils. 'I've always liked music and architecture.' she confided to Phil whose lithe body and enthusiasm she warmed to as they watched the party ebb and flow around the fire, the music hastening dancing, the mixing of the red and white stars and an unruffled comfort in being together.

Rose pulled Ant away, seeing things were going nicely, but not before she had arranged for the three of them to cadge a lift back with Katia whose friend had a roomy car.

So when the red stars had stopped rising to meet their white partners, they clambered into the car to be driven back towards the city. Katia was living nearby.

Phil bashfully got out with her. 'We're going to have a cuppa. I'll sneak in later.' and waved them off.

But it was a long way home. Katia suggested he stay the night. She made up a bed on her floor. They sat on it sipping mugs of tea and talking, unable to find a way of finishing. As the dawn chorus tentatively began Katia sighed and stood. 'I hope you'll be all right, Phil. Do you need the bathroom?'

He nodded and shambolled in to pee and wash his face. She followed. While she was busy, he slipped out of his clothes and into a half-warmed bed to watch her, also clad only in a tee-shirt, slip demurely into hers. He sighed at her buxom almost-visible hips and the luscious mounds made by her breasts. Then he slept deeply, dreaming of showers of stars meeting and kissing in velvet night until sunlight woke him.

He turned. She was looking at him. She smiled. He blushed. He moved his head sideways out of the sun so as to see her more clearly. Her sheet had rucked down as her tee-shirt had rucked up. Her breast swelled, its nipple dark and textured. He was dazzled.

'You look like my brother Sam when he sleeps.'

'I was dreaming of shooting stars.'

'No wonder you were happy.'

'I'm happy now.'

Katia rose and knelt beside him. 'Did you sleep well?'

He nodded. 'I was a bit left out, what with all the stars dancing together.' He blushed, not wanting to say how much he wanted her.

Katia was glad about the blush, she guessed. Glad too it had been such a simple and friendly night. There were few she trusted or wanted to share sleeping with. Enquiringly she lifted the corner of his cover. He nodded happily, rolled away making room with alacrity, opened his bedding and ushered her into his arms.

Katia thrilled as his erection nosed up her thigh. But Phil waited too shy to proceed. He started when she kissed him, finding the oboe-callouses on her soft lips. He caressed her breasts, feeling the peaks harden, matching his desire. Still he waited; there was some illusive gentleness in her holding him back, a need Phil was loathe to break, like feelings he had occasionally experienced sleeping with Ant when they were boys - feelings which entranced him.

Each was reluctant, yet longing. He felt an inner softening as they embraced. 'As if her body is preparing,' he half-realised, 'with a softness I've always wanted.' He carefully rolled her over and straddled her. Her hips lifted, imperceptibly hungry. He slipped in. She was wet. He went deeper until she groaned. He stopped, holding himself as she shuddered, lifting herself. He pushed more deeply. She trembled licked by flashes of orgasm as his huge driving power overwhelmed her. Her softness exploded. Phil was amazed by her ardour. She cried as ecstacy burst.

He thrust, faster and deeper until he fell, his velvet seed washing through her petalled softness, whimpering. 'I love you.'

'Oh, my darling, my darling.' she murmured holding his spent form until each had stopped panting and the quiet they had found by the bonfire, returned.

The sun played in their hair, finally sliding away to poke about elsewhere in the room. They got up and showered, exploring soapy bodies in wonderment. They lunched. She walked him to the bus, promising to meet at Ossian's house in a few days. A few days which dragged, teased by delightful memories. For each had touched an intangible pleasure leaving them breathless.

12-

THERE WAS NO lithe boyish figure lounging under a street tree when Katia arrived after work at Ossian's house. Slightly let down, she rang the bell. Phil opened the door, blushed with pleasure and let her in. Each had been over-expectant; neither could break the reserve the few days separation brought.

He showed her through the lower, living areas, somewhat bare as Ossian had not yet fully furnished them. But the warmth of brick and timber combined with splashes of colour on doors and in the kitchen impressed her. 'I love the glimpse of the back patio and garden and a sense of light trickling through from front to back. I'd like a house like this.' Katia said. Phil secretly vowed that one day he'd make one for her.

He took her upstairs. Katia gasped. It was like being inside a warm animal, there was grandeur coupled with a comfortable human scale and the magic the light evoked, glancing off white plastered end walls punctuated by windows.

On the floor beside the grand piano an oboe stood on a stand. Katia took it and played several notes until the space resounded.

'Play some more.' Phil fascinated that her ears moved when she played, and that with pursed mouth, she looked like a cheeky bird, one he longed to hold.

Katia played some Benjamin Brittain variations on Debussey's *Syrinx:* elliptical sonorities hovering tantalisingly in the studio. Phil was dumfounded. Her music spoke of yearning and sexual arousal, of fluttering hearts and separation. Was Katia telling him how she had felt over the past few days? It tolled in him.

He was sitting on a bean bag in a corner bursting to tell her his own muddled feelings when Ossian came in. Katia stopped in confusion.

Ossian smiled. 'You sound lovely. Don't stop. She's good, eh, Phil?'

Ossian sat at the piano, proffered some music. 'Here's a sonata Tasmin Baker has written for me. I'd appreciate getting a pianist's view of it for once. Let's try it together?'

Katia dragged a music stand over so she had eye contact with Ossian, screwed up her eyes in dismay at the manuscript, pursed her lips and started.

The solo oboe had a long languid introduction. It sounded to Phil it was trying to find its voice as it played phrases and then repeated fragmented versions of them, Then the piano joined-in with fragments, until a whole theme was shared; the movement ended in a resolution sounding clear and confident.

'Next!' Ossian breathed absorbed in the music. The second, slow movement, he started with chorale-like chords making a bed from which the oboe emerged to float a tender song, until ending with a very long oboe note when the piano changed its chordal colours finding a classical resolution into a home key.

Katia turned the page. 'Oh, no! I can't.' she said.

'Have a go.' said Ossian.

It was a gallop for keyboard and oboe filled with muddles and crashing dissonances, syncopation and parallel runs which showed-up how well the players were attuned to each other. It ended in three loud chords under repeated staccato oboe notes.

Ossian sat back and beamed. 'My you *are* good.'

Katia was sweating. 'Wow.'

Ossian nodded. 'I like the way you play it; more cheeky than mine, more risk-taking. I think Tasmin would be happy. Very happy. Could we play it for her sometime?'

They talked about music, about reed problems, about tuning and balance .

Katia noticed Phil get up and leave. 'I must go.' she said. 'Perhaps next week end?' She hurried down and out into the street.

Phil was slouching along already some distance away. She hurried to catch him and took his arm. he scowled.

'What's the matter?'

'I wanted to show you the house.'

Katia only saw his distress. She took him to a cafe nearby, sat in a corner away from the crowd and whispered. 'Phil, don't be angry. Tell me what's the matter, please?'

His face twitched with unhappiness and confusion. He looked at her lovely anxious face and melted. How could she ever be his? He stammered. 'You and Ossian were all over each other and I was there. How could you? I suppose I don't matter much in your sophisticated eyes, a jerk of a student, I . . .'

She stopped his cries with a kiss. It was firm and passionate. 'Phil, I loved you explaining the house you and Ant made. I was very proud of you, very!' She fought back her pain.

'I shared music with Ossian, not anything more. I don't hunt men. I've done all that. What you and I've found, kept me happy all these days. Don't confuse what we have shared, with the other bits of my and your life. Anyway, they are not in conflict. But you have no right to tie me up with your anger. It's your problem. Perhaps you don't care, perhaps you can walk away as if nothing happened. Tell me if that's what you want. I feel hurt; it's not justified; don't you know how I feel?'

The tears in her eyes washed Phil's anger away. He didn't know what she felt; he didn't understand his own feelings, only the dim need to be with her. 'I'm sorry.' he gasped out.

'I love you, Phil. Not only when you're in me, but all the days and nights. I want to be with you.'

Phil sagged. 'That's what I want. More than anything.'

They sat holding hands and smiling through tears.

He never expected love to be so confusing; she found it unsettlingly joyous to be lacking control.

'I'd better go, Phil.'

'I'll see you to the bus.'

She paid all she had for the undrunk coffee and they walked hand in hand to the bus stop talking about the house, about music, about pleasures suddenly clustering round this meeting. They boarded the bus, still talking intently, as unable to separate as they were to join on that first night.

'Fares please.' the conductor called. Katia showed her pass.

Phil looked aghast. 'I don't have any money, do you?'

She shook her head. 'I left it all at the cafe.'

The conductor chuckled. 'Now now. Don't let the bus company intrude on lovers. Oh well, never mind. Let's hope an inspector doesn't board.'

A man sitting behind them proffered a coin. The conductor took it, rang-up a ticket. Phil turned gratefully.

The man waved gratitude aside. 'I couldn't help overhearing your conversation about architecture; You mentioned Ray Rubbo; he's one of the finest architects in the country. I have admired his buildings for years.'

Phil started. 'He's my father.'

'Is he?' the man said. 'I am glad.'

'Is he? Ray Rubbo, your father?' Katia said. 'He's brilliant. Your father, I don't believe it.' She whistled. 'When I discovered his buildings, I wanted to change from engineering to architecture. But I enjoy the mathematics of structures, so continued the course. But I wanted to work with two men: your Dad and Les Stevens. They have turned ordinary building into an art form. To make the ordinary breathtaking is what matters.'

Phil smirked. 'Well now, Les was Ant's engineer for Ossian's house. What I like about him is he never talked down to us, sharing his passion for structure. He's great.'

Katia was flabbergasted. 'You and Ant, working with Ray Rubbo and Les Stevens.' She shook her head in wonderment. 'This is where we get off.' she cried reaching up and ringing the bell. They jumped off, waved to the man and sauntered back to her place.

Once inside he shyly undressed her, pulled his own clothes off and fell with her onto the bed. They recovered, to lie locked in love until mournfully he rose.'I'd better go.'

At the bus stop, coins in hand, he embraced her. She lifted her face to his. 'I love you, Phil. Believe me.'

'I'm sorry. It's hard to know anything anymore. But I love you, Katia, more than anyone in the world. For ever'

The bus trundled up. He stood on the step and blew her a kiss. 'See you in the weekend.'

'For ever and ever.' she called. The dusk and the thunder of the bus shrinking it into a whisper she was not sure he heard. Lightly she tripped back to sniff her bed and revel in his tangy scent and to finger her labia engorged by his ferocious love-making. She smiled. 'It is hard to think clearly now.' She sat alone eating supper and musing. 'His anger must mean he loves me too.'

13-

THE CONCERT DATE ARRIVED for Ossian's first symphony. Most of the family from the valley were there, including Nina who was thrilled to be in the city and to be included in so exciting an event. Miranda had reluctantly left her brood with Wendy and Peter. She was torn between pride for Ossian and regret in abandoning her precious chicks. Will accompanied her, a trifle uncomfortable with the crowds and activity, but determined to show support. He gladly greeted the Deans who had come up from Eliza beach, and the Rubbo's, all of them sitting together in a supporters' block in the front of the hall. He was, they all were, intrigued by Phil's new girl friend, who it turned out was the daughter of Fran, Tim's bassoon teacher. And even more beautiful, Tim decided.

Ossian conducted with skill. He had fought for a programme made up of Vaughan William's sixth symphony, which he regarded as the best English symphony, Prokoviev's suite, *Love of Three Oranges*, filled with colour and action. His symphony began, as Will had advised, with a joyous opening movement, a barren cheerless second movement leading to a resolution in the third so sense, hope and resolve grew into a calm ending.

It was tough fare, two difficult symphonies sandwiching Russian brilliance. But the audience, needled by the press spin over preceding weeks, was very supportive.

Afterwards, many clamoured to congratulate the brilliant maestro; he sent the family on to a restaurant where they would celebrate and stood patiently nodding and smiling at the often inarticulate admiration about him or music in general or his symphony, it was hard to pin the chatter down.

One of the critics winked at him and gave a thumbs-up. Then the queue produced a young woman. 'It was wonderful music. I have never heard such sad emptiness in my life. You were generous to leave us with a little hope.'

The critic looked impressed. 'I quite agree. Masterful. Not only anger, as Vaughan Williams', but abandon; beyond fury or hope. Incredible orchestration, dear boy.'

The woman stood irresolutely screwing up her programme. 'Do you remember me Ossian?'

He started, looked at her for the first time and gasped 'Angelica Salvatori?'

She nodded.

Ossian flushed angrily. 'After all these years? Why?'

She grew upset. 'I came to the concert to hear what you are doing now. I didn't intend troubling you. But the slow movement told me terrible things about you. Things I suffered. I wanted to see you and tell you that it was . . .' she stopped in confusion. 'It was a true and beautiful cry. That's all.' She turned away and pushed through the thinning crowd.

Ossian watched her disappear Everything in him cried out against such a loss. He stammered to expectant faces. 'Excuse me, excuse me.' and hurried after her, took her arm. 'Angelica. I don't understand. But you must not go. Not yet. Please Please come to dinner, as soon as I've finished with the fans. It's only my family. Perhaps afterwards you'll tell me why.'

Obediently she allowed him to ferry her back to sit patiently on a chair nearby while he dealt with the clamouring. Eventually he emerged back into the crowdless silence, wearing a light coat over his black performance clothes.

God, he's still so beautiful, Angelica unwittingly thought as he led her to his car and whisked her off to feasting with his family.

Tim looked round the table. It was a mirror history of his life: his wife and children, Fran who first showed him music and passion, her daughter Katia who seemed connected to Phil Rubbo, Ant's friend, the son of Ray and Kiffy who inspired and reflected his drive to build a better world; their daughter Rose who seemed as rooted in Ant as he was in her, his in-laws the Deans who had been both scourge and support since his tumultuous early years. Then others, who had been supporters all the years both in the city and at Ararat, such as Jiri and Ian - still sad and separated - Eileen Palmer, a fine poet , Kim and Dan, still making golden award films, suggesting new ones with his children.

Ossian arrived at last looking harassed, accompanied by a striking Italianate girl whose shy and intense demeanour proclaimed complexities. Tim sighed contentedly. He knew of complexities; the party abounded with them.

They toasted the first symphony. Ossian rose. 'Thank you all for coming. It's like an Ararat festival. I want to single out two who spurred me on: first my dearest Will, who kicked me into working at a structure and orchestration we argued over so vehemently, as well as bullying me about suffering and feeling; secondly Angelica who turned up out of the blue tonight, the second movement is hers. Also all of you. So supportive, accepting my chaotic life, my comings and goings, my moods, all that. Whatever happiness and hope there is comes from you.'

They feasted. Eventually the staff came in from the kitchen and dined at the other end of the restaurant, occasionally someone leapt up to bring wine; the sweets were on the house. The party fell into an empty street. Tim hugged Ossian. 'Mum, Nina and I will come to your house tomorrow for lunch.' Tim and Sophie were driven to Eliza Beach by Mister Dean.

'I'm sorry, it's rather late.' Ossian muttered to Angelica as he drove her to her street. 'Oh, I have a friend here.'

She asked him to stop at Lettuce Marr's ramshackle house.

Ossian gasped. 'You live there with Lettuce?'

'Yes, I have a room here.'

Ossian took a deep breath and launched into his questions: 'Why did you leave me? Swanning off to Italy. No address. No contact. Nothing all these years? I thought we were true friends?'

Angelica twisted her hands in agony. 'My parents sent me away'. she stammered. 'They ordered me never to see you again. They told me you'd gone away. We moved far away. I tried to find you when I returned. But the boy downstairs in your house said you'd gone on tour. I thought you'd lost interest.'

Ossian shook. 'They told me you were in Italy. I wrote to the address they gave me. No answer. Nothing.'

'I was here all the time. After finishing school, I got a scholarship for primary teaching, leaving home for good. I can't forgive them. I've never been back. They destroyed everything.'

'Everything?'

'Everything. I wanted to play music with you and go to

school, eat with you, talk. I know I was a silly dreamer, but without my dream how could I live? I tried to get on with my life. But apart from the children at school, my social life - parties, sex and all that - is a bit hollow. You are so lucky, having such talents, you've gone on to fame and fortune which I suppose you want; I wanted a dream and it was taken from me.' She looked steadily out of the windscreen at the street shimmering tearfully thinking, He doesn't understand.

She started when he took her hand.

'I know what you mean by hollow: isn't that the core of my second movement?'

'Yes. It reflected my own emptiness and sorrow. That's why I came to see you.'

Ossian sighed. 'What use fame without a dream? You took mine with you the day you left.' His head fell on the steering wheel. 'I've missed you every moment since. My talent, as you call it, was the only comfort. Half of me is dead. No one knows what that feels like.'

She couldn't see anymore. Her despair, her hope, her yearning fell tearfully from her. She fell on him, hugging and cajoling, rocking his tense body until it relented and bent over to join her. She looked up at his weary face. 'Can we be friends again?'

Ossian shivered: having turned off the engine the car had become cold, but inner loneliness chilled him more. Blindly he nodded.

She touched his cheek. 'Will you come in?'

'For a quick cuppa.' (as if replying to Symph or his mother, too preoccupied, too tired to think).

She took him to the house.

'I've had a room here for a year.' She opened the heavy front door and led him into the dishevelled hall. They heard music.

'It's my symphony.' He tiptoed to a door with light streaming under it. He entered blinking at the brightness.

'Gracious me, Ossian. How amazing. I've just come home after classes having recorded the broadcast and here you are. My dear boy it's magical. Music trembling with emotion. My dear. Wonderful.' Lettuce said.

'Thank you Lettuce. We missed you at the party. I'm going to have a cuppa with Angelica who inspired the second movement and then I must sleep. I'm finished.' Ossian retreated into the hall and followed Angelica to her room. He sat on her roomy couch while she went down to the kitchen. When she returned he was fast asleep.

She lovingly removed his shoes, then his coat, black skivvy and trousers and laid him out on the couch. 'He looks so pale, so beautiful.' she decided as she had eons ago when they snuggled on his bed after playing oboe duettes and she burned with first love. Now she brought her duvet and a pillow and tucked him up and then slipped to her own bed. She was teaching in the morning and had to be gone early.

Ossian woke at noon. There was a note and an empty house. He lay on Angelica's bed and smelled its fragrance. He was elated. He showered and dressed and hurried home to ransack one of his father's dog-eared books, finding two poems which said to her what he could not articulate; he set to and made them into songs: the first, *Tempest,* a cry of rage, the second, *Waiting,* a more gentle storm of hope.[*]

TEMPEST

Lion night,
roaring,
claws incising,

humid wind
of hot blood
red wet faces,

livid hands,
slimy rubies
underfoot,

gasps of
the drowned,
the prayful prey,

only whites
of stilled eyes

---

[*]   See notes at end.

shriek

in this
red
night.

The rage was new, for Ossian had suffered unable to blame. The poem unlocked his anger. The singer and pianist stabbed in percussive unity; a short interlude of threatening counterpoint seagued into each verse. "In this red night" finished with low piano notes and the singer talk-singing with nightmarish intensity, beyond melodic expression.

WAITING

The world darkens.
The hills grow stern.
Shadow builds in hollows
until peaks are dulled.
Cloud cloaks sharpness;
high and low engulfed.

I, breathless in
a storm of longing,
with stormy dreams
of our meeting,
of mating
light with dark.

Ah, will
you come
across the grass as
light rain dancing,
enlivening
a parched heart?

In this song the voice waited, disclaiming in near monotones as the piano 'sang' a haunting melody to accompany it during the first two stanzas, then, taking-up the piano's melody it sang the last mellifluous hope, a transformation of loneliness into conviction, turning darkness into a unity of light.

Ossian struggled to complete the songs throughout a busy day. They proclaimed his spiralling feelings about Angelica echoing his fallow emotional development, his dawning realisation of being a boy trapped in a man's habit 'I can write a symphony, but can't find a mate!' he told himself.

At last he finished. He threw a coat on and hurried through the many streets to Lettuce's house. Standing at the darkened entrance, he rang the bell; after a long wait, a light went on and the door opened. Lettuce stood there blinking at him in disbelief. 'Ossian, darling. What are you doing? It's two in the morning. I suppose you want Angelica; I'll get you a key so you don't disturb us. Come in.'

'Sorry.' Ossian said bashfully. 'It's just that I've finished two songs for her and I wanted to play them.'

Lettuce sighed. 'Never mind my dear. Come into the dance studio and play them for me.' She propelled him into a large, bare room with a wood floor, mirrored walls and a baby grand. She shut the door, lit a light over the piano, pulled up a chair and waited while her dearest genius flattened a roll of manuscript, put it on the piano and settled down to play. He sang in his light tenor voice, the rage and then the storm-touched hope. When finished he waited, as he had so often, for her reaction.

Lettuce nodded. 'Ossian, it seems to belong to your symphony: its initial happiness, its despair and its third movement intertwining frustration and hope. It's eminently danceable. I'd love to try it in the morning, would you mind?'

He nodded cheerfully - he enjoyed working with Lettuce; she was a no nonsense, practical person who always made him feel deeply.

She smiled. 'I imagine it as a dialogue: two dancers who are separate and then who join, or look as if they might.'

Ossian looked at her with admiration. 'That's just how it is. I never thought it was a dialogue, but Lettuce you're brilliant as usual. What a dramatic form this will make.'

'Now, dearest Ossian, it's time for bed. Go along up. She might be cross with you at this hour so be gentle. Good night dear boy.'

He stiffly stood and wandered out and up the stairs. Lettuce turned off the light and sat in the gloom, watching the street-lit shadows dance on the mirrors, telling about the ticksy breeze and the stiff-limbed trees and the imperfect window panes distorting images into magic shapes dancing for her until she smiled, rose and shuffled back to bed thinking, Dance-music drives the world, if only we would listen.

Ossian entered the shadowy room. Angelica was curled up in bed. Naked shadow-men caressed her face and arm and danced on the counterpane. He longed to touch her but crept over to the couch where his last night's bedding still lay in a ruffed pile, undressed and wriggled under the duvet. He lay on his tummy pressing his flexing erection into the flexing couch until pleasure swept him into sleep.

In the morning she woke him with a cup of tea. 'Hello, Ossian. Lettuce says they are waiting for you in the studio after tea.'

'Come and hear your songs.'

Angelica smiled. 'I'd love to. Then I must dash. I've a training course this weekend, but I can be a little late.'

Lettuce had classes all Saturday morning. She had combined two students to tackle Ossian's songs. Ann and Richard were about fourteen and had partnered one another before; they were excited to have the opportunity to work with so famous a young musician in what clearly Lettuce considered a unique situation.

She sat them down with Angelica. 'Now I want you to listen to the music and to the words. Let them engage your feelings so we are able to find a choreography of expression.'

She led the discussion about rage and waiting, until Angelica dragged herself away to her course. Lettuce nodded her out. 'In the first song, imagine you cannot see one other; you are enraged by the other's absence, raging in your loneliness, seeing destruction everywhere. You don't need to dance back to back, just remember the other is invisible. Now rage.'

The children danced *Tempest*: fury and loss, danced killing and death until they collapsed on the floor panting. Ossian thought Ann's intensity, extraordinary; he was shaken by Richard's pain, so like his own.

Then Lettuce discussed *Waiting:* stern feelings darkening

the world, echoed by inner storms of longing and dreams about the meeting/mating of opposites: male-female, light-dark, despair-hope. 'Then, Ann, come dancing like gentle rain into the landscape of Richard's thirsty arms.' Lettuce cried.

The children nodded. It chimed with their difficulties growing up and battles with themselves and others. Bemused they rose. Ossian played and sang. Ann rained dancing into Richard's arms until Lettuce waved her arms. 'Now swap: Richard, you rain and dance into Ann's body; Ann, welcome him as a lover, no don't snigger. Just dance coming together and union.'

Ossian longed to rain-dance into mating. He finished playing. Sat dazzled by the flow of the story and his feelings, emboldened by the last nights' proximity as part resolution.

Lettuce had another class. Ann left. Ossian asked Richard to come back to his house to dance some more. The boy grinned and nodded. He was fascinated by Ossian and the mood of risk and pain. He knew it was important. Both felt that.

14-

'IT NEEDS AN ENDING.' Ossian watched Richard in his music room. 'Like falling in love into each other, after all the separations.' He took the boy. They danced towards each other and fell together.

'I can't dance in clothes.' said Ossian angrily.

'You can have my tights.' said Richard. 'I'll wear my underpants.'

They undressed. Richard admired Ossian's erection which incited his own. They repeated the dance.

'I'll be the rain this time.' said Ossian. 'You fall back onto one arm. Raise the other up and hug me until we are face-to-face. Then we'll sink down, one joined body into the grass of the poem.'

He sang the last stanza. Richard fell like a wounded Parthanon warrior; one arm, raised with protective welcome, curled over Ossian who hung stiffly over him pushing his hips and chest over the mute form, gently pushing them together and downward into the grass. An urgency possessed them both. The boy yearned upwards seeking contact, revelling in strength.

Bare legs entwine, bare arms lock; faces strained by waiting, lips meet. Mouths open. They melt. Ossian groans 'Oh. Shit, I've come.' Kisses deeply, hugs and falls inert on the shivering boy who watches the damp stain spread on the bulging tights, timorously touches it whispering 'Gee. That's a lot.' Ossian trembles with lust, obsessively peels off his underpants and takes the pristine sex into his mouth savouring the swelling of Richard's thrusts. His mouth is filled with slime as the boy moans. 'Sorry, I should have said.'

Ossian slid up the softening body and plunged his tongue into the boy's mouth. They shared everything until Ossian wanted more. He took the boy downstairs and pulled him onto the bed, rolling him onto his face and kissing his back and buttocks.

'We need some stuff like *Vaseline*.' the boy said.

'I use it on my oboe.' Ossian stumbled upstairs.

Richard lay on his back. When Ossian returned he lifted his legs onto Ossian's shoulders and ordered. 'Now push your fingers in and stretch me.'

In a flurry of lust Ossian prepared the youthful body. Then, as tutored, gingerly slipped inside. His pleasure was immense.

Richard wanted to please. 'Now fuck me. Pull almost out and then thrust right in.'

'I'm hurting you.'

'No, go on.' the boy groaned as he ejaculated over his ridged tummy. 'I've never done that. Did you come?'

Ossian, still hanging rigid over him stammered. 'Not yet.' He felt the small body relax. Then he thrust wildly.

Richard watched the grey eyes glaze inward, watched sweat blossom on Ossian's skin, watched the urgency of waiting finally burst and the mighty man flop defeated on the sheets beside him.

After resting they showered. Soaping flesh excited them. They tumbled back to bed where Richard whispered. 'Can I do you?'

Ossian savoured the luscious intrusion, was charmed by reflections of his desire in the striving boy enriching him. When he was spent, Richard knelt before his hungry man and offered himself. Later they showered again. Then, almost impatiently Richard lay with Ossian, accepting admiration and exploration as Ossian pondered his lessened wanting.

The quiet intimacy emboldened the boy into admitting his deepest secret: that after his father left home, his mother's brother came to stay. When his mother was on night shift, first he and later his brother, had been interfered with, eventually culminating in penetration and lavish gift-bribes.

'I hate him.' Richard breathed.

'And me?'

'Of course not.' The boy grinned.

For Ossian it felt like love.

Depths of feelings disturbed Richard; all he admitted was wanting what happened. He knew love is for girls, and we are boys.

'Am I as good as your other boys?' Richard asked.

Ossian kissed the soft mouth and eyes 'There's no one else.'

'No one?'

'No one.'

'Never?'

Ossian shook his head and blushed.

'You mean I'm the first time?'

'Yes.'

The boy felt unique, held in such delight. He blushed deeply. He leaned into Ossian's body, snuggling into his warm hug until it contained him. He floundered in love, knew what had happened carried them, as the dance had, into realms which were limitless.

Ossian studied his crestfallen face. 'Shall we dance again tomorrow?'

'If you like.'

They contrived to dance every day next week and most days of the following until hunger was assuaged and other demands began separating them. By that time Richard acknowledged his body-power in hunting, choosing and embracing sexual need.

Ossian grimaced with the discovery his habitual waiting had as keen an edge as the new-found act; the pain of separation, of an interrupted life, was as deep as the pain of unfulfilment. Although sexually fulfiled, he needed a more constant relationship. 'Perhaps shackles are freedom.' he wondered. But the inner boy fought shy of facing anything more complex than intermittent coupling with Richard.

Lettuce viewed the infatuation with gentle concern, feeling although it was genuine, it contained seeds of destruction in an acerbic world. Furthermore, she saw the longing in Angelica needed resolution. When the girl admitted she had loved Ossian since childhood in spite of being brutally separated, and that it had not been consummated, Lettuce felt sure everyone would be happier if Ossian grew-up. 'I'm sure he's a virgin.' she muttered. 'Angelica and Nature might help the darling boy, now Richard has propelled him this far.'

She suggested Angelica invite herself over to Ossian's house with promises of a feast. 'A sumptuous one washed down with abundant wine. Then take him to bed and leave the rest to your dancing bodies.' Lettuce advised.

Ossian was surprised. 'Yes. Do come along, see the house and try out the kitchen.' he said cheerfully. 'Yes, we'll toast the first symphony and welcome the skeletal second.' Angelica arrived laden with shopping and busied herself most of the afternoon. Ossian worked upstairs with an intensity goaded by her presence.

She brought him a steaming mug of tea and a delicious pastry just before he turned on the lights. They sat at a low table enjoying the calm dimming of the day.

He impulsively kissed her. 'Hey, it's nice having you here. The house and I feel better.'

She looked softly into his dove-grey eyes. 'It's good to be here, Ossian.' Longing for much more silenced her. She managed, 'When would you like to eat?'

Ossian savoured the question. Characteristically he delayed. 'What about seven, when I finish working?' He grinned.

'Whatever suits you. I'll wait until you come down. It won't take long to finish and serve-up.' She blushed. He's so beautiful when he thinks about music, she thought. And when he smiles. She nodded. 'Now it's all done. Can I have a rest somewhere?'

'Use my bed.' delighted at the thought of her endowing his sheets with her tantalising scent.

Just before seven he went downstairs. She was fast asleep in an unclenched curve, on her side, her black hair spilling over the pillow, a hand delicately clutching an edge of the sheet lightly lying over her so the contours of her body were evident, as if an ancient Greek sculptor had suggested all her delicious details, her aquiline nose and olive face in perfect repose, the faintest suggestion of the mystery of her womb reflected in its veiled covering. The girl he had found, lost and then dreamed of had returned. The lonely boy inside shouted with glee. 'Yes. Oh, yes. So different from the scheming women who buzz around to sting you.'

Ossian didn't know how to deal with the simple task of waking her. Desire stayed his hand. 'It's gross to wake such loveliness.' he silently raged pushing his fist over his erection so the bed trembled.

He was dazzled as she opened her olive eyes, stretched with feline delight and smiled warmly.

'Are you ready?' she murmured.

Ossian swallowed, his heart pounding his head confused. She caressed the hair from his brow. He trembled.

'Oh, mia tresore.' she whispered sitting up and taking him

like a precious icon into her warming arms. Her tears confused him further. She bent over the edge of the bed and pushed off his shoes and pulled him beside her. She expertly wrestled off his clothes and lay on his bubbling tummy, gazing with admiration at his freed erection. 'It's always been beautiful.' she whispered. She caressed his creamy hairless beauty, fascinated as she had been as a girl, kissing everything.

Ossian peeled off her remaining clothes. Her softness, her warmth, her golden skin, beckoned. Then the boy in him acknowledged she was no longer the girl he'd known. Far more was possible. So, now his yearning might find solace.

As if hearing his silent screams, she lay back and drew him towards her, guiding his penis into her vagina with loving fingers. For a splendid moment they shivered in unison. He lay on her trying to return from that no-space after the storm; she caressed his sticky back until he shrank, and clasped him preventing everything leaching away.

Ossian sighed, rolled off and lay watching her face to discover anger or regret, finding his own joy. He smiled. 'I'm still hungry. What's next?'

Angelica laughed. 'Me too. Let's eat. Ginger prawns are next, then a thick fish soup, creamed spinach with *Vino Verde*, from Portugal, then strawberries with chocolate mousse and a Pino Noir from the Aosta valley, then coffee and liqueurs. Not as good as the first course, but that's all we have. Give me ten minutes.' Merrily she bounded away.

Ossian lay. His bed was transformed. It took him places only dreamers knew of, beyond stars, time itself, places where the boy in him found the man he was, without rancour or regret. It was an inner journey; whether it could exist beyond this moment was unclear. He remembered saying, "the house and I are better with you here."

'I hope it's really true.' he muttered. He shimmied into some loose-fitting clothes and ambled proprietarily into the kitchen.

They feasted. Tongues loosened. Ossian told of his day's work orchestrating some songs and dances for a concert series he was to give next autumn; also some thoughts for his second symphony growing from his new house. Then Angelica told him of her children at primary school, how she played and sang with them and tried to modify their exaggerated bigotry about adult life.

'Sing one of their songs.' he ordered, grinning.

So she did, Ossian adding a bass line.

They finished the fish soup and the wine. Ossian kissed her. 'Can I choose the next course?'

She jumped up happily and grabbed his bulging pants and took him to bed. Laughing, she lifted her legs to his shoulders.

Deeply aroused by memories of such coupling with Richard, Ossian stammered. 'That's a boys' way.'

Angelica blessed him with a smile. 'So what? Let's do it. But I'd prefer the furry place just now.'

He slid in. It was delicious. Soon she climaxed. Soon he followed. She lowered her legs and they snuggled.

She kissed him. 'You and Richard?'

'You know?'

'Of course.'

'You must hate him.'

'No. Silly. I love him because he loves you. I don't mind your loving others. Not if you feast me like this.' She nibbled his ear then sat up. 'Ossian, I've loved you since we first met. Nothing's changed. None of my men equalled your sensitiveness and beauty, or marred the dreams we shared or a note of the music we made. I will always love you, both of you: the naughty boy and the wild man. Just let me be with you sometimes. I don't want to interfere.'

'I want you to interfere, to be here. I love you. I always have. At the very least, sometimes you must come. I'll die otherwise.' He fiercely hugged her.

Fire flared inside Angelica changing dreams, and the world.

They dressed and returned to the feast. Afterwards they went up to his studio and danced to New Orleans jazz in the shadowed space until desire drove them to bed where they joined in the gentlest love-making, then slept like babies.

She dreamed of sheltering in a huge soft cloak, and harbouring precious things in her abundant lap; he, of boyishly playing his oboe leading a triumphant parade of gambolling pilgrims, his music enticing and leading them every step of the twisting way.[*]

---

[*] See notes at end.

15-

ANT WAS OVERWORKED. 'The only good house news is Ossian's new "house symphony". he wailed to Ray. 'The Architecture Department is so demanding. Extending my thesis work. It's silly. All the extra drawings and notes. We built it with half as much.'

Ray studied the requirements and shook his head in dismay. 'Leave it, Ant. You really have produced enough. They can't fail you. It is silly. Your work is exceptional, so is the building. Do they think degrees are given on the weight of submissions?'

Rose, busy with her fashion degree, helped Ant and Phil to render the presentation set of drawings. As each was completed, it was pinned to the wall. The growing exhibition impressed everyone who dared intrude. Katia cast an engineering eye over all the structural drawings, making a few minor amendments.

On pin-up day Ant displayed his thesis. The students viewed it proclaiming it "The Best". Their admiration for the beauty and eloquence of the project was clear. Both the model, the drawings and a wealth of technical reports on structure, materials, sound and ecology excited them. Few seemed aware it had been built but most of them were fond of the slim, shy, articulate grey-eyed boy who had generously shared much of the course with them; To them, Ant was The Best, like his work.

Rose bore the brunt of Ant's exhaustion. But she never left him, dealing with his night-long working, his moods and her own projects and exams. Katia often whisked them out to a small restaurant for a hurried meal. She was dazzled by his brilliance, the fanatical support both Rose and her dear Phil gave him, dazzled to be working in the way she had dreamed of, with the taut logic of structure, a sensual building and with committed designers.

'I can see it comes from your father's stable.' she said one evening to Phil. 'I think Ant's as brilliant as he.'

Phil smiled warmly. 'He is. You should see his own summer house; I'm making a big model. It's spectacular. Hey, you must help us with the structure.'

Katia blushed. 'He'll want to use Les, I'm sure.'

Phil sloppily kissed her leaving saliva on her chin. 'What we usually do is to work-up as far as we can and then speak to Dad and to Les. Why don't you join us. Wouldn't it be fun?'

'Oh, Phil, I'd so love to. Really. Will you ask Ant?'

Phil grinned. 'I already have! Ant thinks you're great. He thought it the best idea. So there.'

Katia loved her mischievous puppy with increasing passion. To be in harness for both work and play left her breathless. 'I love him first because life with him is fun.' she mused after an intense coupling on Ant and Rose's bed between drawings. 'Secondly, he's so sexy, thirdly, everything matters.'

The day of the thesis assessment dawned. A clutch of strangers - experts in various fields associated with architecture - joined the year head, quizzing each student. The "M's" came after lunch. Ant was first.

Ant was called into the studio; the year head sounded harassed. 'Mister Macknight is a talented student. Let him explain his scheme.'

Some of the examiners were shaking their heads. One murmured. 'Clever drawings, hiding shallow thinking.'

The acoustic expert frowned over Ant's calculations. 'The basic formulae are untenable. I told him a year ago! The point of research is to prevent mistakes. As a music environment it fails.'

Ant sighed. 'My research is all documented in a report. The reasons why I adopted another set of measures is explained; the results were confirmed in the engineering lab.'

The head of year tapped his pencil on his clipboard. 'Surely, Kurt, we are examining the process students use, rather than fixing on opinions? Ant has demonstrated he is aware of the problems and took advice. We can't fail him if his advice was faulty.'

Kurt, the expert shook his head. 'Wrong is wrong. The young must learn to get it right. Otherwise the Profession will suffer.'

An engineer from a big commercial practice in the city chipped in. 'If 'Wrong', your buildings fall down young man. Your artistic roof struts will push the walls over. Has anyone ever mentioned the triangle of forces to you?'

Ant coloured. ' Naturally. The walls *are* stable. Yes, there is a horizontal thrust. But the concrete ring beam copes with the struts. The first, 45° struts halve the horizontal thrust onto the second, at 60° which transforms 2/3 of the load vertically, leaving less than 1/3 horizontal thrust.'

The head of year interrupted. 'You see, Don, the student has tried to deal with the problem. Doubtless a visit to you might have saved his building. But it is the architecture, not the structure we are evaluating.'

Don, looked severe. 'Naive architects are the bane of engineers; graduate students must learn the basic theories of support. This is not good enough.'

Ant tiredly hid his frustration. 'Look through the structural report; there you'll find not only theory but design answers. Possibly some of the timber stresses are on the high side, but the roof structure is stable; it not only holds itself up, but can support a hoist for a grand piano.'

The Engineer sniggered. 'Since when have the structural regulations had a grand piano test? Don't be fanciful young man.'

Piers Plingel, buildings editor for a fashion magazine butted in. 'We are spending too much of our limited time on the upper floor which may have merit. I must point out the banal architecture of the ground floor: it's like any boring terrace house any dumb builder could have produced. That is not architecture worthy of the name, worthy of this department or this city. I must protest. Banality is certainly not acceptable.'

Ant was sick of the stream of pompous inanities but he took a deep breath. 'Music demands a certain environment to which the design of the upper floor responds. Living, "The Machine for Living" as le Corbusier so aptly named our design work, Living demands a different environment.* The client wanted something peaceful with a traditional feel as distinct from his work upstairs - thus the key position of the staircase - and garden access - thus the

---

* See notes at end.

relationship to the back terrace and the planting. Banal, it might be, but everyday life can be seen as banal. You might want to live in a glass box filled with artistic treasures. My client is an ordinary man with ordinary needs. The architecture is simple and unagressive. Light and a gentle play of materials enhance the spaces. Quiet is vital in music and in life. It may be banal but it's essential.'

The year head nodded. 'We should commend a student for a simple solution. It takes courage to leave work uncluttered. Ant's interiors seem to me to achieve what he has explained. Now unless there are any more questions? No? Then Ant, you may go.'

As Ant was leaving he overheard a damnation chorus: 'Fail. Incomplete. Technically confused. Too slick for his own good.'

Friends crowded outside. 'Did they like it?'

Ant shrugged angrily 'I failed.'

The gasp from the students was palpable. The news spread quickly. When the examiners emerged for tea the year head was collared and admitted Ant had had a raw deal. 'But Ant is the best.' the students cried. 'You can't fail him. YOU know that.'

The year head nodded grimly. 'Committee decision. What can I do. I tried.'

Quickly students coalesced. Their anger erupted. Suddenly the space outside the examining studio was packed with a ferocious crowd barring the door and shouting to the examiners. 'You'll stay there until Ant Macknight gets his degree.'

The Professor decided to lie low. There was a timid knock at his door and his secretary entered. 'Professor. The press are here. Will you talk to them?'

He blenched. 'Not now, Miss James. Tell them we have the matter in hand.'

The girl giggled. 'Professor it's about the gold medal. A student has never had it before. They want to meet you and him.'

'Gold medal! What gold medal?'

She proffered a magazine. There were pictures of "A House for a Musician", some drawings and a little text about a brilliant young student from Ray Rubbo's office whose building had just won the "Rehabilitation of old buildings" category: Antony Macknight.

But the massed students beat him to the press. They carried Ant out on their shoulders cheering and told the reporters the brilliant student had just been failed and they would be blockading the examiners until they saw sense. 'For a day, a week, a year if necessary.' they yelled. The reporters were delighted. Such a smutty intellectual scandal would sell a few extra papers and spice-up the Arts News on TV. The flux of the "Underdog triumphing" carried them to telephones, desks and news-reading rooms.

The Professor pushed through the student throng, opened the door to the examining and entered. He handed the year head the magazine and eyed the committee. 'Gentlemen, the year head has been trying to tell you, Macknight is our best student.' then turned and left. Outside the rabble cheered, smelling victory and justice.

Ant was white faced with despair. He managed to disengage from the rabid students and hurried home. Shortly Phil bounded triumphantly in with news of his pass to find him over-whelmed with anger. He threw himself at his friend and hugged a wan smile into him. When Rose returned she rang for a cab and took them straight home.

Ray and Kiffy had seen the news. They were livid. As the children reached the house they heard Ray shouting. He flounced out in a fury they had never seen, threw his arms around them all and dragged them protectively inside.

Over dinner they ate and drank too much. But slowly reality, the reality of all makers, returned. Then Ray stood and proposed a toast: 'To our dearest Ant and his very fine building.' They all drank deeply. Ray was still standing. 'All of you must remember architecture, design, fashion, all the arts, are not in reality a matter of opinion, but of fact. The object in use is all we must care about. The WAY we work will fashion it. THAT is the only truth. The rest is shit.'

Kiffy laughed. 'Well, dear, something less smelly, maybe a form of waste matter. To that I would agree.'

Ant stammered. 'And we must never allow ourselves to become experts. In the immensity of the problem there can be no experts. Our struggle is our glory. And . . .' words failed. His face suffused pain until he managed, 'And thank you. All of you are wonderful. If it is a good building it's because you were the team. YOU should have the medal. All of you. I love you.' He collapsed. Rose, who had up till then been shy of showing him affection at home, hugged and kissed him back to some semblance of celebration. Kiffy shortly nodded her sons and daughter to their rooms as if it were the old days. They were too drunk to care about anything but sleep; Phil lay unaware of any other state. Ant held Rose, hiding his bruised self in her embrace, until they drifted away. It had been a bitter fight. In spite of it, Ossian's house was a winner.

Lettuce telephoned Ossian. She had seen the news.

'I had wondered what was going on.' he said. 'There seem to be a number of people hanging round the street. But I've been esconsed here with music matters. I'll drop round to Ant's place and see if he's all right.'

He was button-holed as he left the house by a young reporter. 'Are you the client of the young architect?'

'Yes. He's my brother.'

'How much is his work and how much his office?'

Ossian was shocked by the insinuation. 'It's all his work: the design, construction, details. Everything. I watched him at work. There's no doubt at all.'

The reporter scribbled. 'You know, the University and the Architects' Institute are saying he borrowed it from his office, it's his boss's design.'.

Ossian paled. 'Ignorant people have ignorant ideas. I KNOW Ant is the architect; I know Ray Rubbo would agree. Go and talk to Ray. He'll put you straight. Wicked men must not be allowed to strip Ant of his talent. I'm going to see Ant now. Come, if you want.'

They went together only to find the bird had flown. Ossian went next door and rang Ray while the reporter quizzed Sophia about 'That bellissima family' as she called them. The reporter was impressed so famous a musician had so talented a brother and such a bellissima family as well. He decided it was an interesting story: The Establishment squashing a talented family, might get him onto the front page. So he jumped on his motor-bike and roared off to the Rubbo architectural office to flesh out his story.

Ray was incensed and hotly denied authorship suggesting firstly his office had no fees for the job; secondly, his help was administrative: the back-up of an office for the building stage, and any other advice was of one professional to another; thirdly, the reporter should view the various submissions for approvals in offices in the city which, although bearing his office stamp, were clearly labelled with Ant's name and signature. Calming down he observed, 'It's scandalous; talent is trampled upon by people who are so incompetent they can't even use their senior positions to support youngsters emerging behind them.'

The reporter, similarly oppressed, grinned. 'Thanks Mister Rubbo. And thanks for the pictures of his design and of the family. Ant is being crucified. I'll try to get the true story out. You and he have more friends than you know of.' and roared off to the city, saw all Ant's drawings and letters, rushed back slaved over his piece and grudgingly had it accepted for the front page of the morning's edition. His editor tiredly observing it was a spicy follow-up to the debacle at the University, and that Architecture was a profession of wankers.

In the meantime, Ray's anger metamorphosed into disquiet. That the Architectural Institute had commented, and without contacting him or Ant, was a scandal. He cancelled his appointments and went to the city office where he confronted the secretary whose carelessness and disinterest in architecture was offensive. The Institute had been approached by the professor of Architecture; they had not properly checked, believing Ray and Ant would perpetrate such a smutty act; because, as all the critics voiced, 'the work was like any other Rubbo project'.

Ray was horrified by the cynicism. He stood up to leave. 'Both I and the client will confirm Ant's authorship; you must check all his submissions; issue an apology and retraction within forty eight hours or I will resign my membership.'

SENIOR ARCHITECT QUITS INSTITUTE blazed on the front page two days later with a concise report.

There was an editorial commenting on the mess the profession was in, the parlous state of the fabric of the city and the need for a blood-transfusion of young talent, that education and building design must be improved before it was too late.

What disturbed the president of the Institute was the last liner which stated "Many younger architects are refusing to join what they regard as a corrupt and useless establishment." He knew it was time to act. Unwillingly he gathered his supporters on the management committee and they resolved to dismiss the secretary and revamp the administration, then issue a press release saying The Institute had turned over a new leaf and would in future promote the practice of architecture in every way possible.

The cub reporter was relegated to 'Architectural Correspondent' on a good salary. His column was widely read; he haunted Ray's office; joining the coterie. The mess and the pain had another benefit: both Ray and Ant were sought-after. At the end of the following year when Phil would graduate, there should be ample work for all of them.

It was pre-empted by Lettuce who asked Ant to add to her dance studio a small play room for the children of day students who were training there.

Lettuce took his arm. 'We will pay. The Local Authority is financing us; consult Ossian's friend, Angelica who works with children; do consult Phil's friend, Katia - I don't want it to fall down.' She grinned at her beloved bright-eyed architect. 'Consult whoever you like. But don't steal a Rubbo design. It's an Ant heap I want.'

Everyone roared. Lettuce was solid support.

Ant took a site plan and pictures of the area proposed to the country. He, Rose and Phil disappeared to Ararat for a month both to recover from the gruelling term, escape the newsmen and renew themselves.

Phil asked Katia to take some holiday time and join them. 'It'll be fun.' he urged. 'Ossian and Angelica may come for the last few weeks, so bring your oboe.'

16-

THE VALLEY sighed with pleasure and welcome, reflecting the delight in Ararat itself. Nina abandoned her programme and cheerfully escorted them down to the river, its shrunken summer self sliding surreptitiously in the groin of the land.

'Of course we'll swim.' she shouted, dragging them to the deepest rock pool. Phil felt her beauty keenly: fifteen, blossoming and full of fun deeply aroused his interest. She knew his eyes caressed her; she yearned for that. But it was Rose whom she fell for, her fully fledged womanhood graceful and fecund, her joy, her intensity; Nina, for the very first time was strangled in a thread of jealousy for Ant, her beloved Ant who had been her dream-brother, who now was connected to the one person to whom Nina longed to offer her treasure.

Everyone swam; naked water-babies, the flash of a smile when playfully they collided, the unabashed freedom whose breathlessness tinged everything with a delicious beauty and emboldened them to touch and clutch until the boys' erections began to rise and the girls nipples harden, as they lay basking in friendship and dappled sunshine, watching each other watching sparkles dance over the water and into themselves.

Nina's intense interest shocked Rose. It was reminiscent of Ant's; it whispered of loving admiration, of sharing until she shone. It was a desire tinged with much more than sex, enriching her appetite for everything this peaceful valley offered; it was infectious. So when they returned to the house something angelic bound Nina to Rose.

As the shadows lengthened Ant escaped with Rose and meandered up the rise to visit Will, Miranda and their brood: Nici,6, Kim,4 and Nestor, an adventurous one-year old. Wendy was helping bath them. She looked up happily from the chaos of wet. 'Nearly done. I'll finish and join you in a few moments.'

Miranda slipped out. She made them all tea. They sat on the verandah, the kids gambolled the dogs following, talking about Ant's degree dramas. Rose had made the children tiny and not so tiny tee-shirts and shorts, screen printed with a leaf design made during their trip to the green lake. The children, soon abandoning pyjamas, clad in the Bush, became entrancing bush-spirits; Miranda was deeply grateful.

Will looked admiringly at Rose. 'You've captured the colours perfectly. They'll treasure them. Thanks Rosie It's great to be joined to the Bush.'

Rose looked far away. 'I'd like to go back there. I have an idea for a complete outfit for my graduation collection, using the greens of the lake and moss, sky blue, the ochre of the rocks and fragments of black like birds. Of course it has a private significance: there, we married. But they are blessed colours, I believe.'

'I'd like that.' Ant breathed. 'Maybe when Katia comes we can slip away. Phil won't feel so abandoned.'

Miranda smiled. 'Will you make babies there?'

'Not yet. First, my final year.'

'Hey, what about Ant's house?' said Will.

'We've come for that.' Ant smiled. 'When Katia arrives, my office will be complete. Then we'll finalise it.'

'Is she good?'

'She understands me more than I do.' Ant said. 'She and Les are fanatics: it's all talk of stresses, friction, torque and moments. Quite beyond me, Will-oh. She's one of us.'

'Like Rose.' Will said softly.

'Exactly.' said Ant kissing her lips for so long the children clambered all over him clamouring for attention. Ant sighed. 'Oh, the duties of being an uncle.' and jiggled them on his knee and covered every inch of bare flesh with sloppy kisses until it was time for bed and a story - to calm them down - which NuncleAnt was pressed to relate:

*It was a chilly night. Bunyip was shivering when the chil -
dren let him in. They had such lovely warm tee-shirts and shorts.
Poor Bunyip, even his fur seemed thin that night. So the eldest girl*

peeled off her clothes and said Bunyip should put them on for the long journey.

She was so beautiful naked, the stars gasped thinking a new shining star had been born. It was because she had had such a lovely long bath, so was clean and shiny like a new baby.

Then Bunyip took their hands and leapt into the dark sky: up and up, beyond the world as we know it, beyond time itself, until with a BUMP they landed.

The children opened their eyes. They were such very good children, keeping them tight shut as they had promised, so as not to fall with a BUMP and hurt their heads.

But here, they saw, they could safely fall BUMP, because everything was soft. So soft one had to be very careful moving about in case the ground opened and you fell through.

Yes Kim, like the muddy swamp you made when you emptied your play-pool onto the dirt this afternoon.

So, the children tip-toed over the spongy, squishy ground to a tiny house on stilts.

Yes, Nici, stilts are like legs, house-legs in fact. And these were long, so the children could walk right underneath.
Yes, Kim, far, far higher than your house, where only puppies can run upright. No, the house didn't walk, I don't know why not.

But let me tell you a secret. But only if you promise to keep it a secret?

OK! Well, Bunyip took me there years ago when I was little, just as you are. It was he who gave me the idea of building a house on stilts which your Daddy and Peter are helping me with. Yes, they were with me that time. So, when it's finished you must come and run underneath and see if Bunyip is there.

Anyway, Bunyip was with them in the squishy land. He lifted each child onto his shoulders so they could scramble up and get into the house. Inside was a family of feathery imps who were delighted to share their little house with such handsome and polite children.

It was then that the girl had a brilliant idea. She shyly asked the feathery imps if they had any spare feathers, explaining that Bunyip got cold on his long trips and needed a feathery jacket.

The Mummy imp sprang up laughing. 'My dear Himp' (which is what they call us. Human+Imp), 'My dear Himp, I have *just finished making a warm, feathery coat and we were sitting here wondering what to do with it. You have solved our problem. Let's give it to our beloved Bunyip.'*

The little boy suggested she add some buttons so it would be truly warm. Which she did with alacrity ('Quickly', Kim).

So that is why when Bunyip visits you he does not shiver. He has a warm cosy coat now. Thanks to your clever idea. By the way, you may all keep your new clothes. So they flew home through space as warm as toast, everyone in such finery.

While Bunyip was visiting, Nina emerged out of the dark. She saw Rose sitting on the verandah with Wendy. 'Oh, there you are. I thought I'd find you here.' she said. 'Supper is soon. Come back with me. Ant can follow when he's finished. He knows the way blind.'

After goodbyes, Nina gleefully took Rose's arm and piloted her along the rough track to Ararat. Rose was charmed. She put a friendly arm around the girl. They moved as one through the dark homing on lights in the house. Nina's heart was pounding. At the bottom of the stairs leading from the lake-side level up into the house, she stopped, blocking the way. 'So here you are, safe and sound. Isn't it worth at least a kiss of thanks?'

Rose grinned in the dark, enjoying the game. She leaned forward and pulled the girl into a long hug. Nina shuddered leaned her head on Rose's shoulder so as to be surrounded by warmth.

'Hey, Nina, your heart is racing. What is it?' Rose whispered.

'I don't know.' Nina trembled. Rose held her and stroked her hair. Her face lifted. Rose kissed her.

Nina burst into tears. Savouring the warmth and her intense dreams of union, she clung to Rose, opening her thighs to press closer, as longing, embarrassment and delight swirled her about. Then Rose understood: for it was also her own body's longing, her own response to drowning in love.

'I can't help it.' Nina whispered, as she floated in a wondrous sea of perplexing lust.

'Oh, my dearest Nina.' Rose whispered sadly.

'I wish I was.'

'Darling, you are. But I love Ant. You know that. Oh Nina. Please don't cry. Love is cruel. But true. Yours is so prescious.

But I can only love you as a friend, and as a sister. My dearest, special sister.'

'You don't care.' Nina sobbed.

'I care for you deeply, my darling Nina. As deeply as I do, Ant. But he's my partner. We can only be sisters.'

She held the distrait girl until her weeping subsided. 'Oh, my Nina, we can use love either to kill or to live. Let's make a solemn promise to love each other so our lives are enriched. You may feel bitter. You may hate me for this. But I believe we can find ways of loving which will not split us up: split Ant from me, you from Ant, you from anyone. You and I must struggle with love so it gives us life. Please, please try to understand.'

Nina brushed Rose's cheek with an amazed finger, looked longingly at her fulsome body so miraculously close and sighed. 'I love you.'

Rose stood firm, her own heart beating erratically . 'So, can we be sisters? Two loving sisters?'

Nina shut her eyes. She was suddenly happy. It was not her dream of union. But it was real: a loving contract between two special sisters who loved and shared and would trust and comfort and weep together. Nina wanted much, much more. But what was offered was enough for now. She said softly 'I love you, sister.' They kissed.

Then Nina bounded up the long flight of stairs like a willy-willy and burst into the kitchen so overwhelmingly happy. Sophie blinked in disbelief as she carolled. 'Rose is back. Ant is coming after Bunyip is finished. I'm starving.'

Sophie smiled, thinking, Ah, our little love-child. Happy. She needs company, just as Ant does, the pet. She weighed-up the radiant face. 'Darling heart, set the table. Choose where everyone sits and call Daddy. He's resting in the bedroom I think. Phil has been mooching around studying the village green as Ant now calls it. Better tell him too, will you darling.'

'Mummy, let's have candles. Rose will sit next to me. She'll help me. Here she comes.'

Sophie looked up. Rose had been crying (so had Nina, she saw). Then she realised Nina was in love. She thought, Thank goodness Rose seems to have sorted it out. Sophie smiled at her favourite prospective daughter. 'Are you all right?' Rose nodded and smiled. After Nina had rushed off to gather the feasters she said softly. 'I think it's all right. Just.'

Sophie kissed her brow. 'Treat her gently. She is impetuous and headstrong, like the rest, as you've already found.'

'We've promised each other to be loving sisters which I welcome. Her intensity is awesome.'

'Well, that makes me a Mum-in-law, or something similar. That's awesome too, Rose dear.'

Rose blushed. 'Do you think we should marry?'

'Dear one, it's up to you and Ant. Tim and I have no worries about you.'

'We want to leave it until I finish my fashion degree at the end of next year. We rather like the turmoil of life as it is. But we want to go back to the green lake for some unfinished business.'

Sophie took her hand. 'Rose I have loved you as a daughter for many years, as I have loved Phil. Whatever happens, remember that. Don't feel we are binding you to Ant. Be free, both of you.'

Rose straightened and looked at her tired face. 'Soph, I love Ant more than anyone. He seems to feel the same. We are happy being bound. We are really happy. We're not going to the green lake because of any doubts. Rather, to remake promises. Also I want to study it as inspiration for my degree collection. He feels, I think, more of a man now he's an architect with Daddy. We're not kids anymore. I don't think he has any doubts - I don't. We go with our love and all our hopes intact. It has been a terrible year in some ways. We are damaged and need its peace.'

'That's why you should go.' Tim quietly entered the kitchen. 'You are brave facing those furies. I ran away from them. Came here to hide. Yes, you'll find peace and renew your love and hopes. I'll get Peter to take the 4WD in for service so it's ready for you both. Darling, I'm famished. Can we eat?'

Sophie sighed. He made things seem so easy. But they were not. But she held her tongue. The rest, Rose and she had already tackled, and Nina's happiness confirmed some success. 'Can you wait for the boys?'

Tim nodded happily. 'Yes, the boys are always late. I'll open the wine, shall I?' He put his frail arms around the two women and lightly kissed each of them.

Rose looked admiringly at both of them thinking, They're

battlers, just as Daddy said. They ran away in order to battle-on. The valley is a grand monument to their dreams, as real as Ant and Nina. She flushed. 'Thank you for Ant.'

Tim and Sophie's smiles were drowned as Ant and Phil bounced in boyishly. 'Where's the grub? We're famished.' Nina bustled in and scolded them delightedly. 'Where have you two boys been. I looked everywhere?'

That night, Rose clung to Ant. She felt vulnerable in ways hardly understood. Although exhausted by the challenges occasioned by his thesis, he responded with deeper more focused hunger, with new solidity and support.

Rose woke remembering her father was due to discuss the pavilion he'd designed for Tim and Sophie; in the first instance, for a couple of helpers around the house and garden, but which Ray gently proposed could become their retirement pad when the main house became too much for them to manage - raw thoughts Tim had pushed away.

Ant and Phil were clamouring to talk through their plans for Ant's house and to raise issues about other sites with Ray. One they had earmarked for Ossian; who, through Peter's efforts had leased the neighbouring plot up-river from the Forestry Commission with the condition that no building be erected.

'We have secured the Bush, but not found him a place for a house.' Tim murmured, supporting the idea Ossian be placed in the Village. Phil was enamoured with Ant's project. Having made a big scale model, he spent much time talking to Peter about standardised timber sizes and timber connectors, the most suitable hard-wood deck and how they were planning to connect the stilts, on which the house was raised, back to the rocks with minimum interference with the site.'I love making it work.' Phil said happily.

Ant struggled with the sculpture of landscape plus buildings, their marriage was his chief passion. 'Adding to the earth. It's like burrowing into you.' he whispered to Rose that night. 'Finding how best to fit; how to come together, to enhance beauty, not damage it.'

Rose yearned for comfort. 'Is making houses like making babies? she shyly asked. 'Something new grows from a marriage?'

Ant pushed hugely into her whispering. 'Yes. And making

love. Oh, darling stay here forever.'

But Rose remained troubled; perhaps it was trying to cope with both their lives - his had been acerbic during this first shared year, hers challenging enough on its own - now her father was due: another adjustment; and Nina troubled her: something chimed with her invisible self, overlayed by her growing-up which Nina had exposed; dimly Rose felt it touched deeply on the nature of love itself which she felt ill-equipped to handle.

After breakfast Rose took her headache back to bed. She lay looking at shadows dancing on the wall and nodding cheerfully at her until she fell asleep.

She was woken by the silence, everyone must have gone out; and by her bed sinking slightly as Nina slid carefully in beside her to shelter there.

When Nina saw open eyes, she kissed them 'I'm sorry about the headache; It's my fault. I hope you feel better now.'

Rose lay an arm over the girl's waist. 'It's the fault of life.' and rested her chin on Nina's fragrant hair. 'I can smell the river.'

'I was swimming. I wished you were there.'

'You are a beautiful water nymph.' Rose murmured as warmth spread over Nina's face, thinking, She's young and tender with the innocence of a nymph, before ravishment by a hungry god.

'Perhaps you have your period?' Nina whispered.

'No.'

'I went on the pill, because my pains were terrible.'

Rose seemed to hold her own shadow; to talk as if to herself. 'I know what you mean. I found sexual activity or just sexual excitement reduced my pains from agony to mild discomfort.'

'I haven't started sex.'

'So, do it yourself. To get excited seems to work. You're probably excited now.' Rose said.

'Are you?'

Rose fingered her sticky labia. 'Probably.'

'Try me?' pleaded the girl.

Rose slipped a finger into her vagina. It opened to her touch, wringing wet. 'Yes, you are.'

Nina shivered. 'That's good.'

Rose caressed her naked thigh. 'Don't you do that?'

'No. Will you do it again, please, Rose.'

Rose licked her fingers, found and caressed Nina's clitoris until the girl winced with pleasure and climaxed. Nina fiercely held the fingers in place but her relaxing body let them go. The girl breathed out and fell back with regret that the storm within was becoming a suffusing glow. She was dazzled by a sense of beauty, in herself and Rose.

'Show me what to do.' Nina had slipped Rose's nickers down her legs and was studying her fury triangle as if it would indicate how the levers of pleasure could be handled. Her life-long curiosity about the mysteries hidden there re-awoke She licked her fingers and wriggled them between the fleshy labia. Rose directed them to her stiffening thread, tutoring the foreign fingers to slip gently along it. Nina felt her shiver. 'Am I hurting?'

Rose shook her head and gasped, her eyes unfocussed, turning inward in pleasure as her womb shimmered.

Nina was amazed at her power and the power it unleashed. It sharpened her dreams of union with Rose. When Rose cried, she cried. As Rose sweated yearningly, she sweated. In a waking dream she brought such deep pleasure to her loved one, manipulating the ancient knowledge trapped in her deepest sinews until Rose shivered, gripped her fingers, as she had just done, and cried of soulful delight. Nina had supped such riches off this body, women's riches, sacred, magisterial, earth-shattering. Nina was suddenly terrified: firstly she might never reexperience such joy; secondly, she'd lost everything, her childhood, her dreams, her energy, herself.

'So now you know.' Rose smiled tenderly.

Nina now understood this was repeatable, if Rose survived, she would. Delight, wonder and dread spun her. She snuggled into Rose to hide, and keep the ecstacy, to wallow in a storm of loving feelings with giggles and whisperings as her hair, her flesh her joy were caressed by a warm womanly hand settling the torment.

They showered, soaping, sponging and towelling until flesh glowed. Then they lay for a short while finding enough composure to sally back into the family.

"So now you know." Rose had said it for them both.

That afternoon Nina slipped away to the swimming pool where she fingered herself, and swam. A lusty solidity grew in her body, she walked with her legs slightly turned out as if inviting vaginal pleasures, and pushed her breasts out mimicking Rose.

No one noticed the change. Rose spotted Nina spying on her and when caught, smiling with a brightness charmed by love.

Rose confessed her fling.

Ant was glad her love was enlarging. His had. 'We love each other first; then there are others. It's like ripples on a pond, our green pool - we must throw a stone when we're there. Other lovers are the ripples lapping the bank when the centre is excited.'

Something healed in Rose. It was a combination of Ant's manly love and Nina's girlish love which re-connected bits scattered in growing up.

No one noticed the change in her, except Ant who found a more solid response to his own longing.

A few days later, Ant and Rose accompanied Peter on a tour of M+S Landscapes' jobs. Nina had offered to take Phil up-river to a sandy pool where they could picnic and swim.

'We can lie in the grass and plop in whenever we want.' she promised as they trudged through the tangled scrub bordering the river. It was a bright day. A light breeze scuffed the valley, shadows danced. Only hats, shorts and tee-shirts against the burning sun were required, and a small pack with lunch and snacks.

'The river provides the rest.' Nina said denying a place to a heavy carton of fruit juice Phil proffered.

She led the way; he following, shouldering their provisions and keenly eyeing her buxom form. But his lonesome, lascivious dreams prompted wild thoughts to hang about like flies. On arrival, although she stripped and splashed in, he demurely hung back and lay on his stomach on a towel sunning himself and getting hot under his non-existent collar until, with a mouth full of water she leaped out and drenched him.

Phil gasped and jumped up, his erection bouncing. He stumbled to the waters edge and fell in tickled by Nina's raucous laughter. With an obliterating splash, she fell outstretched beside him and pushed his head under. They fought to hide feelings and to hold each other (As boys do, Nina thought gleefully). She was fumbling with herself and with his body searching in their watery games for a resolution to restlessness.

It reminded Phil of youthful silliness with his sister usually ended when hurriedly they colluded in trying to tidy up the damage as a parent was heard approaching. 'But this is not as carefree.' he mused as they lounged on the grass eyeing one another.

The day seemed to hold its breath. They ate ravenously, slobbered water from a rivulet above their bathing pool and returned to lie on the grass and talk. She was glad he loved the valley, enjoying his enthusiasm about Ant's holiday house and of their dreams of making a village for all of the family around a green behind Ararat. She longed to find out about his girl, Katia but was silent, although couples and coupling engaged her.

He was lying on his tummy again. She grinned and pushed him gently onto his side to reveal his stiffened penis. She thought men's' floppy penises untidy, the meaning in stiffening was interesting if obtuse.

She ran an inquisitive finger along it. The head swelled, opening its fleshy petal, oozing liquid.

'Are you excited?' she breathed.

He nodded shyly.

'I get wet too.'

She held it. It seemed to talk to her. Its power thrilled her. 'Do you like that?'.

He nodded, his open mouth proclaiming pleasure.

It's a bigger version of Rose's, she thought, running a questing hand up and down. He tensed. She pushed him onto his back and straddled his thighs, lifted her hips, leaned forward and carefully dropped down onto his erection, holding herself above him when she had admitted the shining tip, jiggling it further in.

Strong feelings burst. She lost control and sat heavily. It plunged in filling her. A needling pain shimmered. But lust was stronger. He flexed his muscular bottom to thrust in small pleasurable movements. Each gasped.

She stretched out her legs and spreadeagled over him. He was free to thrust more quickly. He panted 'Nina. Quick. I'm coming.' and tried to disengage.

She held him ferociously. 'Go on. I'm on the pill.'

Phil pushed her upwards two hands making space. Stretched to breaking point, he laboured, rising and falling, until with waterfalls of whimpers he climaxed and collapsed, she heavy above him. They lay as the world settled.

Nina watched him recover. 'All that effort for nothing.' and flicked his shrunken penis.

'Nothing.' Phil muttered.

'Just like love.'

'I hope not.'

She rose stiffly. Her vagina stung. Is this how it is with men? she thought wading into the pool.

He watched her. 'She's bloody gorgeous.' he said to himself, grateful and guilty. He felt shrunken, like his dick; he longed for love, for Katia, for the hugeness of dream and body, the joy and tenderness of fulfiled feeding. He shivered, remembering the previous summer and the plans he, Rose and Ant had made.

Each privately decided for now to go it alone.

When they returned to the house Nina moodily went to her room. He wandered into the kitchen to find Will there, talking to Tim. 'I was just saying that Ant's house has an A-frame. So what about yours?' Will grinned.

Tim laughed. 'A P-frame is a bit top-heavy, more like a pregnant woman than a handsome stripling like you.'

'I don't have a house.' Phil said.

Tim looked fondly at him. 'Phil, do you want one?'

'No land and no money. Phil smiled.

Tim chuckled. 'There's land if you want - as described so expertly by Ray and Ant. And your dad is willing to pay for materials if you do the work. So whatd'ya'say? It'd make a teasing thesis, another Rubbo project, another fail.'

They all laughed heartily.

'Are you serious?' Phil stammered breathlessly.

Will grinned. 'I heard them, Phil. It's fair dinkum.'

Tim was serious. 'But, dear boy, it's completely up to you. If you and your lass have other plans, that's fine.'

Phil choked. 'Plans? I? Plans? I don't have any, except to work with Ant and Katia. Do you really, *really* mean it?

Tim put his arms weakly round the astonished boy and hugged him. In the depth of the embrace lay the assurance sought. What a beaming face emerged, what excited arms crushed Will in a blinding embrace as Phil stuttered 'Wow. My own house. WOWEE.'

Will struggled clear and panted. 'I wondered whether a Greek P might work for you. It's a *pi* in our maths, you know, 2-*pi*-R and all that. It's like a big double joined t, 'Π'. Phil, could it be your structure?'

Phil was thunderstruck with disbelief (was Father Xmas real? Yes, they called him Bunyip in this valley). Delight, gratitude, love and a sudden fear he was not skillful enough to emulate Ant. But Will's idea was a fantastic start.

He trembled. 'Oh Will, you *are* amazing. What a brilliant idea, a Greek P. My temple will have a flat roof although the Parthanon has a pitched one. I'm not sure Katia designs goddess-columns. Oh Tim.' He hid his face as a tear sneaked out unbidden. The others smiled cheerfully, deeply happy, welcoming this clever, loyal boy into the family, joining the Rubbos and Macknights, as they had been joined in work and belief for many years.

'Ray will be pleased.' Tim said softly. 'He's quite sure you'll make a fine house. So am I. That little diamond just dropped into the earth will grow into a fine *pi* temple-house. You'd best get out there and decide where it should sprout. Before all the know-alls return with conflicting advice.'

Will leaned into his Tad, worrying about his strength for Will was so much stronger now. They watched the boy stumble dazed to an area beyond Ant's site. There he sat and pondered, unable to count all his treasures, but sure the proximity to Ant, an ancient area of flat rocky ground, had been fashioned just for him. Here, his first sacred act of building should take place. He turned and looked between the rocks, over the river and into the haze of trees and ridges beyond. 'Today did hold its breath.' he said to Bunyip and the Bush. 'So I could be emptied and filled.' He smiled. 'A place in the Bush. My place in the village, in this valley. I don't need anything else. Except Katia. She must help me.'

He rose and sauntered back towards the house. Seeing the mess of tree bits, he took up a waiting axe and began chopping. It was a rhythmic twang. Chips flew, logs snapped. Soon a pile was ready for the fire. One day it would be taken to *his* hearth. What an idea. Grinning, he carried arm-fulls of wood into Ararat, pausing on the verandah.

'Come here, my dear.' said Sophie. She brushed him down front and back, enjoying his firm buttocks and the bulge between his legs covered with wood chips. She brushed hair off his damp face and murmured. 'Thank you Phil. Tim and I are finding it harder every day to do those heavy tasks. Without you boys, where would we be?'

'Do you know about my house?'

'No, come and tell me over a cuppa.'

She was reminded of Ant's enthusiasm so many years ago when he hardly touched the ground. It's the same happiness, she thought gladly. She was pleased about Will's part in it. They all have so much compared to Will, she thought, overlooking all Symph's blessings, Miranda, their children and a growing variety of work. She had forgotten the treasures the valley bestows in her worry about Tim's ailing health.

When Tim's headaches returned, he had a complete check-up and brain scan. Nothing unusual was found. But the hospital decided he needed rest, suggesting he come in on the days that Sophie worked so she could help with the driving, also shortening his hours. The registrar had fixed it so Tim was made a consultant, earning more. So he received the same salary for a shorter day. Everyone wanted him there. His care, knowledge and good sense were vital both to the spirit of the team and to the patients. The way he networked with outpatients, with social services, therapists and rehabilitation specialties was clearly very effective. His annual jazz night when everyone mingled and danced and some slipped into the night for more intimate dancing, was eagerly attended and reported by gleeful orderlies so the hospital hummed with innocent scandal for weeks afterwards. No wonder it became known as 'The Happy Hospital', one which attracted skilled and personable professionals from psychologists like Sophie to nurses like Wendy.

Tim's prognosis was his motorbike accident had long term effects and age might increase his discomfort.

'But getting old is having to try harder, getting tired and having to do less.' Sophie proclaimed. 'We're not youngsters.'

Tim smiled. 'But your cunt is as lovely as ever my darling.'

'But my cunt doesn't cut the wood or drive into town.'

'It always cheers me along, wherever I'm heading.'

Sophie grunted reprovingly. 'Well, let it sit with you, doze with you, rather than your usual tearing about. Please Tim. There's so much life left. Let's enjoy it.'

Tim tried. It was difficult to ignore his restlessness which had happily driven him all his life. But he finally admitted she was right. His body was resisting his accustomed ways. It was time to let-up a bit. So he began to enjoy his children's' lives, enjoying their worries and delights, their loves and disappointments, and to welcome his growing family back to the valley, 'Where they all belong.' he mused. 'And whoever they bring with them, it's the best nurture.'

And he turned increasingly to his oldest love, music. He'd lost his lip, he knew. But he still played well. He longed for Ossian to fly in from his busy life and fill the music space, talk about symphonies, songs and dancing, longed to play chamber music with him and his able friends, longed for the lift such collaborating induced; for then he felt fully alive, singing with the angels.

Later in the living-room everyone drank beer and nibbled small cheese tartlets Nina and Sophie had made.

'So, you buggers have been plotting on our behalf.' Ant said to Will. 'Can't leave us alone, all your meddling.'

Phil laughed. 'Well I have to take my doctor's advice. It will be hard, taking the medicine. But what can I do?'

'Lie down and die in my house might be simpler.' Ant said.

'You wouldn't catch me dead in an 'A' frame.'

'So then, pee everywhere instead.'

Rose giggled, thinking of their unruly water games in the back garden. 'You two. Always flashing your willies and wetting fair maidens and the whole bloody village green.'

Tim guffawed. 'A for 'orses, B for mutton, P for relief. So you accept the neighbour we chose for you, Ant?'

Ant grinned, his whole body grinned. He looked out of the living-room window at the view he had loved all his life. 'It's as good as a Bunyip story. Thanks Dad.'

'You must help me, please Ant?'

'Phil, I'll never equal your help. But I'd love to be involved.' Ant grinned. 'First with a hundred foot wall on the boundary so we can't hear you and Katia having it off. Then a machine-gun turret so I can shoot your mighty prick off and stay dry. And after that. . .'

'And after that let's eat.' said Sophie.

'I'll set the table.' said Ant.

'I'll help.' said Phil.

'No, Phil, let Rose keep an eye on him. You've done a masterly job with the wood, and it's mid-summer.' Sophie said. 'I think you must be planning a high wood wall there's so much.'

'We'll thank you all winter.' Tim filled his glass.

Nina was nonplussed, they were all so silly and friendly and excited. Phil was excited - as she had been beside the river - it was not like this. It was sex, she felt it, yet also another pleasure. She longed to join in. She sat mute, sipping fruit juice. Then irritatedly she rose and went into the dining room, finding Ant and Rose passionately embracing. 'Do that later. We want to eat.' she rasped.

Ant smiled. 'The table's ready. Tell the others.' and returned to press himself into Rose's open thighs, kiss her and pull away happily. Nina hated him. And her. She didn't belong.

'Nina, I put you next to me.' Rose said gently, pulling the girl to her. Nina fell into her arms weeping. Rose caressed her cheek saying softly. 'Nina, do we seem a terribly noisy intrusion? We are happy because we will see more of you and share this magic valley.'

'What magic?'

'The magic it's always had. The magic of us sharing and growing up however painful that may be.'

Nina was unsure whether she wanted them gone, or whether she longed for them to stay. In the long turmoil of the day she was comforted by Rose wanting to be beside her. It was terrible to hate someone she loved. Now, she hated and loved them all.

Languorous days stretched away. They would collect Miranda and the kids, sometimes only Nici and Kim and make their way through the dry whispery grass to the river where they swam and lounged about, watching the little ones gambol, sometimes with one of their uncles - Ant and Phil had both been crowned. When off duty from the hospital, Wendy would join them.

Most afternoons, Will and then Peter back from town, would amble down and flop in the refreshing stream. Then, Tim and Sophie would leave the cool of the house and trip down to join the basking. Kim and Nici discussed all the hairy things as they dallied by a small rock pool they had appropriated for play causing mirth in the adults who gleefully had to agree with their observations that the Rubbos were the best endowed in the valley.

Only Nina was put out. Thinking, All this sex, and they're still little. She surveyed her breasts and longed to be like Rose.

Ant discussed his plan to take Rose to the green lake with

Phil who longed to take Katia. 'Can't we go like last time? Shared time and separate time? I want to be there with Katia. So much.' Phil, confounded by Ant's reluctance, said. 'It would be such fun.'

'Let's discuss it when she arrives.' Ant said.

Phil borrowed a car and drove to the station to collect Katia. She saw him first and thrilled at the solid, sunburned hunk lounging in the shade of the sun-drenched entry looking like a lusty farmer in his bush hat and shorts.

He was surprised how pale she was. Her bright laughter and passionate embrace reassured him.

'You look as if you need a holiday.' he said, taking her case and ushering her to the dusty car where she knelt down and drew a big heart with an arrow and the initials, PR and KB on the bonnet.

Phil grinned. 'We'll see about that.'

They went to the supermarket to collect Sophie's order.

While Katia sat in the hot car, Phil filled the back with boxes, finally ice-creams they hurriedly gobbled, as they drove along.

'Yuk, it's sticky.' Katia said.

Phil leered at her legs. 'I know a small fire dam on the way where we can clean up.'

She looked at him. 'I'd forgotten how lusty you are.' She squeezed his arm.

After turning off onto the rough dirt track to Ararat, he pulled off into trees beside two huge domed rocks and trundled into a clearing with an earth dam half filled with water. He parked under a tree, they removed their sandals and fell out of the car to reach the bank. He cupped his hands and let the water run over her sticky legs, afterwards, cleaning himself, eying her mischievously. They sauntered back, undressing. He threw a rug onto the ground and pulled her yearningly onto it.

'It's the most beautiful thing.' she said placing his penis at the mouth of her vagina.

He went down on her. 'I missed you terribly.'

She took him in and trembled with pleasure. He thrust ferociously and came, freezing inside her as his seed streamed out until he wilted and fell away. They lay contentedly until talk returned. She told him of trying one-night-stands, of missing him, needing him so much, sometimes she couldn't sleep even after masturbating.

'Phil, I love you. I can't help it. There's no one else.' she whispered kissing his lips. 'My office reprimanded me for moonlighting with Ray's office, saying it was "most unprofessional" but I don't care. I told them it was "professional development, an interest in timber structures", but I didn't mention you.' she hugged him.

She prodded him to admit his dalliance with Nina, and all the nights of wanking. She held his floppy member. 'I know how you felt; sex isn't enough; I decided we have sex because we need to express our feelings for each other. Then, it's wonderful, like now.'

'But we just fucked like animals.'

'It was *your* hunger, *your* penis, *your* seed which I took. That makes it fabulous.'

He nodded. 'You're right. You make it so good. Giving you everything, pounding you for being away. Loving you for having me. He swam in her eye-deeps. 'I do love you Katia. I missed you. Let's stay together.' He told her about his π house.

She looked amazed. 'Yes, we'll do it together.'

'And call it *our* house.' he kissed her breasts. The nipples hardened. Dammed feelings flowed. They forgot the heat, the dust and the waning day. They embraced fully.

They were so dishevelled when they reached Ararat that, after unpacking, they showered, so dinner had started by the time they emerged and entered the dining room. No one minded, except Nina who screwed up her nose and looked unforgiving.

Rose grinned at her bashful, happy brother. His joy was hers. She had expected growing up involved growing away, but here it seemed she kept her family as well as joining her beloved Ant. 'I think Katia is good for him. He's the same silly puppy romping through life, yet she settles him bringing a solidity. I hope it works out.' she mused half-aware the solidity of a sexually satisfied man is but part of the working out.

In spite of her craving for time with Ant, Rose was agreeable to her brother and Katia joining their Bush expedition. 'After all, it had been great last time. Now, with Katia, Phil will feel better.' she told Ant, still troubled by the shared prospect of the effect on Phil and Katia of the power of the green lake.

'That is, if they go down there.' Rose said.

'Rosey, if you're happy, so am I.' Ant kissed her.

So, the four talked and planned a week's trek with the

anticipation of something tough, exciting and essential. A rewarding adventure holiday from the strictures of everyday.

One afternoon after playing oboe and bassoon duets Tim sighed. 'Thank you, Katia. Please get back to play with Ossian and me. It's been fun. You are so good. No wonder with a brilliant teacher like your mum.'

Katia had surmised that her mum and Tim had been very close. She asked him about his early lessons with her.

'She gave me a love of music and of myself.' he said.

'She says much the same about you.' Katia said.

'I was such a tearaway, mixing everything in my life to which she responded. It was wonderful. I was besotted with the bassoon and with her. How she coped with the whirlwind I'll never know.'

'Was she with Dad?'

'With him, but not married. I think they had just become lovers at that time.'

'Were you?'

Tim looked at the spirited daughter of his beloved Fran, wondering what she knew. He broke the warm silence.'Your mother was my first woman. I doted on her. We explored all the alien territory of our bodies until we were able to drift apart. All my music and myself grew from that relationship. It was some years before she married or you were born. But Fran is as much part of me as my bassoon. That you are here makes me happy beyond words. I wonder if you can understand?'

Katia smiled, thinking, He is a lovely man, even now. And said. 'I understand passion; its power is essential. But I can't imagine Mum so young and headstrong.'

Tim chuckled. 'Nor me?'

'I hear it in both of your music-making, a clamouring for connection, an enjoyment of ensemble, powering towards resolution.'

'To play and to fuck. Is that what you're saying?'

'I suppose I am. The pleasure of being together.'

'Of playing (at music or sex) together. Yes.'

Then Katia had to tell him about her infatuation for Phil, adding. 'We go crazy together, do anything, everything. He liberates me. I can't imagine life without him.'

Tim kissed her softly. Ah, she is so fragrant, he thought. 'Then you love him deeply. Good. Like us, you also share; in your case the making of buildings. To share part of the world as well as each other is the only sort of love I have ever wanted. It's deep and wild and all-embracing. But clearly you know that. Your Mum and I discovered those connections. It was our starting point. Don't ignore your ecstacy. It matters. You're lucky each of you is at about the same stage of life, so it's possible to find a way of sharing beds, babies, professional lives, whatever. In this, you are so very fortunate. It took me many years to catch-up with my half-formed self so as to be able to marry, to work and to love Sophie.'

'Does she know about Mum?'

'Of course. She was the first to know.'

Katia blushed happily. 'I don't like secrets either.'

'There may be some necessary secrets shielding others from the pain of separateness. Otherwise I consider secrets become corrosive over time.' Tim looked at her tenderly. 'I've been fond of Phil for ever. He's a good boy, by which I mean, true, loyal, full of life. I hope you and he hit it off. Nothing would give me more pleasure my dearest Katia.'

They were sitting opposite each other, separated by two music stands. He stood and went to her and kissed the top of her head. She put her free arm round him and pressed her face into him and looked up into his faded grey eyes. 'Being with him makes dreams come true, like being here with you.' she murmured.

He shyly smiled. 'This is the valley of dreams.' he said softly.

17-

THE JOURNEY TO THE SPLIT ROCK pinnacle crowning the green lake valley was almost uneventful. At the beginning of the section along the last ridge one of the tyres went flat. The two boys laboured to get the car jacked-up and to replace the wheel.

'Luckily, we have two spares.' gasped Ant. 'But now we must be careful.'

It was mid afternoon before they stopped between the towering rocks and, lugging heavy back-packs, started the decent from the windy ridge into the tangle of trees and sheltered scrub in the valley.

They reached the second of the rock pools where they had camped previously deciding it was far enough. With good team-work set up the two tents, gathered wood, made a fire, put water on to boil and then stripped and gambolled into the water.

Little desire was expressed. But supper was speedily prepared and eaten, teeth brushed before the couples scampered to rest. The rush was over. They lay, bodies unwinding in embrace, whispering about everything and nothing until the delicious delay collapsed into an orgy of action.

In the ensuing silence the fire glowed, myriad stars flecked the heavens and a new moon rocked over the dark ridge. Small night creatures fossicked for scraps and snuffled back to burrows licking surprised lips, as the four lovers had. That night they wanted for nothing.

Breakfast was comfortable, the sun warming the camp and casting a hieroglyph of shadows over naked shoulders and out-stretched legs whose meaning danced with the content in four faces.

Rose wanted to go downstream. 'Maybe not yet as far as the lake, but to where there is a generosity of water.' Ant readily agreed, packed a light snack and towels and took her off through the trees.

Katia shook her head. 'I don't know why they rushed away Phil. It seems silly, it's perfect here.'

Good naturedly he acquiesced to her desire to stay, pottering about the camp, gathering more wood, digging a latrine, reinvigorating the flattened fern mattresses in the tents while she lay dreamily on a ground sheet near the smoking fire.

'The smoke joins us to the sky.' she whispered when he came over for a hug and a chat. 'It's the way brightness is drawn down into the blind earth so it flowers.'

Phil was bemused by her mood. 'Are you scared here?'

'Maybe, whelmed by the magic.' she said softly.

Rose had told her of the voices in the bowels of the canyon, of sacred baptism, of their feelings, of bonds and promises.

Katia reeled with feelings for Phil, bright as the sky. The blind earth disturbed her: her senses mixing with her dreams opened her to yearn for what? For union with him? With herself? Did these things echo with previous times when she was washed with ecstatic fullness, dreaming such magnificence she woke in the morning, dazzled?

She had longed to speak of this to Tim, but words and courage had failed so she was only able to caricature her concerns to him. But now, like a waterfall, it engulfed her. She said what the waterfall thundered, what her body cried, 'I do love you Phil.'

He pushed against her. Aroused. Shy about his hunger. 'Isn't our loving enough, my Katia?'.

She shivered as his fingers caressed her labia. 'I know it should be. This love is overpowering. It can't be good for us.'

He attentively pulled off her tee-shirt and suckled her hardening nipples. 'I love your overpowering. It makes life bubble up.' He whispered pushing her shorts down her legs. He wanted to explore her centre, found her clitoris and licked it to life, knowing its pleasure from the caresses she had planted on his erection.

Katia groaned as waterfalls felled her. Blindly she sought to burst into the blue above. She pulled him to thrust far into her. Vaguely she heard his gasping breath as she surfed towards climax, until with a shout releasing birds from nearby trees, she cried all the mystery she contained, feeling his riches spout, finding momentary unity in their striving as his whimpering shrunk them back into the

Bush to lie writ in dancing shadows.

All her questions remained. She rolled over and buried her face in his damp tummy. 'Why can't this be always?'

'Will you promise me it will be?'

She nodded her throbbing head.

'Then, come on.' He leaped up, taking her hand and pulling her up to stumble to the waters edge. They stood side by side dazzled by reflections, seeing an inner place where two sprites stood hand in hand who waded into the water and knelt down, hand in hand, lips upon lips and vowed unity for ever; two naked sprites haloed by sunlight, wreathed in leaf shadow, bathed in water, shining like new-born beings, which, of course, they had just become. They were connected by light and water, their hands, their lips, the earth and sky of their love.

'Come on.' he whispered, wading into the water where he turned and kissed her, then together they knelt and kissed again and fell into the water, one lumpen mass splitting so two drenched creatures struggled back to the bank and sat breathing heavily on a warm rock hemmed in by enormous questions.

'Katia. Did you answer yes?'

'Yes Phil. Did you?'

He nodded. 'Yes, and for ever.'

Phil looked at the girl who had given him everything, and now, the impossible, reflecting how strong her love for him must be. He filled with delighted terror.

'Are they rash, impossible promises?' He lay in her lap trying not to fracture. He was beyond happiness. Her lap was a kind of landfall he'd washed-up on, from a sea-storm of feelings.

Katia looked at his boyish face working with emotion; her's, she acknowledged. She too was beyond tears or laughter. She bent and kissed him. With every withdrawal of lips each whispered. 'Forever. Forever.' until the whirling stilled and the shivering leaves, limpid bird song and the ever-gurgling creek embraced them.

'I only want one other thing.' he said with finality. 'To make a house with you and be there sometimes.'

She laughed. 'That's not enough. I want all of you, our house and lots of babies and working together, wicked, wild, wonderful times, all of them, and all the time. That's what I want.'

He grinned. 'I say Yes to all that, plus being here again, being ourselves, remembering this moment.'

He rolled over and spied her willful grin. Longed to share more. 'When Ant and I were boys we had sex. I began at school. Wanted to go all the way (still feel a twinge). We never did although we slept together. I think I loved him (still do, not enough to upend the balance we've found, I hope). Those shadows lie deep. You must help me face them.' He watched the water lazily scuffed by the breeze. 'I suppose, because of that I'm more of a virgin than you.'

'A beautiful one, my Phil. We come from such different lives, finding in each other a balance? Mine was a riotous growing up. Boys, sometimes girls, in bed, in the bushes, in the surf, in other people's garden sheds, in train carriages. My headlong search for something wild enough to depend upon. Like you.' she murmured. 'I feel safe with you. Perhaps because of your shadows? And because we can be together simply, beyond sex or talk or social games. As well as sharing the complexity of all the rest.'

'I feel that. Here we are together. Sex, and everything.'

'Oh, my darling Phil, isn't it funny, everything and again, everything, and now everything. So many everythings. That's what I want. That's why I love you. You give me all these everythings.'

'Do I?' he was surprised. 'But you give me everything.'

She lay back and shut her eyes. The sun made ruby blotches in them and warmed her breasts and face. She felt his breath on her ear, his tongue seeking shell-shadows inside. 'They are yours for sharing', she whispered. Soon he rolled off to lie beside her. They snoozed. Nothing disturbed them until he groaned.

He leapt up. 'I'm busting for a leak.'

She watched the stream gush from his soft, small spout, hit the rocks and darken them with splashy patterns, watched him shake it elegantly, yet leaving a drip or two gleaming at its fleshy tip, watched her boy/man return, responding to her smile, his sensual lips parted, his teeth gleaming, his cheeky tongue licking as if preparing for another sexual onslaught. She rose, walked a few paces, squatted and urinated. The stream gushing from her vagina aroused him.

She took him to the tent, rummaged in her pack and handed him a thin parcel which he unwrapped to find a livid pink double-dildo. 'I found it in Mummy's cupboard. Do you want me to fuck you?'

After he had greased and pushed one end into her, Phil knelt before her. He shut his eyes as she pushed into him. The pleasure was intensified by her excitement. They thrust and gripped for some time until she gasped. 'Wait, or I'll come.' She lay against his buttocks and rubbed his erection while fondling his balls. His feelings coalesced. With a gasp he ejaculated. His back relaxed and sank pushing out his buttocks to take all the dildo. Then he gripped it with his failing strength so she could thrust against it. He wiggled his butt around so it arced as it drove into her. She emitted little cries as repeated shrills of climax screamed in her. He felt her effort as two or three times she drove, held herself against him and cried as she finally climaxed. He relaxed to allow her to withdraw. She was still kneeling when he turned and gingerly pulled the livid pink rod from her vagina.

Both were blushing from exertion, feelings whirling them beyond normal values or roles into an alien world. They lay speechless in a light embrace. She kissed his eyes, as if what they had witnessed needed salving.

He leaned into her for reassurance. 'That was way out. You're quite a man.'

Katia blushed.'And you are the most beautiful boy in the whole world. Are you OK?'

'It was amazing. Gosh, you came with a bang.'

'So did you, no wonder I'm awash when you're inside. Our shadows are scary.' she whispered.

'Only because we've never looked into them.' he said. 'It's like the first sailors crossing the chartless oceans. What they found was not monstrous as expected, but places like home.'

'I found the man in me, you, the boy/woman.' she said. 'Is it another everything?'

'Certainly. Another home-coming, my darling Kat.'

'Always call me that.' she whispered.

'If I can be your dog.'

Only when it rains inside us cats and dogs.' she grinned.

'That's every time, my Kat.'

'Only when you wag your tail, doggy.' She felt down to clasp the soft velvety flesh. They cleaned up the messed dildo, wrapped it and put it away.

They were lying together when the others tried to slip unobtrusively back into camp. But Phil and Katia scrambled up to happily greet them, glowing with the day.

'Everything all right?' Ant asked easily.

'Fine. Nothing's changed.' Phil grinned, knowing his life and Katia's were different now they'd embraced the shadows.

Rose noticed the shadow of a smile on Katia's face. So we don't need to go into the green lake, she mused. It's influence reaches for us even here. 'You two look very happy.' she said.

Katia eyed Phil. 'We are.' she purred.

Rose had considered the influence of the lake all day. They had settled just beyond the slippery moss slide so Ant could swim there, and draw rock ensembles while she made water colour studies. She produced lots discovering how subtle the colour variations were and how difficult to record accurately. 'The light changes everything.' she complained during a swim and cuddle break. 'Your ink studies are better than mine.' But Ant was impressed. She had worked hard and patiently, looking thoughtfully and struggling to match the colours around her; colours which, it dawned on them, were reminiscent of the green lake canyon: the dun coloured rocks, the dappled creamy brown tree trunks, the rich hues of a variety of leaves, the deep green moss, the straw coloured grass, the blue/green foliage of trees and shrubs offset by the blue brilliance of the sky and rich black shadows.

'The colours of the canyon and its influence are here. But not the lake itself.' Rose said.

Ant inspected her papers. 'Your study reveals it.'

Later she painted him into a couple of water colours of the pool where he was bathing, standing on a rock, pale dun, with leopard-shadow spots. 'A lithe naked faun of the forest.' she murmured. She caught him again sliding down the mossy rocks, feet and hands in the air, his body a strong curve as he slid on his green bottom to splash with a grin into the water of the pool below.

'You've given me a lovely big dick.'

She looked at the real thing and then back to her painting. 'It's how I see it.' smiling at his silly proud grin. 'Anyway, it's not size but use which counts.' she said without rancour. 'Now I'm ready to go down there. Can we go tomorrow?'

'If you'll make love to me like last time.'

Rose sniggered, poked a rude tongue into his ear and whispered. 'If you baptise me again under the waterfall and promise to love me.'

'What will you promise?'

'Never to.'

'Never to do it again?'

No silly, never to stop loving you.'

'You mean the same old fuck, day after day?'

'The same old wife, the same old husband whose orgasms get better and better.'

His face softened. He held her close. 'They do.'

They lightly kissed.

'Ant, I love you more every day. I'm happy. I hope you are.'

Ant looked up into the endless blue; there, a small streak of cloud stretched as if someone had wiped a milky cloth over the sky forming a fluffy grin; it was just his feeling: happiness, tickling him all over, inside and out. 'I would have died if you'd not been there this year. I can go on because of you. I can't imagine life any other way. What we promised here last year worked because of your love. I begin to love you with my life.'

'I feel that.'

'I know you do. You're wonderful.'

'When we marry next year, let's work for a while before we have babies? Your babies will be the most fabulous of all time, wait and see. Is that what you want too?'

'Let's make them in our new house.'

'And bring them back there often so they grow straight and tall like their Dad.'

'And curvey and sexy like their Mum.'

'And free like we have become in this magic place.'

'Dear Symph.' Ant's cheek quivered.

But it worked out differently. For over supper Phil and Katia haltingly tried to explain their union until the others nodded knowingly.

Rose looked at Ant. 'Do you think they should go to the green lake tomorrow?'

Ant looked at her. 'Yes I do.'

Katia and Phil fell asleep immediately missing the gasps and whispers from the other tent. The small creatures of the night, snuffling about for morsels left by the diners, paused, sniffed the air with inquisitive snouts, but soon got back to foraging so the camp site was clean by morning; as fresh as the four young faces that emerged soon after the sun heated their tents, faces crowning eloquent bodies sparkling after a dip, proclaiming the perfection life anoints its creatures with.

Katia and Phil meandered down following the unruly path of the creek until they stood nervously on the rocky ledge it cast itself over to fall into the deep gloomy well to a distant pool.

'It must be the centre of the earth.' he said.

'How do we get down?' she peered around the unhospitable ring of rocks until she spied a faint track probably made by game. She pointed. 'Let's try there.'

He nodded.

They set off, making their way through tangled undergrowth and a mess of rock until they stumbled on what looked more like a flat foot-width thread which wound past a tenacious tree twisting out from a joint in the rock and down to a rocky platform at water level.

Neither was confident in this precipitous situation. By the time they reached the platform, their bodies were screaming with fatigue and muscle tension. Gratefully they flopped down. He bent down, cupped his hands and drank from brimming palms, splashed his face and leaned back panting.

She had stripped and neatly dived into the depthless water. She struck out for the waterfall at the other end of the pool. Standing on a submerged rock chilly needles danced on her head and shoulders. She called. 'Come here, Phil.' The rocks ricocheted with her voice until a thousand voices called him from every point of the compass.

He was startled by the multitude of mighty voices filling the space, loudly calling. 'COME Hear PHIL COME ear MM PHILL-COME ILLILLLMM'. Flocks of tiny birds fluttered like black butterflies in the yawning space.

His heart leapt. He felt the breath of giants on his neck, was challenged by threatening questions which ransacked his reason. His most ancient instincts stirred; he smelled the stench of the sabre-toothed tiger the bellicose god of gloomy caves; heard the boom of the woolly mammoth whose single foot-fall squeezed the life out of any body. He stood naked and undefended as eons of humans had, confronting the terrors challenging their existence.

He saw Katia waving to him from the waterfall. Phil took a breath and dived deep. Away from the lightening flashes of terror into the cold silence of the green lake which held and shepherded him across its serene face until he paddled beside her.

Her head spattered with water. 'Here, stand on this rock.' She clung to him, sharing the penetrating force of the waterfall and kissing his mouth with long sucking ardour until he shook free. 'Darling, the cold will freeze my balls off. Let's go.'

She followed him to the nearby shore. He was shivering. She took him back to the sun-drenched platform and attentively dried him. 'There you are handsome. Let me warm you.' She held him as his shivering faded.

Only then did he blink. 'Something awful happened after you left. I don't quite understand. But I was trapped in the whole history of the world. And then I saw you and it was all right. The history of the world is in me. A part of us still walks naked, still sees the world as alien and threatening, invents gods to lord it over all the rest; but still we're not sure. Darling, Rose told me of terrible truths heard down here. Do you hear them?' He shuddered. 'When I saw you, it became today. Almost. I escaped, diving into the safety of the lake pursued by wild animals I know are fossils. Reaching you saved me.'

'Touching you saves me every day.'

'Katia please don't leave me. I need you to be my love and to love me. There are wild animals. You help me to fend them off. You don't laugh at my timidity or tell me I'm a baby.'

'I don't want to leave you. I promised you yesterday. It was the truth.'

'I know, I forgot. You have no idea what it felt like just now.'

She realised how serious he was; how frightened. But of what, she was unsure, for Phil was usually carefree. She remembered the howling over Ant's thesis: were those animals baying for Phil? Or the uncanny feeling of being watched in the Bush? the scorn scalding her adolescence? professional contempt? their new pain?

She laid him down on their towels, kissed his penis to life, straddled him, looked into his soft blue eyes, leaned forwards, lifted her hips and stretched. It eased into her until all its length was inside. Gently she began moving in slow even strokes, watching his eyes widen as she forced him back into his life-feelings, forced him to respond to the power she was pushing into him until groans of pleasure usurped the shadows.

He gasped. 'Put your legs down with mine. Raise yourself on your toes and put your hands below my armpits.'

She bounced over him for a while until weakening, climaxed. Then he raised her hips on his hands, making a space through which he thrust. Her cries grew to a great shout. He moved faster. With a strangled cry his taut body launched the entire universe into her. The spinning world diminished. They lay supine, beyond the reach of monsters.

She woke to a movement in the corner of her eye: a small bright green snake slithered across the rock and slipped into the water; its delicate head breaching the surface as it swam. She squeezed his arm. He sat up. They watched this visitor from the bowels of the earth reach the far side and disappear.

'No wonder it's green if it swims here.' he murmured.

'It's a sign from the earth . Our snake's nicer than Eve's.'

He stirred. 'Hey let's eat.'

They unpacked and wolfed thick sandwiches filled with cheese and tomatoes and then chewed crisp apples.

'We'll leave our thanks here for the snake.' he said, dropping a crust and two apple cores into a cleft in the rock.

'Phil, let's pack our clothes and climb naked back to the world. We'll emerge from this green womb like being born, and then cover our nakedness.'

She watched him. How his balls hung; his penis swung and his pert bottom flexed as he climbed; how his strong back danced as its muscles held him; how his arms, recently holding her flying through ecstacy, fell from his spicy armpits with their shadow of hair. 'Oh how fabulous he is.' she marvelled as he led her upwards.

He watched her labour up to meet him as he waited beside the gnarled tree half way to the top. He spied her breasts bouncing slightly as her weight was taken on one shapely thigh and then the other; watched her legs enticingly framing her pubic triangle where he'd taken such pleasure; watched her able hands grasp at rocks and roots as she panted up to him with a delightful crease of effort on her unblemished brow, as if she were climaxing.

He placed her back against the tree, put encircling arms around her and eased his erection in. He vibrated, coming quickly. When he plopped out a tiny stream of liquid coursed down her inner thigh. She hugged him. 'Sex before birth is very forward indeed. You are a precocious baby.'

'Some babies need a lot.' he said sheepishly.

'Darling, I'm hungry too.'

Reaching the top, the heat of summer engulfed them. They walked demurely up-stream to the moss pool where they waded into the water, warmer than below, tinged gold rather than green, and very refreshing.

There he told her he'd been taken by Nina in much the same way, and how in those depths of the earth he'd found love changed a rather awkward act into one rich and beautiful so he grew, rather than shrank. 'Your love makes me grow. It's the best of all.

'Always grow.' She sighed. 'It gives me strength.'

Ant took Rose to the green lake next day. They took their clothes off at the top and scrambled down past the tree, down to the shelf of rock warmed by the sun where they kicked off their boots and dived in, surfacing to gasp a deep breath against the chill water before swimming to the waterfall. There, he stood on the submerged rock, Rose hanging around his neck. They painted A on his forehead and R on hers, kissed and promised to love one another for ever, then made for the nearest shore with chattering teeth. Rose didn't tease him anymore about his shrunken sex, or his skin, livid with the needles from the waterfall and the icy water. She felt settled. There was no need for teasing. She felt a quiet hunger to stay connected. Ant felt the same.

They used stepping-stones framed in green grass at the waters edge

'Like the hair around your balls.' Rose said happily.

'A trifle greener.'

Rose giggled. 'Your balls are too rolly-polly to gather moss like rolling stones. That's why.'

'That's your fault. Thank goodness.' he guffawed.

'Thank goodness you love me too.' she cried as she took the

final step up and onto the rock platform to their possessions.

As she bent down for a towel Ant pushed his erection into her opened vagina. She stilled, savouring the warmth rippling through her. Like a breeze over the lake, she thought. He thrust faster. Everything hummed in her. 'Let's lie down, darling. If you can stop.'

Such ecstatic agony in the withdrawing.

Rose lay aware of the distant sky as he entered. He went fully in and stayed, teasing tremors from her. She relaxed admitting all of him in intangible ways which, none the less, each was aware of. It stayed his excitement without driving to orgasm; she drifted on waves of butterflied ecstacy, every pore vibrating with pleasure. It was the softness she had experienced with Nina, a coveted way of loving few men wanted. She imagined the velvet-soft malleable testicles from which Ant's passions came. 'I love his hardness, and softness!' she said to herself.

What endless pleasure. In the depths of the mysterious crater; time, reality, duty, judgement were suspended. Both imagined eating an ice cream on a stick which neither melted nor finished. They became part of slow turning nature, linked to the majestic hugeness of the earth, evolving seasons rather than clock-regulated action.

He felt her generosity-greed melt. It lifted him into a giants' class, cyclopian, seeing only one reality: the gratification of sexual hunger. He was huge, towering over her, over the earth itself, feeding and seeding its depths, making life sing in all their veins, forming the universe, holding its brightness and its darkness until one immense lunge carried him out of himself into her and away, far away to where all conquerors finish.

She embraced this power of immeasurable hunger and her capacity to absorb it. Her richness and her riches grew with every minute tensing of her beloved, occupying, usurping her until she overflowed and carried it throughout the universe she had become. Each spasm was overwhelmingly greater, beyond all limits, beyond what might be conceived or imagined, yet so specific, so focussed she forgot everything in the embrace uniting her to all the rest, with him, the other immortal who held her.

The still surface of the green water wrinkled as a stray tongue of wind moved the waterfall to pock the pool rather than splash onto stones. Then the sky danced and the immobile rocks shivered seductively and its edges shimmeyed with reflections. Everything wilted and trembled and the distant lip of the canyon grimaced like a mouth trying to dislodge a pip. Today it wanted to shout about the victory played out beside its shimmering eye. But only the black butterfly-birds were shaken from their nests, spiralling in the mute space, witnessing creation. The only evidence being two radiant figures recovering, climbing and re-emerging at the edge of the real world.

That day, Phil and Katia mooched about the camp for a while. Then meandered down the water course exploring. When they reached the shelf of rock over which the water fell, they crept close and peered into the depths. There, on a far rock lay two tensing figures.

'Look.' Phil breathed. 'They're making love.' He watched fascinated, never having witnessed it before. He saw Ant's bottom flex to thrust, saw Rose's open legs and face arching back in delight. He trembled with longing, longing to be opened and filled, and absorbed.

Katia saw distress, or perhaps doubt, flicker across his face. 'It's beautiful. Come on, we shouldn't pry, particularly down there.' she said pulling him away. 'I'm sure we look the same.'

'Can we go back?'

'I'd like that.' She took his hand and they hurried back up the creek to their tent.

Undressed he nibbled her neck. 'Let's use the dildo?'

She enjoyed his teasing way of inserting it, then he turned and kneeled, pushing his butt out so she could slide the garish pink-ness fully in. Then she fucked him. He cried urgently. 'Do it more.' It thrilled her. He gripped it so it flexed inside. When her excitement was intense, she fondled and masturbated him to climax and fucked herself to orgasm. She was surprised how intense his need was. 'You really want it, don't you?'

'I long to be filled.'

'Cat and dog. The same sometimes. Darling Phil, it's perfect with you. Perfect.'

They lay united.

After breakfast the following day, Rose surveyed the tangle downstream. 'I want to go back to continue studies of colour and form around the creek. I like its brightness and the teeming life.'

Ant willingly stayed, persuading Katia to help with the structural details of his house.

Phil hung about for a while and then followed the gurgling creek to the mossy rock face where he played before seeking out Rose who was busy nearby, close enough to trip back and replenish her water container. She was glad to share swimming, chat and a snack with her brother.

'Is it too intense?' she asked.

Phil shrugged sadly. 'There are many doubts.'

'Tell me, brother dear.'

'My feelings see-saw from delight to worry. It's worse than when I was fifteen. We managed Ant's thesis; then I was given the land for a house; then Nina made me feel bad; Katia promised - as I did - to love, then I thought it was unreal; then I thought I can't design like Ant, or have a mate like him. Then I was happy here but terrified by the lake; I love sex with Katia but how can it last? I feel so empty.'

Rose was distressed. What had happened to her lovely cheeky brother? They were sharing a holiday making her joyful and him depressed. In a flash she realised he was "little", part boy part man, maybe too much had happened too soon. Yet his declared emptiness astounded her.

Rose sat with him. Their feet dangling in the slothful mid-summer stream. Their nakedness reduced barriers. Clearly the boy needed to talk.

Rose hugged him. 'Phil, you must talk now. Tell me every-thing. It should help. Can we start with your friendships when you were a boy, around the time Ant came to stay. Please risk telling me what it was like being a boy?'

He sat in silence, his face dark. 'It was like being a bomb about to explode. It was mainly about sex. There was no way of deal-ing with it. I liked an older boy, I think it was love although a wor-rying thought. I let him fuck me. It was wild. It released me, but also all my feelings burst; I wanted it day and night. It was confusing being his girl, kissing him as if he were a girl. When Ant came I wanted him too, I loved him uncomfortably, now I love him more openly; he refused to let me in, but we slept together, as you know. It was wonderful sleeping that way and feeling the release he gave me.'

Rose nodded. 'Do you still feel a boy/girl?'

Phil sighed. 'I think so. I don't know who I am.'

'There's nothing wrong with being both.' Rose said softly. 'By rejecting that duality you reject others, like your ability as an architect, as a lover, as a friend, even as a brother.'

'I know.'

'So, let's talk about Phil the architect.'

'I'm not a patch on Ant. He's brilliant. He won't put up with a plodder like me for long. Why should he?'

'He has great ability; so do you, silly. Now listen to me: you *are* a partnership. he tells me without your work with Peter, he wouldn't have a real house, only a paper one. Your ability to systematise all the components is awesome. Don't you see, *together* you can make buildings? You are the left hand, he is the right. Try to work with only one and you'll see what I mean. Why do you boys spend so much energy competing? Why not remember architecture operates just like a family: each person is different, each contributes to family life, or in your and Ant's case, to the making of buildings. Surely you admit you need guys like Katia or Les, and skilled craftsmen on site? *All* of the family make the building. How can you trick yourself into thinking anyone would want you to go? How will you build that way?'

'You can't mean they need me?'

'Of course you silly willy. And Katia needs you too.'

'She's brilliant. It won't last. Sex isn't enough.' Phil sighed.

'What did she say down by the green lake?'

'She told me I made her strong.'

'Phil, you must believe her; truths are found there. Perhaps it's strength she wants to share so you can face the monsters. So, stay together as you've promised! Consider her another partner: where would the left hand be without the right?'

Uncharacteristically Phil cried.

Rose was apalled to see his tears, for since their childhood his cheerfulness had lightened her. 'Oh, Phil, I'm so sorry.'

But he looked up at her with so radiant a smile she almost cried herself.

'Oh, Rosie. It *is* difficult.' he stammered. 'Thank you. I *am* a silly willy. You see so clearly. I still don't know what I am, but at least I'm clear about my partnerships. They matter more than anything else, and having you around.'

They sat quietly. The trees rustled in the hot breath of summer. The water giggled over stones, seeking its running. A solitary butterfly hovered over the damp moss near the pool while the sun burned their backs.

'Let's swim.' Phil rose.

Rose sat pensive. 'We must find ways of ignoring the bad voices haunting us. Voices which condemn you for using your body fully, for extending your love, for being different from others. Thank goodness you are. Listen to Katia, Ant and me when we say you're our beautiful beloved Phil. Listen to Dad when he says you're loyal and talented. He knows. We know. Now, *that* matters.' She gazed at the shadows flitting across the sturdy tree trunks. 'The magic green pool tells us we are true when we are honest, as you are. It tells us invisibles matter, like loyalty and love, skill and a sense of freedom. You believe in these. It shows us we can take everything and then find more, we can loose ourselves and find a partner and lastly, as part of the earth, we are heirs to its treasures. Now that, darling brother, is to be rich indeed. Symph had nothing but he was richer than all of us. That's what Will and Miranda found here. I bet you and Katia did too.'

'And you?'

'That's why I came back with Ant. And why I'm studying here; why invent riches when they're freely available? The magic of this place lies in the colours and shapes, the way the light celebrates shape and form, the majesty of sky, the gaunt, beautiful trees, the golden threads of water. If my fashion collection displays a quarter of that it will be breathtaking. But most of all, the ageless serenity of the lake. We'll each take something of its potion away. I already see a golden thread wound through you (your own talents), something gaunt and tree-like (is it boy become man?) and a deeper blue in your eyes (is it both boy and girl?). You go home the same but deeply different.'

Rose looked at her brother standing ready to splash into the pool. He has a great bum, a long strong back and neck, finely muscled legs and able hands, and a mighty cock. If only he saw that, she thought but said. 'Hey, hunk, Katia is special. I'm so glad you're with her. Remember last summer; isn't she what you dreamed of?'

Phil turned and grinned. 'Yes.' he said, falling like a sack into the water. 'Come in Rosie, here's gold for you.'

Supper was early. The lovers all wanted some daylight. Ant and Rose went down hill following the creek, leaping like graceful springbok from rock to rock until they ventured onto the ledge over which the water cascaded down into the distant lake. They crouched there gazing into the now shadowed depths until an imperceptible grey filled the canyon. They sat quietly, aware of the quietening of the day around them as the Bush grew shadowy. They contentedly made their way back to camp. and a love-induced sleep.

Phil, liberated by his talk with Rose, was bursting to be with Katia. Haltingly he tried to explain about his incompleteness, the boy not yet filled out as a man, of his boyish feelings still partly displaced, of his doubts about his ability in a competitive scenario, of his terrible need (he had never known such longing), the need for her and the influence and inspiration she had become, 'You seem to accept the girl in me and all my silliness. Do you?'

'Dearest Phil, of course I do. It's part of the you I love. You teased me once about being your man. Do you know I always wanted to be a boy and wildly chased after that all my life. Only you have allowed it, because you dared to meet your own longing. I want a partner like you. But there's a terrible realisation: it's easy to be a boy. My problem has always been, to be a woman; one day can I be your woman?'

'I love the man in you. 'He hugged her. 'My problem is the same. One day will you let me be your man?'

His erection grew. She trembled in his arms. 'Our secret project this year - our Thesis: I becoming a woman, and you, a man. Then we'll see.'

'See what?'

'See if it's forever. See if it's babies and building, you know, all that.'

'So, you become a woman and bugger off.'

'IF I'm a woman, then I'll have to stay. There's no other man I want. I promised you that.'

'If you are a woman? If I am a man? If? If?'

'Don't be trivial. Start now. Fuck me how I want, how you want. With the strongest prick in the world, the sweetest seed. I'll find a place for you, the place where only you have been, which only you are manly enough to find: where hearts and minds beat together, women, men, boys, girls and all wild rutting creatures.'

'Sex isn't the answer.'

'Through our bodies, we can unite all those pieces by sharing all we are, giving up ourselves to find more than we lost. We'll work together and sometimes live together. But I believe our bodies are central. If you want me, take me now. Please . . . Ah.'

He plunged in. Sweetest passion reined. He played in her until softened and enraptured, she opened for the rush of life-bringing seed; and, flying beyond himself, he poured it into her.

The last day for all of them was reflective. They had journeyed through their own lives and through the endless breathing of the world, confronting primitive terror, yet finding immeasurable riches; wonder, perhaps, being the first.

The 4WD bucked and rolled over the wind-swept ridge hugging the perilous spine where, far beyond, the earth's rumpled form confronted them.

Phil shyly announced. 'I have two theses this year. You must all help. The university judges one, Katia will judge the other.'

Ant grimaced. 'Get used to it boyoh, there are lots more coming. But they're much more fun.'

Rose caught Katia's eye and grinned, thinking, I'm really glad she's staying with us.

Perhaps she spoke. For Katia whispered, 'So am I.'

18-

THE RUMBUSTIOUS HOME-COMING began when Will's dogs frisked and ferried the dusty 4WD to his verandah then leapt over the jolted campers as they climbed out, joyously leading them to the door as Nici bounded out crying 'Tea's up, tea's up. Pretty Nici.'

Miranda soon followed with a tray of steaming mugs and some rock-hard buns Nici had made, finished by the dogs. There was gleeful chat about the Bush, the voices of the green lake, about love and lust and campfires and the creek which laughed, or sang? as it capered down the valley looking for a chance to fly.

'We all flew.' Katia said happily. 'And some faced tigers.'

'Some of us played with water sprites.' said Rose.

Ant grinned. 'And some of us kissed them.'

Nici took Phil's silence as a needy one and clasped his big strong hand. He lifted her onto his knee and hugged her warmly, whispering. 'One day you'll go there.'

Miranda looked quizzically at the four radiant faces. 'So, you found what you went for?'

Phil nodded. 'Much more.'

Miranda smiled. 'It's always like that. But then, we don't always know why we go there, do we?'

Nici insisted Phil stay to bath her and tell her a story. Katia helping Miranda, saw one year old Nestor suck nip and hiccup milk over her abundant breast until her own twitched and she cupped it with a longing hand.

Miranda murmured. 'I'm having another one. This little king will have to share soon . . . You and Phil?'

Katia blushed. 'One day I want his child. When we've worked things out.'

Miranda nodded.' It can take longer than you think. But it's worth waiting. Was that your promise?'

Katia slightly shook her head. 'We promised love, forever. The rest is unknown.'

'Of course it is. But forever means babies and making a home. You must see that.'

'We need to grow first.'

'I understand. For I remember assuming Will would be mine ages before it happened at the lake.'

'In those ages, perhaps you both grew?'

'Yes, you're quite right. Plus something more: a sort of agreement to coming together was confirmed there. But I'm happy for you: to love such a lovely man is the best start. You must both come here whenever you want. Often. Will and I love you both.'

Bath time was a cheerful riot. Kim and Nici slid up and down the frothy tub until Phil enticed them out to cuddle in big towels then carried them to bed where, with promises to sleeping tightly, he told them the following story:

The lake lay at the bottom of a deep well of rock. It was so deep the sun hardly reached the bottom so only creatures with huge eyes which saw in the dark stayed there.

The water was as green as the soap we used tonight, although it looked black in the sunless depths, it was so still you could easily see yourself, with the sky way, way away; although you see yourself looking somehow different.

Imagine looking. There you are, your mouth, OK. But words slip out from between your lips, telling you things you didn't want to know, like 'I'm frightened of the dark and all the big eyes watching me' and 'What a lovely body I have.'

Then you look again and your eyes are talking. Imagine that. Two eloquent (fluent, expressive, Kim) conversations about 'You are so brave coming into the centre of the earth.' and 'Don't be frightened, because most fears come from inside ourselves and we project them onto what we see.' ('project' means we put inner things, feelings, out into the world and think they are real. (Like when you are angry then Daddy seems to be angry, even if he's laughing.)

Now look again, there in the gloom sits a big furry creature (Yes, probably Bunyip). He's not scary. He tells you, 'Feelings are

*like your hair, or your hands: they go where you go. Like your
body, feelings need to be seen and understood. They are friendly
and useful. Yes, even the big bad feelings.'*

*Then, Bunyip shows you your own feelings. You laugh at
some, feel fearful of others, or feel embarrassed; some feelings
don't seem to belong in the outer world because someone shouts at
you saying 'Keep those feelings to yourself or I'll kill you.'*

*Bunyip says, 'Try to ignore (fail to notice, overlook, Kim)
the shouting and say to yourself, ALL feelings need airing, just like
Mummy airs all the washing: imagine if she put half the things
away, still wet. That would be silly, like putting feelings away
before they are aired and allowed to flap in the wind.*

*Do you know they flap because they are trying to get away
from the wind which tickles them mercilessly? Well, examining
feelings is tickling them so they belly out laughing and plead,
'Please stop tickling us.' After airing them we can snuggle down
with our feelings, even if they are uncomfortable, just like snug -
gling into a warm lumpy bed.'*

*Yes, Bunyip had a lot to say, didn't he. And now it's time
for you to snuggle down and to dream. Do you know that dreams
are the pictures our feelings make for us. I think Bunyip would
agree dreams also need airing. But you must have them first, so
sweet dreams little ones.*

The children hugged Phil for a long time savouring the smell
of wood smoke in his hair. Dutifully they closed their eyes and drifted into a depthless well of eiderdowned rock where they played
with balls which looked like eyes, where mouths sang and they
marched triumphantly across the water as any sprite would, and
arrived at morning just in time for breakfast, or a little before.

Most of the lights were on at Ararat when Phil and Katia walked in.
Ossian was in the music room with Tim, and calling for Katia's
superior oboe playing. Ant was working on the dining table with
Angelica, glad of the break in music to engage her own specialty,
young children; Ant wanted Phil to join their discussions about
Lettuce's children's' playroom. 'Don't you think architecture for
children should relate to them before catering for the adults?'

Phil nodded like Bunyip. 'Of course, just as stories or clothes should fit them.'

Angelica enjoyed their intensity. 'Remember, human relations come first. Afterwards, relations to a building. But a good teacher and able children should be encouraged to use a building: ledges for flowers and knick-knacks, walls for their art work, pegs and door handles they can reach, spaces which allow fantasy and play, for example.'

Ant got terribly excited and jigged on his chair. 'Yes, spaces of every size, inside and out. A building like a Mother. Welcoming, calming, nurturing. Lots of light, views and places to put things and to climb over. I like that, Angelica.'

'Or a Father. Strong, reliable, sexy.' she said shyly.

'Or a child, busy innocent and trusting.'

'Exactly, Phil.'

Ant began to sketch: walls, windows, little figures running and sitting, flowering bushes, cats, fish in bowls, a few big people, toys, books, easels, coats in rows, a little boy peeing, posts, floors: they spend a lot of time on the floor. He followed with plans, talking to Phil about light falling on bent heads, and drawing sections to explain how it might enter the play spaces to which Phil added little galleries for peeping, reading or play.

Angelica was bemused. She sat back. 'Lettuce says you are two talented boys. That's why they nearly failed Ant and why Phil must be very careful. But you needn't worry, her committee is fair, and this is the best discussion on play spaces I've ever heard.'

Supper was animated by talk about music, architecture and the magic of the Bush. Nina was put out by the hilarity and the good-natured teasing sweeping the table.

'Rose is so beautiful. Why doesn't she look? I could be a post for all she cares.' Nina scowled. But the mood was infectious, so when she was included under the topic 'children' she defended all children vigorously saying they were far too old to remember.

'You one footers wouldn't know.' she said rudely.

Tim laughingly sobbed. 'I take a grave exception to that.'

Every one, including Nina, laughed. Sophie winced; it had touched her deepest fears about Tim's recurring headaches.

But Nina completely forgave Rose after she looked in to kiss her good-night. 'I'll finish making your Bush tee-shirt on Sophie's sewing machine tomorrow. I started it at home but ran out of time.' Nina threw all her arms around her and fell smiling (for the first time in ages) into untroubled sleep.

This left Rose hungry. So she enticed Ant into her where they played until, beyond need, they too slept.

Katia, who had touched Miranda's milky breast and emotionally played chamber music, longed for Phil, then slept deeply.

He lay awake afterwards musing on monsters and feelings until Bunyip whispered, 'Most are only projections.' Then he smiled, snuggled into the crook of Katia's sleeping body and fell into the eiderdowned chasm with Nici and Kim who were singing,

> *There were three in a bed*
> *and the middle one said,*
> *'Roll-over, roll-over.'*
> *So they all rolled over*
> *and one fell out . . .*

Phil, anchored to his girl, laughed in his sleep. He liked the idea of three. But three 'whats?' His dream never specified.

Angelica found Ossian's sexual shyness difficult; each wanted the other she thought, yet Ossian wavered. When she caressed him he grew demanding, like a whirlwind screwing through her to the delight of both. He didn't want and fuck like her other lovers; he hung back. 'Perhaps he'd prefer a boy.' she decided.

They were spending early afternoons together, he showing her the haunts of childhood, she delighting in the adventure and in the perfect beauty to be found in hidden flowers, unobtrusive rock formations and the life which blossomed beside the river. Usually they swam, sometimes in deep pools, sometimes basking in rivulets coursing over stones where the water played over them in unabashed ways heightening their pleasure. His erection signalled more she longed for. 'Being with him wakes me up.' she told herself as he reached for her. As if he needs me, she noted relievedly.

After sharing his accustomed places they went up the slope behind Ararat and the village green, venturing into the dense forest Peter had leased for him. Peter and Will had started fencing its northern boundary, and cutting a fire-break there. The fence was of simple three-strand wire design so wild animals could easily get through it when roaming and feeding or escaping hunters.

Ossian and Angelica lay on their backs in a small sunny clearing, cushioned by leaves. The only noise was the symphony of birds, the faint rustle from the trees and the gentle thump of their hearts. Such peace encouraged intimacy. Angelica asked. 'Ossian, do you want a boy sometimes when we are together? I don't mind. I wondered about your unresponsiveness.'

He sighed. In the far blue brightness a hawk hung eyeing every movement on the ground, deciding whether shadow or game. 'I should tell you I'm having some help from Trish Maxwell. I went to see her because I can't cope with you; I know that. And as you put it, I can't say what I feel. With Richard I know what to do so it doesn't matter about saying: what each of us wants is obvious. But you, I don't know and for some reason I can't say what screams in me. I feel like shit. I want to make you happy. I know I disappoint you.'

She looked at the dancing tops of the trees, watching the sun glittering and obscured by teasing leaves. 'Tell me something really bad or hard to say just now.'

Ossian lay as still as a fallen tree trunk. Eventually croaking 'I want you terribly.'

Angelica almost smiled. 'I want you terribly. But tell me something really awful.'

He glanced at her, she seemed serene. 'I want you all the time. My insides hurt thinking about you. It's not normal.'

'I ache every time I think of you. I think it's normal. Only leaving it unsaid is terrible. Say something really terrible, Ossian.'

'I know I hurt you. I don't mean to. It's how I am.'

'It hurts you can't share these things. But my pleasure in being with you is a thousand times greater; it hurts because I long for that. But again, being with you makes me forget. It's wonderful, just being together.'

'So why didn't you tell me?'

'Because I want you to feel free in your life. I hate interfering people like my parents and so many others. Although it's uncomfortable, I far prefer your hesitancy about making love to the greedy way my other lovers used me. I need the space you give me, just as I think you do.'

155

'But our being here. I'm awful, playing music all day. being with my family. I'm so selfish.'

'So am I, if that is what you mean by selfish, it sounds more like having a holiday to me. I am here because I chose to come. I was delighted by your invitation. I like your family very much. I enjoy this place immensely. I love being here with you day or night. This is my dream Ossian, if you must know.'

'To be with ME?'

'Yes, living, playing, working together.'

Ossian rolled onto his side in disbelief. 'But that's my dream. I thought . . . so why can't we live together?'

'Because you've never mentioned it.'

'Why should I?'

'Because if you have to ask for dreams they loose all their magic. If you can't catch and match a dream you're not worth much.'

'If you don't ask you get nothing.'

'Nothing is better than a damaged dream, Ossian. There are compensations, as I've said.'

'Lear said: "Nothing can come of nothing."'

'And Cordelia says "My love's more richer than my tongue."* Don't you know that the richest things are given, not demanded.'

She's right. What a fool I am, he thought. Ossian was silent. 'The richest thing I have is my life: me, my house and my music. Do you really want that? Because it's all yours.' He trembled. 'I long to give it you. To share. I long to be able to say these things and to tell you I'm still crazy about you after years of waiting. I just can't tell you such things.'

Angelica trembled. 'Darling, you just have. Just said all the most wonderful things anyone could say. You *can* match dreams, just as you can make them; no one makes better dreams than you. That's why I love you. You made me dream from the first. When we lay on your bed, when your seed shot, when you kissed my vagina, when we played music together and everyone cheered, when we sauntered along the street doing nothing in particular, when you wrote my agony into your symphony: those are precious dreams.'

'I didn't know.'

---

* See notes at end.

156

'The boy in you needs our help. He's so tongue-tied. He knows music but not life. Not yet. Please show him to me. He's part of my precious Ossian but you let him hide away. I won't harm him. I want to love him just as I love the man. Try to believe me.'

'The boy only feels safe with you. I only feel safe with you. That's my truncated love.'

'Your love's not truncated, it's the image you hold of yourself. Together we can bring the boy into the open between ourselves, not necessarily out into the world, bring him into the open, let him be with us, let him be loved, let him love, where-ever he needs. Become the man~boy you secretly are. That's what I want for you. That is the rest of my dream: Ossian the king and the beggar-boy, the maker and matcher of dreams.'

'How?'

'I don't know, except that talking seems to break the barriers down; also, being together seems to help. It must be understood, never must he be destroyed. Someone wrote "Our creativity depends on being in touch with the child in us." Maybe we will unearth a girl in you as well, wouldn't that be fabulous. Ossian, rely on me to defend the girl, the boy, the man and the woman. No one will harm any of them.'

Ossian nodded. His shorts bulged. ' C C Can I?'

'I want you so much, darling, now, yes now.'

He plunged in, blew up at once and wailed. 'I couldn't stop. Oh I'm sorry.'

She grinned. 'It was lovely. You are so powerful! I felt your seed splash into me. That's all I need. Ask often.'

'Will you also ask me?'

'Sometimes I'll ask you and take it however I want: like a man or like a wild dog. I am so hungry for you darling. It's been a long wait. We have some catching up to do.'

'My boy loves wild dogs.'

She was silent. She took his arm. 'If I'm moving in with you I must have my own room where I can work, have my books. I don't need a studio like yours, but do need a separate space.'

He nodded. 'What about the airy end room in the garden wing which Ant made for children and visitors. You tell him what you want and he will see it becomes your room. But only if I can visit and the boy can occasionally be bitten by your wild dog.'

Angelica laughed. 'No conditions, except if you and the boy do not come, I'll burn the house down.'

'My little ladybird.' His love overflowed. He held her, aroused, eased in like a nervous thief. She gasped as the gentlest pleasure sparkled in her, gasped at his tenderness and the endless majesty of his being there. The tumult at ending was overwhelming: man and boy, girl and woman struggled to free themselves, struggled into unity so blinding that Ossian and Angelica forgot even themselves in the rush carrying them on angels wings into the bright heavens to swoop earthwards, hawk-hungry feeding off each other's amazed bodies.

That evening Ant walked Ossian around the village green, suggesting where his house might be located and prying; he and Rose were intrigued by Angelica's relationship to Ossian, seeing it as a mix of intimate and distanced ('It's as if they love but don't fuck.' Ant had said. Rose tended to agree). So when Ossian announced shyly Angelica was moving into his house, Ant cheerfully responded. 'I'm so glad. You and the house need a companion; in fact, one day you should fill it with others. A family is a village. Then you can belong to one here in the country as well as in the city.'

Ossian felt liberated. 'My boy and I, in place now, thanks to Angelica.' he mused. 'Richard touches the girl in me. Angelica is right, all of me can exist; I need her so very much. And hers is the love I crave.'

'Think of her room as part of, yet distinct from your house; just as your house here on the green is part of yet distinct from the village we are building.' Ant said, seeing Ossian's struggle with privacies, 'Not clashing but coexisting.'

'I'd like a house on a platform, higher than yours, so I can look over Ararat and down the valley, a sky house?' Ossian ventured.

Ant grinned. 'That's a lovely idea. With the rising ground and a backdrop of mountains, your house will anchor all the rest, somewhere we can all have our heads in the air. You and Angelica will have to produce monkey-children, swinging through the air instead of grubbing about like Rosie's and mine.'

Ossian trembled with warmth for his charming brother. They were kids again playing in the rocks. But now the play involved far more than make-believe. Real music, real houses, real fleshly love. 'Ant, I'm so terribly happy.' he murmured as they ambled back to the busyness of Ararat.

Suddenly Ossian was impatient. Angelica was right, There was a lot of catching up to be done. He longed for her all evening, during supper, during the chattering afterwards; he postponed playing music again and slyly dragged her to bed where play and whispering, more play then untroubled sleep carried them beyond the stars, into space and time where heroes and heroines gambolled, where everything was complete; and where symphonies are born.

When it was time to return to the city, Will and Peter drove the party to the train station. In the silence to which Ararat returned, Nina settled; It had been a troubling month, finding painful feelings, stumbling on the pain of intercourse as she imagined; for she was dumfounded by experiencing the pain women bore when men intruded. There must be something more, she thought comparing such awkward coupling with her thrilling embrace with Rose. 'Men are fun to have around, like unruly dogs; I think I want something more, like my old dolly who sits surely on my bed, like the delight which Rose stirs in me.' she said to her reflection one morning before a swim. 'Something between the eyes and between the legs.' she added before she splintered her image by flopping spreadeagled into the lake.

Sophie shared the silence with Tim with double regret: first she had lost her children, secondly he withered perceptibly on their departure. 'Come back soon.' she had cried. Although she knew they would, it was hard saying goodbye; it smoothed the ripples of joy she experienced when the house was full. Yes, it was just like old times. Yet all of them were changing. Furthermore, the valley belonged to them now, it was their lives it nurtured. 'Tim and I are caretakers, just like dear old Symph.' she whispered burying her face in the soft fur of her favourite ginger cat who often snuggled and purred on her when she rested or read in the living room, and who clearly approved of the quiet.

19-

THERE WERE MANY CHANGES in the following year. Phil and Rose graduated with honours; Nina completed her matriculation and was accepted to do English and Music by the University; Timi, their fourth child, was born to Miranda and Will; Nestor although put out was forgiving. Tim and Sophie persuaded the burgeoning family to settle in Ararat and moved into the new pavilion Ray had built. 'It's our small new house.' Sophie mused, 'Its suits us.'

Another building, Ant's playroom for Lettuce, was completed. It caused the same joy as the pavilion at Ararat but collected scorn from nigglers who decried buildings as playthings: Ant (and Phil) had designed a place children could clamber over, hide in, bask beside; "Dangerous for children, fearful for building maintenance!" was trumpeted by parts of the architectural press. But to no avail, it won the (revived) Institute's silver medal that year. Ant and his friends were more touched by the triple gold joy lavished by Lettuce and her company in effusive thanks at the opening ceremony. After several speeches, it developed into a rip-roaring party filled with food and drink and, a variety of dance-items.

Ossian accompanied some of the dancers.

'Now you are part of our dance-family.' Lettuce cried cheerfully. She had persuaded Angelica to take charge of the new play-school. 'Your skill and love for the kids is exactly what they, and we need.' she said during the official interview which was more a confirmation of first strong thoughts than applicants realised.

Angelica's answer to the question, "Why should you get the job?" clinched the matter. 'I've been involved with children, music and dance for some time. Also, I was consulted about the project by Lettuce and by your architect. I would like to be able to continue that work. The children and the Dance Studio are important to me.'

20-

NINA WAS GLAD to be at university. Following on her siblings she felt new possibilities existed there. She was glad two of her favourite teachers, Lyn Barnes cello, and Aileen Palmer English, were in the faculties she joined. They cared about her and excellence. While the youngest in the English Department, she was one of a clutch of young talent in the music faculty, comforted by the welcome another Macknight was accorded. Luckily, Lettuce dallied in re-letting Angelica's room. Nina took it with alacrity. Lettuce understood her need for both independence and mothering; the house was filled with music and dance; Nina, reminded of home, was delighted.

What intrigued her was ambiguity in music and in dance. Neither was solely male or female, both were involved. She had danced with Lettuce before, savouring the role of an aggressive girl expressing a need for boys' energy, kudos and initiative denied by much of the world, for which she strove as her brothers and sisters had. Being the last child she felt deeply the need to be both boy and girl "All the [children] of my father's house." as Viola had claimed in *Twelfth Night,** one of the term's English texts she knew well.

At the Conservatorium Nina joined a string quartet. She knew of the ebullience of the first violin, the competitive generosity of the second, Nina loved the viola's inner voice, easily overlooked, she gloried in the solidity her cello brought to the ensemble. 'It's like "all the daughters and the brothers of my father's house" and mother and father too.' she said to herself joining her three friends to reveal the characteristics of their musical house which, after impassioned argument they called The OstrAu Quartet, because Leos Janicek died in Ostrau after writing *Intimate Letters.**

Nina wrote a short story based on Janicek's quartet. The first

---

* See notes at end.

movement, *Andante* starts with the cruel voice of the cello. Ghostly memories from the viola soften and lead to warmer songs of friendship and first love; the second movement *Adagio*, filled with baby-rocking, disintegrates into fearful expectations and the third, *Moderato,* a carefree summer harvest is overwhelmed by blood and war; The last movement, *Allegro,* dances under duress, trying to keep warm and desperate to forget, dancing towards a future without youth or love, fed by terrible regrets.

'All the passions of love in a cruel world.' Nina explained. She and her cello sang of storms of love and hate, fear and hope. She was unconnected untouched. Nina threw herself into her work driven by a tiny knot of fury. All the children in her father's house kept her aloof, 'I'm only half an apple. Where's my other half?' she whispered into her pillow one night after helping Lettuce with a passionate dance routine about *Daphnis and Chloe.* She had cut her hair, wore boys' clothes, became a striking, wilful Cesario. She was lusted after but she remained a trifle uncomfortable. 'Love letters, but not intimacy.' she moaned to her mute pillow.

Nina revelled in music-making: the intimacy of work, the wordless eloquence and power, the glories of sound she shared with her big brother Ossian who knew and complemented her enthusiasm. She savoured her visits to his house, playing there, eating Angelica's Italian food and agreeing Italian was the language of music and love (Love. If only I could find some, she longed).

Finding words were spears, she engaged in a tussle over love in her English studies. There, she felt pressure to take sides in the phallo-centric battle stirred by literary critics gripping the Department. "Why should men dominate literature? Why should we accept their egocentric view? Side-line them, give women a voice!" was the battle-cry. Nina's knot of anger suddenly had an outlet. She was thrilled by a sense of sisterhood in confronting the enemy, a phallic view of the world, her father's view, the poison making her frustrated. Connected to her sisters she felt powerful. Her inner wildness flowed out into daily life. To see in new ways delighted her. Seduced by sisterhood, she embraced everything feminine, finding a reactive love shyly growing from her earlier relationship with Rose. But there was a worm in the bud: Nina was not sure whether it was Cesario or Viola who eventually seduced her bosom friend, Fiona, one long night of work, drinking and later, with trembling caresses, finding the glory of being played by a sister to a mutual ending.

'I love your drive and inventiveness.' Fiona told her in yearning forgiveness of the violation the next morning. They showered together soaping and stimulating each other until embraced by soapy arms and intruded upon by stirring fingers, each climaxed, cementing a bond which held them, off and on, for that year.

Twelfth Night haunted Nina. Her life became entangled in its feminist flavours. She embraced the view Viola was the power at its centre, Orsino was a wimp, that Olivia had wavering sexual preferences, wanting both the girlish Cesario and her gay brother Sebastian who had been Antonio's lover. Hidden appearances were embedded in the play: Viola as "eunuch" as she described herself when dressed as a boy; the shadow sides of Olivia and Orsino, noble leaders without backbones; Malvolio, the skilled manager, as foolish as the Fool was clever; Sebastian the faggot who fought like "a devil incardinate [incarnate]". Mirror images, like the twins Viola and Sebastian, "one face, one voice, one habit, and two persons." whereas the rest consisted of two faced, unresolved people. Only Viola managed duality, seducing both Orsino and Olivia. It is she who clinches the action by dressing again in "woman's weeds" to marry Duke Orsino (and avoid Olivia). Like her twin brother she engages with the sexual range from boy through to girl, but with integrity; as explained in the conclusion when Feste, the fool, sings about the range of experiences, or "what you will" risk in living life fully (rather than turning a blind eye) accompanied by daily raining; as willy nilly life drowns in difficulties.

'As both Cesario and Viola, I'm finding life difficult.' mused Nina. 'I don't want to wear woman's weeds.' No one, not even a duke minded, *she* would have to decide who she was.

She was Fiona's shadow in the English department; they studied together much to the approval of the feminists who took the first-year girls under their wing, protecting them from phallic influence, and inculcating them into the glories of sisterhood.

Nina consulted Aileen Palmer, the childrens' teacher at Ararat who had inspired Nina to undertake an English degree. Nina trusted Aileen's remark that her poems reflected her struggle, expressing ambivalent doubt about her dreams and relationships. Although shocked to discover Aileen had a girlfriend, Nina poured out her preoccupations about love.

She was little comforted by Aileen's opinion any love could be troublesome, that Viola's strength was her ability to tackle her relationships and to act on her wishes. 'Just as you can.' breathed Aileen one afternoon, cradling Nina's boyish head on her lap and caressing her cheek in gentle affirmation. 'You're not so fragile.' Aileen said. 'I am. I don't have your courage to explore far.'

Nina turned and looked into troubled eyes. 'But you are a wonderful poet. Better than any of us.'

Aileen bent over her blazing face and lightly kissed her forehead. 'Dearest Nina, I don't doubt you will be too. You are connected to two of the great sources: the earth itself and to your feelings; stay with both. Remember, it is fearful to be independent, as any real poet knows. And remember, words can define or damage. That's their power. Find ways of defending yourself, as well as ways of expression.' She looked fondly at her lovely pupil. 'Feel free to come here whenever you want, with Fiona if you need. I have watched you grow. I love you.'

Nina snuggled into her trusted lap and whispered. 'I love you too.' It was a special connection growing from years of sharing.

Nina left Aileen's house with a sense of solidity, as if she'd been playing music, or supped on magic. That evening, before making love to Fiona, she wrote:

> *Alone. Bright without.*
> *You let me take*
> *to inner dark:*
> *beating hearts*
> *greedy cries,*
> *my image merges*
> *sinking in your sands.*
> *Love buoys me,*
> *I see both of us*
> *are blacks and whites.*

'I don't think I feel that.' Fiona whispered. 'I feel the merging. Being together, being one is my need. I want to sink into your sands and stay there.' She paused. 'I love you Nina. My first love. You're so wild, I know you won't stay. But for me it's forever.'

She pulled off Nina's top and began kissing her breasts while exploring the strands of her neck, feeling tension and delight growing. She worked down the lithe body.

Overwhelmed, Nina fell back wracked by pleasure as Fiona kissed her to clitoral orgasm. Later she reciprocated.

Fiona cried softly. 'Do you care? You do, don't you?'

Nina kissed and whispered into her lips. 'Of course I care, silly. I love you too. It's just. I'm so restless. It's my fault. Not yours. Fi, take care. Remember I do love you. I'm alone without you but I do see our blacks and whites, I find us separate. I need the outside and the inside, everything.'

'I know.' Fiona said bitterly, snuggling into Nina's warmth. 'Just like Viola.'

They slept soundly.

In the morning Nina crept down stairs with her cello to start the day with Bach as Pablo Casals had. Usually she sat near the window in the silent dance studio enjoying the empty volume of the room and the quiet street beyond the house where only the leaves of trees stirred the shy sunshine. She knew the unaccompanied cello suites well; letting the mood of the morning choose which to play. Today she felt like dancing so played one comprised of dance movements giving a rhythmic push to the melodies until the space filled with pulsing melody.

Something moved out of eye-shot. A tousled boy slipped into the room. He listened intently, beginning to twitch and bend with the rhythms, raising his arms, his hands, birds flying with polyphony. He's one of Lettuce's strays, Nina thought, glad of the company. When finished she looked-up. 'Did you enjoy that?'

The boy nodded.

Lettuce bustled in. 'Gerald, this is Nina's space. Dear one, do we disturb you?'

Nina shook her head. 'It's OK. We're both dancing.'

Lettuce smiled, fondly attentive.

Nina twice repeated the Minuet and Trio to which Gerald responded. Lettuce watched, occasionally repositioning the boy's arms or twisting his body until he blended with the music.

Gerald grinned panting. 'It's music which topples you. So, I stagger now and again. An elephant-cello attempting ballet.'

Lettuce nodded. 'You catch the grace and the heaviness well.

She pushed the boy out the door. 'Now dear, go shower and dress.' She shook her head. 'Nina, thank you. Gerald has a cruel home and escapes to sleep on my couch.' She sighed. 'He's so sensitive and talented. He has a key. What can I do, he's desperate? But he knows not to disturb you so throw him out if he's a nuisance.'

Leaf shadows danced over the floor. Bach's birdsong still floated in the studio. Nina felt contentment with the "blacks and whites" she had left in bed to find them dancing later.

She smiled. 'Dear Lettuce, I enjoyed it. Gerald reminds me of Ossian whose dancing speaks music. Words complicate, but not dancing. You know. You told me.'

Lettuce bent and kissed her brow. 'Thank you for Bach; It's a lovely start to the day.'

Nina rose. They went together to the foot of the stairs, arms round each other, where Nina stepped away upwards to snuggle her instrument back into its case and to snuggle for a moment with a sleepy lover whose welcome filled the day with song.

Fiona went home for the weekend. Nina settled down in her silent room, studying for English and preparing for Sunday's quartet rehearsal. Propped by pillows she sprawled reading.

Gerald slipped in clutching a bundle of rags. 'Lettuce has lent me a leotard. Can we dance again?' he jiggled awkwardly.

Nina nodded absently. 'Give me a moment. The chair in the bay window. Change. Put your clothes there.'

She was studying *Twelfth Night* for next week's tutorial on mirrors. She flung the book down and swung her legs onto the floor, knocking over her mug of tea. 'Shit.' she cried, grabbing a tee shirt to stem the flood. 'Help me.'

The boy bounded over and threw his singlet down. They stood regarding each other, the damp floor and tea-stained clothes. He was clad only in underpants, she almost as skimpily in a loose tee-shirt.

Although familiar with her brothers, she viewed him with sudden interest. 'Gerald, you're beautiful.' She ran appraising fingers down his hairless flanks and appraised his blushing face, then pulled him into a gentle hug.

'Viola was more eunuch than boy.' she murmured feeling the bulge of his sex pushing into her. She cradled it in her hand weighing it against her vacant crotch.

Gerald stammered. 'Theirs is cut off.'

'Not all of it. Only the balls. So they can sing treble and have safe sex.' her hand was full. 'Castrati sang women's parts in early operas; strange strangled voices and no seed. I guess Orsino kept everything at arms length, including wooing so didn't feel where Viola had bumps.'

'They are half men-half women.' Gerald said.

'Is that what you are?'

'Is that what you are?' Gerald blushed.

Gently she pulled his pants down. She held his spotless erection feeling its responsive length and cupping a palm under velvet testicles, astounded by the "blackness" of them compared to the "whiteness" of his phallus, excited by his pleading body and his shamed face which broke as fluid shot from his penis and he wilted.

They clung. 'I'm sorry.' He looked desolate.

Nina held him carefully; he was precious and fragile. She was ashamed of inciting him yet liked his relief. 'But it was good?'

Gerald nodded into her breasts, flooded with love for this girl-boy who comforted and accepted him, the very first to show him there was no shame in his clamourous dreams.

'They call me poofter because I dance. You're a lesbian, aren't you?'

'I don't know what I am. A sort of eunuch who likes Fiona and you. She watched slime ooze down his thigh. 'Who enjoys words or music or dance; blackness as much as whiteness.'

'Have you ever done it with a man?'

'When I was a girl. I didn't like it much.'

'A man fucked me a year ago. It hurt. He didn't care. He did it and went.'

Her silence held his secret. 'Did it hurt just now?'

He looked up from her beating chest, eyes swimming. 'Oh no. It was. It was amazing.'

'As good as dancing?'

'As good. Better.'

'Shall we go down to the studio now? Get your leotard. I'll help you change.'

He bounded across the room, returning with a scrumpled black cloth. Together they untangled it. She held it open so he could wriggle in. He pulled a strap over each shoulder. It showed his trim form, his neat buttocks, flat stomach and puff of sex.

'Can I carry your cello?' (he wanted to hide his excitement).

She tightened the screw holding the spike. 'It's sharp. Be careful. Don't knock it.'

They tripped down the stairs unobserved.

The dance began. Passions raged: each was emboldened to feel naked, responding without restraint, celebrating freedom in intimacy until bewitched and exhausted. In the silence he flopped on the floor beside the discarded cello. She took his sweaty head in her lap, her hands on his shoulders.

'*Twelfth Night* starts with, "If music be the food of love, play on." You remind me of that.' Nina felt him settle. 'We've been feeding each other. It's the same in the quartet. Come tomorrow and see, if you can be very quiet.'

'Like a mouse.' he glared at the floor with a green realisation she worked with others.

Lettuce entered the studio, and nodded approvingly. 'Dancing? Do it again.' She made adjustments to Gerald's choreography. She sighed.'You're making something very special. I hope Gerald we can persuade Nina to accompany you in our Dance Day next month. *Movements from Bach* should be included. Your partnership is exceptional. It has the magic of living music and dance.'

What particularly surprised her was not a change in the boy, she expected their working would bring that about, but a transformation of Nina's playing. It was richer, softer, rhythmic, full of dance. 'He's touched her. It's more than boyish, a richer, feminine character has blossomed. How wonderful,' she mused.

That night, Lettuce sat with Gerald after he had slipped under the duvet on her living room couch preparing to sleep only wearing underpants, his tea stained singlet in the wash. She enjoyed his slim, hairless body.

He eyed her. 'Dancing with Nina is like dreaming.'

Lettuce laughed easily. 'Well, my dear, for this occasion both of you must stay fast asleep to reap the riches.'

His troubled face softened. 'I really like her very much even though we're both gay.'

'All the best people are half-and-half. Sleep well Dear. I'm glad you love each other. So do I.'

In the morning Gerald opened the door to Eugene, the leader

of the OstrAu quartet. 'They're all sleeping.' He led him into the bare studio. Eugene had an untidy mop of fair hair. His blue eyes were set in a slavic face. He was a bigger version of Gerald both acknowledged with interest. Eugene took out his violin. It was such a small cello. Richly varnished with resin dust under the bridge and a chin support worn by long use matching the ruddy mark on the young man's aristocratic chin.

'Do you play Bach?' asked the boy shyly.

Without a word Eugene started the solo sonata in E major whose virtuosic prelude stunned the boy. Gerald, like a sleep walker, watched Eugene draw such magic out he felt faint. On and on glories shimmered until deep inside, where no one had been allowed, Gerald sang. Eugene took him swirling and spiralling. Riches blossomed; they fell, mouths open, drinking them in. 'This music is the food of love.' the boy knew. Blue-eyed love regarded him, siren-singing to the end. They shared its ecstacy.

Gerald had felt before what music told: shrill terror, sly regret, carefree flying. Gymnastic ecstacy shone like Eugene's violin and his blue eyes. But this time something lacked, something discovered in Nina's Bach: a soft solidity.

Eugene winked. 'Could I have a glass of water?'

'I'll make a pot of tea. Is that all right?'

In the kitchen after the tea pot was filled, Eugene put an arm around the boy's shoulders. 'I'm glad you like the sonata. It's one of the best. Filled with life.'

'And hope.' Gerald murmured. 'Is it difficult?'

'Of course. The best always is: music, love, dreams.' Eugene smiled, touched by Gerald's intense admiration.

'Dance too.' Lettuce cheerfully breezed in following the scent of fresh-brewed tea. 'Good morning Maestro.'

'As difficult as Nina.' Gerald whispered shining with the blush Eugene had lit.

'So, you've met our Gerald.' Lettuce inclined her head. 'He's staying here for the moment. Dancing with Nina. Exceptional.'

Eunene shot a sharp look at the boy. 'Well, I know he likes Bach. A dancer, eh?'

'Yes.' Nina sidled in. 'He's special. Eugene, you played like an angel this morning? See, you can.'

She smiled so fondly Gerald winced. Embarrassment.

Delight. Flying. It blew him away. "The food of love!" he thought excitedly, the door bell interrupting them.

Sam bounced in like an excited puppy. He busied himself getting chairs into the studio, arranging concernedly for a jug of water and four glasses.

'Five.' advised Nina, wanting to include Gerald.

'Let me help.' the boy sprang up.

Sam grinned and supervised chair and music-stand positioning, drinks and the hanging of abandoned clothes on the pegs inside the front door just as Ilya, the second violin arrived panting with lateness, anxious to put it behind him and begin the rehearsal.

'They're working, so keep quiet.' Lettuce advised the boy as she pushed him into the studio and closed the door so the rest of the household would be undisturbed.

Gerald sat on the floor listening spellbound during the Haydn.[*] 'He wrote it for a violinist, Johann Tost. It's in the plain key of C major but is far from plain.' Eugene murmured to his admiring boy audience. 'Listen to the Bohemian gypsy music in the first Adagio. That quality permeates all the music today. Dvorak, Janacek, Haydn, Ravel have all been tainted by gypsy violins.' He turned to his friends. 'Now, let's do it without the music And, Gerald, you must tell us how it sounds.'

Gerald's heart beat wildly. The four seemed to be playing each other. 'It's like when Nina made me come.' he told himself, knowing such a thought was unspeakable. Then he noticed how strongly each instrument sounded, how they swapped and shared, how scratchy, how warm and sweet, how lilting the melodies had become. And how unified the sound. It's like hugging, he thought.

'When you make one sound, you all breath together.' he burst out. 'It's great.'

Eugene raised his bow. 'Play the Adagio more like a steady sung choral so the wild gypsy tune escapes from within it, as if God can't contain its luscious life.'

'I like it better.' said Gerald eventually. 'There's more beauty. More freedom. More of you all. It seems to fit with the rest.'

They took a break. Eugene spoke of *The American* by Anton Dvorak.[*] 'It once was called "Nigger" because it was influenced by

---

[*]   See notes at end.

170

negro music. But they changed the name.'

'Words change.' said Nina. 'One day you won't be called poofta.'

Gerald wriggled.

Eugene watched him. 'I was called that at school.'

'It means 'misfit' to those unable to do anything.' said Sam.

Ilya got ratty during the Dvorak. 'It's far too romantic. There must be devilish gypsy rhythms driving it throughout, not all these slushy rubatos which aren't in the score. There are numerous changes in note values and accent. Let's play what's written. That's enough.'

But playing it straight was difficult. In the end Eugene persuaded Gerald to beat time with his spare bow on the back of a chair to keep them together. 'A dancer knows about time. Let's put our music away.'

The muddle of the music cleared. It felt easier to play. It sounded better without the music. The morning flew.

Everyone in the house lunched on Lettuce's soup, bread and cheese and fresh fruit.

Lettuce took Gerald aside 'They're good, don't you think?'

Dazzled, he nodded. The intensity and intimacy, the nakedness he'd found with Nina was in their work. He witnessed the struggle. Now he knew he had to work in the same way. It was neither bad nor gay, rather, it was how to find meaning in sound and movement. Sam was right about "misfits". Music and dance (and love? he wondered) mattered far more than labels. He would not cringe any more. He wanted to fly. 'They're brilliant.'

Lettuce smiled. 'I'm glad you agree.'

Two weeks passed. Every morning Gerald waited for Nina, leotard in hand in case she was amenable; he learned to judge her mood: sometimes he crouched quiet as a mouse as she fought her cello, or her after-dream mood or doubts (the boy wanted to share), or when she wanted to be alone.

Sometimes she helped him change, and he danced to her singing cello, danced only for her, eye seeking eye until the final cadences when intensity was relieved by silence and breathing.

She could torture him. Each knew music's inevitability after teasing out their "whiteness and blackness". After one ungenerous session Nina relented. 'Sorry about this morning. We could do Bach this afternoon. I'll be here. If you like.'

Gerald was bruised but wanting to comfort her, to tell her nothing mattered, she was wonderful. He said, 'I'll come at three.'

At three he slipped into her room. She smiled wanly. Without more ado he pulled off his clothes strewing them on a chair then tip-toed over, proffering the leotard ball for untangling. She took it, letting it fall to embrace him, feeling his bulging underpants homing into her crotch with unspeakable longing. Hers his. His hers. It pushed against her mound of vaginal hair. In her shifting hands he flexed his buttocks, the eloquent kneading mounds the rapist had plundered.

She opened her empty thighs. He groaned and burst. She held his slack body as life returned. It relieved her. But only a bit. She fought her feelings of want, trying to concentrate on his calm. She did not want another in her life. Nina kissed his soft, boyish face, spying the manly wet on his underpants. Her turmoil stirred.

She spoke as Viola, '"As I am a woman - now alas the day.-
. . . O time, thou must untangle this, not I; it is too hard a knot for me t'untie."'

'You don't look like a woman.' he murmured as he shimmied into the leotard.

'You make me feel like one.'

'Perhaps you are.'

'You're a man with me.'

Gerald, the dancer hugged her, reviving their companionship in dancing. A prelude to their duette downstairs.

Lettuce found them resting in the studio: he, radiating belief, she, doubt.

'Gerald let's have tea. Will you go to the shops and buy us some of those Jewish dark chocolate-coated ginger biscuits Nina likes while I make a pot?'

The boy cheerfully streaked out of the house while Lettuce shepherded Nina to the kitchen, gently sat her down. 'Tell me, Nina dear. Is he too much?'

Tears welled. 'No. Yes. It's me, messed-up. The dance is fine. It's the rest.'

'His demands?'

Nina laid her head on the kitchen table struggling with her tangled feelings. 'He's so patient, so vulnerable, bubbling with life. No, it's not him. I don't know what to do with myself. He takes all my shit. I feel so empty.'

'Does he fill you?'

'Not really. We don't go that far. I don't want it.'

'How do you know? When you deny the man in him, you deny something in yourself. Perhaps you think you are not what you are. Normally I wouldn't condone such a relationship. But you do need each other. It's not a matter of age, rather of exploring the very beginnings of the desire each of you, from such different backgrounds, has cauterised. Let him help you, as you're helping him. I'm going to Ararat shortly. Come along. Bring him. There, with the wisdom of the trees, you might find how to go on. My dear, both of you deserve that chance. Time helps but often it needs a little push.'

'A little push with what?' Gerald asked bounding into the kitchen. 'Oh.' he blurted, seeing Nina's distress. He put a tentative hand on her spiky hair. 'Is it our dancing?'

'No dear, being a woman (or a man) is difficult. We must help Nina to help you to help her to be close, loving friends.'

'We are.'

'She needs more than that.'

Gerald blushed (So do I, he realised). 'Is it pulling off the labels Sam was talking about?'

'Not only dancing, living too.' Lettuce sighed. 'And, talking of living, let's start with a hot cuppa.'

Nina looked up at them both almost smiling.

What compounded Nina's unease after taking Lettuce's advice, was the continual feminist harping; many of her friends criticised her involvement in a male quartet playing music by men: 'You're so subjugated you look like them. We must liberate ourselves from the phallocentric culture imprisoning us.' they urged.

Aileen robustly defended her, remarking in her English tutorials. 'We should free ourselves from all ideologies so as to relate, with all the riches this brings. Remember Christopher Norris' *Text and Ideology* which concludes, "[Literary] scholarship [is a] casebook of endlessly dissenting views." Literature and life must involve dissent, not slavery.[*]

She published Nina's poem with a comment supporting Norris in the faculty journal which raised hackles: "Blacks and whites is a traitorous attitude." one reviewer thundered.

'But you aren't any happier.' complained Fiona, saddened by the distance growing between them.

'I know.' grieved Nina. 'But freedom has a cost.'

'It's true: you do play with men and boys; you do look like a boy. But I love you.' Fiona cried.

'Love can be dissent but not slavery.' Nina answered. She was wrung out, needing to escape to her beloved valley where she could reconnect with the child inside her and with the child in Gerald and with the trees, the snaking river, all the other reliable children of the valley.

One morning she sang to Gerald before she played:

> *O mistress mine, where are you roaming?*
> *O stay and hear, your true love's coming,*
> *That can sing both high and low.*
> *Trip no further, pretty sweeting;*
> *Journeys end in lovers meeting*
> *Every wise man's son doth know.* [*]

'High and low, but I'm wobbly.' he said. 'And my Dad's no wise man; he's a monster.'

'It's about separation and life-journeys.' she said.

'And love.' he grinned.

'And wishing for, "Stay and hear" 'now' is plenteous.'

'What's plenteous?'

'It's what we have in Lettuce's house; what the valley has: lots of happiness, plenty. That's why we want to take you there. We'll sing both high and low and really dance.'

'And do what we want?'

She nodded determinedly. Knowing she was in ernest, he felt plenteous for days.

---

[*] See notes at end.

21-

ARARAT had a sprawling, easy air. Gerald felt at home. Nina's parents, clearly delighted by her visit, included him in a relaxed if appraising welcome (She had brought girl-friends there previously). He was reassured by Will's enthusiasm for dancing; he savoured Miranda's homeliness and the childrens' shy curiosity. 'Nici is so like Nina. Kim and Nestor chase after her just as I chase Nina.' he mused, as glad as they to scamper about and explore the valley. Their innocent happiness infected Gerald until he glowed. Nina found it hard to balance this bright, boyish spirit with the dark sexual urges driving them both.

'Are we all apples cleft into blacks and whites?' she wondered watching them all, stripped to underpants, dancing to Lettuce's recording of *Bolero* by Maurice Ravel, sizing what bloomed between his legs with nervous longing as he sprang into the air, as if into her.

Everyone dined early, at the children's hour. Afterwards Nina, sure of familiar ways in the gathering dusk, took Gerald around the lake and down to the river. The water chucked and shone greyly in the gloom. Trees sighed. Her heart beat uncomfortably. She put her hands on his hips and drew him into an embrace. They were trembling. He kissed her with butterfly shyness. She felt the clamour pressing urgently at their crotches. Clumsily she undid his belt, unbuttoned his jeans, took it out; she knelt to quench its fire in her mouth, to be reassured about desire while cradling the ultra soft sacs, scenting excitement until with a tremor he sluiced velvet into her mouth.

'Oh.' he whispered.

She relinquished the shrinking god and swallowed the almond-tainted seed. 'Do you like the taste?'

'Not much.' He sighed.

'You smell great.' she murmured, rising to ferry some seed into his mouth and hold him as his energy returned.

'Don't you ever want to come? It's not fun for you?'.

She hugged him gratefully. 'I don't mind. Yes, I do. I love your excitement. The release. The aftermath. Later?'

They ambled up to the house, their clasped hands impassive, suppressing expectations of their first experience of black-white love.

Later, she gasped with physical delight. 'Fantastic.'

He responded to her body as he did to her music, dancing over it, skillfully pausing where he sensed excitement until in extreme pleasure Nina trembled with the onset of clitoral orgasm. Yearningly she pulled him up and into her. The beauty and power she had fondled the previous weeks slid inside. She was filled with its shimmering presence, buoyed to unimagined heights of ecstacy. Too soon his power crumpled, leaving her with diminishing waves of orgasm echoing the cloud-bursts erupting before his own.

They slept. Woke and made love again and again. Neither the night nor ordinary time could contain their passion. Yet towards morning, they slept deeply, purged of want.

In the morning they were nuzzled into a dazed awareness by Nici and Kim. Nici squirmed into the warm space between them while Kim crouched on the foot of their bed reflectively holding his penis and regarding the bigger hairy creatures, he unconsciously knew, had danced all night. That choreography lay in the Bach Movements danced and played after breakfast which he saw as clearly as Lettuce.

'I'm going to dance like Jerry and Daddy. You are too.' he told his Teddy. 'But you must grow up first.' Teddy accepted the news gladly.

'Is there something in its presence which makes me open?' Nina muses, aware of the wet warmth of her vagina. 'Am I feeling what women feel?' Why do I worship it? Do I project my longing into it because I see it rear up hungrily and can calm its yearning? I'm in charge, therefore I love? And yet not in charge at all, just as happy. Do men long to be filled? Do men also worship it - I think they do. I sense his drive to shoot, equals mine of wanting to be filled.' she ruminates. 'Here are blacks and whites, yet I sense although the journeys are different our destinations are similar.' She smiles and presses her throbbing vulva for reassurance. 'Forcing our passivity or action as if alternatives is a scourge welded to masculine and feminine. Obfuscating naked beauty as rude, immoral, unseemly is another scourge reinforced by the dual use of our organs for sex and passing waste as we become aware of in childhood until everything related to those precious areas becomes kucky. For churchmen to pretend our deepest pleasure is secondary to making children is obscenely unreal. But there is merit in acknowledging over the centuries, much disease has lodged there.'

Nina feels the solidity of a tree trunk. 'Viola and Lettuce are right saying "That you do think you are not what you are." So many naked, copulating boys in my childhood, too few opportunities to witness or to imagine sisters or mothers making love; certainly the phallus dominated our lives so I dreamed-up my own to become what I was not, and grew confused about the subterfuge unlike Viola, a confusion which bred fear later reinforced by pain. I remember bleeding, regarded as natural by everyone; but my plight seemed a threatening imposition; another discomfort. In a world where appearances dominate, the invisibles of my body were overlooked, devalued, becoming unreal. No wonder I turned to similar bodies for relief and reinforcement, parading Cesario as equal, as lover, as friend. No wonder I was restless (unhappy?)' She muses watching clouds metamorphose from fantastic shape into fantastic shape or thin air.

'I turned myself and the phallus into myths, when the reality is all of us want and share the destination, arriving there differently: some whitely some blackly, making love, or music, or families, or poems. We must each do what we can. Our various destinations should be as clear as the previous ones. To legislate who does what, who wears woman's weeds, who, boxer shorts is to lose sight of essentials. For "The rain it raineth every day" so let's sing "Hey, ho" and get on with it.'

That afternoon Nina and Gerald meandered through the rank grass down to the river. The hurrying waters charmed them. They leaned against a ragged tree-trunk.

He stammered. 'I'm happy dancing, talking, walking

in the Bush with you.'

'Me too. You're wonderful.'

'So are you.'

Hastily they undressed and he eased in; after a few swift strokes he flooded her. They settled, sheepishly helped each other to dress and then collapsed onto a flat rock to fill with the dancing songs of the river, the sighs of trees and with contentment.

Nina was emboldened by his equanimity. 'Tonight, will you fuck me like a boy? You've done it that way?'

Blushing relief in unveiling his shameful vice, he nodded. 'We need slippery jelly.'

'Do you mind my being a boy?'

'I like everything with you.'

'I want everything.' she whispered, pulling him into so tight an embrace he gasped.

'Why me?'

'We do things together. I don't know, I trust you.'

'You do things with Eugene.'

'Silly. He's different. Anyway he's gay.' she frowned.

'He loves you, It's the way he looks at you.'

'No. We work together. Nothing more.'

'He's well-hung.' he sighed longingly.

'Trust you to see that.'

'I watch you all. Ilya suffers and works, Sam smiles and works and Eugene dreams and follows your every move.'

'And me?'

'You show your magic prick to them. Four weird boys making music come alive. Each of you is brilliant, particularly you.'

'Somebody said that to you.'

'I talk to Lettuce. I never ever tell about us. Not to anyone. But I see a lot; you showed me how to watch. And you are brilliant. Your playing and the way you are, boy~girl, or as you say, "blacks and whites". I trust you as well. As much as Eugene does.'

'Don't say that. I'm happy now. Leave me alone, Gerald.'

'Lettuce is arranging a scholarship so I can get away to dance academy. Anyway, I'm a kid. No use to you.' His smile faded.
She cried because love was tender and because it was true. Yet she clung to their dream half-aware it was indispensable.

He saw the river water running away .'Sorry.' he said.

She looked at him with new admiration in his ability to step into his future. 'I'm not sure I'm much use to you. But I do love you.'

He was mortified by her tears. He glowered at the water-smoothed rock. 'Oh Nina. I do too.'

They leaned together, separate. Sadly happy in the calming Bush, the only 'unchanging'. But not the only comfort.

The chuckling stream matched their sadness entwining it with threads of sweetness drawing them back to the house where, after supper, Nina offered a Bunyip story to the children, Nici (7), Kim (5), Nestor (2ish) and Gerald (14+), if they solemnly promised not to tell and not to peep as they flew over the sleeping world to places beyond time itself where Bunyip took his trusty helpers:

The small boy was standing by the window when a furry shadow landed on the cill. Not waiting for a scratch he opened the sash. All the children joined Bunyip, sitting with feet swinging over the ledge. He looked fondly at them. 'We don't go far tonight. Just up the valley into the mountains from where the river bursts. For there is the problem. There has been a landslide. A complete change in the hidden valley from which all our waters gush. To you it will not seem strange. But for the many dwelling there, the changes are fearful so all of us must struggle to help them find their old cheerfulness. Otherwise they cannot till the land, keep it fresh and fertile. Then all the waters will be swallowed up and everything will dry and die. And that would never do.'

The children held hands, Bunyip in the middle. They shut their eyes and the cold fingers of the night wind ripped at them. They shivered and moaned as they flew up into the sky. 'Oh dear' said Bunyip. 'You need furry coats. Luckily Mrs Bunyip has just finished making some so first I'll take you home.'

They swooped down and into a gaunt tree leaning over the river slightly roughed-up where someone had leaned recently and rubbed off the bark. 'I'm sorry about the mess.' said Bunyip. 'This is our holiday house. We've just moved in. Children, meet Mrs. Bunyip.'

Naturally they stayed for tea and delicious wild-honey scones piping hot from the oven. Miraculously there was a coat for each of them, although the biggest boy's arms projected from rather short sleeves like a scarecrow, and the smallest boy lost him -

self in voluminous folds so it looked as if his coat had a life of its own, carried on invisible feet and waved by invisible arms.

What with the hot tea and the big coats everyone was as warm as toast when they set off again on their mission to save the world.

The hidden valley looked a mess. Trees lay up-rooted, rocks strewn about as if by an angry giant; much of the under - growth was flattened and stones which had once been houses lay in untidy heaps around which tramped their weeping owners cry - ing 'What's to be done? Catastrophe. Hopeless. If only . . if only.'

'You see what I mean!.' Bunyip whispered .'You'd never believe they were the happiest folk in all the world.'

'Let's help them rebuild the houses.' said one of the children. So together they began moving stones, making walls, adding stone on stone on stone, singing all the while and telling huge fibs that each stone was a hot scone, a big hat, a steak tartar (whatever that is), a lumpen muff for the coldest winter, frozen shit, and much else far too rude to relate.

Soon many more were bustling about remaking their shat - tered lives. Soon all the children were shouting. 'Here's a lumpen muffin. Here's some frozen pooh. Here, take this hot scone and put it way up there so the roof can sit on it.' Soon there was singing: "There were ten in a bed and the middle one said roll over and they all rolled over and one fell out/ there were nine in a bed ," and so on. Soon all the houses were finished, all the songs and fibs too. Now there was laughter. Also sighs which troubled Bunyip who asked the children to discover the cause.

Eventually someone muttered. 'It IS good to have our houses. But they are different. Everything is different. If only we could get the old days, the old ways back, THEN we'd be happy.'

Bunyip sighed. 'I know you think the river is always the same, but it's ever changing. No one can step into its running water twice. Life is more subtle than a river. Yes, your lives are different now. But if you care to look you'll find you've made a lovely village with safe play spaces for your babies, with comfort - able places for the oldies to lean and chat, wide spaces for teenage larking and snug houses for Mums and Dads. Look how clever you are. Be proud. Make use of all this, you really are much better off now than you were earlier. Ask your children.'

All the children cried happily 'YES. MUCH BETTER.'

One of the teenagers grimaced. 'It's hard to change. But in the end it's worth it.'

Another grinned. 'Try to stop it, you can't. Change is life. You should enjoy life by embracing change.'

'Children are so wise.' said Bunyip, kissing the now cheer - ful folk whose cries of gratitude hung round his clever helpers as together, they were whisked back to bed and to sweet dreams.

'Teddy wants to change.' Kim told his lovely aunt Nina as she tucked him up afterwards.

'So do I.' whispered Nina kissing his rosey mouth. 'But sometimes we need help.'

Nici insisted that Gerald carry her to bed. She twined ivy arms around his embarrassed neck and kissed him. 'Goodnight scarecrow. I'm glad you came with Nina.'

He flushed kissing her eager mouth. 'Are you? So am I.'

He followed Nina back to the living room where Will had lit a fire warming their chat. Gerald enjoyed the banter mixed with sincere discussion, like occasions at Lettuce's place, so unlike the contempt in his home. The fire burned low burnishing faces with its glow. Coals gleamed and broke imparting stories to the boy who sat on a rug between Nina's embracing thighs, an almost adult-child.

Lettuce was glad of his contentment, glad too he seemed to have tamed Nina's independence so she could snuggle up to him. 'Maybe to better face the emptiness she complains of.' Lettuce mused. She smiled at Nina's first public intimacy with a boy. 'Are you two something like the end of *The Taming of the Shrew* : "Now, go thy ways; [Gerald] hast tamed a curst shrew.\ 'Tis a wonder, by your leave, she will be tamed so." Well my dear?'

Nina coloured at the barb. But Lettuce's gentle demeanour, and years of her loving care, helped her to answer. 'I do feel that wonder. Dancing and trust have tamed us both. You are a dear naughty dear.'

Lettuce chuckled. 'My antlers are not rusty yet. Your dance and music, grown in trust, are so eloquent it should win Gerald a place at the Academy if all goes well at our end of term Dance Day. Furthermore, do you hear another sound in your playing, something softer yet insistent, a real feminine force?'

Nina nodded. 'Isn't it funny that my giving in to him has made me more, not less of a woman?'

Lettuce grunted like a pig nosing a truffle. 'Of course. Because you are a strong Kate who WILL be tamed because of her love and music.' She rumpled the boy's hair. 'And my lovely poofter is become a man. That's another wonder.'

'You . . . .' breathed the boy accusingly.

Nina whispered. 'I was telling Kim just now sometimes change needs a little help.'

Lettuce laughed.

Back in their room, Nina carefully undressed him wanting another look at the intruder beforehand.

'Are you sure?' breathed Gerald bursting and, not waiting for much of a reply, positioned her kneeling on the bed where he pushed greasy fingers into her anus, pulled a condom on and gingerly entered.

She reassured his trembling. 'Wow, it fills me. Is it exciting for you too?'

'Oh. Oh, yes.' he gasped in extreme pleasure, coming.

'I'm on fire. It was fun, being a boy.' she whispered, cradling his spent form in her hungry arms until, kissed back to life and on his back, she straddled him and took in the phallus.

Nina gasped as it filled her. She began lifting her hips in regular movements as waves grew, crashed and grew. She gripped as it thrust peeling off privacy. Riding with ecstacy everything burst. Weak with longing she whimpered 'Turn over. You must. You must.'

He had stiffened himself so she could ride. Now, holding slippery bottoms, plugged together, they turned over.

His body, arching between outstretched toes and palms, began to bounce. Frantically each strove, panting and moaning towards climax. She involuntarily lifted her legs yearning towards his hammering hips, drowning with entwined cries. 'Yes. Love love love LOVE YOOOOU.'

The boy, first enacted boy then woman then man; the girl, first boy then man then woman; each accomplished the ritual stages towards maturity. They slept embraced in hedonistic dreams of love's teasing music.

The next morning, Sunday, leaving day, there was music

and dancing in the music hall. Afterwards, while the children went with Peter fossicking for gum nuts, leaves and bark for their Biology project, Gerald offered to cut wood. Miranda interrupted with a refreshing drink he quaffed on the back verandah before leaping back onto the wood pile to finish off. He screamed and hurled himself backwards onto the verandah, blood oozing from his shoe.

'You've spiked yourself. Stay there, I'll ring Wendy. Luckily it's her day-off.' Miranda called running to the phone, also calling Will. 'Sweet. Help Jerry. He's jumped on one of the spikes in the formwork left by the builders. It looks bad.'

Will shuddered. The long nail had penetrated the foot, coming out the top. Carefully he carried the pain-torn boy inside, laying him on the livingroom couch. Wendy soon arrived with her nursing implements. She looked grimly at the damage. 'Will, get Tim here. And bring one of your big pliers. We'll have to get it out first.'

Wendy summonsed Nina telling her to reassure Gerald while she and Will struggled to hold the shoe, pull out the nail and remove the shoe and sock. By which time Tim arrived. He nodded his head approvingly. 'Well done, you two. Stem the flow with antiseptic and bind the foot to prevent swelling.'

Wendy found a needle and anti-tetanus injection. 'We need to take immediate precautions . Tomorrow I'll take you with me to the hospital for an X-ray to see whether the bone is damaged.'

Tim nodded. 'Someone can take Nina in our car to pick the boy up and bring him back, unless he needs an operation. Even if all is well my dear, you must rest for some days before returning to the city. I'll give Lettuce a doctor's note absolving you from school which she can take back. Nina, what about you? We will gladly care for Gerald if you want to go.'

'How long? What if I can't ever dance? I *must* get a scholarship to The Dance Academy. I must.' Gerald's tears welled.

'He's dancing at the end of the month.' Lettuce chimed in. 'If he's fit.' She was shocked by the boy's tears; never had he broken down. She watched the blood spreading through the bandage in dismay. 'Don't worry. We'll think of something.'

'I can't go home. I've no where. I can't . . ..' he sobbed.

'I'm staying.' Nina cried helplessly.

Tim, his face white with memories, looked at Will. 'We have all loved Gerald's visit. The children's delight is a measure of our feelings. You can stay here dear boy. It'll not be the first time we've taken in the homeless. I was one myself. So was Will. Peter too. Work it out with Lettuce. Remember you belong here, whether you come or go.'

Gerald, confounded, shivered and wept.

Miranda waved at them. 'That's enough. The boy's in pain. First deal with that. Then the hospital. Then the rest. Gerald, stay here. Tim's right, you're already a member of the family; we're pretty wild, but you'll not be eaten.'

Tim vanished. He returned with two pill boxes. 'Yes, they should leave. This is Wendy's preserve. Gerald, you must finish all of these anti-biotics, to speed healing by inhibiting infection, so you can dance again, and here are pain-killing suppositories, one, twice a day, deep in the rectum, strong without causing biliousness. Only the slight indignity of bearing your arse and being fingered. Dear one, the pain will quickly be quelled.'

Then he remembered Doctor McKay and Sophie who had ministered to his damaged rectum as a boy at Eliza Beach, handed the suppositories to Nina and, leaving Wendy in charge, shepherded the rest out.

'Lift your hips.' Wendy murmured. She pulled down his jeans and underpants noting his spotless member with a tiny pang. 'Up with your butt. Nina, push it in the full length of your finger. Sorry Gerald, but they are the best.'

The boy winced with pain. He groaned through a wan smile 'It's all right, she's paying me back.'

Wendy guffawed. 'Oh, so you deserve it; the suppository, not the wound my dear. Now rest, keep your foot up. I'll pick you up at six in the morning. I'm on the early hospital shift. You'll have to wait for a bit: X-rays, the bone specialist, then bandaging. Nina, you should leave here about eight o'clock. I can't promise he'll come back with you'.

She noted the agony in both young faces. 'Would you like a moment to yourselves?'

Nina nodded. Wendy kissed each tearful face and slipped out to join a subdued tea-party in the kitchen, hugging Nici and Kim. 'Wait dearest, Nina and Gerald need a little time together. Then you can help them to be brave.'

The children brought them tea. They looked wide-eyed. Suddenly fragility estranged them from their old, confident selves. Gerald's distress was frightening.

'It's only a silly foot.' Kim said.

'Maybe he'll never dance again.' Nina said.

'Or walk.' whispered Kim.

'It's too early. Time, and the hospital, will untangle that question.' said Lettuce. She kissed them and departed for the city.

Nina took Gerald to their room where his brave front evaporated. He crumpled and wept. Despair usurped his dreams and prowess. Now he felt he was nothing. Nina lay beside him and hugged him, burrowing her head into his limp body so as to hide from the looming monsters, and to protect them both.

There was a knock on the door and Sophie entered.

Gerald struggled to separate. 'Sorry.'

'May I come in? Don't move, darling, hugging is often the best medicine of all. You're so frightened I wanted to talk to you.'

She sat lightly beside them, caressing two sets of damp cheeks, and running a finger over the big-dipper edges of their sculpted ears. 'Gerald, I'm so sorry you're wounded. None of us wanted to dent your happiness.'

Nina turned towards her mother whose gentle tone lessened the gap which had lain between them since adolescence.

'I want to tell you a story, a sort of Bunyip story like the one you told Nici which she relayed to me about getting old, which I complain about.

'We have all noticed her provocatively hanging onto Gerald, you poor boy, trying to be friendly but aware of the sexual innuendo. Gerald, I admire the caring way you handled her. She is like her mother, she seizes people she loves whereas Nina remains distanced. You see, my dears, little Nici is as aware of change as you are, at this time of her life exploring without the complications of sex. Gerald, you are old enough to see her behaviour differently. Also she (and I) like the new village you have become, Nina.'

Nina shivered. 'New village? Me?'

Sophie nodded. 'Children make little distinction between fictional and real meaning. You know that. Nici understood it was as much a story about her although it grew from your concerns. We're all pleased you and Gerald have built new selves, in spite of the yearnings to remain unchanged. We delight in your exploring and enjoying all the nooks and crannies of your new selves. The lesson is embedded in your Bunyip story although consequences are skirted. You were uncomfortable, Gerald when I entered?'

The boy nodded shyly.

'It was a natural defence of privacy of feelings, but I wonder whether part of the discomfort is because coming here for a fuck has turned out to be more complicated?'

Gerald and Nina blushed.

'Complications such as you, Gerald, becoming the children's elder brother, sharing their activities with great spirit and by cutting fire-wood (damaging yourself so we're all challenged): joining in family life. We love you for that believe me. And Nina, instead of rushing back to University, stays to help you and us. This is the tangled web of relationships growing from love. Bunyip reminds us change effects everything, inner and outer, acts and appearances.'

Gerald pushed hair off his eyes. 'Are we different, then?'

'Do you feel different?'

'Yes.'

'Then you've changed. Hopefully the new village is a better one. You should look around carefully. You seem to be tackling a huge bundle of change just now, which brings me to my story:

There once was a boy who finished a degree in Music who, instead of engaging in a brilliant career teaching and performing, abandoned music for another career, Medicine, because he wanted to change the world.

One day he was run over by a huge lorry which split his head like an eggshell, leaving it in pieces, his brain trembling, unprotected. Injuries so gross no one thought recovery was possible, everyone believed he was now a vegetable.

He had a wide range of friends one of whom, a doctor, put a team together and fixed the damaged head so it mended, in an operation which, nearly forty years later, remains a mile-stone.

But although mended, the boy had lost his spirit. He walked about like a zombie; he was 'absent' having no expectation, no hope, no joy, unable to love or to live by employing your cud - dling, comfort or tears. He was clinically cured, yet dead.

Bunyip took him to the country, far away where he met

and played with small children who in simple ways gradually made him respond. So, he was slowly cured. I say "simple ways" but that obscures the complexity of the cure. But all I can tell you is by first relating to and then loving the family who took him in, this boy began to revive until he dreamed of returning to his old life.

When his girl came to collect him, she saw little change so she wanted to go. But they persuaded her to stay. In time she found his love and beauty again (and her own).

They returned to their old life as if nothing had happened. Yet the terrible damage and the long cure reminded them both just how mysterious change is, how mysterious is love and how lucky we are to be here.

'Didn't that happen to you and Daddy?'

'It's his story.' Sophie said softly. 'You and Gerald must watch the ancient video of Ossian and Will's dance about it. Then consider whether you should be so fearful about a nail in your foot. And know why all of us are sure whatever Gerald makes of his changed life it will be for the best.'

Long after Sophie had left, Nina gingerly stripped Gerald, licked him erect and carefully straddled him. Shortly he came; she lifted her hips so he could insert fingers into her streaming vagina and tease up orgasms. Lying contentedly beside him she whispered. 'It's even better with a hole in your foot and a bomb up your bum.'

Gerald winced; his foot, his whole body, was throbbing. But happiness counteracted the pain.

Will drove them back from the hospital where Gerald had been pronounced free of serious damage. 'Tim's and Wendy's treatment is perfect. Rest and see the physiotherapist at the end of the week.' he was told.

'You're a duck . .' Tim proclaimed a couple of days later. '. . who's taken to the Ararat water.'

Gerald had thrown himself into work (It was such fun he thought the term a misnomer). He shared some of Nici's lessons with Tim or Sophie or Nina or Peter, dealing with maths, sociology, English, biology and geography. Never had he adventured through such rich landscapes with so much study and argument. 'I've never made love to my teacher.' he grinned gleefully at Nina one afternoon when she seduced him as a wild man.

'Another nook and cranny. Oh, G I need you.' she held his spent body as it softened.

Gerald was drafted to help Will with dancing activities everyone participated in. For a few days Gerald sprawled on a couch cheering them on; he learned to be gentle with Kim and Nestor, remembering how as a tiny tot he'd been bullied by bigger kids. They warmed to his skill in talking through music so dancing followed. He was bemused by Tim's bassoon. 'Such polite farts,' he bubbled. Much to Tim's amusement he hobbled up and began a rude bum-dance, as Nestor called it, which incited Tim to additional farty notes, until the two small boys gleefully joined in.

Gerald was stunned by the dance video. 'That's how I want to dance. You're brilliant.' he said. 'Why did you stop?'

Will smiled. 'I found other ways to express myself I suppose.' Gerald's admiration prodded him to admit worshipping Tim as a boy. 'I still love him. Some things can't be said. That's why I danced them. Nina has courage and uses words, Tim and Ossian use music, Nina also. Her various talents are what we seek here.'

Gerald gasped. 'Is love part of the curriculum?'

'Of course, the mind and the body and our feelings become talents when engaged with love.' Tim replied coming behind him and embracing him. Gerald shivered with excitement. He longed to be loved. Here, he was held in its soft thrall, in uncontrollable joy, falling for everything.

Nici half-knew his ardour and clung to him for it. She often lay with him in the afternoons when pain gnawed, reading and talking, running errands with tea and messages while Nina practised in the music room.

One day she supervised his bath, laughing as he awkwardly splashed in, his damaged foot in the air. 'Like an emu bathing.' she decided. She inspected his body in silence as she dried it. 'Make yours stiff like Kimmy and Nestor.' Taking his penis in her hand she marvelled as it grew, too immersed to be shy. 'Does Nina like you because of this?'

'I like her because of it.' he whispered red-faced. 'No more, Nici, please.'

Nici saw his confusion. 'Do you let her?'

'Yes. But that's different. We should stop. Let's be friends,

Nic. It's best to try to be happy, eh?'

'Will you live here always?'

'I'll come and see you often and often, if you like.'

Nina watched him dress and then led him hobbling to his bed. She lay close and hugged him for a long time as he was in pain. 'We all want you to stay. We love you so don't cry.'

He gasped. 'Love is hard. And leaving. And life.'

'There, there. Don't cry.' Nici snuggled and cooed.

Nina discovered them fast asleep. She was shocked by his tear-encrusted face; shocked by the dazzling smiles they greeted her with; shocked by her envious thought, Are *we* as beautiful as that? Shocked with the realisation the woman in her was now driving.

Gerald's cure was manifold. The hospital proclaimed him out of danger, sending him home with exercises to strengthen the damaged tissue. He was as loathe as Nina to leave and readily agreed to prolong their stay a week.

'IF you both work.' cautioned Lettuce gladdened by their happy telephone call.

Nina then rang Aileen who gave her tutorial and lecture work. Then she invited the members of the OstrAu quartet down for the following week-end with the tempting explanation, 'For once Mohammed must come to the mountain.'

They worked resolutely. One break she took Gerald along the river, the suppository suppressing the pain, their spirits danced with the busy water.

'This is where I started.' she pointed as they rested, rugged-up against the chill wind, to a grassy hollow where Phil and she had had intercourse. 'I swam there all my life. I want to show you.'

He wanted her. More than sex. More than he could say. Blindly he hugged this fabulous girl who had helped him become, what he was not sure. But he felt born (coming-out was not quite a sacred enough description), he had found a happiness unimaginable; not only feeling wholed, but the joy of sharing all his selves while feasting off her various selves so together they were a jig-saw of boy-girl-woman-man.

She marvelled at his worship; it reflected, uncomfortably, her own. For she had explored him, mastering her disdain, tapping into her lusty curiosity until - with Lettuce's support - she risked letting him in only to discover the depth of her longing, her satisfaction and her growing love with its celebration of he-ness and she-ness, the "blacks and whites" she had only dreamed of. 'It's the he-in-she I shared with Fiona and the she-in-he in Gerald, working with the he and the she in each of us which brings a solidity.' she said to herself watching illusive emotions twinkle in his boyish face so she wanted to hold the baby and the giant.

'You make me beautiful.' he whispered. 'Can boys be that?'

'Boys are babies and giants. The huge and the fragile, ugly and beautiful which I feel with you.'

'Is that what girls are?'

She caressed his face, then felt down his tough dancer's body, down his firm thighs and hips which sometimes bruised her, lingering on his swelling fly.

'I am glad it wants me.'

'I need to be inside you.'

'Then we can speak ourselves.'

'Then it begins to make sense.'

'Perhaps it's the only thing that does?'

'I love you, Nina. Can you love me a little?'

'I do, silly, don't you know? More than anyone. You give me so much. Sometimes it's all I want. And I worry about being trapped yet free. It's, it's . .'

She watched a late butterfly delicately clinging to a reed shaken by the wind until relaxing, it allows itself to be blown away over the river to vanish in the tangled Bush beyond. 'It's being able to be full of myself. And loving you till it hurts.'

'"A hole in your foot, a bomb up your bum."' he guffawed.

'Exactly.' she moaned. 'You've become my better half.'

'You're mine.'

Long, fragrant kisses. Overwhelming desire. But they do not strip. There is more they want to say. So they long and laugh, waiting for the velvet cloak of night to delve in and deliver themselves. With this frisson, work is thoroughly done.

Feeling a new freedom, each connects more easily. He savours an erotic closeness to Tim and Nici. She relaxes with Miranda and her mother as well as allowing the innocent intrusions of her clamouring nephews and niece.

The bright steadiness of the welcome settled the OstrAu quartet members who were a trifle nervous about confronting both the legendary bassoonist and his brilliant son Ossian.

Miranda and Nina prepared supper for everyone. It was a noisy feast. Eugene seemed withdrawn and retired early. Wanting to comfort him Nina gave-up her early morning slot in the music room. Cheery talk continued, but shortly afterwards she slipped away with Gerald; neither, able to wait any longer.

Inspite of, or because of, the night's delights, Gerald woke and slipped out of bed shortly after dawn. He pushed a suppository up his arse, clambered into clothes and padded to the music room.

The floor near the high windows was smeared with early shadowed sunshine. The back of the room was still gloomy. Gerald lay on the floor waiting for the pain to dull, watching the shadows shorten and the majesty of grass, trees and water shine as the sun rose far to the invisible left over wooded hills whose haze he and Nina had enjoyed.

Eugene came in unseeing. He layed down his violin case, sauntered to the window and moodily looking out as life blushed into the serene landscape. His head rested on the glass. His shoulders and back expressed unhappiness. Gerald, unlocked his instrument and took it to the grieving man. 'Eugene. Play and feel better.'

'I'm not good in the morning.'

'Play.' the boy whispered.

'There's nothing that says it.'

'Then you put it into the music.'

They looked at one another. What stirred blushed their faces. The boy retreated to the neutrality of floor, lay down and waited. After a silence the violin screamed out fragments of the joyful prelude to Bach's solo sonata in E major. This was overtaken by a glittering tearful gasping fragment of melody gradually overshadowing the Bachian stream. Then a reflective waltz, of gentle clarity once again blotted out by the the same tears. The third movement began with jokey pizzicato, leading to a childlike dream finishing tearfully with a yearning fifth. Then all hell broke loose. The violin screeched and sawed, crying, lamenting, bleeding waterfalls of fragmented melody blundering towards an inevitable cadential ending. Then silence.

Eugene looked at Gerald. Each near tears. They knew such

suffering. Like the suppository, the music had dulled the pain.

'Fantastic.' Gerald whispered. 'The most fantastic music I've ever heard.' He got up and awkwardly took Eugene's arm. 'Let me dance it,? Eugene, play it again?'

'It's so difficult. I don't know if I can. Eugene drew a few deep breaths before plunging into Hell.

Gerald was spellbound.

After recovering Eugene muttered. 'It's the second solo sonata in A minor by Ysaye, too hard to play in public.'

'You say so, but you're magnificent.' Nina said as, with Will, she stumbled down the stairs to Gerald.

Eugene sighed. 'So, you want to dance?'

Gerald stood looking out into the awakening world. He flexed his body and nodded.

The music lifts the dancer into high-flung pirouettes, flying cartwheels and gyrating steps, arms out-flung over the entire space (unbound life) until stilled by the first pause when, gripped by death agony, he escapes again flying into life. The second pause brings freedom constricted, and enfeebled escape ending in a choreography of flight.

The second movement: the dancer waltzes gracefully with sensitive gestures but increasingly frail, finishing as a broken bird on one leg (the undamaged one) with bent knee to which the head gradually reaches, to rest there as the figure sinks on one leg with its last breath, head dying on a crooked knee. Stillness accompa - nied by a long interval of a perfect fifth on the violin.

The third movement astounded Nina and Will:

The dancer bounces to the bouncing plucked strings, it is all knee-work, the arms tight to the body until bowing recom - mences, when the arms drift out like awakening branches until the 'Dies irae' (a very ancient melody of death) intrudes to push the tree-dancer down back to the floor to sit immobile, avidly listening and watching the violin sobbing out its longing, as if at this point only listening is possible. The music slips back into a beat of three with majestic sighs of death and a yearning, prolonged octave. Only then, the dancer rises signalling the last movement.

*Allegro furioso whips the dancer into a fury of gymnastic
activity, leaping over the entire space, flying with cartwheels and
somersaults, spinning in circles, almost falling, arms flying out in
martyrdom. A spiky Dies irae unleashes clouds of invisible spears
or bullets; the unprotected body raked and shivering. The last
recapitulation of the opening thrashes the dancer with all the pain
of impact He whirls round , throws himself through the air, driven
back, back, back towards the player, dying with each backward
leap until with the final chords he falls dead at the violinist's feet.*

The boy lay as dead, panting, quite wrung out. Eugene
picked him up and carried him to a couch where, smiling slightly
through his pain, Gerald reassured them he was all right.

Eugene bent over. 'Thank you for dancing me. Thank you for
making it bearable, making it visible.'

Will wept. 'My grief exposed. And to dare leave the music
un-danced is real bravery. It was the most amazing performance.
Ossian and I are amateurs compared to you. You both do the impossible. Nothing in the world could ever be better.'

Nina crouched over Gerald and whispered. 'Is it that bad?'

He floated in grey eyes. 'Not now, having you. But.'

Eugene blinked. 'Yes it is.'

Nina looked into the shimmering blue of his eyes. 'But you
have everything: beauty, talent, feelings and the most amazing
technique. Eugene?'

He shrugged. 'Always emptiness.'

Will shuddered. He grasped Eugene's shoulder. 'Don't listen
to those voices. There is never nothing. I wanted to tell Nick
Jacobson. We *can* find a door out, a freedom-door. Never, never,
never give in!'

Eugene was deeply touched. They cared and knew his pain.

'Breakfast.' said Nina hopefully. She helped Gerald to stand.
They made their way slowly up the stairs with Will. Eugene packed
his violin in its case and followed. The attentive way Nina helped
her wounded boy cut him. 'If only someone would help me.'

The involvement of the family mollified Eugene. It was
crowned by the admiring children. He softened under their squirming limpet-like attentions. Gerald was a tiny bit put-out, but Nina
made up for that.

Ossian listened intently to the Ysaye sonata. 'There is another quality beside what one calls style. I am reminded of pianists who are drawn to Chopin because of the pianistic naturalness of his music, also the arid flurries in the natural flute writing of Qantz. Each reminds me of Ysaye where technique brings an additional quality to its style in much the same way that Bach's fugal skill takes *The 48* beyond his baroque style.'

Eugene wallowed in musical intimacy with Ossian. 'I think I know what you mean.' he said excitedly. 'There are places where I feel, Yes, music and technique coincide, when it's the violin rather than the composer who speaks.'

Ossian grew excited. 'I wonder whether that 'other' speaks to dancers, whether the voice of the instrument gets limbs and minds working? As if unconsciously they hear that coincidence you mentioned? Ossian looked carefully at the score. 'I've been thinking about naturalness for ages. You have focused me. Thanks. I'm working on a concerto for chamber orchestra and string quartet where each instrument has an opportunity to speak for itself. Could Lettuce choreograph it? I'm a one-eyed wind-player so would you help me with the string parts?'

Disbelievingly Eugene nodded.

'I'll get Nina to bring you over to my studio.'

Eugene, still smarting warmly from the squirming children was doubly flattered. 'I'd love that.'

'I wondered if we then might have a run through down here - a music fest weekend - with a scratch orchestra and the OstrAu members? Trees, the only audience.'

Eugene blushed, here was a real dream, an unselfconscious performance. (One of those doors Will had spoken of).

Everyone returned to the city refreshed.

Lettuce's school Dance Day approached. She wanted Gerald to dance the Ysaye. But he insisted on dancing Bach. He and Nina were so happy Lettuce relented with the challenging proposal the day might finish with Ysaye. 'If you can manage so much.'

'Yippee.' cried Gerald. Both? Brilliant. I can do it.'

'Lettuce kissed him. 'Yes, Gerald, you *are* very good.'

Lettuce put the word around to the Trustees and the critics a treat was in store for them. All the children had heard the rumours about the transformation of that scowling boy into a real dancer.

Because everyone participated, because it was the school's annual show-case, excitement shimmered. Gerald was apprehensive because teachers from the Dance Academy would be there assessing scholarship options.

Just before he went on Nina pulled him into the green room, fell on his neck, caressed his tense body, kissed him passionately and whispered 'My sweet, you'll be fine. Dance just for me because I love you.'

Some of the older children winked. 'So that's why he works hard . . . hard - I bet, ha ha, she keeps it up.'

But his intensity, his coaching work with Lettuce and his enthusiasm led most of them to wish him luck. One or two even had inklings of how much he needed to escape to the Academy, so cheered him on.

The Bach performance, a sensitive series of elegant Baroque dances danced with grace and inventiveness won warm applause. Lettuce, bringing them bouquets as they bowed whispered. 'No problems, my dears,' and led them to the edge of the stage for a last bow. Gerald was untroubled for the rest of the event, before the Ysaye.

Eugene was unsettled, running late, as he seldom did.

Lettuce provided a moment for the two to settle as she made her annual speech about the school concluding, 'Now to finish we have something special: two talented performers who have pushed their art to limits of what is possible. They will risk everything here, because we are one family. Sometimes those dancing on tight ropes fall. That is no shame. Remember Gerald recently had a serious accident. Also, Eugene would not normally play this hugely demanding sonata in public. But I ask you all to consider the magic brew of mixing live dance with live music, consider how wonderfully each illuminates the other, consider this basic tenet of our belief in collaboration. The arts, like life must involve all disciplines, all aspects, all peoples: narrow mindedness out-performed and great risks taken towards a new reality.'

The virtuosic performance was watched with horror and wonder. The impossible shook them all: its beauty, its rage, its fiery death, its life beyond words. The dance critic wept. Others blinked in tearful disbelief. Like love or life or dreams, the impossible had happened. Hope and beauty reined.

There was stunned silence when Gerald died at Eugene's feet and the final chords ended this glimpse of hell. Then, a roar: feet and hands and voices. Lettuce was sure the roof lifted. She stood watching her two young gods take hands and walk to the front of the stage whether weeping tears or sweat she couldn't tell. It was a triumph. She watched them bow and disappear into the wings.

There, Nina stood weeping and laughing. She held the two fragile, wonderful men soothing and calming beating hearts. Then she gently took the violin and bow and pushed them back into the thunderous applause. Eugene's baby was silent. Its fit had passed. The power hidden in its varnished shell, slept. It was the power she held between her legs when she played music or love. A useless and essential thing which must be skillfully played to entice its magic out. "Blacks and whites", she knew them now.

Nina was radiant when the two returned. She looked at them so hungrily they began grinning during the last bow: "Blacks and whites" coexisted, they also realised.

22-

ANGELICA'S HAPPINESS was full yet she occasionally allowed the tiny urge to have children. One lazy morning, she cuddled her man. 'I am so happy, now, with my prince and beggar boy. So happy.'

Her prince, or was it the beggar boy? straddled her and whispered. 'So, will you marry me?'

Angelica gave a little cry. 'Oh my own treasure, YES.'

He thundered into her filling her with warm stars until they were too twinkling to say anything else.

Rose suggested they combine weddings; first at the registry office and then a joint celebration. Ray and Kiffy paid for a honey moon at a nature reserve where Rose and Ant could swim, sail, tramp along the coast and into the interior. They had a hut with a timber walkway onto the beach and a bar-b-q outside where they cooked and feasted with swarms of mosquitoes, hungrily busy on still nights. Not that that worried the honey-mooners much.

Tim and Sophie agreed to Ossian's idea of honey-mooning in Venice. Angelica was over the moon, longing to explore the glories of that floating city with her dearest man, using her other, their other, language. 'Italian, the language of music, of love, art, architecture, cuisine.' she whispered. 'Oh my darling one, can our life start? Are we together at last? Will you make a *piccolo* Ossian and a *grande* symphony for us all? He will play music in your studio and then learn about the world with Lettuce and me.' Laughing at the generous disbelieving smile lighting Ossian's face.

She wanted nothing else. She engulfed him in her love.

Tasmin Baker and his close musical friends noticed a new energy in Ossian's music. 'In this shitty world, he manages to find solace and to remind us there is still much to embrace and enjoy. He champions life, bless him.'

23-

OSSIAN AND ANGELICA were whisked away from the wedding celebration to the air port where they boarded a plane to Venice.

They landed. The day was whipped by a fretful wind scuffing the grey lagoon, rocking the motor boats waiting to take poetic passengers to the "towered city" beyond the mist.

Ossian had been reading *The Stones of Venice* which had convinced him they should approach the floating city not by land but by water, and via Torcello, "Mother and daughter, both in their widowhood" as Ruskin wrote.[*]

'It has to be a sad start to our time here, remember, our future also started sadly.' he murmured, leading his wife to a *motoscafo* at the ugly concrete quay of the Venice airport. 'Look. See "the multitude of towers scattered among the shapes of clustered palaces, that fretwork to the southern sky."' he spoke as Ruskin.

Angelica looked lovingly at his wind-buffed face thinking, If Venice is half as beautiful as my husband, I'll be satisfied.'

But there was nothing to be seen. Only the grey expanse of water marked by lines of stakes, many at crazy angles, marking the invisible channels across the lagoon. A steely wind cut their faces, shivering the face of the freezing lagoon so the reflected poles became squirming sea snakes straining from each pole leering towards them as they passed. Low smudges of mud oozed and broke the leaden water, places for sea birds, not the heavy tramp of pirates or of other men. Then a higher smudge broke the monotony.

'Torcello.' breathed Ossian. Its famous tower proudly proclaimed this human outpost in the watery wilderness. High reeds massed each side of the channel. Beyond a ramshackle landing a few rooves and a small stone bridge became visible for a

---

[*]   See notes at end.

few moments until engulfed in reeds and lengthening distance as the taxi pushed onward.

Angelica uncomfortably slipped backwards into past times. Times of pirates, of treasure, of hide and seek, of huge ships' booty and the mysterious silence of restless water reminding her of the beginning of the world:

> In the beginning . . . the earth was without form . . .
> and the spirit of God moved upon the face of the
> waters, and God said. 'Let there be light.' and there
> was light . . . and God said. 'Let there be a firmament
> in the midst of the waters and let it divide the waters
> from the waters '. . . and it was so. *

She was witnessing the beginnings of the world and of their marriage, from the magic sea where dreams spring, of all their hopes and fears in the nothingness expanse of their lives. In her struggle for Ossian into her adult life, Angelica had abandoned her Italian connections to become wrapped in a swirling dreamy landscape they learned to embrace; but now everything coalesced. She blushed with fire whipped by the breeze as well as with the intensity of her inner spirit. All realities existed: the real and the reflection, mist, mud and firm land, dreams and the every day, separation in their unity, joy after pain. She knew he shared her ecstacy.

'Look there. The towers of campanile and palazzo.' he whispered as a long shadow metamorphosed into Venice as the bells and palaces she had sought in him glittered and chimed as she clung to him weeping so the hardy boatmen were less surly helping them to disembark, one delaying his snack-break so as to whistle-up a small motor taxi which would take "The bellisima honeymoon children" to Calle Larga 22 Marzo - the stop nearest their hotel.

The driver was a boy, blue with cold whose gentle smile heartened the weary travellers.

'That's my brother's name.' Ossian shouted into the wind as Antonio deftly spun his boat around and bounded along the ugly coast of quays and the rude backs of buildings, past the glowering Arsenal through its dockyard canal and out into the glory of the main St Mark's basin where he then sauntered following the Riva degli Schiavoni quay past The Doges' Palace, past St Marks' Square

---

*   See notes at end.

and on into the busy traffic of the Grande Canal spurred by his excited passengers to point out the finest landmarks; emboldened both by their eloquent Italian and their joy.

Antonio had just inherited his sickly father's boat. It was fun being your own boss. But lonely work. He was hungry. He longed to share the vitality of his passengers; yearned to be warm and fed and keep his childish dreams of well being poverty and a cruel winter were stripping him of.

Antonio slowed the boat, turned into a narrow canal called Rio della Albero between two palazzos with lacey marble facades and wended his way to landing steps beside a low footbridge where he threw a hawser over a spike, took their bags and ferried Ossian and Angelica along dusky narrow lanes and into the courtyard of a small hotel around whose minute garden a number of blocks of rooms were situated.

'Yes, Signor Doctore e Signora Macknight are expected, and welcome.' the concierge cooed, waving a bent old man to take their bags to the honeymoon suite with a view of the Grand canal (if you stood on a chair and peered awkwardly out of the window) while the pair ordered hot cappuccini for themselves and Antonio, despite the startled expression on the barman's face (boatmen belonged on the water not here he believed). Angelica took the bashful boy and pulled off his nylon jacket finding only a threadbare shirt. She grimaced and said in English. 'Ossian we must get the boy a jumper. He needs it.'

But he understood and blushed with shamed pleasure. Ah, she is an angel, he thought, saying. 'Shall I pick you up tomorrow and show you the official as well as my private Venice?'

Ossian demurred. 'Antonio, please give us a day. Come the next day. I want just to mooch around on foot. It's my way of arriving.' He handed him a scrunched-up bank note - the fee plus a handsome tip.

Antonio smiled, grateful no change was required, delighted with the tryst with his new friends. He was hugged goodbye by each. Filled with longing and cheer, he bounded back to his boat impervious to the cold. His smiles enticed many others into his craft before the day was done. He was charmed. Pleasure danced in his dark Venetian eyes mirroring the canals.

Love danced in the honeymooners' eyes that evening after

supper. They stood at the window of their room watching the mist gather, obscuring buildings and haloing lights, softening the bare trees in the bare garden. Angelica caressed Ossian's neck and ran questing fingers down into his crotch delighting in his arousal.

He stood as soft hands stripped him of his clothes and soft lips trailed over his skin and his wife's ebuliant hair tickled his thighs as she nestled savouring his stiffening.

Soon they bounced the bed until suddenly he erupted and fell on her.

'Always want me like this.' she whispered. 'Oh, Ossian it's wonderful with you. Here together. At last. And no dead letters.'

He kissed her gently, their lips delighting in responsive contact. They drifted away into a misted sleep and only wakened when the maid brought in their breakfast trays.

After breakfast they donned warm clothes and ventured out, crossed the misty Calle larga 22 Marzo and made their way down the crooked Calle delle Veste to the Fenice Theatre recently restored after a disastrous fire.

'Let's book for Rossini's *Figaro*. You'll love its highjinks.' he told her.

Angelica nodded happily. 'Then I'd like to buy you some trendy clothes to hide your beauty from other admirers.'

Ossian grinned. 'They're all talk here and no action. I'd like to buy you something swish to show-off yours, since we have those posh red chairs in the stalls.'

They had coffee and pastry in a busy cheery Trattoria nearby where they booked dinner after the opera at the end of the week.

They sauntered back to the shops glowing along the March 22nd Calle where Ossian accepted a blue-black high-necked soft wool jumper, a tight, stretchy pair of trousers, matching sox and a well-cut leather jacket; and Angelica blushingly accepted a long slinky deep purple dress which fitted her so beautifully it had to be accompanied - advised the shop assistant - by a leather and silver belt, navy stockings and a richly coloured head scarf and matching stole. They found a thick rugged purple-blue jumper on the 'Sale' table which they took for Antonio, also three woolly hats, one for each of them.

Since all the bags were to be delivered to their hotel (not quite the standard expected by the assistant) Ossian and Angelica wandered unencumbered in the direction of the Accadamia Bridge along winding Calle's, on bridges humped over winter-sheened canals leading to open Campo's lined by high mouldering tenements from which children erupted to run and play football until hunger drove them indoors.

Ossian and Angelica discovered a small restaurant packed with long bare wood tables. They squeezed in with all the rowdy locals and ate a hearty lunch washed down with wine from a generous glass jug, proclaiming every order for food.

The locals' curiosity over so handsome and Italiantate a pair was eventually rewarded when she admitted they were just married and on their honeymoon; the wine flowed faster than water and the big-boosomed proprietor supplied free *tiramisü*. 'It means pick-me-up.' Ossian gurgled to his tipsy wife. Toasts were drunk until everyone tumbled out and weaved canal-like away, the honeymooners dancing along the narrow calles and out into the spacious Campo S.Stefano, relieved it was no longer used for bull-fights.

They were taken with a shop jutting into the square.
'Look at those clothes.' cried Angelica in amazement.They guffawed over the extreme wildness of brilliant glittering cod-pieces, elephantine suits, weird shirts and dresses which made carnival dress seem conservative. Everything was gross, as if made for over-sexed puppets in some appaling tragicomedy.

'Rose would freak-out.' said Ossian laughing in admiration at the theatricality of the collection. 'I'll buy the codpiece for Will.'

But Angelica was far away hop-scotching over the paving stones. He bounded after her.

The dance led onward, following arrows saying 'Accademia' to its imposing wooden bridge. They stood at its centre overlooking the Grand canal.

'Now THIS is Venice.' Ossian breathed watching the business of boats crowding the grubby water and the drunken palazzos and other buildings marking its course. 'It's a modern day Canaletto. Ugly, beautiful and lively.'.

They crossed over to inspect the facade of the Accadamia Gallery.

'It's closed. We'll have to visit another day. Now, let's take a *vaporetto* back to St. Mark's Square.' cried Angelica happily. 'And explore that end before going home.' He bought tickets. They clambered down the floating pier to await a Number 1 *vaporetto* sitting in the front seats, eyes watering in the chill wind, with a very few other hardy travellers, as the boat bustled down past the motley buildings miraculously having so many features in common there was a sense of unity in ebullient variety.

St.Mark's Piazza had stacks of wooden tables at various points which someone told them would be set up should *acque alte* (flooding) occur. The basilica was almost empty. It brooded in gold~green tessellated shadow, its undulating floor dancing with multi-coloured marble shapes. 'Gabrielli and Monteverdi wrote music here exploiting its difficult echo.' Ossian whispered.

'It looks as if it were carved out of solid, rather than being constructed from myriad bits like other buildings.' breathed Angelica feeling for the solidity of her man in reassurance of his uniqueness. Ossian turned, smiled and kissed her. Then they left to explore the twisting lanes lying beyond, bursting with trattoria, gift and souvenir shops, clothes and antiques, finding in Laga San Marco a gallery filled with sculptures made of glass.

'These would look well in my studio, lit by the sun.' Ossian said to the girl at the desk. 'I'll return later.'

She offered a special discount on several sculptures of musicians and booked for them the *Trattoria alla Scala* nearby which specialised in local cuisine and personal *campiello* service.

They returned to their hotel to shower, to make love and to fall into a soft doze warmed through and through.

That evening they dressed in their new clothes, donning warm coats for it was chilly. They window-shopped all the crooked way to Piazza San Marco and sauntered along the collonade watching the *bora*-whipped tourists gawk at the campanile and be blown towards the wider wilderness of the waterfront and Harry's Bar.

Angelica and Ossian waited for the clockwork Moors to strike the bell in the *Torre dell 'Orologio*.

'We must hurry. Our table is booked for now.' Ossian said.

'Don't worry, darling. Venetians will not begrudge a few minutes.' said Angelica smiling, yet shivering so they hurried away to supper under the stairs.

'Luckily not under the stars.' Ossian mused stumbling into the small warm, pink and cream trattoria filled with pictures and shining glasses, where the Maestro took their coats and breathlessly led them to a table, delighted with so elegant a pair.

'They are foreign film stars.' he whispered to his wine waiter who was nonplussed enough by their Italian to probe.

'No. Ossian responded. I'm a musician, you may have seen one of my CD's. I'm not working here, this is our honeymoon. Our Italian? Well my wife is half-Italian and of course it's the language of love and of music.'

The establishment preferred the truth. Romance and Venice had long been coupled. Anyway, CD's were a music-equivalent of stardom, they agreed. Such radiant well-dressed beauty enhanced the trattoria , their story bringing tears to romantic eyes and extra wine from many of the neighbouring tables.

The Maestro attentively recommended local fare: *fegato alla veneziana* and *risotto nero,* with *Raboso,* then *fritto misto di mare, salate misto* with *Prosecco* which sparkled in long elegant glasses, going straight to their heads. Both began muddling English and Italian to everyone's amusement.

A swarthy gipsy entered with a basket of freezing clenched red roses (from some distant clime). Ossian was prevailed upon to buy one for his lovely new wife who blushed like the flower and secretly squeezed his leg under the table.

The meal finished with *due espressi* and a tart lemon pie, all they could fit in. As they left the Maestro cautioned them about a predicted winter high tide which might submerge Piazza San Marco. 'But around La Fenice the land is higher. Your feet should stay dry.'

Angelica murmured. 'My parents run a small trattoria, but it is not in this class. We've had an exceptional evening. Thank you. Yes, we'll certainly come again. Good night.'

They ambled back along misted, twisting lanes, crossing humped bridges over the restless waters gnawing at quays and foundations. Ossian paused on one small humped bridge to savour the seductive patterns, leaned into Angelica's undulating body and kissed her with unending passion. She felt his erection arching through layers of clothes ignoring the chill in its hot desire. 'I love you, Angelica.' he whispered overwhelmed by mist.

'I have everything I will ever want, only take me back and fill me.' she whispered, looking into his soft grey eyes and burning with love making the rose tremble in her excited fist.

24-

THEY HAD HARDLY BREAKFASTED when Antonio was announced. They ordered him up to their hotel room, stripped off his ugly plastic work-coat and presented the boy with his new jumper. 'Fantastic.' they crooned as Antonio blushed and stammered firstly refusal and then thanks. He joined them in the mirror deciding to his genuine surprise they *all* looked rather handsome.

'We are the three wise kings of Venice.' Ossian cried hugging them both. (It sounds finer in Italian). They donned their new woolly hats and strutted down past startled hotel staff out into the calle, to the boat moored beside the Albero bridge. Antonio turned his boat in the narrow congested canal and puttered away into the *Canål Grande* pointing out the famous facades, the Rialto bridge and beyond to the railway station. Then Angelica persuaded him to motor to the famous equestrian statue of Colleoni.

'Bartolomeo Colleoni beside San Zanipolo on the Rio dei Mendicante.' Antonio said mentally forming a complex plan of the canal-journey. He returned along the Grand canal; nearing the Rialto bridge made a left turn into a minor canal beside the post office building and expertly negotiated the over-occupied canals, under bridges where often they had to duck down, to eventually arrive at a landing stage in front of the city hospital shared by the church of Santi Giovanni e Påolo which dominated its narrow campo.

'I thought it was called Giovanni e Påolo, not Zanipolo.' said Ossian. 'Someone's made a mistake.'

'We Venetian have another name for it like many other things.' Antonio smiled. 'Welcome to our private Venice. Look, there is Bartolomeo and his horse.* Visit the church too. I'll wait for you.'

---

* See notes at end.

Angelica and Ossian clambered out.

'Wow. Look at those facades.' Ossian gasped. 'Look at the false perspective and how the collonade of semi-circular arches unites the facades of the hospital and church. Coducci was the architect. Ant told me I had to pay special attention to his work. He is the genius of delicacy Ant says. He designed San Zaccaria and the cemetery chapel on San Michele where Stravinsky lies.'

'It's like Venetian lace-work.' said Angelica.

Their inspection of the statue, the famed general riding resolutely into battle was hurried by the chill *bora* which blew them into the cavernous church where music echoed.

'That's Gabrielli.' Ossian whispered. 'But not very accomplished.' He sighed at the blunders of pitch, notes and muddied stereophony. But he led Angelica to the western wall to show her Paulo Veranese's painting of the *Adorazione dei pastori*.

'It's a rude two-story manger.' she murmured.

'Filled with bloody angels.'

'And all those muscled workmen and a couple, or three kings? Mary is matronly, Joseph grandfatherly, but the baby is cute looking past his mother towards his future in the sky.'

'I think Joseph is energetically hugging the lowing cow; the donkey behind will carry Christ into Jerusalem in due course.' Ossian whispered.

'Darling, Joseph is old, the accepting (infertile) partner of the Virgin.' she said. 'The donkey and cow are in most manger pictures. Look at the left hand shepherd bowing or dancing, about to step onto the lamb so scrunched up as if leg-tied (tongue-tied), trapped by the sacred ordinary.'

'The slaughtered lamb of God? And the straining man with the walking stick. John a baptist-shepherd? looking away into the same enticing sky as the baby but frailer; as mortal as the lamb, as focussed as the baby, aware of the irony of the celebration: opulence in so ruinous a place. The jewels of Venice sparkling on the mud.' Ossian said, becoming irritated. 'Darling, can I see what on earth they're playing.' He strode down the isle towards the high altar and a band of musicians with early music instruments.

Ossian frowned at them. 'Gabrielli did not write that.' The leader looked up at so authoritative an opinion, thinking to silence it, handed over a facsimile of the Renaissance score. But the stranger looked keenly at the score, nodded and said. 'You see, here and here and here, the sackbutts have G Sharps; the annotator has mistaken the sharp sign as a quaver sign, easy enough; but it is above, not beside the note. Change the timing and the pitch and it will sound wonderful.'

There was a hurried conferring. Pencils were produced, changes made. Ossian then raised his hands without a thought and conducted. The sound rang through the shadowy heights of the nave with a far more enchanting timbre and improved ensemble. Everyone smiled.

Then he borrowed one of the reeded instruments and blew. A loud sweet~harsh sound filled the church. 'That's how you should finish together.' Ossian said. 'You need to strongly support the sound with a very tight diaphragm. Stand up and try the last *tutti* again.'

A sweet roar filled the church making everyone there stop and turn curiously at this call.

The German students were dazzled by the music Ossian had winkled out of them and implored him to make further changes.

'You probably know that Gabrielli had to contend with an insistent echo in St. Mark's. He used the architectural space distributing his musicians to mimic each other and to accompany the echoing basilica.[*] We should separate so the audience can see and hear two distinct sources; and play slightly slower *marcato* to allow the echo here to creep back and enhance your sound.'

'Let's move our chairs.' said the leader doubtfully (knowing such a distance would make ensemble impossible).

Then Ossian carefully tuned them to the least variable of the reeds, waited until they had settled and conducted the entire piece without a score, dancing and directing so every single player felt he was the sole concern of the conductor, and played every phrase as required by eloquent direction. Then at the last *tutti* the band stood and roared out the ending section so the stones and the light danced and the vast spaces sang. Two old women fell to their knees in prayer responding to the voice of God.

The leader shook his head. 'So you know the piece?
'I looked at it with you beforehand.'

---

[*]   See notes at end.

'But that's impossible: to memorise it at a glance.'

'Not for me.'

All the band were silent; astounded. Music had been wrung from them by this slight, handsome man who knew exactly what to do. One of the cheekiest ventured. 'Vould you conduct us tomorrow in ze concert?' His friends all nodded appealingly.

Ossian couldn't resist. 'Give me the scores. One last rehearsal, then we'll see.'

He took a bundle of music and embarassedly joined Angelica who was watching.

'I'm sorry darling. Forgive me?'

Angelica laughed and hugged him. 'Silly billy, of course. You have made this dreary old barn sing. Anyway, how could I deny you such a dream-come-true?' She dragged him into the cold outside where Antonio was shivering in his shivering boat. Bartolomeo and his bronze horse shivering in sympathy.

'Antonio, you will bring Angelica and come to the concert tomorrow at three. There will be free tickets for both of you.' Ossian said as the boat thrashed down the canal and watery music ricocheted off stone walls.

They ate a snack at a bar near the Albero bridge. Then Antonio bounded off looking for passengers while the honey-mooners went back to their hotel where Ossian studied the music, then crept into bed beside his warm wife, finding solace and sleep.

The following afternoon Antonio stuffed his ugly coat in a locker on the boat and allowed himself to be led into the church wearing contempt-proof armour, his sea-purple jumper. Politely they were shown seats towards the front, with one of the stone columns of the nave at their backs.

Ossian explained to the audience the programme had been changed, that all the music from northern Europe would come first, with the players in one group, followed by the Venetian pieces, when the band would split into two sections, the customs of the times the music was written.

Antonio enjoyed the singing folk flavour of the first half; he smiled in admiration as Ossian dance-directed the musicians, smiled and shared Angelica's pleasure and pride, smiled with the childish whimsy tickling him. The second half was different. Sound came from two far places and mingled with the huge space like a loving argument, almost a battle, leaving him increasingly breathless. Its warmth and the slightly warmed church softened the hard knot from work and poverty growing inside him.

The final music was Giovanni Gabrielli's *Concertante for San Marco*. Its dazzling arguments, mirrored both by each set of players and by the building, flung him about on waves of wonder. Antonio almost saw the little speeches, the ripostes, the teasing and the sleepy almost profound echoes holding him in thrall. He looked this way and that, left to right and then up to the shadowy heights of the nave, snared by singing threads. Then the players stood.

Antonio struggled to stand and, restrained by the gentle hand of Angelica, looked around noticing the audience remained seated. He shrunk into his uncomfortable chair as the combined choirs of instruments blurted out a magnificent unified hymn of hope filling the cavernous church and embracing him, shouting that the glories of Heaven were here on earth and he, Antonio could partake. He hung his head and wept. Someone gently took his hand and squeezed it companionably; someone stayed with him as the audience clapped and eventually left, until he was able to stand and be led by Angelica to the Rosary Chapel where ordinary men were packing up instruments and music stands, and talking in normal cheerful terms.

Ossian felt his joyful distress keenly (had it not been his own for so long?) He smiled. 'I'm so glad you came, was it what you expected?'

Antonio shook his swimming head, trying to wake from a dream. 'You made angels sing, angels were here.'

He loved this man who not only respected him but for whom angels sang. All his longing flowed as Ossian hugged him so angels sang again telling him he was treasured. From that moment Antonio began his double life: angels now inhabited Hell.

Guided by angels his boat ferried them to a concert party near the Rialto Bridge in the Alla Madonna, a traditional Trattoria on Calle della Madonna where a long table had been reserved and where the musicians and their friends feasted late into the night.

The talk around the table was mostly in English. Antonio was struck by the easy way his two friends slipped from one language into another, struck too by the general view of Ossian's brilliance. 'Everyone thinks what Angelica and I think of him. They love him almost as much as we' he mused. Wine loosened his tongue; he told them of his careless if grim childhood, his pranks with his best friend Frederico, his troubles with the priest who decried sexual awareness, his father's failing health and his inheritance of their *motoscafo.* Water, intangible riches and ruin seeped into his life as it did, Venice; the richness of the crumbling city contrasting with the poverty of his family.

Antonio was shocked at the naked freedom of Ossian's childhood. 'You often saw your sisters and your parents naked? I never was allowed near mine. I rarely bathed with my brothers when no highjinks were permitted.' He listened in disbelief to Ossian's stories of love and sex in the family.

Ossian warmed to the boy's admiration and disquiet. 'I fell between the stools of child and adult, avoiding sex either with boys or girls until I met Richard and Angelica.'

Antonio was as dismayed as he was elated by Ossian's view love not gender rules love-making, and, that the other non-verbal communication - after music - is bodies in love. It's an angelic rule, he thought, shoving it, with angels' songs and hope, on the angelic side of his life, realising their disdain of judging him was part of their freedom, 'Freedom of thought, of act, of life.' he said to himself wistfully.

Antonio wolfed the food; but a deeper hunger, sharpened by his experience in San Zanipolo, gnawed; he yearned for angel-food (whatever that is) to lift him to realms beyond the daily grind.

He stumbled over expressing his deepening feelings for these two friends yet he shone with pleasure. He would have felt out of place in so polished a crowd, but he blossomed under the influence of the general good-cheer and the rich food and drink. A hidden beauty was drawn out of him by the general admiration. He knew angels attended them tinging everyone with joy. He could see it in faces, hear it in the garrulous good humour, feel it boiling inside him so he wanted to shout with glee. 'Angels exist in Hell.'

But Antonio sang instead. An itinerant guitarist sang some local songs. One of them, about a gondolier and a girl was tuneful and short. Antonio cried. 'What about the rest?'

The singer grinned. 'It's too rude for this company.'

'Then I'll sing for them.' Antonio nodded to start the guitar and added all the verses about love, sexual frustration and its fulfilment which Angelica translated to the delight of the company. Ossian listened intently, soon humming a base line to supplement Antonio's feather-light baritone and the pulsing chords of the guitar. The applause was as much for the risque message as the handsome singer.

Ossian was glad. 'Well done. You sing sensitively and highlight the meaning, as any good performer should. Your vernacular songs have given me a musical idea, so you'll have to take me to a shop selling manuscript paper in the morning. But now, Let's drink to love and boats.'

In the early hours, Antonio and the angels gingerly took Ossian and Angelica back down the swaying *Cånal Grande* and up the unruly Albero canal to the small drunkenly bucking bridge near their hotel. Angelo told them he'd sleep-over in a room his family had behind La Fenice. Yes, he would take Ossian to buy music paper in the morning, but not too early. Drunkenly he kissed them both; he seethed with unfamiliar energy lustily aware they shared it as they had shared the evening with him. Filled with the songs of angels they all stumbled to their beds too tired for anything else.

25-

OSSIAN WOKE EARLY and gave the freshly penned words of his song to Angelica to correct the Italian while he jotted down the skeleton chordal structure of the guitar part. Antonio arrived sheepishly late and took him to a not so distant music shop for manuscript paper. Antonio stood beside a piano in the shop while Ossian played and sang to him. It was a ravishing song, filled with floods, reflections, stones, stars, and intimations of love. He blushed, overwhelmed by attendant angels. Antonio burned with lusty dreams. His brilliant friend not only understood the secrets of his city but lasciviously understood private dreams. So when Ossian asked to see his room, he breathlessly took him through labyrinthine ways, up a twisting stair and into a small room, bare but for a bed and chair, blind except for a petite dormer window breaking through the sloping ceiling into the sky.

When Ossian kissed him, Antonio abandoned himself to his wild feelings. He frantically pulled off his clothes and fell on his knees, hands seeking belt, fly and buttons, fighting to reach the springing power bursting there. Ossian pulled off his outer clothing. They fell hungrily on the cold bed. Antonio was dazed by caresses and kisses, overwhelmed by his man's need. On his back, he lifted his hips. Questing fingers pushed and opened the secrets in his anus. Although he had never before given himself, inklings about coupling buoyed him. Attentions to the sensitive areas surrounding his sex crazed his desire; he shivered with abandoned apprehension as his man first prodded and then forced his way in. It was too late to resist; they became joined; loosing yet taking all; feeding off, fed by clamouring angels and bruising ecstacy.

Antonio cried with pain and flung ejaculations into a slimy sea on his tummy. His lips were overwhelmed by kisses, his mouth filled with wagging tongues. He looked into the soft grey eyes. Aware of Ossian's struggle, unfulfilled, he lay defenceless. His inner world was rent by thrusting forces reaching a huge pitch of tense stillness as Ossian erupted; he was washed and filled; then the power leached away. They lay bemused until Antonio, revived by his lover's many caresses, jockeyed behind his kneeling body, was invited to complement their coupling.

'Please be very careful. You're so big.' Ossian whispered. It was a delirious exchange of power, the man sported a boy's erection compared to the thick heavy manly member of the boy.

Ossian's ecstasy was intense. This boy/man engulfed him. He swam in angel-music flaming like hell-fire as everything died.

'I love you.' the boy whispered.

'You're wonderful.' Ossian breathed licking his boyish cheek 'How did you know what I wanted?'

Antonio smiled slyly. 'I didn't! You danced into me as if you were conducting.'

Ossian chuckled. 'I've never conducted a band like you. You make the most fabulous music in the whole world.' He took the limp penis in awe, felt the weight of its heavy sacs. 'It's beautiful. You keep it a secret, I never guessed. Thank you for giving it to me. Its power is awesome.'

The boy was proud. He nestled into Ossian's warmth. He realised the angels in that gloomy church had told the truth: the gifts of the world could be his; now he understood, for he had supped. Antonio was flooded: happiness, love, pride carried his double-life towards a future; inner Venetian riches enhanced him. Life was undeniably tough. But living freely mattered most.

Ossian stopped the boy at the door and drew him into a long tender kiss until each blushed with arousal. He is passionate like Angelica, but fragile with longing like me, Ossian thought.

Antonio floated in affection. 'Come on, I'll take you to the bar where the gondoliers hang-out and where we'll find a guitarist for your song.'

'Our song.' Ossian said as they tapped down the bare stairs and into the street, where the boy, ablaze, spear-headed their twisting journey to a bar overlooking Rio del Santa Maria Giglio filled with smoky talk and bored gondoliers.

'You want blind Allesandro.' the gondoliers all agreed.

Antonio nodded. 'Yes, I know where he lives.'

'Have a drink. Go later. Here, join us.' the burly men plied their angel with wine until clamouring guitars egged him on to dance and his head spun with the cruel goading of the boatmen (who thought themselves a cut above any *motoscarfo* lad, even one so handsome). Antonio diva-danced like a disabled puppet.

Ossian sat transfixed. 'Men like this cannot celebrate beauty. They suppress their feelings of childlike awe. They want to win rather than worship. It is the lowest form of poverty. They defile Antonio rather than bless his grace, transforming him into a freak.'

He rose unsteadily and braving the contemptuous anger of the gondoliers, rescued the befuddled boy and ferried him outside and along the calle and down the familiar humped bridge over the Albero canal.[*]

Antonio staggered blindly to its centre leaned over and was violently sick, crying out his disgust. He fell emptied against his heavenly friend who attentively took him to his hotel room. There, he was cleaned-up, undressed by two pairs of hands, and carefully put to bed where he drifted uneasily into sleep.

Angelica understood her husband's unabashed tenderness and the love marks on the boy's body. She kissed him forgivingly, noticed his frenzied composing in the bar, reflecting his ardour.

She squeezed his arm. 'These extremes of passion - your tenderness and the gondoliers' brutality - will unsettle Antonio. He need to pull back from both.'

'Can we defend feelings without blunting them?'

'Certainly. He must escape brutality. His love for you is blinding him. We must talk to him about being more careful.' Angelica said gently. 'My dearest, you, as evoker of angels, must be very careful indeed. Angels, unlike fire, not only burn one's fingers but one's soul.'

A twinge of guilt was enticed out by Angelica's understanding. Ossian's cheek trembled as he fell through the maelstrom of defeated glory Antonio had released. He recalled their last two-sided kiss and whispered. 'Oh, Angelica, oh my love. Kiss me.

---

[*] See notes at end.

Please?' A confusing Serenissima fog; his stumbling with ecstacy.

Her lingering kiss proclaimed she loved the boy in him, honoured all his manly gifts and blemishes. He touched unity as he had with Antonio. Music poured out in a flurry of love. He acknowledged he had burnt his fingers when Antonio burnt his bridges. There was no going back. But love and care and Angelica's guidance were essential if all of them were to escape unharmed.

Antonio woke when they entered. Angelica announced they were taking him to dinner and ordered both men to bathe. She pushed a coy, underclad Antonio into the bathroom with Ossian. Delightedly they soaped each other. Antonio's peeping eyes stung with shampoo, he had his hair lathered twice and his genitals three times. He cheekily reciprocated until every part was purified.

Dried and glowing he confronted Angelica in only his bulging underpants as Ossian dressed and hurried downstairs to telephone the Trattoria for a reservation.

Finally alone with her his heady good humour evaporated. She sat beside him on the bed when he muttered. 'You know, don't you. I'll go straight home. You hate me.'

Angelica stroked his muscled thigh. 'Antonio, we share something very precious: a love of Ossian the miracle-maker. How could I hate you for that. Do you hate me for loving him? Of course not. Love is not ownership; you must know that, love is a complicated mixture of relationships~feelings~loyalties. Your love for him is as unique and possibly as necessary as mine. I can see what you have given him and I see changes in you he must have influenced. Don't you see?'

The boy blushed with sexual alarm and passionate agreement; he was at sea again: more or less naked, and in a turmoil of elation. She knows. It's all right. She loves me, I long for her. Wonderful, wonderful, his tumbling thoughts whispered.

Hiding from chaotic feelings he fell shivering into her lap

Angelica fondly stroked his shampoo-fluffed hair with a pensive palm, bent and kissed his cheek. 'You must be careful with him, he is as vulnerable as you; I trust you in this. And, my Antonio (he grew ravenous) you must be very careful for yourself. Not so much with him, but alone out there in the world. Those sailors nearly trapped you with their cruel game. There is evil in some shadows in Venice and traps are sometimes hidden by the light. You must avoid them. We would die if anything happened to you.'

'You love-birds must hurry. We eat in half an hour.' Ossian teased on finding them.

Angelica restrained the boy; for a second time she stayed his alarm, her gentle hand telling him to wait. 'We're trying to sort out some of the dangers of love and life. And some of the joys. There are joys, my Antonio?'

He grinned, nodded and rolled, displaying his lust.

Ossian squeezed his tented erection. 'Dear Antonio, it's the best in the whole world, but enough now. You'll have to manage it later. I've found it usually works.'

Angelica laughed. 'Usually, yes "usually", but only after food for thought and stomachs.'

Laughing, they helped Antonio dress. He was radiant; his new jumper enhanced his floating halo of hair (so much nicer than gelled); he strode arm in arm with his friends along changed yet familiar paths. Now he dared to see both laughter and pain.

With different eyes he spied an altered world of shadows and of light. Richer, more alarming, images of self. Angelic light and devilish shades.

It was a delightful meal. They fondly parted after feasting. Antonio earnestly promising to get the blind Alessandro to the gondoliers' bar in the morning.

26-

ANTONIO AND OSSIAN sauntered through a dusky morning mist making Venice secretive and indistinct.

'Is there time to make love?'

'Of course.'

They hurried to the tiny attic and romped.

'Does it always get better?'

'Yes, always.'

'Will you miss me?'

'What do you think, will you miss me?'

Their leaving kiss was fuller, more equal, more transparent. Each felt fulsomely fed. Reeling with pleasure they meandered to their rendezvous with the great guitarist Alessandro, who had always walked in darkness.

The bent old man sat quite still at a table, an empty jug of wine at his elbow, a guitar case on the bench beside him.

'So you are the Barbarian who makes angels sing and who spirited the lad away yesterday from the vultures - who are unforgiving and of the opinion the lad is screwing cash out of you because you're screwing him.' Alessandro put out a hand, felt Ossian's tense face and then the flaming face of Antonio. 'Good. So we understand each other. Music dwells with love.'

He sent the lad off for another jug and additional glasses saying softly, 'Antonio is a good boy. You know that. He had a brutal childhood, a drunken father, beatings, starvation and all the other blessings of poverty - like most of us here. But he remained clean, know what I mean?'

Ossian placed a hand on the wiry old fist on the table. 'I love that cleanness. My song is about us in Venice, him, me, my wife, his *motoscafo* and the city. It tells of love and water, stones, threats and unisons of need.'

He pressed the gnarled fist. 'I agree, music is the food of love and feeds off it. Few admit that. Music also is movement, colour, form. Antonio was the first to tell me it is the voices of angels; only an angel knows that. I hope we can persuade him to sing it eventually; he has a lovely voice and a sensitive ear.'

The old man bent wearily over the table. 'Only fools talk of angels.' He growled. 'So tell me what I can do for you.'

Then Ossian went through the chords he had arranged into similar riffs. The old man nodded. Together they sang chord sequences. Again the old man nodded and drained his glass. Soon the jug was empty.

Alessandro grunted 'Where's me guitar?' He fumbled for the shabby case.

Ossian struggled to his feet. 'I must piss; I'll get a refill, and for you Antonio, *acqua minerale con gas.'*

'Best ask for *acqua gassata* otherwise the vultures will swoop on you. Toni, you still have a bit to teach him.' Alessandro chortled.

Ossian returned. The old man was lovingly bent over his instrument, caressing sounds from it and shaking his head in disbelief. But he was note perfect. Then Ossian hummed along with him until Alessandro stopped. 'Let's do it then.'

Ossian asked if he would play the melody and some support chords of the two last lines to link the three verses and start with the melody plus chordal support of the first two lines as introduction. 'Like reflections in a still canal.'

Alessandro grunted. 'Never seen one. Guess repetition would suit you?'

Ossian laughed.

Antonio gasped at the unbridled pleasure of the collaboration. It's like making love. It gets better, he thought as the guitar carefully announced the beginning with Alessandro's "reflection" of the opening lines.

They played and sang quietly, intent within the hub-bub of the bar. Antonio watched them meet each other. They responded with voice and string, releasing the sturdiness of folk music, the melismas of Monteverdi, Bachian and Stravinskian chord progressions. He felt the love, the hum of angels. He was dazed by their eloquent virtuosity. It dawned on Antonio Ossian's song was a love song; he floundered in embarrassed disbelief.

Motoscafo

Cullami come la tua barca;
canta dell'acqua e dell'amore,
della laguna increspata dalla brezza,
del cielo stellato, di nebbia velato,
scuro e tenero come i tuoi occhi
ed il fiato appannato dall'inverno!

Rock me like your boat;
sing of water and love,
breeze-roughed lagoons,
of a sky of mist and stars
dark as your eyes,
as winter-clouded breath!

Cullami come la tua barca
riempiendomi di calore
come l'aria si riempie di campane
ogni giorno, ed ogni volta
che il cielo si vuota di stelle
e la laguna diventa agitata!

Rock me like your boat
filling me with warmth
as the air fills with bells
every day, and every time
the sky empties of stars
and the lagoon roughens!

Io canto dell'amore e dell'acqua,
dei tuoi occhi e delle pietre luccianti,
di stelle e sogni velati dalla nebbia!
Cullami come la tua barca;
abbracciati ciondoleremo uniti il capo
inondati dall'amore!

I sing of love and water,
eyes and shining stones,
stars and misted dreams!
Rock me like your boat;
tethered we'll nod as
one, awash with love!

Antonio watched the two become one breathing instrument shimmering with sound, expressing the sense clarifying with each play-through. 'My boat, my eyes, they are like shiny stones. We do fill each other with warmth, rocking with love. Yes. We are dreamy stars.' demons shouted in his reeling head.

But the two players went blissfully on.

Antonio wilted.

Seeing his distress, Ossian stopped. 'What is it, Antonio?'

'It's about .. How can you sing it aloud in public? It's about you and me. Being here.'

Old, bent Alessandro, reached out blindly and touched the

trembling boy; he prodded him tenderly. 'Of course it is.' he said gruffly. 'All the best songs are love songs, but no one knows to whom. Anyway, Ossian has written you a triple love song, it is also to our sinking city, also to his wife. It's Everyman's song, yours and mine. Antonio, you must understand all artists and lovers take risks. That's why they hate and fear us. Somehow dreams are invincible. When you have truly loved, then you will understand.'

Ossian leaned over and kissed his furrowed brow. 'My Antonio, angels risk damnation, we only face censure. I wrote all my love into it; you must bravely defend it, as you must defend yourself.' He paused. 'My treasure, the vultures already accuse us of being filthy perverts. Does the song worsen their opinion or their judgement, or the truth?'

Antonio blushed with fearful rage. 'They'll change nothing.'

'You are quite right.' Alessandro sighed. 'Now I see you understand risk is an illusion. For only what you deeply feel empowers you; don't you see? Even an old blind man sees that. Now, let's "tell it to the mountains" as that Negro slave song advises.' He shouted over the alcoholic din. 'Hey all you boating laddies, I've got a new song about us. If you shut up we'll do it for you. Brothers, it really is our tide-lapped city, our boats, our loves. Come on. Shut up. Listen.'

The bustle stilled. Men crowded around the old blind guitarist muttering. 'All right then, let's have it, trying to shoo Ossian and Antonio out of the way.

Alessandro rasped. 'Belt-up fellahs. It's their song too. My friend Ossian will sing it this time - Antonio will do it later - If you're ready we'll start.'

Into the expectant hush the guitar softly sang, continuing its undulating melodic chords like the illusory images on troubled water or changing clouds in a windy sky. All the keen-eyed boatmen understood. They had read such signs all their lives.

Then a thin, yearning voice spoke liltingly about boats, warmly about love, breathlessly about the windy lagoon, trembling with thoughts about soft, dark eyes, entrancing them until the solo guitar sighed an echoed end.

Then the voice grew firmer and tolled like bells and shivered with fear as rising waters engulfed the tune and the music sighed and bubbled like water seeping out of gullies in low-lying piazzas until only a lone guitar had voice.

Then, full of sexual longing, the voice sang of water and lust, of starry lovers rocking and nodding in union, awash with love like the city awash with *acqua alter* but undrownable, as inextinguishable as Venice itself. Finally the guitar, a lonely watcher over the floods of water and love, confirmed the victorious lovers in their unsinkable city. Alessandro sat quite still, head bowed, sniffing a few tears.

Ossian squeezed his bony shoulder. 'Alessandro, a thousand, thousand thanks.'

Antonio looked on, amazed. 'You saw the angels Alessandro? I again heard them.'

The impressed crowd returned to their drinking, rowdily ordering a barrel of wine for the musicians.

The old guitarist finally spoke: 'My dears, only fools see angels, fools like me. Antonio you have caught a fantastic fish. Never let him go. Ossian, the lad touched you; what you've said is miraculous. I'll never forget you, or a single note of your music. Today I saw God. He is dark and fills the void with music few of us ever risk hearing.'

Alessandro then turned to the lad. 'My Toni, I will never doubt you again. You were right, he is god-sent. Brilliant, quite extraordinary. You have made my day, no, my life. Dear boy, take risks, but very carefully. You have a long time left. The angels can't protect us all the time.'

Antonio looked into Ossian's soft grey eyes, at his fair skin and elegant body. Never had he been flooded like this. Love drowned him, wave after wave. It was not a fish but a man he held in his heart. Nothing could be more wonderful, a special man, his angel. He shook his head. 'I'll protect the angels. And I *will* be very careful, I promised one yesterday.'

Antonio gambolled around Ossian as they made their way to the hotel. He fell about like a puppy, all smiles and wagging. He carolled. 'Alessandro will meet us in three evenings time at the Trattoria Mariani on the south of Campo San Giácomo. He wants me to sing with him as well as you. He says we should get money and lots to eat. Oh, Ossian I love you-our song.'

Ossian grinned at the wild energetic boy. 'There, you see, no one knew it was our love-song? Only us. But your happy dance is a give-away, it's as much a love song as mine.'

Antonio whooped in agreement and gambolled on. Soon they were back. He offered to pick them up after the opera that evening

'Come to the Trattoria, say about ten and eat with us and I'll sing you some of Rossini's gorgeous songs.' Ossian tempted the happiest boatmen in Venice before he bounded off to earn his keep (and his family's).

'We must pay him for all the taxi trips and guiding.' Angelica said to Ossian, after making love, when they lay planning the remaining week of their honeymoon.

'I can't find a way to pay him. Particularly after the vultures' remarks. He refuses anything. It's as if he fears I really am paying to screw him. He's like musicians who find it hard to separate business from music and are ashamed taking money for a gig. I thought I'd take him to a bank. My accountant told me in the early days to save a little; Antonio must do the same, in spite of his family's need.'

Angelica sighed. 'Darling, you're right. So we must force him to make the distinction. His love and care, our feeding and help-ing him are in another realm. Nothing to do with business. He's starving himself because he's in love. The dear boy. Let me talk to him.'

27-

TEATRO LA FINICE looked a jewel in the dark; spilling light onto the tiny campo beyond its flight of entry steps and glistening the gathering mist. Ossian and Angelica left their outer coats in the cloakroom and went into the intimate red and gold auditorium. A young usher showed them their seats with deference; clearly such a beautiful couple, fashionably dressed, were visitors from some distant and fabulous world. When another member of the distinguished audience spoke to him, status was confirmed.

A man shook Ossian's hand. 'I saw you in Saint Giovanni. It was a very fine concert. You drew magic from the players.'

Ossian smiled. 'Thanks to its finely tuned echo.'

Angelica chipped in telling him about the informal concert in three evenings time in campo San Giàcomo. 'Come and hear Ossian's latest piece, a song to a Venetian.'

The man promised to bring his entire tour-party.

The Barber of Seville was a cheerful riot. What surprised Ossian was the beautiful singing of one of the minor parts. 'I'd like to meet that girl and tell her she's wonderful.' he said to Angelica.

Keighley was touched by his admiration. She readily accepted their invitation to dine next door. 'I sometimes eat there afterwards.' Keighley said as they trooped through the mist towards the bright welcome of the Trattoria whose maestro quickly added a place to their table for three.

'Our friend, a *motoscafo* owner is coming.' Angelica said.

Keighley was Canadian. She had struggled to get into European opera. Her sparkling pleasure hardly obscured her lonely struggle or her relief in speaking English. She quickly discovered Ossian's musical obsession and his deep knowledge of the music of drama and dance. She was almost unbelieving when he told her she had a stupendous voice, technique and musicality and deserved to star. She readily admitted knowing Mozart's "Marriage", in fact she had studied most of his operas which, she heartily agreed, were great beyond measure, as Ossian put it.

'Come and sing then.' Ossian said, getting up and opening grand double doors into a neighbouring space abandoned after Carnival where a piano stood mute and palled. He pulled off the heavy sheets, sat and played the introduction to Cherubino's aria to the Countess and Suzanna in *The Marriage of Figaro*. 'Imagine a fresh on-the-edge-of-sex child, in love; every-thing around him dripping with lust: chairs, sofas, women, guitars . . . an unbroken, breathless voice, dreams still unblemished by adult darkness, confronting his two magnificent angels.'

Keighley looked startled, nodded and sang with a clear, bell-like tone high in her register and a richer tone for lower notes - a mix of innocence and desire (Just as Antonio capered round me this morning, thought Ossian).

'You make the piano so like Cherubino's guitar.'

'Judicious pedalling.' he said as a bright-faced boy in a blue/purple jumper, eyes shining like sea-drenched stones through a wild thatch of dark hair looked in and waved. Keighley, already trembling with music-making was dazzled by Antonio; struck by Ossian's loving smile of welcome as he murmured. 'Antonio is our Cherubino.' He shouted " *Buone sera mia Tresore.'*

Then he turned back to the keyboard. 'Let's do The Countess's solo aria, full of yearning dignity and doubts.'

He played the orchestral introduction. Keighley swallowed and sang a mellifluous, rich and longing aria.

In the silence afterwards Ossian gulped. 'I love passionate women.' He brightened. 'Let's do Suzanna and The Count, you know, the yes/no duet? Filled with confusion, teasing, sexual innuendo and a pure spirit of life.'

There were shadows at the doors as a rather light-weight if impassioned Count put a cheeky maid servant through hoops of temptation and authority, challenging her flustered yes's and no's, swinging from irritation to desire which had hardly died away before polite applause wafted into the chill dark.

Ossian grinned. 'Dare you sing the Queen of the Night now?'

Keighley chuckled, nodded nervously, cleared her throat as the piano giggled and challenged the austere pomposity of the Masonic HQ in *The Magic Flute*.

It was breath-taking: the very high notes floated like bells, the intemperate rage of the Queen and the cascades of silvery notes, contemptuous laughter tantalisingly hidden in prickly anger, all the glories of a Queen of the Night. Ossian gasped. 'Bravo.'He led the sweating girl back into the light and warmth of the dining room and tangible admiration.

'Keighley, you are great.'

A wizened critic agreed. 'I will tell them about your brilliance in my next article. Good luck with your career.'

Others sent wine and flowers to the table waving their gratitude across the lively dining-room.

Antonio was speechless. His beloved man could call-up angels anywhere. The glitter on the moody lagoon, had been caught by voice and piano like sardines caught and preserved in oil-filled jars for feasting. Such riches inspired him until his heart beat faster, his eyes shone, he sweated and smiled and loved everything (just like Cherubino).

He taxied Angelica and Ossian home first, kissed them heartily, making a soto voce tryst with Ossian in four morning's time for love and banking; then he ferried Keighley to a landing near her room, leaped out and manfully helped her onto the shore to hug and kiss her a delighted good night. She was too tired to respond to his youthful ardour, but his warmth and the joys of the evening buoyed her for many days.

Ungainly *vaporetti* took them across the gloomy lagoon. On one occasion to Murano where they visited a glass factory behind a rambling warehouse stuffed with hideous glass sculptures.

'Changing that lump into so eloquent a goblet is like giving a formless dream meaning.' said Ossian as they watched a small gnarled man with puffed lips blow into a lump of molten glass.

In a nearby shop they bought a glass clock for the kitchen with colours as rich as jewels; Angelica found some tumblers of clear glass which had been squashed and misshapen while soft, embedded with red and blue molten sheets and finished with cheeky faces.

'Like children besmirched in food.' she giggled.

Another day they visited San Michele for a double homage, firstly to Coducci who had designed the facade of the chapel on its quay and secondly to Ossian's hero, Igor Stravinsky on whose black polished grave he put a rose and whispered. 'I remember. I also look for a Diaghilev or da Ponte to transport my music to heaven.'

One morning they inveigled Antonio to join them on a visit to Peggy Guggenheim's palazzo on the Grand canal. On its gondola steps stood Marino Marini's bronze equestrian statue, *Angel of the City.*[*] On a comfortably small rotund horse sat a little fat man, arms and legs spreadeagled, face upturned as if pleading with the other angels to applaud his erection sticking upwards like an unclad stick, a risen tower looking for a city, which had been well masturbated judging by its golden patina.

Antonio grinned. 'A well-fed if frustrated angel I love his sense of freedom.'

Antonio was struck by a painting by Emilo Vedova called *Image of Time*, a black hellish place filled with clockwork shapes.

'As if, however we spend our time, we will be tortured by bloodied machines.' he shivered.

'And layed in geometric graves like Peggy and her dogs outside.' Ossian pointed.

Angelica watched Ossian confronting *The Antipope* by Max Ernst: three female figures, one imprisoned in a coral-like pall, another, a horse/owl clad in a tattered red gown. From its rent protruded a succulent breast and tummy complete with neat feet and matching red court-shoes. A third, clad only in a pink frilly tunic, embraced by a deathly female herm and a staring black horse-once-female-unicorn judging by the wound on its forehead and black breasts under a jewelled armoured collar, all trampling on a fossilised seascape. 'It's a wild dream of sex and war, of a dead filigree entrapping us and the world so all that's left are horses, birds and women.' he murmured. 'Is there no place for my music?'

'I now see that Art helps us to see.' said Antonio as they drank coffee in the Museum cafe where he clutched two tubes with prints, one for him.

---

* See notes at end.

Angelica took Antonio to an untidy shop in the campo near his house where she pressed two sets of warm underclothes and a couple of shirts onto the boy who was too shy to try anything on 'in public' as he called it. She took him back to the hotel where adroitly he changed in the bathroom and displayed his new layer. Angelica then slipped his new shirts over his head. 'See how they match your trousers. You are such a smart sailor now.' He bashfully stood beside her looking in the mirror. He grabbed her and gratefully kissed her and nuzzled into her breasts until his arousal pushed against her. Angelica minded far less than he. Antonio was distraught with untamed desire, the expected rebuke never came; neither managed to separate, or dispel his longing.

He kissed her so violently they fell onto the bed. Angelica removed his new, nakedly white long-johns and held his impressively large sex while the boy shivered and spurted streams of seed everywhere. Antonio whimpered with shamed weakness. Angelica bent and took his magnificent shrinking member into her mouth, licking it clean. He began to undress her.

They soon lay naked. 'I've never touched a woman, I love you, I want . .'

She stopped his mouth with a kiss. 'Touch me where ever you want, yes, everywhere, yes like that, oh yes.'

Emboldened, he explored, amazed as he excited her. He grew again. She rolled onto her back and guided his engorged penis in, an undeniable fist claiming her. When he thrust she shivered. 'Yes, oh yes. Oh Antonio Yes. Until in a flurry of struggle, he exploded. She was engulfed as he died.

Afterwards they dressed. Then she sat with him on the bed, kissed his hands and face and whispered. 'Happy?'

The boy blushed. 'Are you?'

She said into the fragrant cavern of his mouth. 'Antonio, it was the YOU I love: firm yet gentle, cheeky, sensitive and overpowering. You're beautiful.'

He sat disbelieving. 'It was beautiful being inside. You made me feel it was in both of us, and afterwards I was . . . better.'

They sat in contented silence. 'I thought you hated me. Why did you let me?'

'Because you wanted me, because of love and Ossian and La Serenissima . . I don't know. We both needed to say those things.

Me in order to understand what you and he get up to; You, I suppose, wanted to know what he and I share?'

The boy was transformed by a shimmering smile. 'Yes, all of that. But mainly because I wanted to know you. I have wanted, without realising, ever since the beginning when you smiled at me at the *Fondamenta Nuove* when you hired my *motoscafo*. Angelica, you are my angel; Ossian's too. I would die for you.'

She saw her chance. 'My Antonio, you will die unless you separate our friendship from making money. Ossian and I don't love you for money, anymore than you love us. All our gains are loving not moneyed ones. Don't you see? We dine you, buy your clothes because of love. You take them because of love. We talk and walk, make love and music, and explore together because we enjoy being together. But when you transport us, it must be paid for: the cost of the boat, the fuel, the licenses, all; plus the needs of your family. We are terribly upset you refuse our money. It seeps into the other things we share. Don't you see, love can never be in any contract? Please let us pay you so we can all go on loving freely?'

Antonio suddenly felt small and poor. But his angel was not patronising him; her tears proclaimed they had shared something sacred and beyond the market place; what he took she had given freely because . . (his head swam) because she did love him as he loved her. Then he understood there were two currencies. Then he nodded. 'Yes, I do see. You are right. Sometimes I get muddled.'

'The greedy world muddles us, my Antonio. We must keep it at bay so love can be strong and clean.'

'It is.'

As he was leaving she thrust a wad of notes into his hand.

'I don't deserve all that.'

'You deserve it a thousand-fold.' she whispered reaching up to kiss the ravishing stones in his sparkling eyes. 'Keep some for the bank Ossian will take you to tomorrow, if you've energy left.'

His laughter hung in the air long after he had vanished back to the canals.

Angelica pleaded that Ossian take her back to dine at the *alla Scala* hoping its attentive opulence would soothe the doubts Antonio had planted. Ossian's mood is similar when he returns, although more carefree than mine, she thought.

It was a fine and soothing meal. The trattoria was as empty as Venice.

'You must go now.' the proprietor anxiously hovered. 'There will be water in The Piazza. Be careful.'

San Marco was lapped by water issuing from the gratings in the piazza as if the world was silently sinking below a primordial flood. Ossian and Angelica, the last survivors, scrambled up onto the line of tressels erected along the northern collonade and ginger-ly made their way to the relative dryness in front of the post office.

'Tonight. Antonio could sail us right to the door.' he said as nervously they navigated back to their hotel where the concierge waited to usher them in and barricade the entry.

In the morning Ossian recounted his dream to Angelica:

> *I wasn't sure whether to join the parade. I went to get petrol but put the car in the wrong place. That garage seemed impossible so I looked for another.*
> *There was a big glass structure housing a huge, open machine. It seemed an appropriate place.*
> *Then I was in a super market. There were a lot of kids who remonstrated 'Why don't you join us?'*
> *I cheerfully walked in shopping streets thronged with shoppers and parades of theatrical Carnival folk.*
> *Then I was in a mobile boat hoist, its four sets of wheels carrying a void, where boats could be held and transported. It had stopped because, its driver told me, 'There are no staff.' So, I offered to find some, and set off walking along a bank where I met my wife and a girl who agreed to join us. I was happy thinking, This is better, now the journey can continue.'*

'Your dream is filled with ordinary people and voided machines, reminiscent of asexual images - those of a child compared to an adult - which you held when we first met: mechanistic empty people.' Angelica murmured.

He nodded.

'Is it Venice thronging with life? Are the absent boats those of Antonio whose boat you long to fill and be held in, long for the completion of its function as a container, a boat-womb which allows proper life-journeys?'

Ossian nodded. 'I'm struck by the change of vehicles, car for boat, for boat-hoist, as if the dream asks what is a proper craft for negotiating life. Also the management of a "godlike conscious carriage" by feminine staff in order to journey the unconscious flood as the jungian, von Franz tells us.[*] Music, boats, reflections, love and magic make-up much of my experience here in Venice; at last, my dream has become life. A boat within a boat-womb: having the experience of intimately sailing with Antonio, and with your knowledge, your knowing is the protective womb. I wonder about the cradle holding the hull in the hoist; cradles for boats and for babies; does the journey across the land make me into a baby, or show-up my childishness? The dream shows the necessity for boats, children and loving staff as we sail the life-flood.'

Angelica hugged him. 'Maybe the dream girl with me is your inner girl, visible at last. Or a memory of me.' She needed to caulk her boat, leaking with sexual demands and whispering doubts, yet she said. 'All the children and the girl might be those you have always trusted and savoured, snuggling up with them and telling them Bunyip stories, as you must with the kids we'll have. Ossian, it's your funny way of being at sea, for these machines make sailing over dry land possible just as we could have sailed rather than walked last night. Stories make invisibles as real as children feel them to be. Being childish may be the only way we can sail over the land.'

Ossian smiled. 'Or anywhere else. Stories, *and your love* bring the impossibles back into our lives. I will tell our babies stories if you will love them in your special way.' He rolled her over and stuffed his erection into her with the same energy as Antonio. She cried a little joy. They were swept away into gently lapping oceans.

---

[*] See notes at end.

28-

OSSIAN AND ANTONIO walked through the drab wet *Campo San' Angelo* en route to his tiny bare room.

'Tell me, Antonio how you feel about what we do.'

'It is only with you; I never touch others.'

'Does it worry you?'

'I want you.'

'But does it trouble you?'

The boy looked pensively at bedraggled pigeons shuffling hungrily at their feet, grey birds on grey stones under a grey sky. He studied grey eyes, embarrassed by their hunger - and his - and stammered. 'Don't we make music?'

'Yes, and love. But at a cost the vultures have judged. Soon I leave; we should talk. Let me say, you've filled me with your beauty and power so music bubbled out of me with everything else.'

'Out of me too.' Antonio broke his troubled silence. 'I feel dirty and happy. I want you and Angelica. I'm a cheat. But I can't help it. Oh, God, I'm sorry.'

'So, you're a cheat like me.' Ossian murmured.

The boy shook his head and looked distastefully at the crumbling walls trapping his life and sighed. 'Why I love you both is because you let me have what you have, show me equality. You talk *our* hopes and risks, *our* love and making, I'm scared. I know it's right. What we do pains and disgusts me yet it's amazing, like flying into a dream where everything is possible, being a man, even being a woman or a musical boy, even loving and being loved.'

'So the cost of this flying is fear and pain.'

'I'm used to it. But yes; and bits are inside.'

'And the rest?'

'Being strong and happy, wanting to burst.'

'That's inside too?'

'Some pops out.'

'Making a mixture?'

'That's the problem. Not everything inside helps.'

'I understand. But tell me, do you want to go to your room now or not?'

Antonio's face trembled. 'If you want. I want to be with you, that's all I know.'

'Oh my Antonio, I enjoy you, even knowing it probably does me more good than you.' Ossian said ruefully. 'But today we must say goodbye. Say with our bodies what is too painful and fragile to express any other way, make promises with our bodies for ever. And then you must let me take you to the bank and get your business sorted out so there is a future. There, we must mix love with business but without guilt or rejection.'

Antonio nodded. 'Angelica lectured me about the two currencies. I understand now.'

They continued in silence; undressed and caressed in silence until the boy spewed streams everywhere and groaned with delight, opened his body to its centre and willed his angel-man in, to bruise and release velvet to shrink into a defenceless thing, then, to be similarly bruised filled and abandoned. 'It's not exactly what I want!' each mused in tender glowing embrace.

'I'll never be the same again.' the boy whispered into Ossian's spicy armpit.

'Nor will I.' Ossian said, grateful for the inner sweet boy and the outer towering man holding him.

That evening Ossian, the sweet boy-man with the bent, blind Alessandro performed before a motley audience. They sang familiar Venetian songs including Ossian's new song which he and Antonio sang. Wine flowed. It was a rowdy departure when Antonio stumbled outside and fumblingly prepared to ferry his friends home deaf to entreaties they should walk.

'Better to drown from booze inside than in the Grand Canal.' Ossian lisped falling with Angelica into the bottom of the boat as its unwary captain backed into a wharf and broke his motor.

Alessandro spoke to the Mariani Trattoria owner whose

brother obligingly promised 'To sort out the fuck-up, in the morning.'

So, they walked. Antonio grieving over his damaged boat as well as grinning with the fun of the evening, the coins and compliments received.

Antonio wanted to lie all night with his wild friends but, drunk though he was, he held his tongue; although his embraces were eloquent.

He slunk off to his room too ashamed to go home, firstly because of the damaged boat and secondly the spectre of aping his drunken father would upset his mother. He preferred to sober-up before confronting her. Yet lying in his freezing room gleaming in his new underwear, hugging his pillow into warmth, he drifted away on waves of happiness. 'Bad and good things are inside, bad and good things are outside. Angels are in Hell.' he said to his bemused pillow as they kissed each other lustily to sleep lapping around him as softly as the flood at the foot of his tenement.

The flood receded. It was time to go home. Antonio insisted on taking them to the airport. 'Marizio the mechanic fixed the engine also serviced it. He says it's strong and reliable enough for any long journey. He has found me another old boat we're fixing. My best friend Frederico who is bored lugging bags at the station will drive it. He's excellent. We'll be partners.'

Ossian grinned. 'I'm glad. You're better with a partner, either in bed or in the boat; like singing. But seriously, to share makes sense. Get a card printed reading *Antonio & Frederico: Reliable Motoscafo Hire.* Use some of your bank money and get mobile phones, then you can stay in touch and take bookings. I might even ring you from home just to hear your lovely voice.'

Antonio was crestfallen; his happiness and luck had blosomed with Angelica and Ossian, and his chaos of feelings grown from lonesome despair into perplexed hope.

But Ossian comforted him. 'Life is very like music: we must practise for good performances; think of our time together as practise time. You're getting better, with two boats and a new partner. Like your singing, life's improving.'

Three figures stood in the freezing breeze on the ugly

concrete pier of the airport. The man and boy clung and intimately kissed goodbye; the woman and boy melted into a loving embrace emerging tearful. Antonio wept in the warmth of his lover, his angel, the quiet presence which had sustained him; he wept with a lover's gratitude and sweet sadness, realising other angels remained, as Alessandro had predicted.

He watched them wheeling their cases into the terminal building; confronted by new arrivals, point to where he waited well clad now against the wind, his departing angels providing other customers. Helping them aboard softened his grieving. Antonio turned his *motoscafo* around and headed across the vacant lagoon towards his unseen widowed Venice.

The ticket clerks were apologetic about the Macknights having no seats because of double-booking by the airline. 'All we can do is to offer you an up-grade.'

Angelica seethed. 'You must put us together. This is our honeymoon.'

Stops were pulled, staff bustled, phones rang. Eventually the supervisor handed her two seats in Business Class 'With our complements and best wishes.'

Ossian sat ignoring the bustle of departure, grieving as well as wondering for the first time about the future. Torn from his Venetian dream he retreated into music. As the aircraft taxied and leapt into the sky, he sat hunched over manuscript paper pouring out another song. He mutely handed Angelica the poem he was setting:

> **SEER**
> *You give him all he wants.*
> *He turns into you.*
> *You turn into him -*
> *wheels within wheels,*
> *the ancient clocks*
> *tock drip waters -*
> *and embracing, escape;*
> *green hands hold nothing.*
>
> *You give her all she wants.*

You turn into her
to solve an ancient puzzle.
You clock out, blind,
free yet embraced,
emptied of want,
half knowing that she,
not he, knew ecstacy!

She trembled at his tears. 'Aren't you as happy as I am? The "You" is Antonio?'

He nodded

'The "He" is you, the "She" is me?'

'I know you were lovers. The seer is Teireseas, blinded for revealing women's ecstacy. Your ecstacy. He did give you what you want.' Ossian murmured.

'Gave you what you want?'

'Some.' Ossian was silent. ' I don't know.'

'Don't know?'

'Some, yes. But you are the rest.'

Angelica saw his pain. Bravely she managed to say. 'Your poem is correct but you misunderstand. Yes, he gave me everything. All my men gave me everything. But only one makes ecstacy shimmer through me; the one who first kissed my girlish vagina, whom I first loved and who filled me one night before we feasted and again afterwards and again and again, and beyond count on our honeymoon. While you were "wheels within wheels" I waited. Happy and sure you would return to stir my ecstacy, as you always do. My darling, there is only one. Your heart tells you the same. Look what it's written.'

Ossian wept.

A stewardess worried. 'More drinks, nuts, flight magazine?'

'We're fine.' Angelica hugged her fragile husband.

Ossian sobbed. 'I can't bear leaving. We were so happy, you, me, my boy, my girl. Never before. I don't want to loose them.'

Angelica held him. 'Darling, we brought them to life there. Now they live filled with the wonders of that floating city. Like your shadow, they'll attend you always. And I will, if you'll let me.'

'All of us together.' he gasped.

'Yes. All of us including our babies and all their little friends, two and four-footed.'

'There is only one.' he said softly.

'And a few loose wheels.' she said happily.

'For the cart for our journey.'

'A rocking horse to pull it.'

'With a space large enough for making love.'

'And an orchestra to serenade us.'

'No orchestra. I'll sing to you. It's simple really. Just the words, "I love you!" to a little tune.'

He turned back to his new song. It soon shimmered with ecstatic orchestration, a tick-tock percussion under the flowing woodwind, melodies and bundles of string sounds sighing with content, reminding them of the misted lagoon where life begins.

29-

ANGELICA STEPS BACK from the glass torso just unpacked from the Venice gallery. It stands in a niche in Ossian's studio where sunlight slants down so light bursts from it, flecking the walls and floor with Venetian jewels.

Ossian glows. 'Darling it winks wickedly, reminding me of "The sad slapping of the water on a tethered boat, the distant clanging of a fog bell" as James Morris writes.'[*]

His wife puts a tray down. 'I prefer your poem: "Fill me with your warmth / as the air fills with bells / the sky empties of stars / and the lagoon grows rough."' Angelica's body is graced with glowing beads of coloured light.

She hands him juice in a glass beaker squashed by its maker, wrapped in red and blue glass and given a cheeky face. ' Here, mia tresore. Our Venetian family.' She kisses his cheek. He turns to embrace her, fully kissing her. Both are bathed in dancing jewels.

'Ossian, are you glad to be back?'

He looks into her rich olive eyes remembering Antonio. 'It's as if I found you in Venice. I *am* glad we're here. It was such a happy time, you, Venice, Antonio, all the angels. You were right, they have come home with us.'

Angelica surveys his peaceful studio embellished by Venetian light. She says in Italian, 'Yes it was happy, my treasure. 'She goes contentedly downstairs to prepare supper.

The chink of dishes gladdens him. He calls. 'Can we eat early, my angel; I want the extra course tonight?'

Her laugh hangs in the air. 'So do I.'

'So do I" sing the airy angels.

Ossian sits at the piano and scribbles on manuscript and

---

[*] See notes at end.

plays fragments. Angels dance until he's finished. He looks dreamily out through street trees over rooves. Fleecy clouds float. Their softness warms his crotch. He smiles. 'I missed the trees.'

Ossian had substantially finished his psychotherapy. But a dream about death so troubled him Trish Maxwell agreed to see him. 'It's about music and death; odd because it was neither ecstatic nor sad, a statement from the unconscious as you would say.' Ossian said. Then he told her his dream:

> *I'm lying on the bed beside an elderly woman under the covers. I'm reading and writing music. Her hospital-like room has a number of neighbouring beds, unoccupied. A minder, a male nurse, stands nearby looking out a window.*
> *The woman has a spasm. The minder hurries over and lies on top of her so as to settle her. I am pushed off the bed onto an adjoining one. Feeling a useless encumberance, I go to the other end of the room where I continue working. I scribble on a large manilla envelope.*
>
> *When I return to the bed the nurse is singing the dying woman a Bach chorale from one of his cantatas.[*] I join in adding all Bach's ecstatic decorations and embellishments surrounding the core choral melody, like haloing a saint.*
>
> *She settles peacefully, her body moving slightly to the rhythms of the melody, an inner singing. Although I can only sing one of the parts (the choral or the embellishments) when I stop singing one for the other, <u>both</u> are audible, a sort of joining of outer brilliance with inner core. Eventually I finish. Then she is dead.*

'She has waited for me to finish singing. I should be fearful about death but we are peaceful. How do both parts sound when I can only sing one? Am I writing a letter (from Venice?) on the envelope? All the beds are like a hospital/hotel sort of place? I'm too

---

[*] See notes at end.

busy to see out of the window. I'm troubled by this death, what is it ending?' Ossian stammered. 'My honeymoon felt like a beginning, not an end.'

Trish left his questions for a moment. 'Death in dreams often marks a change, a new beginning after the end - the 'death' - of an older situation, such as your leaving a young self behind; or old relationships, such as with your parents, now you have married: youth is abandoned (dead) replaced by maturity, the ability to express both youthful and mature feelings which "embellish" the youthful core. This is not forgotten, you hear (acknowledge) the youthful choral core although it's surrounded, drowned-out by the complexity of the adult life you're engaged in. Ossian, we have often discussed your fear of losing your inner boy; the dream seems to be advising you although something has gone, you are aware of and harken to it, it's gone but not lost. Both parts of the melody remain, you can sing either!'

Ossian started. 'Yes, it feels like that. Am I writing to you from Venice telling you so?'

Trish let him feel an answer. 'You wanted to see me, to "write to me", to sing to me, about your dream. You should consider all the empty beds: they represent a mixture: possibly beds you keep empty of rivals; or other bits of yourself, other beds you've made to lie on, other voices you will also hear enriching the chorale of life. Maybe they represent all the other bits of you, "dead" before your dream, that you can hear but don't need anymore?'

Ossian sighed. 'All these deaths.'

'Rather farewells, like Antonio who lives on in another place. May I come back to the theme of change. It seems you are burying your muse because you've learned both to know her music (which you sing together in farewell) and to know yourself.'

'Change is so hard to deal with.' he muttered. 'The horizon is just as far away, there are just as many unknowns; the knowns build up but are not much comfort.'

Trish Maxwell looked at his handsome clouded face with affection thinking how sensitive and expressive he had always been. 'Ossian, I think your dream is saying you can confidently say goodbye to the lonely naive boy, now you are a husband - a man with his musical band (or ring), bound to a wife - and with talent, with experience and skill. You're able to part with the old and to keep working, even on the back of envelopes. As I said, it is behind you but not lost or forgotten (or repressed). Furthermore, the dream suggests elderly women like me can peacefully be allowed to drift away on clouds of godlike music, knowing what you've become.'

Ossian blinked a tear. 'So I must say goodbye?'

Trish waited with sad pleasure at his gentle achievement of having been able to grow-up. 'Goodbye to the old Ossian and his therapist, yes. But come again if you feel the need. For as you say, the unknowns are multitudinous.'

'So it's a good dream?'

'All dreams tell truths. This one says, "wake-up".'

Shortly afterwards she watched Ossian walk meditatively away below her window. He looked up, saw her and threw her a trembling smile of rare warm thanks.

Some dreams and some people are all important, she thought.

30-

OSSIAN HAD MADE SUPPER between musical preoccupations. Angelica arrived late and ate distractedly. 'Darling, I'm afraid I'm pregnant.' she said. 'I got muddled in Venice, what with the late nights, the wine and our many adventures I often forgot the pill. I've thought and thought. But it is a fact. I'm sorry. Dear one?'

Ossian grinned. 'Well, we were busy.'

She studied his happy face. 'You don't mind?'

'Well, it's done.' he said softly.

She gripped the table. 'I can't face having it cut out. Oh, Ossian I know you wanted to wait until our summer house in the valley was ready, when we felt the time had come, but . . '

'But it's done.' he said. 'I won't let them kill our baby either. You and surprises, first you muscle in on my concert, then my bed and now you make me a father. It is another of those empty beds in my dream. Now, tell me, are *you* all right?'

Tears trembled. 'Perhaps it's not yours, although I feel it must be.'

'Antonio's?'

She nodded. 'It was around that time. But only once where-as we made love very often, the chances are small. But I want so much to have it. Darling?'

He looked into her and Antonio's lustrous olive eyes - stones of Venice. He travelled back there. Wind, water, towers in the mist. He shook his head. 'We'd mixed our seed. It's funny but I don't care too much. It's more important our baby is Venetian; filled with reflections, angels and ecstacy. What matters is you and it. My wonderful family. Now you mustn't get upset. Angelica, my treasure?'

Weeping, she rose and went to him, embracing him, chair and all, crying. 'Oh, Ossian, I so, so love you. More every day. It hurts, the happiness of my love.'

Ossian wriggled up and stood carefully holding her. 'Can we still . . feast?'

Angelica rained kisses on his face. 'You must. He wants to shower with you every night as he has all his life. Oh, darling: lover, husband, father; you really are everything. She blessed his desire, overwhelmed by manly power and her longings all of which she held in her arms. 'Yes Ossian, it's done. I'm yours forever.'

'Shall we call it Alessandro, or Alessandra?' he grinned impishly.

'It's yours to name.' she sobbed blushing.

'Ours, my treasure.'

'Lettuce told me you'd want it. She said I must bring it to work, babies belong in the play school, children must learn about mothering them in as much detail as about dancing. She's a pet. She ordered me to the doctors and made me promise to tell you right away.'

'Hey, you can't have him every day. I have to teach him music. That's as important as dance. You ask Lettuce.' Ossian cried happily, drenched in more kisses. They abandoned the table and hastily retired to bed.

The next morning Angelica was clearing away so Ossian answered the phone. Afterwards he sought her in the kitchen. His stricken face terrified her.

'Wendy is dead. Killed in a car crash coming home from her shift at the hospital. Will says Peter is broken. They are caring for him in Ararat. The police told him she was pregnant. Angelica, first Dad's accident at that age, now Wendy. I'm frightened.'

She held him until his trembling eased, rocking him gently in her arms. 'We must go to them. I'll telephone and make the arrangements.' But she couldn't tear herself away for some time. Facing death alone is impossible.

Ossian looked miserably out of the train window watching the familiar muddle of back yards, streets bustling under bridges and the uneven regularity of the catenaried wires hiccuping over poles, today in sickening rhythms of pain softened by Angelica's concern and the solidarity of Phil and Katia who travelled with them.

Ossian felt struck-down by the forces his father fled, of

which he had become apprised as a boy; they had circumscribed his life. It was a terrible blow after his Venetian flowering to realise there was no escape. Suddenly everything seemed pointless. Yet when he saw the bloom in his wife and remembered the life she carried he was drawn away from doom towards something comforting if unreliable. It's so distressing, no wonder we want to pray, he thought. Otherwise Hope is all we have to combat the terrible idea of Chance. We, as with the Greek gods, are powerless.[*] He read:

> *Love: a skinned animal hanging from a hook, its pain and its pleasure both senseless. The future is maintained by other things than those we devote our whole life to. According to the Chinese, the future lies behind us. As when on a journey we sit back to back with the driver. Then the past, the road we have travelled, is all that's ahead of us. And we will never see the driver. We will never sit side by side with life. Only its back will warm our backs for a while, until we get there.*[*]

Our baby is the warmth of life, he thought. He lay on Angelica's lap as she also read before passing it to the others.

Katya rested a hand on Ossian's tense back and whispered urgently against the rit-rit-rattle of the train. 'Music and poetry are not only warming, but are mirrors reflecting what has happened and what's to come.'

Ossian savoured the warmth of lap and hand. He turned to look up at Katya thinking, She's another Wendy: passionate and warm. 'You hold a mirror for us.' he said and smiled so warmly she blushed, taking Phil's responsive hand and squeezing it as if it were his phallus, saying. '"Senseless", but essential.'

Angelica shivered. 'Our pain might be senseless but sharing it is an essential combat to the cold of mourning.'

'Both of you are precious because women are better connected to birth and death, your mourning songs have acted as mirrors linking past and future in various cultures for many ages.'[*] Ossian stammered. He looked at Phil who was embarassedly kicking the opposite seat, perplexed by the sensuality of grief and the lack of

---

[*] See notes at end.

laughter drawing them back to the magic valley where love and their future were rooted.

Will met the train. He was standing on the platform shrugged against a breeze and the dumbing pain. He fell into Ossian's embrace. He looked up. 'Where's Jo? She's on the train.'

They surveyed the stragglers until a trim woman detached herself and joined them. 'Hello, you lot. It's strange to be back. The station seems shabby now; I remember it as more enticing. Perhaps it's years of neglect.'

Jo kissed her two brothers and Katya, turning appraisingly to Phil. 'Phil. Do you still have water fights? Hey, what a man you are.'

Phil grinned. 'Sometimes I chase Katya around the bathroom; it's as messy but no one minds.'

'No one ever minded, silly.' Jo said. 'Where's Ant?'

Phil nodded reminded of the tragedy. 'Ant and Rose drove down with my parents to spend a little time with Peter.'

Jo took Will's hand. 'He must be devastated. As you must be, my Will. Take heart. We are all here. It's sad we meet only to deal with catastrophes.'

Ossian shook his head. 'That's not so, Jo. We're often down. Watching our houses grow, keeping an eye on old and young, sharing life here. We are becoming village folk. It is you, absent for so long, who's a stranger.'

Will held onto her. 'You'll be shocked by Tad, he's frail now. Mum fusses. Even the smaller house is a trial for him. He says it's the recurrence of his accident. He's been badly hit by Wendy's death; raving it's her parents' fault: the racing car they gave her, their constant prying into her marriage. He's raging about their insistence she be returned to the family vault. Peter is too upset to argue. He cries a lot. Never goes back to his house. He says the memories there kill him.'

Jo held on. 'So, will Peter go back to his old flat above the office in town?'

'I don't know. He's with us for the moment.' Will let her hand go, picked up her bags and led them to the car. Tiredly he accepted Ossian's offer to drive, and squeezed into the back extra seats glad of Jo's proximity. She held his hand most of the way home.

Ossian fought back his tears comforted by Angelica's grip on his thigh as he negotiated the dusty tracks all the way to Ararat where Miranda and the wide-eyed children met them. Ossian with a heavy heart, knew they would insist on a Bunyip story that evening. He felt his grief was no beginning for a children's adventure. Yet he knew sharing it was essential.

Jo was still weeping when she left Peter and went to her parents' bungalow. She was apalled in the deterioration of her father and her mother's stoicism. "Rage, rage against the dying of the light"* she yearned, blinking at the valley melting in her tear-drenched eyes.

'My darling, it's been a long, long time since you were here.' Sophie whispered, caressing Jo's streaked cheek and pouring her a triple whisky.

'To your fantastic career.' qualed Tim.

'Fuck my career.' Jo said. 'I'm coming home. You might as well know, I'm pregnant. There isn't a man. Only me. That's how it turned out. But I'm having a kid before it's too late.'

'Oh, my darling.' Sophie groaned, almost smiling.

'About time.' said Tim grimly. 'The region needs a competent doctor. It's one thing trees and rocks don't do so well.'

Ossian stood awkwardly at the door. He went to his mother. 'Angelica is pregnant too. We've not told anyone.'

Sophie gave a little cry. 'I never thought you'd be a father. Oh, Ossian. Wonderful. Wonderful. Two babies.' Then she remembered Wendy and sobbed. 'Why can't we be happy? I thought it would be different here. It nearly was. But life battles death everywhere.'

Tim threw a hearty arm around his handsome son and blew a kiss to his wife. 'Darling heart, what matters is who wins.' He kissed everyone in sober benediction and poured another round of stiff drinks murmuring, 'Just this once.'

Jo gulped it straight down. '"Do not go gentle into that good night", Dad. For Peter and I, we *all* need you.'

Ossian chipped in. 'Alessandro needs a grandad.'

Sophie put her arm around Tim's fragile body. 'He's not going anywhere. But losing Wendy has hit us all.'

Ossian tried to smile. 'The valley has prospered and we've grown from a family into a village here.'

'Of course we have.' said Tim.

'And there's still room to grow.' said Jo softly.

'I do hope so.' breathed Sophie draining her glass.

Over dinner, Peter groaned. 'There's not a single comfort.'

Jo started. 'Being here with us?'

Peter shrugged helplessly.

'You'll find not everything is dead.' Will said. 'I did.'

Peter, remembering that horror, shook. Tim's tears softened it. 'Yes, you are here, all of you I'd die otherwise. For the first time in my life I tend to agree with Mum and Dad Sloan who tell me it's an act of God. No wonder I abandoned him.'

Tim sniffed angrily. 'A fast car, a dangerous road, an exhausted driver. That's the cause.'

Peter froze. 'That's what I believe. I should have stopped Wendy working. But she disliked being alone out here. She loved the busy hospital. She was a star. A falling star.' He was silent.

'And, what a star.' said Tim.

Nestor nudged his brother Kim. 'There are many people in the sky, can we see Wendy?'

Seven year old Kim looked at his Daddy.

Will shook his head.

Ossian roughed his hair. 'Nestor, what a wise thought. Many people believe the stars are what wonderful people like Wendy become. Nobody just vanishes. One day when we look up we'll see her twinkling. Bunyip may be able to point out exactly where she is.'

Their nine year old sister Nici sniffed, sorely missing her second Mum. 'I want her here, not in the sky.'

'Darling one, of course you do.' Sophie said.

'We all do.' whispered Peter brokenly.

'Stars matter.' said Ossian struggling.

'They're the night-time people.' said Nestor who, at four, already understood his uncle Ossian.

'Spirits of sacred majesty.' said Angelica mixing her catholic past with Nestor's bewitching present.

'A memorial to their great gifts which enriched our lives.' said Ossian, thinking of his muse Orpheus, while Nici and the rest remembered Wendy.

The children were flagging. Little Tim and baby sister Semele were already abed when Nestor whined. 'Uncle Ossian, please bring Bunyip to bed.' Nici took Rose by the hand and dragged her to the bathroom to supervise teeth brushing. Then the three children tumbled into Nestor's bed making shivering mountains in the covers with two plateaus for their beloved Rose and Ossian. Unusually they remained silent for so long Ossian, bending down, found the leg of the bed and scratched with his fingernail.

Kim whispered surreptitiously. 'It's Bunyip.'

The boy let Bunyip in. Everyone saw he was upset. When the children were all sitting on the window cill holding hands Bunyip said. 'Tonight you must be brave. A terrible thing has happened. We must prevent tragedy by making a miracle.'

The children sat swinging their legs, looking down the darkened valley lit only by a scatter of stars, small far away eyes which kept watch on everything so no harm would come.

Bunyip explained a "tragedy" was a happening, making you cry and cry; and that a "miracle" was a magic occurrence mak - ing invisible things visible; like hope and love. 'Like the night which lets us see the stars.' someone whispered.

'Exactly.' growled Bunyip, taking their hands and spring - ing into the night, shooting through the freezing air far, far away, beyond the valley, beyond time itself, even beyond the stars. Not that the children saw, for their eyes were tight shut as they'd promised. But they felt the wind tear their faces, felt the distance arching under them as their furry friend carried them towards tragedy, and before he had told them anything about miracles. But they knew he would. For by now they trusted him completely.

They landed on a bleak ridge which finished abruptly in shear cliffs falling into a depthless abyss, and, on its other side, grew into a jumble of shadowed outcrops of rock jagged and uninviting like screams frozen into tortured shapes. The only sound was the moaning of the wind.

The children were freezing. Bent double against the cruel wind they followed Bunyip into a small cave where he rummaged in a pile of furs, finding each of them a warm coat with a fury hood and a pocket on each side holding pebbles.

'I suppose the stones stop us being blown away by the wind.' someone said.

Bunyip nodded. 'With these coats you can fly. Removing pebbles will make you lighter so you can rise up should you be carrying a load. Remember, pebbles in the left hand pocket make you rise, ones added to the right make you fall. So you can navi - gate, changing them from one pocket to the other. They are bal - anced now. Try. Take a pebble from the right and put it in the left. Your feet will leave the ground.'

Of course, one of the boys transferred a handful of pebbles from right to left and rose knocking his head on the roof of the cave. Even with a hood on it hurt. But he was brave and hid his tears.

'Put pebbles from left to right pockets and come down here.' Bunyip called. When the children had gathered round him he said. 'Your bravery, like not crying from a bruised head will be important if we are to make miracles happen. You'll be scared. But if you keep your heads and think, I'm sure you'll find ways of making them happen.'

Then he told them in the many caves which punctured the crags above the ridge, lived a tribe called Im; that the Im had found ways of living deep within the caves where they were safe from the wind and from falling. For they were very light and the cliffs treacherous, anyone blown away fell into the depthless abyss and was never seen again.'No one can argue with the wind.' Bunyip said.

'That's because we can't see it.' the girl said.

'Invisible, but its effects are real.' said Bunyip. 'It's like hope, sadness or love. They're also invisible, but have a real effect. The problem is not with argument but management.'

'You can't manage something you can't see.' said the girl.

One of the boys chirped. 'We can manage the wind with pebbles. We look after ourselves and let the wind howl all it wants.'

Bunyip beamed. 'Both of you are correct. Invisibility and control. Maybe we can't see the wind, but we can feel it; we can deal with its effect if we think and act carefully.'

Everyone nodded. Then Bunyip explained the Im had unthinkingly let some of their little Ims stray so the wind suddenly

blew them away over the cliff and down, down into the abyss.
Lost. Bunyip shook his head glumly. 'Such unhappiness. Lost for -
ever. There are so very very few little Im. Most of them blown
away. My impression is they feel it an impossible imposition of
impending doom, an implosion of fate, immoderate and unimagin -
able.'

'Can't we look for them?' The children bravely said.
'Maybe because they are light, they have lodged on crevices?'

Bunyip gasped. 'Finding them would be miraculous. The
cliff is depthless. Invisibles such as fear and hopelessness will tug
at you like the wind; it is dark and lonely. No one knows what lies
at the dreadful bottom. It's improbable you could ever return. Only
your impassioned cries would remain to whirl around the cliffs fill -
ing the wind with immeasurable moaning.'

The boy said. 'IF it would be a miracle to reunite the little
Ims with their mummies and daddies, let's forget the impossible
and try.'

All the children nodded energetically.

They had never seen Bunyip cry. They were scared. As he
dried his eyes he whispered brokenly. 'I love you. You are so
brave. So beautiful. No one else could do it. You MUST be very,
very careful - full of care - care for the Im and care for yourselves.
I'm too scared to face the eternities of cliff and wind; so are the Im.
But I'll tell them. But whatever happens, afterwards come to that
far cave high in the mountain, look, up there! Fly there with or
without miracles. That you risked everything by trying will be hon -
oured. By them. Certainly by me, dearest children.'

Nervously the children practised rising and falling and
moving around the cave. They were heartened by growing skill
which brought with it a secure sense of being in control, before
venturing out into the fierce wind.

'Let's imitate the wind: blow around and about, whistling
through crevices and around bulwarks of rock, mitigating its effect
by judicious use of pebbles.' said the clever girl.

'And spy out for anything looking like a little Im.' added a
clever boy.

'And be very careful with pebbles and ledges of rock so we
are not smashed by them.' added another thoughtful boy.

'And disappear forever.' said the girl.

All the children shivered. Not just from the bitter wind but from the idea of dying. They all agreed with the one who whis - pered. 'I want to go swimming tomorrow, and eat breakfast and go walking with uncle Oss and aunt Angel and Rose and Phil and run in the long grass chasing shadows and come home to play music, see Mummy and Sem and Timi and . . .'

So very gingerly each took one pebble from their left pocket and dropped it into their right so imperceptibly each hovered and drifted downward, swinging with the wind whining and curling across and beyond the endless falling face of the cliff.

Down, down the children drifted, tossed by a petulant wind, feathers in space. The ridge where they had landed with Bunyip grew a small distant wriggle of rock above them. Below yawned depthless space filled with groans and sighs and emptiness.

'It's the place of death.' the girl called to her two brave brothers as they settled, like dying souls, ever downward, search - ing for the slightest sign of life.

It grew darker, a throttling dark which took their breath away making them shiver. Until, clouded in dense grey night, they agreed to put a pebble back into left pockets and stop falling, to hang immobile.

'We may as well return. There's nothing here, All the Im are lost.' one of the boys called to his almost invisible companions.

They each transferred another pebble from right to left pocket and imitating the wind began to cork-screw upward into growing light, beginning to enjoy weightlessness and the slow circling like lazy eagles lying on a current of air.

One of them shouted. 'Look. There. Something moved.'

Three eagles swam towards a precipitous ledge where a pair of frightened eyes regarded them and from where a minute whimper issued.

The children held hands (as if Bunyip were guiding them) and then one of them reached over and skillfully picked up a shivering little Im who clung tightly to his rescuer, too scared to look or cry.

Carefully they again transferred stones from one pocket to another. Slowly they rose, eagles in graceful circles of flight, until one of them shouted. 'Look. There's something up there.'

The three eagles circled closer and spied another terrified little Im who was soon clinging eyeless and voiceless to her res - cuer. More stones were transferred. A lot more; because the addi - tional weight impeded rising. But eventually, almost back at the ridge, they saw, or thought they saw, a tiny flicker of life on a narrow, jagged ledge smaller than a table and slippery.

'Another Im.' the girl shouted in the vast space which sucked up sound so it became a whisper. It was nearly impossible to navigate, as the wind tossed them about like leaves on a flood. 'It's important to stay calm.' she called, edging towards the terri - fied little Im. As she took his hand he slipped over and slid down the ledge. Only a frantic struggle stopped him falling and vanish - ing forever. Crying and rigid with fear he hung onto the girl's shoulders, pulling them all downward, into black eternity.

'Throw stones away.' screamed the eldest boy.

Luckily it worked. They slowed. They stopped falling and began imperceptibly to rise again towards the light, towards moun - tain heights and home. The wind tore at them shrieking like ram - pant monsters. Cliffs snapped their sharp teeth hungrily. Everything spun round the children's bemused heads as, with cumbersome grace, they managed to pilot their clinging ballast to the mouth of the Im cave.

There, a host of tearful Im sobbed. Through their splintered vision is was as if three clouds hovered and dropped down to them, clouds which each carried a treasure so precious none of the Im dared think it a true vision. 'It's only a cruel dream to taunt us about our grievous loss.' they sobbed, moaning like the wind which, to the childrens' surprise waned as they reached the cave so quite easily they descended to land with a rude bump, spilling their pebbles.

A great cry went up. 'Look. It's Imbecile and Imbroglio and Imbalance. Bunyip told us the children were miracle-workers. It's true. It's true. Oh, thank you, thankyou thankyou.'

In the deep safety of the cave a mighty feast was prepared. While the wind howled menacingly, there was dancing and

singing, speeches, funny clowns and jugglers and many stories.
Much laughter. Of course much feasting. There were quiet
moments of grief, for many were lost. But joy is infectious as are
the Ims' gratitude and adoration. So it was with faces flushed with
food, success and praise the children finally took Bunyip's furry
hand and leaped into the immense void to travel back to their cosy
beds.

'We know, don't we, that whatever the catastrophe, there
are miracles, if only we look carefully enough.' Bunyip pro -
claimed. On this, everyone agreed.

Rose carried Kim, a warm ball, to his own bed; Nici, clinging
to Ossian like a little Im, flew to hers through stormy winds.
Sparkling eyes closed. Soon all the children were floating like eagles
on currents of dream their laughing and crying echoing in an
immensity of space.

'It was a complicated tale.' Rose said as they made their way
back to the living room.

'The detail was complex, but the story was simple.' Ossian
said. 'Children understand the story and feel depth reflected in the
detail they may not understand. It's like Mozart's *Marriage of*
Figaro: most miss the delightful complexity the orchestra is engaged
in. It supports the story often in ways only half-heard.'

Rose hugged him. 'You made a miracle of stars shine in our
eyes.'

Ossian smiled. 'That's the reward.' he said gently.

Entering the living room was like falling down the Im precipice.
Rose was shocked by the discussion about Jo's pregnancy. Not the
fact of it, rather something savage in her independent stance mixed
with an anxiety rarely visible. Jo, whom men would die for, alone?
Running back home?

'You must take Symph's house. It is perfect for a family.'
urged Miranda, just as shocked as Rose. 'Although over-crowded,
we left it unwillingly. We were so happy there. And later when you
work your child must come here to us for lessons and company. The
arrangement worked for us. It still works.'

Jo felt keenly the up-ended relationship with her little sister,
now central mother, from whom she sought mothering. Jo felt

scarred by the tangle of success and failure in her own life; and the singeing of her hope and inextinguishability. Nothing had mended her fear, caught from Sophie when Tim had been wounded rescuing Will in the flood. Sex had been a temporary answer; so had work. But fear still gnawed. Both the frailty of her father and the approaching end of her child-bearing capacity unleashed a realisation of mortality. The death of Wendy confirmed that nothing was for ever. Jo shared with Peter, something unconsolable.

'It reminds me of Ossian's story, of the joy in the return of the Im treasures, inextricably mixed with the pain of losing others; under the busy din of life lies an almost silent stream of pain.' Rose explained to Ant when at last, they cuddled together in bed. She snuggled into him.'The green lake told me so but I didn't listen.'

'The continuity of the waterfall which baptised us pressed its message, we must jump into life and swim with it.' Ant said fondling her hips.

Rose felt for his erection, savouring its energy, then positioning herself so Ant slipped in. She forgot her pill again, felt it lengthen and swell, felt its luscious movement sprinkle her with galaxies of ecstacy until they exploded into depthless sleep, swimming, swimming with lapping life unwittingly made.

The event celebrating Wendy's life had been arranged by the hospital both in gratitude for the family's involvement there, and because of Peter's antagonism to the church.

The small chapel was ebulliently decorated with flowers. The coffin stood under the rose window at one end. A small group of nurses clustered around the organ console where Ossian played and directed their singing. Many of the staff were there. Many from the town, including the police and civil officers and many clients of M+S Landscapes. Peter's partner, Glen Murkett and his entire family with Peter's entire family sat at the front with all the Macknight family, close friends and the parents and sister of Wendy who were touched by the size of the crowd. The pain of the community was palpable. The speeches were short, the tributes heartfelt. Grief leaked out of every act. Even in an institution used to damage and death the loss was unspeakable; there was no need to ask "For whom, tolls the bell?" The sung twenty third psalm of farewell was underlain by sniffs and sobs:

*THE Lord is my shepherd; I shall not want. He
maketh me to lie down in green pastures: he lead
eth me beside the still waters. He restoreth my soul:
he leadeth me in the paths of righteousness for his
name's sake. Yea, though I walk through the valley
of the shadow of death, I will fear no evil: for thou
art with me; thy rod and thy staff they comfort me.
Thou preparest a table before me in the presence of
mine enemies; thou anointest my head with oil; my
cup runneth over. Surely goodness and mercy shall
follow me all the days of my life; and I will dwell in
the house of the Lord forever.*

Four undertakers silently carried the coffin out leaving the
chapel unbearably empty. Tim took Peter's hand. The family
followed, slowly ran the gauntlet of sorrowful eyes, then went
downcast to the Senior staff canteen where a reception had been laid
on. The ordinariness of the place underscored the loss but at the
same time forced a recognition that life continued.

Many left Peter saying, 'Do come and see us.' Many kissed
his pale fraught face or reassuringly pressed his hand. His sister,
Mary hovered white faced, shadowed by their speechless little
brother, Joseph, a spotty-faced school leaver. Tim stood like a
rampant lion guarding his flock until Sophie and Miranda took him
and the children home. Nici lingered pleading she'd come with
Daddy and Uncle, later confessing to Peter, 'To dwell in that house
is not enough, is it? We want Wendy in our house.'

Peter broke down and cried and Daddy said. 'The psalm
comforted many. Darling, of course you're right. Peter is crying, not
because you hurt him but because what you said is true. It may take
a long time until he can live there again. I hope he'll live with us.
We must tell him how much we love him and not to abandon us
altogether.'

They took him back to Ararat where he walked beside the
waters of the serene river and through the fecund pastures he had
made, and supped at tables a long way from enemies. But Peter
seldom laughed.

He felt punished for the duality of his love. Now he saw Tim
having life slowly squeezed out of him. Peter's struggle, his love, his

dreams, his achievements, all unsubstantial. Grimly he reengaged with the everyday, stunned the other love of his life was dying, unaware how lonely he was until one of the children touched his frozen feelings with an unconscious craving for connection drawing him back into their life.

Peter's house lay abandoned. It reminded fresh-faced Kim of a fairy story, the castle trapped by thorns, holding a princess who died spinning. Peter squatted in his town flat distancing himself from Ararat and all the hope and regret it represented.

'Uncle Peter is also dead.' Kim said.

His aunty Jo, big with child, comforted him. 'When someone you love dies, it's as if something dies in you as well. It takes lots of time and lots of our love to live again. One day you'll understand.' But she hoped, unlike her own teenage confrontation, death would effect her little nephew differently.

31-

TIME PASSED. The Village, with a few gaps, now encompassed the Green: Ossian, Angelica and Sandy (Alessandro) came regularly; Ant, Rose and wee Sid for many weekends and holidays, Phil and Katya often accompanying them. Jo and her daughter Sam (Samantha) savoured the companionship, the busy weekends filled with fun and games and work: for the family still made little distinction between all these activities. Many of their visitors both taught and relaxed there as they always had. It brought a new lease of life to Tim, who, although frail, hungered for such a crowd; Sophie smiled and sighed, but with less gusto: 'It is not our problem now.' she mused. Family life clamoured louder than her fears about death.

Sophie was surprised with what pleasure Tim received the news of Phil and Katya's marriage. 'I have always loved the boy; he's so like one of ours, untamed and spirited.' Tim responded, adding archly. 'Fran's children are special.' Then, in case there was troubled water, he poured the oil of suggestion that they offer some initial finance for building Phil and Katya's house. Sophie chuckled.'Your old empire-building remains undimmed my darling. It's a lovely idea. I'm sure the children will agree.'

Both Phil and Katya were delighted. 'At last, we can build our very own shack.' they chortled.

Phil looked serious. 'Ant and I think you should join our practice. You could imitate Rose by running an independent consultancy if you want, since most of the work is architecture, not fashion or engineering. Now we'll be one family, it makes sense?'

Katya laughed. 'Making our own buildings is what I want most of all, almost as much as you. It's a repetition of our first night together, when you slept in my room: being together without complications; not that I want to avoid them now, dear one. But to work together without complications and then to make love~make a home~a family, now *that* is the same perfection as our first meeting.'

'I wanted you madly.' he said.

'I wanted you. But I knew important things should wait a little.' she said.

'We both needed space to be independent.'

'Space to grow, Phil; space in which our love could grow.'

'There is so much of us at Ararat, could we celebrate our marriage there?'

Miranda and Will good naturedly agreed. 'It will be much easier for Dad.' So, a weekend containing a party of celebration, followed by Phil and Katya camping for a week near the green pool was planned; there, once again, vows were exchanged and they were blessed by the spirits of the earth.

Some time afterwards on a visit to inspect the progress of their own shack, Katya visited Tim and Sophie to advise on a sagging timber beam in their pavilion (on behalf of Les Stevens) and to share a cuppa with them.

'The beam is weak because it has a knot in a prime position; we must reinforce it with a strut - which would look good.' she suggested. 'I'll get our builder to pop in and do it.'

Tea became entangled with the children who often visited GraniSo and PopTim where they felt welcome and comfy. They were playing at weddings. 'Like yours.' they explained as they gambolled around the grown-ups sipping tea.

'I'm going to marry Sandy.' Nici proclaimed. 'And Kim is marrying Sam.'

'But they're family.' Katya smiled.

'Yes, like Mummy and Daddy.' Nici bounced on her knee.

Sophie shook her head 'Well, my darlings, it's true that marriage grows from love. But although we think of Will and Miranda as brother and sister, Will originally came from another family.'

Nestor stopped bounding about. 'Like Phil and Katya?'

Katya nodded. 'Yes, like us.'

Nici stilled. 'Will Nina and Sam marry then? They share the same bed.'

Katya gasped. (My brother bedding the elusive Nina? she thought).

Sophie tweaked Nici's nose. 'Darling not all love leads to marriage; sometimes we meet someone we want to be with for always, then we decide to marry.

'Well, they play together all the time and then they sleep, isn't that marriage?' Nici grinned.

Sophie blinked. 'Darling, we must let them decide. In our family we want each of you to find a stranger who becomes loved enough for you to want to stay with, and you should feel free to choose by your own inner rules, using all those feelings you are finding and expressing. It takes time; think how long Katya and Phil have been together before they wanted to marry. They too worked and slept together. Certainly it's a start; you're right. But as you will find, selecting a partner takes a lot of time: time which can be fun as well as difficult.'

Tim guffawed. 'Nici, you are a wise little minx, just like your gran and your mum. Do you know poor gran had to wait a long time until silly old me realised I had to marry her. Certainly you're right: our minds and our bodies must join in working and loving, also something else - I have no name for it, poets might call it our souls - must also unite before we can marry.'

Sophie hugged the abashed child. 'What's necessary today is you're exploring feelings for each other; the same feelings which, when you are older, will help you decide about a partner. The game is very important. But you all know that. It's a feelings game and should be played along with action games such as running or swimming or climbing trees or building huts . . . all the other games, part of the work you do.'

'Life, yours and ours, is about all these things.' Tim said quietly. 'Ant and Katya and I might call it building. I think Gran would say relating.' Then he grinned. 'I'm jealous of Alessandro. Why can't I marry you?'

'You're too old.' cried Nici happily flinging eager arms around his neck while all the rest tumbled over him clamouring for a story.

'After your drink.' he gasped.

'Come on Sid, while you do a pee, I'll get the jug of juice.' prompted Sophie alerted by the wee boy's bursting bladder jig.

'Let me help.' Katya rose.

Sid craved help. He wanted Aunty Katya to take off his pants, to admire his willy and watch him spray the WC bowl (inside and out) then shake it dry before dressing him; it somehow related to marriage he felt, sharing pride and shyness and all the relief afterwards as the pressures eased, so he could snuggle back into the writhing heap of children, happy and scared as Bunyip flew them through unfathomable space to unimaginable places where work and play and marriage coalesced.

That night Katya caressed Phil whose erection was reminiscent of Sid's (in a Bunyip story things meld together). She cried softly 'They offered me a baby at the green lake. Can it be now? Oh, my darling I want you to fill me. Unless you want to wait.'

'Wait for what? It's another to live for.' he whispered.

She covered him with kisses as if it were the first night of their honeymoon.

Tim wondered had he told the children his last story. Now he'd begun to consider his own. He was reminded of his beginnings reading a German folk tale about Saint Christopher:[*]

There was once an big brutish man who insisted on serving the strongest king in the world. He did. Until one day, hearing his master muttering incantations against the devil, the man offers his services to this more powerful one, until one day he saw the devil blanche as he passed a cross: clearly THE force in the world. When he enquired about serving omnipotent Christ he was told to live by a broad river and help anyone who wanted to cross. Being strong, he carried all sorts across with little difficulty.

One day he hears a childish voice but finds no one. Then he spies a small, frail boy who pleads to be taken across the river. The man nods, picks up the feather-weight and strides into the water. But with every step the child becomes heavier, almost drowning them. Struggling to the farther shore, the man gasps, 'How is it so light a burden gets so heavy crossing the river?'

The child smiles. 'I am Christ. You carried the world across the river. Go home. If you don't believe me, consider the dead stick

---

[*] See notes at end.

in your garden. It's flowering to prove it.'
　　This is how the man got his name, Christopher, the Christ carrier.

'Chris picked me up and carried me to enchanted islands of sex, aggression and sleep where the hero Ossian went, according to Yeats, leaving me only when he saw Sophie would help contain "the foul rag and bone shop of [my] heart".* Will he carry me away to sleep for good?' Tim asked as the world whirled around him one afternoon.

A surly wind rattled windows, or was it a missed tram rattling away from him? For there was Chris. Tim struggled up waving. Then eased into the car. 'Leave the tram. Take me home.'

'Of course.'

Or was it Bunyip? Tim saw a furry arm out of the corner of his eye, felt the tug of chill as they lifted into space.

'Look down, one last time.' Bunyip said.

Far below them the valley lies. Children play under trees nodding with dusk, light glints on the lake and falls from windows issuing like music from within. Beside the snaking river lovers rock and cry in passionate clasping, olive trees stand sentinel where Peter had planted them in golden contours of wheat. Creatures lope towards nests and food, a car stirs dust to smoke from a twisting dirt track linking a nestle of rooves on the escarpment nudging the ark-like house he and Sophie had built. So much changed since the early days of Symph. But not grossly, given its life of thought and conviction. Love and truth still reign there. And would for a long time. He is reassured; Symph would be too. It is Enough.

He fell like a stone back into the chair.

Sophie found him dead when she returned. She cried a little, sitting with him as the evening gathered and the millions of eyes twinkled and cried in the sky, until she couldn't see anymore.

Then she rose and stumbled to Symph's house where Jo and Sam were living. Jo read her face as her mother croaked. 'He's gone, Jo. Gone. It's over.'

Sophie sat mute as Jo later telephoned Peter in town, and

---
* See notes at end.

nodded as she was relayed his intentions to make all the arrangements: undertakers would collect the body only after all the children had farewelled him in his own house.

'First, Will and I will lay him on the sofa. After that they can take him.' she announced firmly. She was comforted Peter would be coming that night after making the arrangements and contacting all her scattered children.

'I'll make a bed up for him here.' Jo said sadly, a little fearful of being alone after her mother insisted. 'I must go home to watch over my Tim.' Sophie trembled as she departed to tell Miranda and Will, glad of the dark to weep in.

It did not have the savagery of the sudden loss of Wendy. But a terrible emptiness haunted them all.

Nestor drew a picture for Gran of a scruffy tree. 'PopTim was a tall tree, like this. We are all the little ones around him.'

'It's a precious picture. I'll put it on my wall.' said Gran.

'I think he was a big tree under which we all sheltered.' said Nici, manfully trying to join image and grief.

'Yes, Dad is transformed, like Syrinx, into one of the trees.' said Ossian. 'Now with the wind's help, its whispering tells us his preoccupations, gives us messages, like Bunyip's scratching at night.'

Sophie blanched and murmured. 'Tim would have reminded us of that. Oh darlings, I will look at Nestor's picture of him and listen to his songs and love you all. It's some comfort.'

Nina agreed. She had been unable to shake off Sam who accompanied her from the city, and held her sobbing body tenderly for several nights until she escaped from her desert of feelings and into their unexpected tree-clad love, when the girl in her could hope, and a man and woman find solace.

Angelica offered her body to her grieving husband, it was everything she had. They regretfully made love, hope gleaming in the dark of despair as another life commenced.

Will was devastated by the loss of his godlike father. 'Perhaps we should go and get married. Then no one can get at us.' he whispered.

Miranda licked his salty stubble. 'I will, my Will. But it's all the same to me together with you here in our valley, darling heart.'

There was a gap in the family forest. More light, perhaps, but a great tree was grievously missed.

Sophie still welcomed the younger children. They visited as before, shyly returning to play and to fight and to find grace in Granny's shade. 'Children are more constant.' she told Tim one evening some months later. 'I'm glad we had so many. It must be fifteen or sixteen by now you wicked man.' But her lonely bed dispelled sleep; she dozed during the day now. But why not? Dreaming and life were already entangled.

One evening, as had become usual, Peter returned to Symph's house. Jo gave him a frosty can of his favourite beer before carrying Samantha to bed. She kissed her daughter, still glowing from a long steamy bath and whispered. 'Good night, darling. Shall I leave a light on for you?'

'Only so I can go for wee wee.' Sam wriggled. 'Uncle Peter is here. He'll keep the Horribillies away, won't he.'

'Of course. But darling, please leave him to sleep in the morning, even if his door is ajar. I know you like to cuddle him. But the man needs his rest, as you and I do. So wait just a little.'

Jo turned off all the lights in the bedroom wing, except a dim night-light in the hall so Sam could go fearlessly to the toilet. Then she went looking for Peter and to arrange their supper.

The house was empty. Jo found him on the verandah, head against a post, weeping. Her heart in her mouth she tip toed up to him and, without a word, took his rough strong hand.

'Sorry Jo. Sometimes I can't go on.'

'I know.'

'It's not fear, its something worse . . .'

'I know.'

'Do you?'

'Most of my life. That's why, as a girl, I needed you.'

'That's why I came back through the flood.'

'I often wondered.'

'Often?'

'All the time. Surely you've not forgotten our promises?'

'Such a long, long time.'

'Eternal friendship.'

'Yes. But is it enough?'

He turned. She willed him to take her in an enveloping embrace, feeling the dark warmth of his beating heart. Feeling desire grow until all the years streamed away and she whispered to his unasked question. 'Can you really want such damaged goods?'

'Can you want me? Oh Jo, you can be free, as you've always been.'

'Not without you. I know now. If only you knew how hard I tried. The farther away I got, the more I wanted to return to my dream. It was much much later I discovered you were my dream. You always had been, ever since we were drawn together and that time you let your seed spill. Then, growing up I forgot. I looked all over the world and never found another dream. But when I returned, here it was.'

'Here?

'Yes. You and the valley.'

'Will you, um, with me?'

Jo shivered. 'Yes, Peter, Yes.'

He picks her up and carries her as he might a featherlight angel. She reaches behind them and opens the fly-wire door. When he leans on the inner door to shut it, she again reaches out and switches off all the lights. He carries her through the dusky house without colliding against anything or tripping over stray toys, sure in this familiar labyrinth.

In the bedroom they hastily undress. She lies open for him. He hangs over her almost in disbelief until she whispers urgently 'Yes, yes, yes!'

He falls into her. So deeply each gasps. They tremble involuntarily. Joined at last. In a darkness filling with dreams they struggle home.

*

NOTES on some of the texts cited:

Page:

15: Erno Dohnanyi - *Variations on a Nursery Song*
for piano and orchestra, Op.25.

41: *L'Orpheo,* Claudio Monteverdi's opera, 1607.

64: Robert Graves, *The Greek Myths,* Lond: Penguin,
1955, 3-a.1:
*At the beginning Earth emerged from chaos and bore
a son, Uranus (sky) who fondly showered mother earth
with fertile rain"*
The Olympian system represents the mingling and
settlement of the Greek peoples.

93ff F. Oeser & A. Fujikawa, *But, Persephone and other
poems,* Lond: The Sicnarf Press, 1996:
Waiting p77, *Tempest* p85.

103 Reminiscent of the end of Frederiko Fellini's film *8 1/2* .

106 Le Corbusier, *Towards a New Architecture,*
Lond: The Architectural Press, 1955.

156 *The History of King Lear* (Quarto text) see 1.1.
All references to Shakespeare are to *The Complete
Works,.* Wells & Taylor (eds), Oxford: OUP, 1991.

161 William Shakespeare, *Twelfth Night* 2.iv,120ff.
The play permeates section 20.

161   Leos Janacek, String Quartet no 2, *Intimate Letters.*

170   Joseph Haydn, Quartet Op 54, No..2 in C Major.

170   Anton Dvorak, Quartet Op.96, No.12 in F Major.

174   Christopher Norris, *Post-structuralist Shakespeare: text and ideology* in *Alternative Shakespeare,* John Drakakis (ed), Lond: Routledge, 1988, p47-66.

174   See Feste's song in *Twelfth Night,* 2.3.37ff.

198   John Ruskin, *The Stones of Venice,* Lond: John Allen, 1906.
      Ruskin finally arrives in volume two, see Chapter 2, p.12:

      2:: Then look further to the south. Beyond the widening branches of the lagoon, and rising out of the bright lake into which they gather, there are a multitude of towers, dark, and scattered among square-set shapes of clustered palaces, a long and irregular line fretting the southern sky. Mother and daughter, you behold them both in their widowhood - Torcello and Venice.

199   See The King James Bible, *Genesis,* ch1: v1-7.

205   The monument to Colloni by Verrocchio is graphically described by E.H. Gombrich in *The Story of Art* Lond: Phaidon, 1956, p213.

207   Giovanni Gabrielli wrote a lot stereophonic music for St. Marks, much for brass choir. The piece here described is imaginary.

214   The vernacular for 'crossing a bridge' is 'to go down'. See: Mary McCarthy, *Venice Observed,* Lond: Penguin, 1972, p 273.

226   Marino Marina-*Angel of the city*. See rear cover.

226   L.Flint & E, Childs (eds), *The Peggy Guggenheim
Collection,* NY: Solomon Guggenheim Foundation,
1986: Ernst, p135, Vedova, p301, Marini, p 311.

230   Marie-Louis von Franz, *The Cat, A Tale of Feminine
Redemption,* Canada: Inner City Books, 1999,
particularly pp 34, 73 & 99.

237   James Morris, *The World of Venice,* NY: Harvest,
1974, p204.

238   The dream involves Bach's cantata BWV 140,
*Wachet Auf, ruft uns die Stimme . . . (Awake! Cries the
night watch . . .),* fourth movement choral sung by the
tenors with obbligato strings, "embellishing" it.
Trish might have added since Ossian is a tenor, it
has special significance; the title "Wake Up" is
another message: to leave off dreaming old dreams
and embrace what he has become. Abandon old night
for a new day. Trish left him to work this out.

243   M.I Finley, *The World of Odysseus,* NY: NYRB, 2002,
p.146: *Homer having made the gods into men, man
learned to know himself.*

243   Katerina Anghelaki-Rooke, *Beings and Things on their Own,*
NY: BOA Editions, 1986, p36. *Excesses of the Future.*

243   Gail Holst-Warhaft, *Dangerous Voices - Women's
Laments & Greek Literature,* Lond: Routledge, 1992, p2.

245   Dylan Thomas to his father:

Do not go gentle into that good night,
*Old age should burn and rave at close of day;
Rage, rage against the dying of the light.*

254   King James Bible, *Psalm 23.*

259   Metaphor = to carry over; Christ-aphor = to carry Christ.
       See John Forrester, *Holding as metaphor* in
       Val Richards (ed), *Fathers, Families and the Outside
       World,* Lond: Karnak Books, 1997, p41ff.

260   Daniel Albright (ed) *W.B.Yeats - The Poems,*
       Lond: J.M.Dent, 1990:
       The Wanderings of Oisin, p1ff. (Oisin, the Gaelic form
       of Ossian).
       The Circus Animals Desertion, p394.

Have you read the series?

CHANGES 1 - A New Life.
CHANGES 2 - Trios.
CHANGES 3 - Baptisms.
CHANGES 4 - Greening the Valley
CHANGES 5 - Resistance.